Machine Sickness

Book 1 of the Eupocalypse Series

Peri Dwyer Worrell

Also by Peri Dwyer Worrell:

The Eupocalypse Trilogy:

Machine Sickness (this book)

Watch It Burn

Catallaxis

The Savage Earth Trilogy:

Sea of Lies

Savage Remnant (upcoming 2026)

Reclaiming Earth (upcoming)

Poetry chapbook:

Breathe Together: Conspiracy and other poems of the plague year

Poems and short stories in magazines:

"No Cook," in Mystery Weekly

"Verge," poem, Westerly magazine

"Taming What Infests Us," poem, Crack the Spine Literary Journal

"Safe in the Sunshine," poem, The Five Two website

"Itch," short story, HOZ Journal of Speculative Literature

"Tongue," short story, Aggregate

"Plexus," poem, Tiny Seed Literary Journal

"We Both Know That Ain't True," The Dime Show Review website

"Things You Learn," poem, Prospectus magazine

"The Butcher's Dog," short story, Hiraeth *and* Wyldblood magazines

To subscribe to the mailing list, click on the "subscribe" link at www.eupocalypse.com.

Dear Reader:

Thank you for making the wonderful choice to purchase this book.

This was my very first novel. I wrote it in in 2016 (interesting fact: I originally wrote the book with a female POTUS and had to quickly rework the relevant book chapters after the election!).

I'm revising this foreword in 2025 as COVID-19 and the nightmare that was 2020 fades into the background. There are only superficial similarities between the plot of the book you're reading and the reality of a worldwide pandemic. The biggest difference, of course, is its focus: the machine sickness leaves people unaffected, at least directly. The coronavirus, on the other hand, affects only people, leaving untouched the machines and materials on which our common civilization rests.

On the other hand, the passages in which Dr. Davis explains how germ-covered everything is, including human hands, seem almost prophetic.

If you enjoyed it, please take a minute or two to leave a review on the retail site where you bought it, or on the Eupocalypse website.

If you'd like to be notified when Book 2 of the Eupocalypse series, *Watch It Burn,* and later books are released, please visit eupocalypse.com and join the mailing list. Be sure to whitelist Eupocalypse.com so the e-mails will reach you!

—Peri

For Steve

Table of Contents

Prologue

Huang Min gripped the railing impatiently. The approaching small cargo boat seemed to be taking forever! He walked to the other end of the platform and frowned at the oblong puddle of black oil streaming away from beneath them. It wasn't easy to see, unless you knew to look for it. But eventually, someone would sail through it, or spot it from the air, or one of the crew he'd paid off the books to spray dispersant on the spill would talk, and the secret would be out.

If word got out about the leak, he'd be finished! Not only his position as manager of the Bohai platform, but his career and possibly his freedom were in danger. His Party connections could only help him so much, and overlooking a major oil spill might be too much of a favor to ask.

He walked the width of the platform again and saw that the boat was much closer.

When the craft finally reached the platform, he was relieved to see his old friend Chou Yang standing on deck with the crate he'd been waiting for.

Yang set the crate down before Min, who opened it.

Inside were 72 bacterial culture plates, spotted with colonies of flourishing growth.

"These are the same type I used last time?" Min asked. "The color looks different."

"The same. Guaranteed," said Yang.

"Same price?" Min pulled a bundle of hard currency out of his coverall pocket and thumbed it.

"No. I had to double the price."

"What! I can't pay that!"

"You don't have much choice, do you?" said Yang, patting a gun-shaped lump in his pocket.

"This is robbery." Min pulled a second bundle from an inside pocket and began adding it to the first.

"This is the last time we'll be able to procure this product for you," Yang said. "Our source is drying up. So, you need to figure out how to prevent these leaks before it happens again."

"Yes, yes. Thanks for the advice." Min grudgingly handed him the cash.

Yang saluted him and boarded his own boat. Min watched his wake build as he sped away. He turned to a waiting spray tank of ocean water and began opening the culture plates and dropping them in, one at a time, and stirring the tank with a paddle.

Soon he was done. He extended the hose of the tank and began to spray the bacteria-water mixture directly on the spill.

"I hope this works like last time," he muttered to himself. "Now all I can do is wait a day or two and see if the oil dissolves away."

I.   **Valediction**

She was startled as angry voices burst through the half-open door: a blustering, clearly irritated older man's *voce basso*, and the higher, sharper, nasal voice of her assistant, Tim.

From outside the door, the deeper voice: "I just need to talk to her for a moment. She'll be furious if she learns you turned me away!"

Unlikely, DD thought. She didn't recognize the booming voice with its distinctly Midwestern accent.

She squirmed in her lumpy University-issued chair. *What time is it?* She had half an hour before her planned escape. A car trip to her new lab in Houston, then back—by way of Baton Rouge, where she'd give this talk.

Ignore them. She set her jaw. She needed to blow this presentation out of the water! She clicked rapid-fire through her slides on the computer.

Click! Things she loved. Click! Things she hated.

She loved microbiology with an aching passion bordering on rage; she loved the progression from dispassionate scientific process of elimination to the inspiration, cultivation, and tinkering (however much her colleagues hated that word!) to yield a finished, living technology.

But within the stodgy, constricting edifice of academia, there was no way around being forced to follow way too many rules, suffer way too many fools, and do way too many things she utterly and completely hated.

To wit: presentations.

Deirdre Davis had relentlessly practiced, but public speaking still fed her insecurities like the warm summer-afternoon thunderstorms of Northern Florida cultivate creeping patches of mold and twining Virginia creeper on walls and fences. She tried visualizing her audience in their underwear, but DD was so detail-oriented she got distracted picturing what each would wear. *Matching lace bra and panties on her? Boxers on that guy? Torn cotton hipster and tank top? Colored briefs, or tidy-whiteys?*

She felt small and squeaky, despite her average height and build. No matter how often she practiced the timing on her jokes, the punchlines tripped over the tension in her voice and fell flat.

She took a deep breath.

Hell with it, it's not going to get any better than it is now. DD dragged the presentation onto her thumb drive and pocketed it.

She glanced around her cramped office. She stepped heedlessly over a variegated nest of writhing insulated cables. Her office was in a timeworn, brick University building, handsome and elegant, but ill-suited to the needs of a wired age (unlike, say, the luxury office space attached to the new football stadium). The floors and walls were encrusted with plastic cable covers and aluminum conduits, flashing wi-fi routers and signal boosters tucked like cockroaches upside-down under shelves or perched like vultures atop "EXIT" signs.

She froze and eavesdropped on Tim, listening to him play door dragon, guarding her time. Finding an assistant like him had been providence for DD. He staved off the endless bureaucratic distractions of a large research university with ruthless efficiency—*so lucky to have him!* He was smart and meticulous enough to all but write her grant requests and research proposals for her.

And this! This was the entertaining part: listening to him deploy his razor-keen deportment to give someone the bum's rush who badly needed it.

"Really?" Tim answered the visitor. "That's odd, because she ordered me to let no one in to speak with her. What institution do you represent?"

"Now, you don't have to make life difficult…" began Mr. Midwest in a conciliatory tone.

"YOU are the one making MY life difficult, Sir," Tim interrupted. "I'm afraid I must insist that you leave. You are more than welcome to give me your information now, or not; that's your decision. I'm sorry," head toss, slight smile, "but you aren't going through that door."

That whipcrack in his voice even as he "Sirs," "sorrys," and "welcomes," is enough to make people want to punch him.

"Fine," the older man choked out. "Here's my business card. Let her know it's an issue of major importance."

"Thank you, Sir. Have a wonderful day," said Tim, his tone suggesting he'd prefer the visitor fall into a trash compactor rather than have a wonderful day.

DD had gotten many complaints about Tim's curtness. She found him prickly and cold herself. She'd tried to break the ice multiple times, talking about music, games, or family. Once years ago, when he was new, she invited him to lunch. When she arrived at the restaurant, he was already there. He sat rigidly at the table with its red-checked cloth, nostrils flared, bolt upright, almost quivering. He'd brought a mini-legal pad, and one of the distinctive razor-tip markers from his desk (which he insisted—*insisted!*— no one else touch). On the first page of the pad, he'd neatly written the date, and under that:

"1.".

That "1." was as far as he got. It was also as far as DD got, prying fruitlessly at his shell. Although DD was nobody's diplomat (*Mom, may she rest in peace, said I was "always one to call a spade a goddamn shovel"*), she could make friends with most people, but not Tim. She was especially curious about why he'd dropped out of a pre-med program in which, his recommendation letter said, he'd excelled.

But she couldn't argue with Tim's performance: once he had learned the ropes, not one grant had been turned down, not one study design had been returned for major revision, and any materials she needed were at her fingertips almost before she asked. In the years since he'd been hired, she'd

16

rediscovered what it meant to have personal free time. If she'd had to smooth over a few ruffled feathers now and then, so what? *A sensible trade-off in my eyes.*

Before which eyes now, Tim held out a business card, presenting it formally with both hands, even including a tiny, almost imperceptible bow of his slender torso. DD nodded back.

"Hm. Nice card." She fingered it. Heavy linen stock, color logo with subtle foil accents, embossed lettering: PMZ Therapeutics, Minneapolis address. "What did Mr., uh, Fleck want?"

"He wouldn't say. I told him he could tell me anything he could tell you, but he wouldn't." Tim shrugged dismissively.

"Good work, Tim. He can e-mail or write if he legit needs something." She shrugged. "Did the grad students get the cultures packed for the trip?" She tucked the card in her purse.

She hadn't heard of Fleck's company, PMZ therapeutics. It wasn't unusual for private biotech firms to try to recruit each other's star researchers, and DD was considered tops in her specialized field of xenobiotic degradation. But they didn't usually go about it by cold-calling in person at their intended candidate's office.

He has to be new in town, she thought, *it doesn't take long for most people to pick up at least a slight drawl in Tallahassee.* Despite being the capital of the teeming, diverse State of Florida, Tallahassee had more in common with

Birmingham than it did with Miami: Live oaks dripping curling grey Spanish moss; azaleas detonating magenta in the springtime. on suburban side roads, shops posted ammunition prices on their outdoor signs; and a little further out of town, spray paint signs hand-scrawled on plywood advertised "HOT BOILED P-NUTS."

Oh, well. I'm happy in the South; I hate cold weather. She'd studied the Lakehead oil-spill site in Bemidji, Minnesota, for her Masters' degree, and she'd been miserable from October to April. The horror of taking a deep breath and feeling her nose fill up with ice crystals! They'd have to offer her a choice position and a thermospheric salary to lure her back to the spiteful winds of Minnesota!

Besides, DD was already—finally! —getting rewarded for her years of hard work. As her reputation improved, she'd been able to negotiate her terms of employment beyond the usual academic bargaining stance of "take it or leave it." In her last contract with Florida College University she'd retained certain patent rights, and one of them was panning out.

Ever since the Deepwater Horizon spill, investors were keen to fund improvements in green technology for oil clean-up, and for once in her life, it looked like she was in the right place at the right time. She was leaving that same afternoon, with her back seat full of cushion-packed culture plates in insulated boxes start her new lab at Amrencorp, an oil company headquartered in Houston.

18

But it her career prospects in the company hinged on selling the technique to the C-suite suits at Amrencorps's annual leadership retreat in Baton Rouge. Hence the dreaded, but obligatory, presentation.

"All packed up and labeled," Tim said. "I put the biohazard labels on myself." DD nodded. Even though she wasn't shipping the cultures this time, just carrying them in the car, he had put the usual triple-circle biohazard warning labels on them anyway, from force of habit or out of his characteristic perfectionism. The biohazard labels were mandated when shipping any living material by mail, *though in this case, there's no good reason to label them as hazardous at all*. These bacteria were simply genetically-modified variants of bacteria found in the soil in at least ten billion locations on the planet, right outside most people's doors.

"The tickets..." began DD.

"...E-tickets, hotel reservation, and car confirmation sent to your phone and e-mail. Here are the paper print-outs." He magically produced a stack of paper from nowhere, neatly stapled together, with a Post-It on top saying "DD Houston Trip October" in his own neat handwriting. DD smiled. She thanked her lucky stars again that Amrencorp had agreed to hire him to accompany her, and that Tim had agreed to move to Houston.

"Thanks, Tim!" She paused to look him in the eye sincerely. "I appreciate our good working rapport. I don't know what I'd do without you!"

"Struggle," he smirked, turning on his heel and tossing his head again.

True enough.

II.   Red Ring

Amit Viswanathan removed his bifocals and rubbed his eyes, displeased at the interruption. He was genetic biochemist, an internationally renowned legend in his circumscribed field, the first to be awarded a patent for a microorganism in both the U.K. and the U.S.A. He sat on the Stockholm Environmental Council, the NATO Industrial Advisory Group, and advisory boards for both the N.I.H. and N.R.C. He'd received awards from ten different national governments and been published in more distinguished academic scientific journals than he cared to count.

So, why did some clinician in China think Amit could help him with some dirty-needle problem at his local hospital? The caller was very persistent.

"Alright," Amit told his secretary Juni via the intercom, "I will speak to him. It seems that is the only way to get him to stop calling." He picked up the handset on his corded desk phone, turned his back on the pressing documents from the Gujarat CRISPR-Cas9-based recombinant-vaccine project, and let his gaze wander over his office's expansive view of Chicago's broad boulevards, as yet free of snow, but scourged by the snapping autumn winds.

"Hello, this is Dr. Viswanathan."

The slight, stuttering lag and tinny, distorted voice confirmed the call came from far away, carried around the world by fiber-optics or beamed between satellites, perhaps both…*who knows, nowadays?*

"Doctor Viswanathan, I am Doctor Chin. I ask you help me." *Great, not fluent in English, and I know only one word of Mandarin, nǐhǎo. Too late in the conversation for that.*

"Yes, Dr. Chin. What seems to be your problem?" He made his voice soothing, abetted by his lilting British-Indian accent.

"Dr. Viswanathan, thank you help me. We have problem—" series of incomprehensible sounds from the connection, "infection nosocomial. *Pseudomonas putida* 45 patients infection. Urine tract, pneumonia, peritonitis, septicemia." Static crackled with a high-pitched faint buzz behind it. *At least the Latin medical terminology is the same in all languages.*

"I understand you to say you have *p putida* infections at multiple sites in multiple patients, some life-threatening? Is that correct?"

"Correct," the crackling voice said. "Best way *pseudomonas putida*?"

Stifling his irritation, Amit realized he did know something about it. He answered, "I believe there was a prior outbreak in Japan, perhaps fifteen years ago. I recall seeing the article, but I'm not sure where it was published." *Don't confuse him, simple words for a basic English speaker.* "I remember, broad-spectrum beta-lactam antibiotics worked well in that outbreak."

"Broad-spectrum beta-lactam?" Crackle, crackle.

"Broad. Spectrum. Beta. Lactam." Slowly and distinctly.

"Thank you, Dr. Viswanathan…advice this matter." The Chinese took a breath and seemed about to say more, but Amit cut him off.

"You are welcome, Dr. Chin. Good luck."

Amit was annoyed as he hung up. He wasn't a physician. He had no desire to be one. This Chinese chap was a good illustration of why: like most health-care workers, he imagined his time was too valuable for him to waste it doing his job properly. If he'd bothered to search online for *p putida* infection, he would surely have found the article himself.

Amit considered searching the literature himself, just out of curiosity, and to confirm his vague memory was correct. But he was running behind already on the vaccine project. *P putida* rarely infected humans, so it was a novelty when it occurred. That was, perhaps, why it had stuck in his mind. Amit was quite familiar with *p putida* because it was the organism he himself had genetically modified to create the first patented living thing in history. Amit wondered briefly why the Chinese doctor was able to find the literature linking him, Amit, to *p putida,* and then to locate him in Chicago, but was at the same time unable to find the article about beta-lactam antibiotic treatment himself. It must have taken a bit of sleuthing to track down his office number.

Strange.

But anyway, that was over with. He turned to his desk and was almost instantly engrossed in the bureaucratic minutiae of the Indian Department of Biotechnology.

III.   Microbiologists: You Can Dress 'Em Up...

Lafayette, Louisiana is not a luxury resort spot of the Southeast.

She kept her eyes peeled, watching the rear-view and side mirrors for changes in the people hanging around the gas station she'd been forced to stop at, the gauge almost on E. The name of the place was Quick Stop N Go. The two old guys in baseball caps sitting on plastic lawn chairs, sipping from paper bags, were obviously no danger. The kid (too young for adult jail and court) sitting on a milk crate by the compressed-air dispenser was just returning from his third casual stroll, each stroll taken with a different friend, in the ten minutes she'd been there.

DD frowned at her phone; it had three bars, but the little wheel kept spinning and her mail wasn't downloading. Sitting here, sporting her white skin and her relatively new SUV, was just begging for trouble. On the other hand, she had to pee. She'd held it as long as she possibly could. She got out and locked the car door behind her, then skittered to the rear of the station. The door to the single, unisex restroom was unlocked. In fact, to her dismay, she discovered it didn't lock. She slipped her hand in her pocket and checked the location of her KelTec, a little .32 caliber lightweight half-plastic semiautomatic, perfect for concealment under warm-weather clothing.

She entered the bathroom and, on first sight, almost turned around to leave again. But on closer inspection, it was clean, just thoroughly stained by rusty water, and poorly-lit by a single naked bulb. It appeared to have been recently hosed down, in fact. It smelled of bleach, and miracle of miracles, there was a fresh roll of toilet paper. She *really* had to pee. She pulled the KelTec out of her pocket and squatted over the seat, sighing in relief. As she pulled up her shorts, the little handgun happened to be hidden in a fold of the fabric.

One of the old guys from out back suddenly walked in, then startled when he saw her. He backed out the door quickly, "I'm sorry! I'm sorry!" he repeated over and over as he stepped backwards off the curb outside, leaving the door slightly ajar. She calmly tucked the gun back in her pocket, securing its little clip on the pocket edge. She saw no soap or towels, rinsed her hands in the stained sink, and walked out flapping the water off them. The guy was still there. He apologized again, and she answered, "Not your fault. No big deal."

She reflected as she got back in her car that he didn't even know how close he'd been to death.

But then, who among us knows how close we are to death? All the time. She fastened her seatbelt and turned out of the crumbling driveway of the gas station. *We drive our cars as though it were the most natural thing in the world, but it's lethally dangerous. For the young, it's the most likely way to die. That kid back home last week, just sitting at a stoplight on his motorcycle, when a TV-van driver rear-ended him at 60*

26

miles an hour. Gone, like that! His parents and friends weeping on the evening news. And how many accidents, assaults, overdoses has Jessica survived? I don't even know anymore.

When she reached Baton Rouge—a huge yellow and purple banner on the side of a building urged, "Geaux Tigers"— she felt a little safer. Her phone app guided her to the hotel where she was giving her talk. She checked in at the circular front desk. While she was waiting for her key, she looked around. taking in the iridescent purple and green taffeta curtains around the orange and turquoise leather sofas of the central lobby lounge. *Pretentious.* She wheeled her suitcase, crate of culture plates strapped on top, up the hall to her room. She let herself in with her keycard. The room was no less ostentatious than the lobby: niches with impractical-looking vases; a room divider made of futuristic, internally illuminated glass shelving; a sofa upholstered in nubby fabric patterned in more implausibly bright colors. The bathroom was decorated in floor-to-ceiling fake-fossil tiles. The flow of water in the sink and shower was controlled by peculiarly sculpted glass-and-chrome fixtures of obscure functionality. There was no light switch in the bathroom. Instead, motion detection turned on the lights (and turned them back off after a few minutes). *I can imagine stumbling home drunk to this room and being totally confused, unable to figure out how to take a shower and turn off the light to go to bed.* The bed was soft but supportive, though, and the pillows were faux down, so she was satisfied.

But she was hungry. She took the elevator back down to the lobby, ducked into the table area of the bar-restaurant and accepted a menu from the waiter. Artichoke-spinach dip and arugula chevre salad were on offer, with entrees of duck and salmon grilled, blackened, or sauteed with a variety of sauces, seasonings, and vegetables from every continent. The prices lacked decimals. *I enjoy a lavish meal as much as anyone. And it's work-related, tax deductible. Maybe even expensible; I haven't figured out how that works yet.* She grinned.

She selected white wine, a Pinot Grigio, by the glass. For starters, she ordered a seafood bisque. She wasn't in the mood for anything complicated, so she ordered a straightforward steak, rare. Just as the waiter walked away, a very large woman in a very fuschia business suit slid uninvited into the chair opposite her and stuck out a hand.

"Susan Deyle. Do you mind?"

DD found that she actually didn't, despite being an introvert. Her rubicund sartorial flair notwithstanding, the woman had a charming smile and a pleasant voice. "Not at all, make yourself comfortable. Nice to have company." She shook her hand. "DD."

The waiter returned with DD's wine, and Susan said, "Oh, I don't drink any more." In the awkward ensuing pause, she guffawed, "but I don't drink any less, either!" She had red wine. The two women sipped and chatted while awaiting their food.

Susan was a corporate attorney from Des Moines, meeting with a client and a representative from her company's German subsidiary about a series of multimedia instructional-design materials they were publishing.

"Are there international copyright issues with international publishing, like you do?" inquired DD politely, only vaguely interested.

Susan was munching on a truffle-stuffed mushroom appetizer, but she paused, holding half a mushroom on her fork, to respond, "Not as much as you might think, as long as you have someone like me to keep the jurisdictions in mind. There are international treaties and agreements to keep everything clear."

"I suppose there are international regulations for everything nowadays. I expect Germany is a lot more cooperative than China, for example?"

"I haven't dealt with Chinese regulations much."

"I don't think most Chinese deal with Chinese regulations much, either," laughed DD. "Some of the culture shipments we get from them look like they were labeled by kindergartners using crayons."

"What kind of samples?" Susan inquired politely around a bite of food, only vaguely interested.

"Soil and ocean bacteria mostly. There UN regulations we follow, but they're Category 2. They could theoretically make someone sick, but not likely."

"Sounds dangerous! Couldn't it start an epidemic?" Susan's eyes widened.

DD laughed again. "You obviously have the same illusions about microorganisms that most people do. Did you wash your hands before you came to dinner?"

"Of course!"

"Did you get all the bacteria off your hands?"

"I should hope so!" Susan sounded a little indignant.

"Wrong!"

"What?"

"If you used pre-wrapped soap from your hotel room, you probably lowered the number of bacteria per square inch on your hands from several thousand to several hundred. If you used a liquid soap dispenser from the bathroom, you might possibly even have *increased* the number of bacteria on your hands, depending on how long the soap has been sitting."

Susan stopped in the act of surreptitiously pushing an escaping mushroom onto the tines of her fork with the side of her thumb and tucked her hand under the table instead.

"The last time your skin was actually sterile," said DD, "was when you were still *in utero.*"

"I'd rather not think about that while I'm eating..." Susan was frowning at her food.

"Oh, but it's a good thing!" DD plowed on ahead. After two glasses of wine, she was warming up to her topic with the passion of a true microbiology geek. "Your immune system needs to be constantly challenged! The bacteria on your skin and in your gut and respiratory tract are constantly conducting non-stop drills for your blood cells and antibodies. It helps to keep them sharp. Most of the bacteria growing on, and in, your body are harmless, but when a bad type comes along, your body responds immediately because it's had constant practice.

"The really neat part, though," she went on, ignoring Susan's lack of interest and her growing expression of disgust, "is that the same process is going on in the dirt at your feet, and even in the ocean, at the same time.

"For example, the Gulf of Mexico has oil deposits beneath its surface—"

Susan's eyes showed a spark of familiarity. Something from the news! "Yes, the oil wells, like that big oil spill a few years ago, the corporate oil platform that had all those legal claims for compensation!"

"Right," agreed DD, "well, those oil deposits are seeping oil all the time. Gobs of it. Nobody's really sure how much, because here's the thing: there are bacteria that live in the ocean and *eat the freakin' oil*!"

Susan's brow furrowed. "Wait, but, then, why did they have to spray all those chemicals on the oil spills to dissolve them?"

"Did they?"

"Huh?"

"Well, when a huge, deep spill like that occurs, at first there aren't enough bacteria to consume it all. Even doubling every two to six hours (which is about average), it takes weeks for a big enough bloom to occur for the natural *cycloclasticus* and *colwellia* bacteria to make a dent in the oil accumulation. But, by the time enough of the oil plume had made it to the surface for them to be able to spray it with chemical dispersants, the bacteria had already consumed a huge percentage of the hydrocarbons. In fact, it looks like the dispersants might actually have slowed down the breakdown of the oil instead of speeding it up!

"That's what I'm working on now. There's a variety of bacteria called *pseudomonas putida* which grows in the soil just about everywhere. It eats oil like nobody's business. And it's used in industrial processes, enough that we have a really good handle on how to breed it to do what we want." *That's enough. No need to go any further and breach Amrencorp's nondisclosure. Besides, she's obviously squeamish.*

The waiter took DD's empty soup plate. "Still working on those?" he asked Susan, who waved for him to take the half-eaten plate of stuffed mushrooms away with a distasteful expression.

A moment later, a fine strip steak appeared before DD. Susan's came too; she looked at her pasta, redolent of parmesan and covered with thick, pepper-flecked white sauce, and turned a little grey.

DD took pity on her and changed the subject. "So, what entertainment plans do you all have for your visiting Germans? I hear they love the American South!" She picked up her wine glass and gave a lighthearted grin. Susan rose to the bait, glad to have a new topic, unrelated to contamination and decay, to discuss while she ate. She outlined a weekend of barely business-appropriate Big Easy debauchery, her appetite returning.

32

The conversation turned to family. "Do you have children?" asked Susan.

DD felt her smile fall off. She plastered a phony one on and said, "One. A girl. She's gone a lot. How about you?"

Susan was off and running, proudly enumerating her three children's accomplishments while DD died inside by millimeters. *I wonder where Jessica is right now?* DD changed the subject to movies as soon as she could.

At the end of the meal, chattering gaily, they agreed to keep each other's little secret if they both indulged in the chocolate mousse cake.

IV.   **Bohai Platform**

That week, a joint law-enforcement project of Interpol, the World Customs Organization, and the Pharmaceutical Security Institute, code-named Operation Jupiter, struck multiple pharmaceutical smuggling and counterfeiting schemes simultaneously throughout Southeast Asia and the China Sea. Unnoticed, in the thousands of tons of hundreds of different drugs seized, was one specific, solitary shipment. This shipment was not, like the others, capsules or tablets packed in plastic-lined bulk containers to travel hundreds of miles for repackaging. It was not, like the others, included in shipments of other, legitimate goods. It was not on a vessel headed for a known transshipping port like Hong Kong or Yangon.

It was, in fact, approximately three-quarters of a ton of powdered ceftazidime, a beta-lactam antibiotic, hastily packaged in milk canisters, on a converted fishing boat, intercepted a few miles away from, and on course to, the Sheng Li 6 oil drilling platform in Bohai Bay. Certainly, no one involved in the drug seizure operation knew that Sheng Li 6 had been completely and quietly evacuated, and the well capped, the week before. The evacuation was officially reported to be due to an outbreak of unspecified illness aboard, which had supposedly incapacitated the 100-man crew, ruining the unit's productivity for that quarter. And when a minor typhoon swept through the bay a week or so later, and the rig collapsed catastrophically and unexpectedly during the storm, no one particularly noticed except those who were

34

directly involved, such as the accountants of the Sinopec corporation.

One of those accountants was Hen Li, who'd been working for Sinopec ever since earning his dual degrees in accounting and international business at Georgetown. Li left his desk, slipped into the courtyard and took a cheap cell phone out of the inner zipped pocket of his backpack. He'd shared his freshman dorm room, and countless bottles of craft beer, with a roommate, his buddy Lee Flatt. Lee was an extremely patriotic American, who later switched from international business to law enforcement with a minor in poli-sci. After graduation, Lee had gone into international intelligence analysis, and Li had returned to China to work for Sinopec. Li had run into Lee at a conference in Geneva a couple of years ago.

It was Lee and Li, the old act together again! After an evening of alcohol-steeped reminiscence, Lee had pressed the phone on Li.

"We need to keep abreast of what's happening in China, on the ground. I know you're not in on anything top-secret, but sometimes people notice changes in patterns that can tell us more than all the government press releases and hacked communications we can get ahold of. Just a quick call. It's not traceable, I promise."

Li had hesitantly accepted the phone and promised, for old times' sake, with a thrill at the chance of getting caught (and against his better judgment) to call Lee if he noticed anything odd.

And this was certainly odd.

V.　　Not the Avon Lady

DD awakened in fright. Unsure where she was for a tick, she also didn't know what had woken her. Her eyes focused automatically on the only light in the room, the line of light from the hall *(Hall. Hotel. Hotel room, right.),* where it came in under the door. The light was interrupted by moving shadows. Someone was in the hall, and whoever it was pounded on the door. DD realized, then, that this was the second time for the pounding; it was what woke her. She turned the clock on the nightstand: 5:15 a.m. She wasn't expecting anyone. She was suddenly fully awake.

She opened the nightstand drawer and took the KelTec out. There was a round in the chamber; she'd racked it before going to sleep. She was wearing a loose knit nightshirt. Sitting up on the bed, the gun on her lap, finger outside the trigger guard, she shouted, "Who is it?"

Her mystery visitor shouted back, "Dr. Davis?" She recognized his voice from somewhere, even muffled by the door.

Deep voice. Accent...Midwest. Where?

Oh! The recruiter Tim had brushed off. *What the Hell is he doing here? At this hour?*

"Who is it?"

"My name is Ronald Fleck. I need to speak with you. It's urgent."

"Mr. Fleck, I'm not prepared to speak with anyone right now." *Be a bitch.* "You'd better get away from my door or I will call the police."

As if the police would be any use! By the time they got here, he'd either have broken down the door, or be long gone.

"Dr. Davis, you really want to talk to me."

Odd phrasing. Vaguely threatening.

"No. I *really* don't. For the last time, leave me alone!" She put as much authority into her voice as she could, trying not to slur with a tongue still thick with sleep.

He didn't answer. He didn't budge either. She could still see the shadow of his feet beneath the door. He rattled the knob. She picked up the room's cordless phone and pressed zero with her thumb. The front desk clerk answered.

"There's a man at my room door to who won't go away. I'm alone in the room. I need security."

"I'll send them right up." The desk clerk sounded bored, like this wasn't the first time he'd dealt with this situation.

"Thank you." DD hung up by pressing the button on the phone.

Fleck tapped on the door with one knuckle. DD was standing a few feet away, the KelTec in her right hand and the phone receiver in her left. The metal loop latch on the door was closed, but the door frame was just wood, and the screws would give way if he used enough force.

How big is he? I've never even seen him, just heard his voice! She wanted to see what he looked like, but she didn't want to get too close to the door, in case he actually did kick it in.

"Dr. Davis," Fleck said, "I'll wait for you down in the lobby. I urgently need to talk to you,"

"Please. Leave." She outright snarled through a dry throat. *Can't be any clearer.*

He paused a few moments more. She put her finger on the trigger, raised the gun.

Mercifully, the shadow of his feet moved across the doorframe in the direction of the elevators. She quickly closed the distance to the door, dropping the phone receiver on the sofa, and pressed her eye against the peephole. She saw nothing but the opposite wall of the hallway.

She realized her heart was hammering. She put the phone back in its cradle. Any hope of falling back asleep was gone. Breathing deeply, she decided to go ahead and begin her day. She attended nature's call, brushed her teeth and hair, and splashed her face in the sink.

She was patting her face with a towel when a firm knock came at the door. "Security," a voice said.

Right on time.

She pressed her eye to the peephole again and saw a uniformed rent-a-cop who didn't look old enough to drive. She opened the door halfway to speak with him. His uniform pocket and patch said Thurston Security.

"Somebody tried to get in your room, ma'am?" The kid's eyes darted around the room behind her awkwardly. He finally settled on looking at her face.

"Yes, he was pounding at the door. Woke me up out of a sound sleep."

"Someone you knew, ma'am?"

Implication: boyfriend?

"No, not really. He was a guy who tried to get in to see me at my office in Tallahassee last week. Said his name was Ronald Fleck. I was shocked he'd trailed me all the way here to Louisiana. I have no idea what he wants."

"Did he threaten you in any way?"

"No."

"Is everything okay now?"

"Yes. Wait. No! He said he'd wait for me in the lobby!"

"I'll keep an eye out for him. What does he look like?"

"Honestly, I have no idea. My assistant ran him off at the office before I ever saw him. I do know he has a deep voice and a Midwestern accent, though."

The rent-a-cop rolled his eyes. He assured her that he'd be around the hotel all morning; she should definitely call again if he bothered her.

Definitely. I'll call for your heroic assistance.

Out loud, she said, "Thank you," and shut the door behind him.

VI.   Best Laid Scheme

Tim Schneider finished his daily morning run and let himself back into the apartment.

Sam immediately approached him, arms out, but Tim adroitly side-stepped. "I'm disgusting, let me shower," he said, slipping into the bathroom of their one-bedroom luxury apartment and swiftly closing and latching the door. Sam, left alone in the living room, immediately stripped naked, picked up the baggie of white powder resting on the glass and steel coffee table, and began to cut it into thin lines on a black-lacquer-framed mirror. He picked up a cut straw and was about to snort, when the heady odor of Dolce and Gabbana men's cologne wafted under the bathroom door suspended in whisps of steam. He closed his eyes and savored it instead.

Out stepped the cruel love of his life, naked and gleaming with moisture, his wet dark hair slicked back, the barest trail of hair down his chest and belly.

"Your phone's been blowing up."

Tim glanced at it, snorted, "DD again. She can wait." He tossed his wet hair, raining a drizzle of cool drops on Sam's face that weakened his knees. Sam was pathetic, he admitted it; he had a weakness for anything intoxicating, like Tim's beauty, or cocaine. He put his hand over the bruise on his own ribs. Tim was disgusted by the slightest blemish or mark, even if—especially if— he was the one who had inflicted it.

"Whoa! Take it easy!" Tim said. "That coke has to last us! How much did you do while I was gone?" His brown eyes glittered with resentment.

"Oh, sweetheart," Sam said. "Don't be mad at me!" He got up from the sleek Nigel Coates settee and put his hand soothingly on Tim's forearm.

"Fuck you!" Tim said, twisting his wrist out of Sam's grip and flinging him face down on the thick wool rug. Sam struggled to rise. Tim grabbed pulled him to a kneeling position. Tears ran from Sam's eyes…

Tim stood up as soon as he regained control after coming. He picked up the mirror and had a small toot in each nostril, then picked up the baggie and swept the remaining lines into the bag with the razor blade. Sam reclined on the floor watching him, sniffling, red-eyed still from weeping and gagging, but still full of senseless adoration.

"I don't see why you're so cheap with that stuff. It's not like you actually earn the money to pay for it," Sam said. He didn't know how Tim had the nerve to embezzle the way he did and still look his boss in the face every day. Sam admired Tim's courage, cleverness, and self-discipline. He knew he, himself, would have been arrested within days, due to his transparent fear of getting caught.

"You have no idea what I do to earn that money!" Tim said. "You think it's easy posting all the expense disbursements and invoice payments so they balance and don't show the missing cash transfers? There's not one person in a hundred who could understand what I do, much less do it!"

"...and that's why you'll never get caught. I know, I know."

Tim pinched the zip lock with his fingers, sliding them crisply three times to be sure. "Plus: I have to put up with that arrogant bitch DD. She was going on again yesterday about how we have such a great 'working rapport'. She gets the credit and I get the shit work, and the shit pay. As if I actually even gave a fuck about her stupid bacteria! If it weren't for me keeping her data files straight, she'd look like an idiot."

"Don't be so mean. If it weren't for her, would Amrencorp be paying us to move to Houston?"

"It IS nice to finally get out of redneck Tallahassee. But who knows what Amrencorp's lab purchasing system is like? I've only just started digging around in their computers today, when she messaged me the passwords. I've never even worked in a big private corporation before."

He turned and bore down on Sam, looming over him, warming to his topic, lecturing, "I *do* know, let me remind you, that the Sinopec people *aren't* interested in buying any more of DD's cultures. I can't order the grey-market starter cultures in bulk anymore because we have the hybrid bacteria breeding true in its final form, and those transactions were the easiest to skim cash from. It may be a few months until I can figure my way around Amrencorp's accounting systems, and until I do, we won't have any income above my salary— and whatever job you get."

"I have four interviews scheduled when I get to Houston after visiting my sister."

"The point is, we are going to be short on cash. So, go easy on that snow!"

"I know. Sorry." Sam sighed. "What time do we leave tomorrow?" He knelt and reached for his boxers.

"I thought we'd pick up the rental car around two," Said Tim. "I can spend the morning learning more about the Amrencorp system."

"That system will be your little bitch!" Sam grinned gleefully, sidling up to Tim.

"We'll see about that." Tim waved him off. "I can drop you off at your sister's in Atlanta by dinnertime, spend the night, and I can catch my flight to Jupiter the next morning to see my mother."

"Ah, yes, Mommie Dearest."

"She's really upset that I'm leaving Florida. You'd think Houston was a million miles away, the way she acts!"

"Well, you are her little *Timmy!*" taunted Sam, sticking out his tongue and frisking into the apartment's one bedroom. As Tim, piqued, started after him, he slammed the door in Tim's face.

VII.   Not Candid Camera Either

Great. My big presentation is today and I'm short on sleep. She cast a wistful eye at the bed *No point at all in lying back down after that.*

She started the coffeepot. In the bathroom, she bent over the counter, grimacing at the dark circles under her eyes. She attempted a smile. *Unimpressive.* She gave up and jumped in the shower.

There, she thought about her unwelcome visitor. Recruiters in the sciences weren't commonly so aggressive. She'd heard friends in the computer sciences, in Silicon Valley, tell stories about forceful headhunters like this, but microbiology? In Louisiana? Not so much. The warm water streamed through her hair and steamed her sinuses open. She scrubbed her face and rinsed the sleep out of her eyes. Finally, she stepped onto the hotel-towel bathmat, buffed her hair and body dry, and set to applying her makeup.

Rituals calmed her, and like most women, she had a routine that defined the start of her day. *My eyes are puffy, even given the sleep debt.* She blended concealer with her fingertips, then poured the coffee and set it to cool. *Focus on the talk. I am amazing and enchanting. I am brilliant and confident.* Eyeliner, damn, smudge. Q-tip, corrected. *The data are perfect. The technology will be a step beyond anything used before. Just have to convey how excited I am, then let the data speak for itself.* Lipstick. Blot. *Smile. Not too much. Confident smile!* Powder brush. Light mascara. *Scientist, not bimbo. But this* is *the South.*

The coffee was now perfect drinking temperature. She gulped it and poured another. The caffeine began to leach into her brain as she dressed in a grey blazer and skirt, white blouse, and black pumps. String of pearls and pearl stud earrings. KelTec clipped inside the waistband, looking like an insulin pump or cell phone clip. She walked up and down the room, swinging her arms, flexing her toes inside her shoes, breathing deeply.

Ready!

She looked at the clock. Sighed. Slumped.

It's still only 6:53. I don't speak until 8:00. I could have used another hour of sleep. There's free breakfast in the lobby. She took two steps toward the door and hesitated. *But that guy Fleck said he'd wait for me.*

She logged into her laptop. She stuck in the thumb drive and flipped through her slides. She sipped a second leisurely cup of coffee. There was a rough spot on the thumb drive's silver casing; it must have been scratched by keys or something in her purse. Everything on the slides looked great.

The clock said just 7:06.

Well, what the hell! I might as well get it over with and find out what he wants. Better to confront him in a public place. I need to eat a little protein, so I don't get shaky.

She left the loop lock engaged and cracked the door slightly open, looking and listening for Fleck. No sign of him. She shut the door, flipped the metal loop, and opened it all the way. She leaned out into the empty hall and looked both ways, then stepped out, clicked the door shut behind her, and scuttled to the elevator.

In the deserted lobby restaurant, she had her choice of tables and first pick at the buffet. A bored-looking clerk, tapping at a keyboard at reception, was the only person in sight.

A waitress offered the coffeepot, but DD switched to water.

I could stand to be more alert, but any more coffee and my hands might shake. She got some eggs and whole-wheat toast and sat down to eat.

Of course, once her mouth was full, Fleck materialized, right on cue. "Dr. Davis." Beige trench coat, grey eyes. Sandy blond hair, receding at the hairline. His build was medium. His colorless, nondescript looks fit right in with the featureless accent she'd come to know.

She swallowed.

"Mr. Fleck." DD barely acknowledged him. She scooped more eggs into her mouth and chewed steadily. She gazed at a space about a foot above and behind Fleck's head. She sipped her water.

Fleck broke the silence. "May I?"

I win.

"Go ahead." DD nodded at the empty chair across from her. He sat.

"Dr. Davis, I represent a group which has great interest in the work you are doing."

"Your firm has unusual recruiting techniques."

He sat up straight, and his expression and breathing changed.

He's not a recruiter? Don't tell me he's selling lab supplies. But he definitely didn't seem like a salesman either.

"Actually, that's not why I wanted to talk to you."

No shit.

"Oh, really?"

"My group has a contract with TERI. We are aiding them in the investigation of an oil rig collapse in the Bohai Bay, off the coast of China."

"The Energy and Resource Institute?" A well-reputed environmental NGO. "And?"

"We would like to access your cultures to see if they match the bacterial species found in that collapse."

Do I look like I was born yesterday? "I'm sorry, those cultures are proprietary. I held the patents until last week, when I transferred them to my new employer, Amrencorp. All the cultures are now at my lab in Houston," she lied.

"I couldn't give you access even if I wanted to. Which I don't." Firmly.

Another abrupt energy change, with body language to match. He settled back, and his face went blank. If DD were green and guileless, she'd have instinctively leaned forward to recapture his interest.

She didn't.

"Thank you for meeting with me, Dr. Davis," said Fleck, abruptly standing.

He'd been easier to get rid of than she had expected, which led her to believe he'd turn up again. Her mouth was dry and she felt a little queasy.

Nerves.

She breathed deeply as she watched Fleck walk out the front door of the hotel. *What does he want? Surely the story about an oil rig collapsing is a ruse? I can look it up online later, I guess.* She breathed deeply, calming herself before signing her breakfast chit and heading down the hall to locate her meeting room. Once there, she was glad to have something to do: she fiddled with her projector and microphone until she was sure everything was working right.

VIII.   The Windup. The Pitch!

"Some background," she began.

Her first slide said BIOREMEDIATION.

"Until Viswanathan won his Supreme Court patent case in 1980, the idea of using Obligate Hydrocarbonoclastic Bacteria to clean up oil spills at an industrial scale was just a dream."

Her second slide showed a big, blobby-looking "OHCB," which then turned animated and began swimming around the screen, gobbling up black dots and splotches Pac-Man style. Forty men and three women in boring suits sat at cloth-covered tables, some with pads out to take notes, but most steepling their hands or sipping coffee drawn from the urn in the back of the room.

"These organisms, which destroy oil, are naturally-occurring bacteria. They live in areas of natural oil seepage and they have been subsisting on the hydrocarbons there for millions of years."

Diagram of an underwater oil deposit seeping through the ocean floor.

"These organisms compete with one another for survival and multiply dramatically whenever a big 'bubble' of oil reaches the ocean floor."

A slide showing three micrographs in succession: one with ten bacteria, one with 100, and one in which the bacteria occupied the whole circle of the picture. The slide captured the audience's eyes as DD figured it would. That's why she'd picked the false-color images with lots of bright yellows and oranges.

It had taken her hours to dumb down this presentation. She'd dragged four non-scientist friends out to lunch and made them watch it. Once their eyes stopped glazing over, she figured she'd gotten it right. Not that these people were stupid, but they were not scientists. They were the executives who would decide the fate of her new technology and the future of her career.

They sat erect, fidgeted, and frowned at the next slide: the iconic satellite photo of the Deepwater Horizon leak, occupying a big fraction of the Gulf of Mexico. That photo had been on the evening news every day for months and the resulting legal fallout cost, and was still costing, the unlucky oil firm in the billions of dollars.

"During the Deepwater Horizon spill, dispersants were sprayed on the oil."

A simple chart was next: bacterial population versus dispersant concentration. A line sloping down. "The dispersants used were toxic to the naturally-occurring OHCBs living in the Gulf. In other words, the solutions we applied made the oil closest to the surface stick around longer."

An underwater photo of a plume of oil, spiraling into the darkness of the depths. She paused for a moment to allow the audience to spot the two divers near the laser dot from her pointer. One was adjacent to the plume and the other in the foreground, but still tiny. It took a moment to comprehend from the perspective how massive the plume had to be.

"At deeper levels, where the dispersants could not reach, my colleagues and I were able to test and monitor the bacteria levels. We were searching for the bacterial species most capable of dissolving the most oil, the most quickly."

A cartoon of a bacterium holding a trophy.

"And the winner was…*pseudomonas putida*. This bacterium can break down 30% more oil in a 24-hour period than the next-fastest organism."

A dark blue slide, entitled, Problems. Bullet points appeared one by one as DD listed them:

"The problems with this OHCB are that: it has a narrow temperature range at which it can thrive; it is extremely vulnerable to the toxic effects of dispersants like Corexit; and it is vulnerable to ultraviolet light, confining it to deeper plumes and seeps."

A new slide showed the twined strands, like strings of pearls, of colonies of a different bacterium.

"Enter *Alkinivorax borkumensis*. This is the most common hydrocarbon-degrading bacterium in the world, existing in 80% of the planet's oceans. Due to its resilience in different temperatures and conditions, it out-competes the other OHCBs in most ecosystems. This bacterium is a survivor."

Another slide, *p putida* and *a borkumensis* side by side. The images blurred, swirled in a psychedelic mass of color, and resolved into a new image:

"Presenting: *Pseudoalkanivorax davisii!*"

"This is a new, genetically-modified species of oil-destroying microorganism. It could not have been produced using older, plasmid-based genetic engineering, or even the newer CRISPR. The technique was developed in my lab, a highly confidential technique which now, thanks to your persuasive efforts to recruit me," *pause for polite chuckle*, "belongs to Amrencorp. It produced a previously-unattainable hybrid of the two organisms, cherry-picking the genes for high oil consumption from one, and for a wide range of survivable conditions from the other."

The next slide showed three basketball-court-sized tanks of seawater, fifty feet deep, in a gargantuan hangar-like warehouse. One of the tanks was completely wrapped in a mile or so of black plastic, producing blackness within; one had a heating unit mounted on the rim, like a Brobdingnagian hobbyist aquarium; the third had banks of ultraviolet lights suspended over it. DD pointed all these things out.

"Each tank was contaminated by 5% crude oil by volume: 1,056 barrels."

Photo of two workers in coveralls, standing at the top of a steel staircase on a steel platform, dumping a barrel of oil into one of the tanks, a row of barrels waiting behind them.

"A standardized culture of *pseudoalkanivorax davisii* was introduced."

A worker in coveralls holding a metallic hose, sort of like a pressure-washer, spraying something into a tank. The surface of the tank was mottled with black puddles of crude.

"After seventy-two hours, hydrocarbon concentrations in all three tanks had dropped below target levels."

A smiling worker, standing next to a man in a lab coat holding a clear glass beaker of only faintly cloudy water.

"Ladies and gentlemen, this means," DD paused for effect. She had their complete attention. "Not only can we clean up spills, we can clean them up before anyone even knows they've happened."

"Questions?"

As one, the suits began clapping. Smiling faces, nods of approval, excited side chatter among them. DD could tell this was something they'd been wanting for a long time. She'd solved a huge public-relations problem for them, by solving an environmental problem for everyone. She puffed her chest a little.

Savior of Amrencorp, savior of the planet. Nice to be appreciated. I think I'm going to like this corporate gig.

She powered down her laptop and disconnected from the hotel's projector. As the first after-lecture questioner came up to introduce himself, she pulled her USB drive out of the computer and dropped it in her pocket; her thumb came away sticky. She wiped it on her jacket without thinking, unclipped her lavaliere mike from her collar and set it down for the hotel's AV guy. She paused to shake hands with several attendees as she finished packing up.

IX. Ferry Tale

DD cruised down Seawall Boulevard. The architecture of Galveston's main drag ran towards two extremes. First, exquisite Victorian houses, interspersed with charming 1930s Craftsman bungalows. Second, the architectural style, which DD privately thought of as *Brick Elephant,* based on Texas's distinctive red limestone: columns, porches, turrets, gables, bartizans, all intertwined in an arbitrary, massive, ungainly red, brick-and-limestone salad.

She observed that, once one got a few blocks away from the bridge, Galveston seemed quiet, especially since it was Saturday night. Perhaps its storied days of seedy bar fights among oil roustabouts, fishermen, and merchant marines were only a ghost from the past.

Or perhaps I'm just in the wrong neighborhood to see it.

Galveston was less than an hour from downtown Houston's grit and gaud, but the air was breezy and the climate sunny. The quiet atmosphere was vividly unlike the Gulf Coast beach cities in her native Florida, which had been gradually swallowed by commercial tourism and hemmed in by retirement condos in the last few decades.

She'd met her new lab staff when she delivered the cultures in Houston. *What a pleasure that was!* The people she'd be working with were cream of the crop, and motivated.

The lab facility was brand-new, and her office was at least as nice as the assistant football coach's at FCU.

She'd built some extra travel time into her schedule, just in case; DD believed in over-preparing. It left her with extra time on her hands now.

Fortunately, she loved to travel. She'd never seen the Texas Gulf Coast before, so she decided to make a weekend of it. There was a car ferry from Galveston to the Bolivar peninsula; she planned to stop for the night on the peninsula and move on in the morning.

The route to the Galveston ferry terminal was well-marked, though her phone's GPS was also fine. At the boarding station, she obeyed the ferry crew, who gestured with neon-yellow gloves for her to take lane number three. She pulled her little SUV in line, where it was eclipsed behind a customized Ford Expedition, and lilliputianized next to a Silverado 3500 *(yes, I'm in Texas, truck capital of the USA)*. She cut off the engine. The sun was two fingers' breadth from setting and the bay water was choppy, with steely gray waves in sharp regular rows like a bastard-cut file. The fall air was fresher, now that the sun was low. A dolphin's supple back flashed, gleaming among the waves. Pelicans circled and dropped, lunging into the water with flapping feet.

The ferry's motor was running, a slowly oscillating bass growl she could feel through the soles of her feet and up into her hips. She returned to her car and checked her e-mail: *nothing pressing*. She watched a tiny tugboat push a gigantic oil platform towards the cluster of refineries ashore. A group
56

of laughing children ran along the beach. She glanced back down at her phone, then looked up and slammed her foot on the brake in panic, briefly disoriented to see the dock pylons moving past her as the boat left its berth. The ship's start had been so gradual she hadn't felt the movement.

She got out of the car again. There was an odd hole in the hem of her jacket, like a cigarette burn, and she didn't smoke. *Damn, I really liked this suit!* She tossed it into the vehicle and circled the walkways around the deck. Reaching the rail at the bow, she stood next to a bronze-faced Hispanic family: dad, mom, and three girls with silky long black hair, the youngest's in two long braids. The sunset contained utterly saturated, extravagant streaks of lemon yellow, apricot, and lavender. Another latex-shiny grey fin and back flashed and were gone, back below the whitecaps, even as she exclaimed aloud, "Dolphin!" The family scanned in vain, the little girl bouncing on her toes. DD smiled, thinking of her own innocent little girl, years ago, and a familiar pang of grief-guilt-fear shot the smile down, just as fast.

The lights of Houston twinkled to life on the horizon below the sunset. She checked her phone again; five full bars of coverage, but still no response from Tim. *I'm just being a twitch.* But she wanted to confirm she'd used the right data in that report. She'd changed the inclusion criteria at the last minute, and edited the spreadsheet and saved it, but she had an irrational fear that she'd used the old data file, like the niggling worry that you left the oven or the iron on when you left the house. Tim could check the save dates and tell her for sure. She shrugged; it was late, it was the weekend, he would be busy packing to move, and she wasn't likely to hear back from him until Monday. The lay people she'd presented to would never notice, but an error in the report file that was going up on the web page could potentially come back to bite her in the ass later on.

Oh, well. She might as well let it go for the moment and enjoy a restful weekend drive up the beach. She'd never been to Bolivar peninsula before, but she figured that, like most beach towns, it would be full of hotels and restaurants.

The ferry approached the dock. Another dolphin's fin crested and was gone. She got back in her car, turned the key, and attended the process of being ushered off the boat by costumed traffic directors. There was a park-like rest area by the dock: bathroom, small office (closed), and cement walkway along the top of the seawall. Mercury-vapor lights overhead had come on automatically, casting a pinkish tinge that melded with the sunset. A tiny yellow-white hangnail of sun remained unconsumed by the horizon. A few quiet people fished off the seawall. They'd left some things behind on the concrete picnic tables: a straw cowboy hat, a tote bag. *So: petty crime, not an issue here.*

She pulled in, used the restroom, got back in her car, and Googled "hotels bolivar texas." Two. *Hmm.* And the lack of lighted signs on the long, straight road ahead told her she might have erred in assuming she could easily find a place to spend the night. *At least I've already eaten.* The first hotel listed was the Seaside Motel, advertising $35/night, a price which pretty much said that the price was the only thing to recommend it. *Nope!*

How about the Down By The Sea bed and breakfast? She tapped the number to dial. The phone rang and rang, and then what sounded by its clicks and static like an old-fashioned mechanical answering machine picked up. She hung up and drove down the long, lonely strip of highway to the Seaside Motel. The hotel was identified by a yellowed plastic light-box sign above a concrete central pool, surrounded by a chain-link fence and a few rusty steel lounge chairs. The doors and trim had been painted a distressing glossy Pepto-Bismol pink which had been slopped over plenty of wood rot. The general *gestalt* of the semicircular structure, considered as a place to sleep, grabbed one by the lapels shrieking, "BEDBUGS!" Two cars were parked by the office's dirty plate glass windows at one end, and only one guest car was parked in front of the motel proper.

Meager occupancy for a Friday night.

She hesitated a few moments, her hand resting unconsciously on the gun concealed at her waist, wondering if she should see if the rooms would be as bad as they inevitably were. She felt a bit of lurid curiosity, but she didn't get out of the car.

She pulled out and drove down the interminable highway towards the gray horizon.

Now it was getting really dark. *Not many lights out here.* Rather than drive around and sightsee on the peninsula, *which doesn't seem to have many sights anyway,* she'd better zero in on finding a place to spend the night.

She pulled out her phone. She dialed the number for Down By the Sea again. Still no answer, still that archaic answering machine.

"Hi, my name is DD Davis. I'm on the peninsula for the night and I was hoping you had a room available." She left her number. The turnoff for the B & B was two miles ahead.

The light had faded from all but the farthest western sky and the first stars were showing. She couldn't see Houston's lights from here. She followed the glowing map on her phone, turned right on Alberdie Street and almost missed the sign for Vista Boulevard, but there it was: the B & B, marked by a tiny, colorful, painted-wood sign. It was a big beach house on high timber pilings, surrounded by a weathered deck. Just as she closed the navigation app, the phone rang. She answered, and a woman's voice said, "Is this DD?"

"Yes, this is DD."

"This is Joanne Jebali. I'm the owner of Down by the Sea Bed and Breakfast. We do have one room available…"

DD interrupted, "Great! I'm right here!" and stepped out of her car. She sprinted up the steps to the front door and rang the doorbell.

"Excuse me, hold on a minute, I need to get the door. Then I'll give you directions," Joanne said. "Don't go away!"

"No, I don't need directions." Joanne was perplexed as DD tried to convey that she was in front of the B & B that very minute, but the light came on in her eyes after she opened the door and saw DD holding the phone to her ear. They started their acquaintance with a laugh.

One of the best ways to meet someone new. Joanne's sharp brown eyes crinkled in the corners with delight. Joanne was perhaps 60, *old enough to be my mother.*

Joanne welcomed DD into a living room with glorious picture windows facing east over a spacious deck. The overstuffed furniture was too big for the room, which was decorated for Christmas. *This is late September! Early? Or Late?* The artificial Christmas tree's needles were highlighted with fake frost which had gathered grey dust on its tips. *Last Christmas, then.* Adding to the room's overall clutter was jewelry: stacks of sterling silver, semiprecious stones, and beaded hand-made adornments were laid out on every horizontal surface.

"Don't mind the jewelry. We're getting ready for the Jane Long festival in downtown Bolivar tomorrow. It's great fun! People dress up in pioneer costumes and we have talks and demonstrations. You must come!"

DD allowed as how she might come. Joanne swiped DD's credit card and DD filled out a short form. Joanne gave her a metal key. Joanne pointed out which of the maze of decks outside to follow to get to her room. Her Michigan accent was touched by gravel, from neither smoking nor cheering at sports events, DD would later learn, but from a ventilator accident during her career as a nurse; a patient's ventilator had exploded in her face, throwing spores everywhere, leaving Joanne's chest full of the spores of a virulent fungus. DD's room was in a separate, smaller building, connected by a high, weathered, wooden walkway to the main house.

"How much luggage do you have?" Joanne asked. "The stairs are pretty steep to lug suitcases up. I just had an elevator put in." She pointed to an expansion-mesh cage at the edge of the deck.

"Thanks. I do have a pretty big suitcase. I'll go get it." DD went out the front door and pulled her car out of the narrow street and onto the slab foundation beneath the home, which was built on stilts, like many houses in hurricane-prone beach towns. The area under the house was set up as a shaded patio, with porch swing, outdoor furniture, and a grill. She wrestled her scuffed, hard-sided spinner case out of the car, and rolled it to the elevator cage. But she couldn't see how to get the elevator to come to her. She looked all around the entrance, puzzled, and was about to give up and just lug her case up the stairs backwards, one step at a time, when a friendly male voice interrupted.

"Need to get that on the elevator?" The accent was a Texas twang with something else overlaid on it, something DD couldn't quite place. She looked up; the deep voice was attached to a dark-haired man with a congenial smile who popped his head over the deck railing. Before she could answer, he disappeared, and the next thing she knew, he was clattering his long, muscular legs down the flight of steps at the back of the slab. He grabbed a philodendron vine climbing

62

one of the wood stilts and ripped it down, revealing a giant red toggle switch. "Here's the button," he said.

"Let me guess," she pointed, grinning, to the top of the switch, "up," pointing at the bottom, "and down." She found her gaze angling up at him coyly, without conscious intent.

"You got it!" He stepped back to allow her entry.

She pressed the button and held it while the elevator clanked its way down. "Thanks," she said, suddenly awkward, "those stairs are a little steep."

Once the elevator stopped at the bottom, the latch on the steel door clicked. He opened the door for her and set her suitcase inside. It was dark below the stairs, but she could see he had a square jaw, broad shoulders and a lean physique in jeans and work boots. *Hmm.*

"I'm Jeremy Robinson," he introduced himself, offering a handshake.

She took his hand. Strong but gentle grip. Calluses. "DD," she smiled. He smiled back. She stepped into the elevator and found a toggle switch like the one on the post.

"Thanks so much, Jeremy! Goodnight!" He shut the expansion-mesh door; she waggled her fingers at him and smiled. She pressed the button and the elevator lurched up to the patio.

She rolled her case along the deck to the room, clutching her key. There was a row of houses between the B&B and the ocean, but she heard the waves, rolling into the shore and chanting a soothing, slow song with a random, swirling rhythm. The room was snug, white wicker and a canopy bed. The bathroom had a jetted tub, which she filled with a smile. By the time she finished a sybaritic soak, she was logy and drowsy.

It was only 9:00 pm, but it had been a long day; a few of the cultures she brought to the lab had been, strangely, double-labeled in Tim's neat handwriting. She'd had to guess at the hybrids and pure strains, based on the colony configurations on the culture medium, and so they'd taken a little more time to organize than she'd expected. She had met her new lab staff. Trying to learn their names and get a clear first impression of these people, on their best behavior in front of their new boss, had also been taxing. She smiled, though: they impressed her at first meeting, all sharp and inquisitive. Then came the evening's drive, and despite the short length of the trip, she was beat. She cracked open the window and drifted off to sleep on top of the covers, listening to the sound of the waves.

X.   TGIF

Dr. Viswanathan pressed his intercom button. He'd asked Juni to put the international call through to Chakrindar at the Bureau ten minutes ago and hadn't heard from her since. Ah! The intercom button failed to light up or make its usual beep when pressed. The phone system must be down. He looked up and realized the overhead light had gone off at some point. He had failed to notice because the sun's evening rays were streaming in across Lake Michigan, which was visible as a slice of turquoise-green between the skyscrapers. It was a chilly Fall day, and if the power didn't come back on in a few minutes, he might as well go home because it would soon be too cold to work in the office. He stepped to his office door and popped his head out. Juni was standing in the corner, feet in a spreading puddle of cold coffee on the floor, the handle of the pot warped beyond recognition in her hand. The cheap white-plastic drip coffee maker itself looked like a cake that had fallen.

"Juni?" He asked, which snapped her out of her obvious shock. She tried to put the coffee pot down, but the handle stuck to her hand. She pushed it off with the other hand, but like the American folktale someone had told Amit about a Tar Baby, it just stuck to her more. She grabbed for a roll of paper towels, but they just stuck to the gooey plastic residue on her hands. Dr. Viswanathan took a step towards her just as her left shoe came apart, causing her to turn her ankle. She sat down abruptly in the puddle of coffee, bewildered.

He strode over to her and put his hand out to take her sticky one, bringing his other hand behind her arm to help her up. Then *he* slipped, he thought at first in the wet coffee, but as he scrambled up he felt a squishy pulp under his knees and shoes and noted with astonishment that the false-wood laminate floor was turning semiliquid where the coffee had spilled. He was down on one knee, Juni was still sitting on the floor holding her ankle, and *this could not possibly be happening*!

But it was. Some bizarre solvent must have spilled. Or something. There was no smell, and his skin wasn't burning, but anything that would dissolve two different types of plastic so thoroughly and so fast could be quite toxic and shouldn't be trifled with. The wisest course seemed to be to get out of the office, put Juni in a cab to the hospital, and go home. He could call building maintenance from his cell phone. Then, he'd forget about it and enjoy his weekend.

"You'll want to have that X-rayed; I'll get you into a taxi," he told Juni. She nodded, fixing him with her doe-like brown eyes. He asked protectively, "Can someone meet you at the hospital to take you home?"

She nodded again. "My brother. I can go to the urgent care center at the hospital a few blocks from his apartment."

"Very good. Let's get you up…" Awkward, with his feet wanting to slide in the liquefied laminate. He felt awkward, too, touching her, a woman and his subordinate; it grated against his traditional Indian upbringing. But he had to grasp her firmly to get her upright; Juni was a trim but solid-built black woman, only an inch or two shorter than he. With effort, he managed to help her up onto her good foot. The other shoe gave way now, fortunately without injuring her further, and she hobbled along in her stocking feet, leaning on him for support. They reached the elevators—of course, those weren't working either, due to the power outage. Strangely, the emergency exit lights over the stairwell weren't lighted either; he thought they were required to have a backup power supply. Into the stairwell they went, finding their way by the dim light streaming in through the narrow, east-facing windows. Seventeen stories. It would be slow.

So, they began.

The stairs were populated by a few others who had decided to leave; he presumed everyone else in the skyscraper was dutifully waiting for the lights to come on: hourly workers eager to get their full 40 hours' pay, others too lazy to walk downstairs, waiting for the elevators to start working again, or perhaps a few people wanting to finish some item of work before the work week yielded to TGIF. Two athletic young men in khakis and matching-logo polo shirts saw Juni's plight.

"Here, let us get you out of here!" Before Viswanathan knew what was happening, they'd locked hands and lifted Juni up between them, easily carrying her down the steps. He watched them disappear around the next landing and continued to make his own, slower way down the stairs behind them.

By the time he made it down to the ground floor, his aging knees aching a bit from the downstairs climb, the two young men were nowhere to be found. Juni's pantyhose looked moth-eaten, shredded as high up as her knees. She had a gaping hole in the hip of her polyester skirt where she'd sat in the coffee. The right sleeve and cuff of her jacket was full of holes as well, where the coffeepot must have splashed. She was standing alone on the sidewalk, leaning against a wall, toe of her injured foot down, confused and shocked.

He flagged her a taxi and helped her in. She named the urgent care center near her brother's house, and the driver took off.

XI.   Sand in Shoes

DD woke up with morning rays already sloping through the blinds. *So much for watching the sunrise. I needed the rest!* She jumped into sweatpants and tank top and strode out the door, following the deck around to the main house. Things she'd missed in the dark the night before caught her eye: low bushes covered with vibrant yellow poppy-shaped flowers, on the sand fifteen feet below; random pieces of driftwood on a steel coffee table between two deck chairs; a giant seashell set on the railing, filled with pieces of colored, smooth-polished sea glass. She opened the wood-framed glass door and stepped into the common room of the B & B.

"Good morning!" chirped Joanne. "Did you sleep well? Would you like some coffee?"

"Coffee," DD agreed, taciturn until she had her cup, making a beeline for the carafe on the kitchen counter. "I slept well. The sound of the ocean is soothing." She turned and realized she and her hostess weren't alone in the cluttered, cozy living room. In a corner chair by the fireplace, half-hidden by the dusty Christmas tree, the man who'd helped her with the elevator was lounging. He gave her a charming little smile as their eyes met, and DD felt her pubic muscles twitch involuntarily.

It's been a long time, hasn't it? She smiled back, giving a half-wink, then flicked her eyes away. She focused on fixing her coffee.

Years.

"Breakfast is ready!" proclaimed Joanne. "French Toast and sausages!"

Jeremy rose from the chair; DD noted an athletic grace which belied the age attested by the tanned crow's-feet by his eyes and his callused bumpy knuckles. She placed him in his mid-forties, a few years older that she. He was cradling another of Joanne's big ceramic mugs, and he sat at the head of the table, she on his left. He heaped his plate with sausage patties and French toast; DD took two triangles of toast and one sausage patty as he spread his with a thick layer of real butter and drowned it in syrup. DD couldn't help envying him; he appeared to be one of those people who could eat anything he wanted without getting fat, while DD had to watch every bite and exercise daily to maintain a healthy weight. Perhaps it was because he worked hard, while she was a knowledge worker. She was pretty sure he had an outdoor occupation; he was lusciously tanned and his forearms were cut with wiry muscle where the sleeves of his long-sleeved T-shirt were pushed up to the elbow. His hair, though dark and wavy, was coarsened by wind and sun.

"Are you leaving today?" he asked between bites. That accent…Texas, but also…New Zealand? Scotland? Boston? Very faint—*maybe if he talks a little more—*

She smiled, leaned forward. "I'm not sure. I was planning on it, but this spot is so nice, I might stay an extra night." Yes, an answering shift in his posture, a brightening, when she said that, and her smile widened a little of its own volition. She lifted her cooled mug to her lips and took a big gulp of the bitter coffee, blotted her lips with her napkin, and sighed, appearing nonchalant, before asking, "How about you? Are you headed on down the road today?"

"Oh, I live here," he said.

Oh. Not what I'd figure as Joanne's type. Too young, for one thing. In response to what must have been a puzzled look, he explained, "I live in Galveston but I'm staying here at the B&B while I help Joanne fill in around the foundations, after Gertie." DD hadn't noticed the slabs being exposed. Hurricane Gertrude had whirled up the Texas Gulf Coast the year before, a Cat II, which all the structures in the area were built to resist, but it had hit during a high tide with a huge storm surge.

"I didn't notice them being washed out, but then I'm a city girl," DD offered. "So, are you in construction?"

"Landscaping," Jeremy replied. "I don't know if you noticed, but that's my truck parked up by the main drag." DD had, in fact, noticed the gravel-filled dump truck parked on the asphalt before the vacant storefront on the corner.

She'd lived in Florida long enough to know that probably meant the road shoulders were soft sugar-sand that couldn't support a heavy vehicle. Flash back to a night in grad school, a solo impulse trip after one of her many tumultuous breakups, from Atlanta to check out the Spring Break revelry in the Redneck Riviera. She had pulled over to consult her road atlas (before the days of Google Maps and iPhones) onto what appeared to be a solid shoulder. And found her wheels useless in the loose sand. She'd tried wedging everything she could find—driftwood, lumber, her jacket—under the rear drive-wheels for traction, but wound up digging deeper and deeper holes with her tires until the belly of the car came to rest on the sand like the carapace of a sea turtle. She spent the night on the bench back seat of her ancient Plymouth Belvedere and woke up, at the moment of a glorious sunrise, to see a wrecker pull in ahead to rescue her.

She rose, raised her arms and stretched—*caught him looking*—and spoke up to Joanne, "Is my room available another night? I really like it here." *With the relocation bonus from Amrencorp on this culture project (not to mention the prospect of royalties if...when...it pans out for commercial distribution) I can afford a little splurge.*

"Sure," the landlady said, "I'd love for you to stay another night."

"Great!" said DD. "I think I'll go out for a walk on the beach before it gets too hot." She slid out the door to the deck and headed for her room to change her clothes. She willed herself to relax and act indifferent, all the while straining her ears for a step behind her: *none*. She had her key out well before stopping at the room door. She closed the door and shot the deadbolt. She changed out of her tunic and leggings into quick-dry nylon sport shorts, sport sandals, and a tank top, twisted her dark hair up, and stepped back outside.

She made her way around the deck and down the weathered wooden stairs. A breeze blew landward, carrying a rich aroma. Her acute nose began to catalogue its components automatically: salt water (though of course what she smelled was the iodine, since sodium chloride was as odorless as pure water itself), decaying vegetation, feathers—interesting, with no birds in sight—unrefined petroleum, and the distinctive aroma of *cycloclasticus*. She walked down the short street, past RV campers and beach-retreat homes of people a great deal wealthier than she. One had a rustic sign saying, AN OLD FISHERMAN LIVES HERE WITH THE CATCH OF HIS LIFE. Seashell wind chimes hung above sculptures of driftwood and tarred rope on the concrete pads. The stilt-raised homes were status-symbol beach houses for wealthy people from Houston, but humbler lots forewent the house completely and had just a concrete pad and a high sun deck, which doubled as a shelter for a motor home.

When she got to the beach proper, she saw that the low-growing shrubs with the bright yellow blossoms formed a matrix that held low dunes in place. The tide was low, the beach wide. The sand was darker in color than that she was used to seeing on the Florida side of the Gulf. She scanned ahead of her feet for tar balls (nasty to step in barefoot) but saw none. *The cycloclasticus I smell must be breaking them down.* She saw a line of flotsam washed up at the high tide mark and noticed draggled feathers sticking up from the sand. *Must be a nesting ground nearby.* One more aroma accounted for.

Right? Or left? To her left, a jacked-up pickup truck was parked on the sand about a quarter mile away, but she didn't see the occupants. She turned right instead. Half a mile or so south was a cheerful apricot-colored house across from a head of sand pointed into the water; that was her mark. She started towards it, savoring the sun on the left side of her face. The mid-morning temperature was just right for a walk, with a breeze that was cooling but not icy, and she settled into a soft-kneed, easy pace on the sand. Low wavelets broke with soft sighing sounds. A lone pelican cruised by, south-to-north, perhaps fifty feet above the waves. She swung her arms, making huge snow-angel circles, trying to release the road tension from her neck. She paused and shaded her eyes.

The distant truck's occupants turned out to be a white man and woman, now seated on a blanket and watching a small beige child play with a pail and shovel. DD spotted the oil rigs, just far enough out that one could see them only on the clearest of days, like today. And there was something moving near the rigs, a boat, too far out even to get an idea if it was a small, slow, close craft or a large, fast, far one.

She reached her goal point, the orange house, and decided to walk further. She picked a wooden picket fence, between the dunes and the beach, about another half-mile along. But first, she bent and put her hands on the ground, exhaling as her thighs stretched. She shifted her weight onto her hands and felt her calves come to life, walked her hands forward, and held a plank for four deep, easy breaths. She lowered her belly to the sand, then lifted her head and shoulders, using only her back muscles. She took another deep breath, then pushed up with her hands to arch like the cobra who lent the *asana* its name. She stretched flat, arms

74

overhead, before walking her hands back to her feet, standing upright, and saluting the sun with joined palms.

Her mood popped through the clouds of worry that had been shading her, clear as the sunlight, and she smiled the rest of the way down to the fence, her turnaround.

XII.   Heads Up!

The POTUS turned away from the cameras and microphones as soon as he finished signing the bill. His efficient staff led all the congressmen and lobbyists involved in drafting the bill out of the Oval Office. POTUS asked Steve, his primary handler, "Now what?" He expected to be ushered by his Secret Service detail and the rest of his retinue to the Marine One helicopter in order to be transported to Andrews Air Force Base, to board Air Force One, as usual, for a flight to...he wasn't sure today. He'd be briefed en route. But the Secret Service agents weren't moving. In fact, they'd formed a protective cordon around him, very close, very tense.

"What's wrong?" he asked. This was the White House, after all. He couldn't

be under threat in this room, one of the most secure spots in the entire world!

"Problem with the helicopter," someone said, a Secret Service man or a Marine, he wasn't sure. The guy turned his face into his collar and began murmuring into the microphone.

"Mechanical trouble? Terrorist threat? What the fuck? Tell me!"

"Well, we're not sure whether to believe it ourselves. But it appears that the fuel in the aircraft has been compromised."

"Compromised? How?"

"We're not sure, Mr. President. But we're getting word from Andrews that the fuel in Air Force One isn't optimal either."

"What? But do they even take the same type of fuel?"

"No, that's right, they don't, Mr. President." He insolently put his hand up to silence the President, pressed the earbud in his ear; they all did, in fact, and all appeared to be listening intently. Just as he started to object, bodyguards grabbed both his elbows.

Steve was walking backwards in front of him. "Mr. President, we need to go to the secure room for an emergency briefing. Right now. GO! GO! GO! GO! GO!" He turned and led the way, catching up with the door sentries who were getting the same message.

Before the President knew it, the wedge of Secret Service agents had formed around him and hustled down the hall outside the Oval Office; even if he'd wanted to break free, their rock-hard athletic bodies were no match for his sedentary spread, despite his height; in fact, he could barely keep up with them without stumbling. They steered him down the hall, towards the secure White House safe room maintained for the direst emergencies.

XIII.   What Happens at the Beach...

DD reached the short street back to the B & B from the beach in an ebullient mood. Swinging her arms, she reveled in the warmth in her limbs that came from a brisk walk. She pushed her hair back where it had slipped from its knot, damp in the cool breeze. As she approached the steps up to the deck, who should be leaning against the bannister but Jeremy? *Too easy.*

"Good morning." Jeremy smiled. He was standing hip-slung, trying to look sexy without looking like he was trying.

"Good morning," she whispered, taking his hand and gently tugging him after her as she mounted the stairs. *Life is too short to waste time playing games.* He hesitated just a moment before surrendering to her lead.

She stopped in front of her room door, smiled, and reached into her sports bra for the key, watching his eyes follow her hand. She opened the door and stepped inside, standing in the middle of the room and turning to face him. He smiled, came inside and shut the door and locked it.

She pulled off her T-shirt and wedged off her running shoes, leaving herself standing in sports bra, shorts, and socks. She stepped towards him and undid the snaps on his Western-style work shirt (*only in Texas do you see men wear these for work!*), one at a time. His chest was lean and lightly furred with dark hair; her pulse quickened as she flattened her palms on his bare skin.

He pulled her close and lifted her onto her toes, kissed her. Soft lips, hard kiss, just shy of painful. Her tongue as it swept over hers had a barley taste, and he wore some sort of citrusy aftershave. She grabbed his belt with her hands and pulled him tight against her, wrapping one leg around his calf, and he pivoted to fall on top of her, on the bed.

He slid his hand under her sports bra. *Yeah, that's it.* She moaned and fumbled for his belt buckle. While she undid that, and then his fly, he worked his kisses down her throat, savoring her workout musk, then applied his mouth to her breasts. She sighed, reaching for his trophy, but he quickly stood and dropped his jeans. She looked him in the eyes, lifted her hips, and pushed off her shorts and panties. He gave a little growl and dropped on top of her; his skin was beyond delicious against hers from thighs to collarbone. She sucked his tongue. He nibbled her lips, jaw, earlobe. She pressed her softness against his hardness. He broke away and she felt momentarily cheated and empty, reaching out for him with blind urgency.

He stood, working his boots off so he could step out of his jeans and underwear. She lifted her head to look. *What am I getting?* As he stood back up, his cock was thick, curved, medium length. He slowly stepped towards her and she beamed with eagerness. She sat up and grasped it, rubbing her cheek against its velvet while squeezing the shaft and feeling the steel beneath it.

Nothing like that texture.

The aroma, male hormonal yeasty warmth, suffused her senses. He took her head in his hands, but pushed it away, then pushed her back on the bed. He fumbled with a condom (*He's taking too long*). She wrapped her legs around him and squirmed her hips, rocking him against her. He paused, kneading her breasts, then backed his cock away from her clit and slowly, ever so slowly, eased into her. She sighed and squeezed, smiling at the low moan that elicited from him; he pulled back and thrust...hard!

Shit, he's going to come too soon... but he didn't. She found her muscles knotting up in rhythm until, abruptly, surprisingly (*I never come the first time!*), she climaxed in an iridescent burst of pleasure. Waves coursed through her, her shoulders shuddered against her will, and she was barely conscious of him coming as well.

Just like in the movies.

He rolled beside her to lie propped on one elbow, smiling and running his hand absently up and down her body.

Well, that was that. Simple. Purely physical, and wow! Not that he isn't nice, but.

She smiled at him fondly and ran her hand through his hair.

I wonder if Joanne will mind if I cancel that second night?

Two hours later, she was in her car, suitcase in the trunk, driving up the Bolivar peninsula to a reggae jam with a huge smile on her face.

I haven't done that since college. I guess middle-aged hookups are much better than college hookups because there's no pretending; you really, truly don't care if there's a future.

A flock of brown birds, thrashers maybe, broke from the yellow-green bushes. She caught one in crisp silhouette against a far-off rainstorm headed her way down the highway, and the image began to echo in her brain, generating a wave backwards through time: bird, egg, bird, egg…

An old-fashioned foxtrot came up next in her eclectic playlist. She reflected that perhaps ten generations had passed, since this music was first written. Ten generations of humans; maybe 500 generations of thrashers; and how many thousands of generations of bacteria? She started to calculate in her head.

About 3 hours for one generation, eight generations a day, 240 generations a month…over half a million generations.

Half a million generations ago, the ancestor species of humans, gorillas, and chimpanzees were just beginning to differentiate from their common ancestors. Now, humans were directing the evolution of bacteria (Viswanathan had shown the way on that). Now people like him, and DD, weren't just selectively crossing creatures for the way they looked or acted, but snipping DNA for specific genes, encoding specific enzymes, which turned on in specific circumstances.

XIV.   Just Another Breakdown

After their usual breakfast picnic, Ryan and Lori were ready to start their days. Lori worked evenings at the hospital, sticking patients for labs, and Ryan, mornings at the Sears tire shop. This morning ritual, coffee and sausage biscuits on the beach, was their one time to be together for sure. They didn't see much of each other, and once you figured in the loss of their food stamps and subsidized Lifeline phone they made a little less money, but their schedule meant one of them could always be with Missy so they didn't have to put her in daycare. But it meant they sure depended on the old truck. When it wouldn't start after he'd cranked it five or six times, Ryan popped the hood. The primitive engine was clean as a whistle. He'd just replaced the distributor cap his last day off, Tuesday, so he figured he must have left one of the connectors loose, causing one of the plug wires to fall off.

No, the sparkplug wires were seated on each plug where it sat in the classic V8 engine block. The battery terminals sparked when he tested them by bridging them with a quick tap of his screwdriver. He traced each spark plug wire back to the distributor, then began to flip the clips off the distributor cap. There was something sticky on the plastic of the cap, and he wiped it off on his frayed jeans. He gripped the cap and then recoiled, as if burned…the cap collapsed in his hand as though made of clay!

"What the Hell?" He exclaimed.

"What is it, honey?" Lori asked, tossing her bleach-blond pony tail and looking back over her shoulder. She was still half-in, half-out of the king cab, where she'd just buckled Missy in, her hand lingering on Missy's soft afro puff.

"I ain't never seen nothing like this before," he said. The cap was still firm at its base, so he pulled it free. On the inside, it looked like cottage cheese. Some of the contacts were coated with soupy plastic, and others were sunken. Too far away from the rotor to make contact, for sure. Lori had walked around the truck and now pressed her cheek against his upper arm as she peered inside, furrowing her brow.

"What the heck happened to that?" She asked.

"I don't know honey. But the truck ain't starting until I get a new distributor cap. Can you call your mom to pick us up? She can take you home and me to the parts store in Galveston. Shit, I'll have to call in to work! There goes my overtime! Sorry, baby! I know you were looking forward to having that new microwave."

XV.   Fully Upright and Locked

At the Atlanta airport, tempers were frayed.

Long lines of people waited to receive scrawled paper vouchers for meals from harried ticket clerks who were helpless without their computers. Tim, hung over from his prior night's partying with Sam's old school friends in "Hotlanta," stopped next to one such line and listened to an expensively coiffed and bejeweled woman in her 30s raise her voice. "What do you mean you can't accommodate me? Do you know who I am?"

Tim murmured, "She doesn't know who she is? Why is she wasting everybody's time?" A geeky blue-haired teenage girl standing in the line heard him. She turned around giggling, and he cut her dead with his trademark disdainful eye-roll.

The monitors showing arrivals and departures had been exhibiting multicolored confetti for quite some time. The the power to the displays was abruptly cut; they all went black. The overhead lights went out, but the big windows of the concourse admitted daylight. A flight attendant zipping down the corridor, pulling her rolling travel case, staggered as the plastic handle on the case broke cleanly in half. The case rolled towards Tim, who pretended not to see it and lifted his foot as though pulling up his sock, kicking it and sending it somersaulting. The flight attendant limped after it on a busted

84

heel, still gripping the useless handle. It made Tim feel better for a moment.

He spun and glided towards the exit, glad now he'd been checking luggage, and so had parked his rental car instead of returning it before checking in at the kiosk. If he'd done things in the usual order, he'd be stuck here with all these idiots. He could still retrieve the car from short-term parking and drive to Miami, worry about his suitcase later. He'd picked up some Adderal from one of Sam's buddies last night, so he should have no problem at all making the drive straight through.

XVI.   Moving Out

A leisurely day's drive, around New Orleans, through Mobile and Pensacola, and along the straightest and most tedious stretch of Interstate in the southeast, delivered DD back to Tallahassee. The lush greenery, which had so enchanted her when she first moved there, now looked more like a patina of green decay, covering the corruption and backbiting that underlay the political and academic scene. She'd stayed long enough to see what went on behind the Spanish-moss curtain, and that was really, *really* long enough. Then, she'd stayed longer.

She exited the freeway onto Monroe street, passing the cheap motels, dilapidated half-vacant shopping malls, and tattoo parlors. She approached the downtown, the Capitol neighborhood, with its older retail buildings, renovated into lavish offices for law firms and lobbyists. The offices were interspersed with gleaming luxury condo buildings and hotels, inhabited during the feverish few months of the legislative session by lobbyists, State of Florida legislators, and the call girls (and boys), caterers, and drug dealers who tended their recreational needs. The buildings were near vacant the rest of the year, mocking the homeless people who trundled their goods down the street beneath their windows.

She turned right onto Tennessee street, passed a few blocks north of the Capitol building (its erect towering shape flanked by the rounded domes of the two legislative houses, giving rise to decades of smirky jokes about the Governor's hard-on) before reaching "the strip" of college bars and the

86

vomit-flecked sidewalks in front of them. She continued past the University, turned right, and headed up one of the slight inclines Floridians call "hills" into the more upscale fringes of the student ghetto, where the faculty lived.

Her house was a 70s modern with a timbered, vaulted living room, walled on two sides in glass, and a stone fireplace. She noted, with approval, that the realtor's sign was on the lawn as they'd agreed. The sign proclaimed, "MUST SEE INSIDE!" The interior was impressive; DD had gradually remodeled the entire place and redecorated with the finest materials over the years. Amrencorp had provided a generous relocation allowance, which meant she was in no hurry to sell and could hold out for a good price as long as necessary, even until next August's crop of new academic arrivals. Everything was packed up in boxes, sheets of Styrofoam, and bubble-wrap for the movers, except for two suitcases in the master bedroom. The bed was still made; she was leaving the big king four-poster behind, along with a few other items, to help in staging the house (and also because there was no room for it in her sleek-but-small new Houston apartment). She plopped down on the big bed for a few minutes' contemplation. The thumb drive in her pocket poked her hip and she pulled it out. It was sticky. She pinched it and it deformed, like stiff clay or putty. *Odd. I wonder what happened to it? I'll have to check and see if it still works. Later, when I turn on my computer.* She set it down on top of a box.

She'd lived in this house for 15 years, since her one marriage had ended in divorce, and its lights, smells, and sounds were beyond familiar to her. She'd picked the colors of the paint, the granite for the counters, the shape of the moldings, the material of the drapes. She glanced at her hands, trying to remember which nail she'd lost when doing the tiles. The garden would probably turn up the occasional Lego or Barbie limb, from her grown daughter Jessica's childhood, for seasons to come. *Thanks, old home. You were a good home. I'll miss you.*

Before she knew it, the sun had set and it was starting to get dark. The dusk weighed on her emotions. Thinking of Jessica had transported her mind down a melancholy path. *Lord, give me the serenity to accept the things I cannot change, the courage to change the things I can, and the wisdom to know the difference.* She closed her eyes and sank into meditation, repeating the serenity prayer over and over until she felt the burden lighten off her shoulders like angel wings.

Her eyes popped open. She was done with her day; it was time to relax. She stripped and stepped into the bathroom. A single bar of soap and a bottle of cheap dollar-store shampoo remained, but all her other toiletries were in her car, and she didn't feel like getting dressed and going out to get them. *I can skip the skin and body care regimen just this once. Just get clean.* She turned on the hot water. She brushed out her shoulder-length deep-auburn hair and stepped in. She luxuriated in a leisurely shower, purring a hum which turned into an aimless song. At long last, she toweled off and put on an oversized T-shirt which hung to her knees.

88

She ordered one last meal of Chinese food delivered from her favorite place, Emerald River. While she waited for dinner, she combed out her hair. When the doorbell rang with the food delivery, she opened the door and snatched the brown paper bag. "Keep the change," she said, over-tipping the elderly Asian man who brought it. There was a stack of boxes next to the bed, and she laid out the white cardboard cartons on top. She slid her legs under the covers and settled herself in with a book, for a final cozy night in her customary, private cocoon.

XVII.   You Have the Right

Tim was feeling the Adderal, enjoying the way it carries you when you get tired and everything is vivid and crisp on the broken-glass edge of the drug. After the long drive down I-75, through the eternally under-construction portion between Macon and Valdosta, he was exulting in cruising the rental convertible with the top down, on the sunny oceanside highway towards his mother's house in Neptune Beach. One last visit before heading out to Texas and a raise. Not only that, but the Amrencorp purchasing system, judging by what he'd learned from his remote probing, appeared even more vulnerable than the one at FCU!

He shook his head. Why people created such insecure systems in the first place was beyond him. At FCU, over his years of service, he'd unearthed several people less adept than himself trying clumsily to skim cash or pad their expenses. That was, of course, a chance for some petty blackmail, killing two birds with one stone as he acquired small favors from others while he protected his own personal watering hole. He had been doing FCU a favor, as he saw it, by maintaining full attentiveness to their areas of vulnerability, and guarding against some outsider wreaking *real* havoc in the college's finances! Now he was going to perform a similar, unrequested but vital, protective service for his new employer Amrencorp (keeping a well-deserved fee for himself, of course).

He looked in the rearview mirror and saw flashing lights. He glanced at his speedometer: 68 in a 35. He chuckled. High spirits! He grimaced at the thought of the speeding fine and pulled over, smoothing his wind-ruffled hair.

The cop walked up to the passenger side of the convertible. Tim kept his hands on the steering wheel.

"Do you know why I pulled you over?"

"No, sir," Tim lied. "Why?"

"How fast were you going?"

"My speedometer said 35."

The cop didn't even dignify that with an answer. "License, registration, and insurance please."

"Reaching into my pocket for my wallet, Sir."

The cop took the proffered cards and walked back to his car. "Asshole," muttered Tim under his breath, once he was out of earshot.

After a few minutes, the cop walked back up to Tim's car door. Tim brusquely held his hand out for his papers, glancing away, but the cop snapped a handcuff on his wrist instead. "Tim Schneider, you're under arrest. Get out of the car."

"What? What for? For speeding? That's ridiculous!" Tim shrilled.

"There's a warrant for your arrest. Get out of the car!"

"On what charge?" Tim demanded.

"Grand Theft. I'm not going to tell you again."

"You must have the wrong Tim Schneider," he began, but the cop stepped back, opening the car door, and yanked the handcuff chain hard enough to make Tim emit a strangled scream as he was dragged out, belly down on the asphalt and gravel shoulder, losing a loafer and scraping his shin hard on the doorsill. His face was ground into the pavement by the force of the cop's boot on his neck as he handcuffed his hands together behind his back.

He was yanked upright and put in the back of the police cruiser, the cop's hand on his head, just like on TV. There was a second cop, who recited the Miranda warning, also just like on TV. Tim sat in sullen silence, staring daggers at the police through the mesh partition, as the cop car pulled off the shoulder. Tim looked down and saw black oily smears on the front of his expensive new designer T-shirt. Someone must have just happened to have an oil leak in their car, right over where the asshole cop threw him down. Great! Blood would wash out with the right cleaning products. This looked like it would stain permanently.

XVIII. Spaß und Spiele

Susan watched the Germans gyrate on the dance floor. One thing she'd learned in dealing with the company's German subsidiary was that the stereotype of the Germans as strait-laced and repressed was only half-true; when they cut loose, they cut *all* the way loose. She'd switched to tonic water early in the evening and was babysitting six men as they got sloppier and sloppier.

They'd started out at some authentic local clubs playing blues and zydeco, and the foreigners had professed to be delighted, but soon enough they seemed uncomfortable with the glances their increasingly loud German conversation was earning. They made their way to the Hard Rock Cafe™, where they could have a safely familiar international experience.

Susan dabbed some lipstick on and smoothed her hot-pink sequined size-18 tank top. Gunther wobbled over and flung himself on the bench next to her, lifted his beer towards his buddies, and hooted. He turned to Susan and high-fived her. Susan grinned and slapped back, hooting along.

Friedrich and Joseph wandered towards them, and Susan surreptitiously checked her phone. Eleven forty-five. She took a breath to shout out a suggestion that they make their way back to their hotel rooms, but at that moment, the music stopped. In the ensuing silence everyone froze, awkward in the strobe lights. Murmured conversations began.

A headphone-wearing tech sprinted across the suddenly quiet dance floor and disappeared into the bowels of the bar.

The four other Germans drifted over, muttering amongst themselves too fast and soft for Susan to pick up.

"Well," she said, "looks like the party's over for tonight!"

"Oh, let's wait a few more minutes," Friedrich said. "I'm sure they'll get the music going again!" Susan stifled a sigh. Friedrich and Joseph had been flirting with two college girls since they got here, and the girls disappeared into the ladies' room when the music stopped.

The other four, though, had no such prospects, and were more than ready to leave. They persuaded Friedrich and Joseph. Susan summoned an Uber and they headed out the front door. Just as they cleared the entrance, a cracking crash startled them. Gunther dived for the ground.

"Ha! I keep telling you the US is not guns everywhere like you think!" said Joseph.

"No, see, the sign fell!" Friedrich pointed at the plastic front panel from the Hard Rock™ sign over the door, which had shattered on striking the ground.

"Uber's here!" called Susan, waving her phone, "Jacob, in white Honda minivan." They stepped over the plastic shards and headed for the white minivan that had pulled into the parking lot. Susan felt her dressy heel stick to the sidewalk, "Damn inconsiderate!" she grumbled. "Gum on the sidewalk."

Waiting for her charges to load into the van, she turned to glance at the naked fluorescent lights where the plastic panel had fallen. The lights flickered and winked out; the whole building had gone dark. "We left just in time!" she said.

Their Uber driver, Jacob, a dark-bearded man, wheeled out of the lot. "I'm going to go up Bienville to get on the freeway. I-10 is blocked up through the Quarter here because of some kind of breakdown." They wove their way along the picturesque, gritty streets, and Susan couldn't help noticing that there were a number of cars pulled over or parked with their hoods up, and a number of lighted signs with holes in their panels, several buildings whose power seemed to have gone out.

"How random," she said. "All these power outages, but it's not a whole neighborhood, just one here and one there…"

But then they were pulling onto the freeway, driving in the left lane because the right lane and shoulder were sprinkled with broken-down vehicles, and a few in the left lane too.

Just as they crossed the 17th-street Canal, the van hiccupped. Susan caught Jacob's eye in the rearview mirror. Two little lines sprouted between his eyebrows. "I just filled up before I picked y'all up," he said.

The van's engine coughed, chugged, quit. Susan gasped. The driver struggled with the dead power brakes and steering, managed to coast to a stop diagonally, half-on the shoulder. The Germans were buzzing in their language in the back.

"Everybody out!" the driver commanded. "Stay together and everything'll be fine." Susan opened her door, shifted her weight to get out, and felt her foot slide on the floor. She looked down, and the carpet under the foot that had stepped on the gum had a hole dissolving in it, and she was sliding in a gooey mess. She lifted her foot out and found that the entire bottom of her shoe—her *favorite* dressy high heels!—was gone, the heel flopping loose, her bare sole on the asphalt. She turned and stepped each foot in turn up into the van, unstrapping her shoes and leaving them behind, while the Germans clambered out.

The men stood in an uneasy cluster. Susan stood on the pavement, eyeing the glints of broken glass on the shoulder with trepidation. She noticed Joseph scraping his sole on the ground, lifting his foot to inspect it. Jacob, the driver, had his hand in his pocket, holding something that looked heavy for its size. "This ain't the best neighborhood. Stay together and we'll be fine."

Susan wasn't too worried. Six big men, even if they did look like Twinkies in a tray of Yodels, wouldn't look like easy pickings. She looked left and right. It looked like most of the drivers of disabled vehicles were vacating the interstate as individuals or in small groups. The drivers whose cars still ran were driving doggedly along in the far-left lane. One had four flats but was still grinding down the road at 25 or 30 mph.

Jacob led them towards the nearest exit, the one they'd just passed. Susan, barefoot, shortest of them all, and overweight, slowed them down, but the men didn't complain. They were overtaken by a pair of teen boys, sagging, loc'd, and speaking a dialect of English that Jacob knew fluently from childhood, Susan could just make out, and the Germans barely recognized every tenth word of.

"You be with them?" one of the boys asked Jacob.

"I be driving them. Uber, man. You hear me?"

"They be foreign?"

"They be German. But she from here."

"Terence. Shug. You hear me."

"Jacob." Fist bumps. Nods to Susan and the Germans.

"Watch yourselves, cousin."

"You too, how."

The lean young men strode off. Their group followed at their retarded pace. They passed a pair of police cars, lights flashing. Two cops were leaning into an empty vehicle, two were waving flashlights at the oncoming traffic. Why that vehicle, of all the dozens stopped along that stretch? Who knew? The police looked as confused as they were. Susan walked towards one of them, "What's happening?"

"No information for you, ma'am. Keep moving along, get off the freeway. It's dangerous."

They crossed an overpass, and the neighborhood below arrayed itself in all its seedy glory: convenience stores, vape shops, bars, pawnshops, all lighted and glowing beneath the street lights, flashing traffic signals, strobe lights in windows of head shops and strip clubs.

As they reached the head of the ramp, the overhead freeway lights cut off all at once. They blinked in the darkness. One of the cop cars passed them, going the wrong way on the divided highway, siren screaming, lights flashing, weaving its way from the shoulder to the traffic lane among as cars pulled over between disabled vehicles to let it pass. The second police car lagged, lights flashing, but hobbled by two flat rear tires. As its lights faded in distance and the other car's siren became a distant whine, the first sounds of breaking glass came to them. A passing car's headlights caught the German's uneasy glances at each other. A lawyer, an accountant, two junior executives, a QC analyst, and an IT consultant, some of them gym-fit, but Susan was willing to bet none of them had been brought up on mean streets.

A couple of them had keychain flashlights. "I'll save my phone battery just in case," Susan said. She took her phone out to switch it off. "Hm. No signal. Here we are in the middle of a big city and there's no signal." None of them had any cell signal, though their GPS still worked. They switched their phones off one by one.

Jacob led the way, Susan in the center of the group of Germans. As they reached the bottom of the ramp, they heard the chilling sound of woman's screams. The shrieks went on and on, punctuated by abrupt interruptions that could only mean a hard blow to the face.

"None of our business," Jacob advised. "Stay back until they're done."

The six foreigners glanced at each other, glanced over at the underpass where the screams were coming from. Maniacal male laughter echoed between the woman's shrieks of pain and rage. The visitors moved together towards the ramp, Susan lagging behind.

"Do *not* do it, you idiots!" Jacob implored them. "You don't know. You gonna regret it. Damn it! Come back here!" They ignored him. Jacob had pulled his firearm, flicked off the safety, and was following at a distance, reluctant.

"Fucking cops see a nigger with a gun they're gonna shoot me and sort it out later, fuck."

Joseph and Friedrich, the two youngest and fittest, broke into a jog and reached the tunnel first. Friedrich had a flashlight and its faint beam showed a woman, now just sobbing hoarsely, on her stomach on the sloped concrete embankment. A number of youths, five or seven, he couldn't count, stood around watching one of them rape her. The flashlight allowed someone to draw a bead on him; a shot ricocheted off the ground near Friedrich. The cowards then ran off squawking and hooting like the animals they were.

Friedrich stood, motionless. Joseph glanced at him questioningly as the other four caught up.

"*Ich habe mich angepisst*," Friedrich whispered.

Joseph laughed loudly. Jacob gave him the stink eye and walked over to the woman, raising herself to her hands and knees now, still racked with sobs.

"Hey, you're okay now." Jacob said. He stashed his gun in the small of his back, took off his sweat jacket, and held it out to her to cover herself. She took it without looking at him, shrugged into it. Once she'd zipped it around her tiny bleeding frame, she looked up.

"Thanks."

"It's nothing. Can I do anything else for you, sister?" She shook her head, knees drawn up, wiped her bloody nose on the sleeve of Jacob's hoodie, realized her hair was a mess and tried to shape it with her palms.

"She should come with us, don't you think?" Susan whispered.

Jacob nodded, glanced at the Germans gleaming blondly in the darkness. "Yeah."

Susan held out her hand and the woman took it, rose to her feet. "My name's Susan."

"Maya."

"Maya, lovely name. Are you hurt, Maya?" Susan lifted her little keylight and inspected the girl's face. An eye was starting to swell shut and the scrapes warned of purpling bruises getting ready to rise under her caramel skin. She swept the light down and the girl's knees were raw meat, a gruesome caricature of a child who's skinned her knees skating. The color soaking through the sleeves of the grey sweatsuit suggested her forearms were the same. "Can you walk?"

"I can walk. I think my wrist might be broken." She held out her left arm to show a hand pointing off at an unnatural angle.

100

"Hospital six blocks north. Safer there." Jacob took the lead again and the group set off again, hampered by the limping barefoot women and Friedrich's spraddled gait

XIX.   Hey Now, You're a Rock Star!

The next day, DD rose with the sun, tossed the Chinese food containers in the trash can by the curb, and drove to the Circle K on the corner for a coffee. The movers were due at 7:30, so she sat on the steps and waited, enjoying the birdsong outside and watching the morning walkers and joggers.

Her phone rang just as the moving truck pulled up. She checked the screen: her new boss, Dr. Jack Herbert. Not a scientist, but a man who'd spent his career wrangling scientists for various corporations, mediating between their rarefied world and the more pragmatic world of business.

"Hello?" She answered.

"Hi, DD?" Asked Jack.

"Yes. Hi, Jack! What can I do for you?"

"DD, I just wanted you to know: we had the first actual field usage of *p davisii* today. So far, the results are great!" He trilled the R the word "great" in a jovial way that reminded DD of the old Tony the Tiger commercials.

"Really? I didn't think the lab staff would have the cultures cranked up already! That's fantastic!"

"Still used to the academic pace of life, aren't you? We don't let grass grow under us at Amrencorp!" Jack chuckled.

"Where was the spill?" DD asked.

"In the Gulf near Houston. We're 24 hours out from the initial introduction and the oil in the samples is 20% below your projections."

"Twenty percent? Hot damn! I hope you're following my sampling protocols closely, so I can look at the numbers when I get there!"

"Of course, DD! You're a rock star around here now. What baby wants, baby gets!"

DD smiled. "OK, well the movers just got here. I need to go. Keep me posted if anything else exciting happens!"

"Will do. Bye, DD."

"Bye, Jack." She almost did a little dance. Not just because the tests were succeeding, but because she was getting positive feedback in a way that never happened among scientists. In her old world, she'd have had to spend months writing up the results and preparing them for publication, justifying every protocol and process to peer reviewers, before getting even the most guarded recognition. She was self-motivated and cerebral, or she wouldn't have lasted so long in academia. And she'd had her share of insincere flattery flung her way in other contexts. But this praise, backed up by action as it was, felt surprisingly good.

DD put her phone away and eyed the moving crew hopping out of the truck. Six men, from teens to mid-20's, all in superb condition, and all already shirtless because of the heat. *Nice! Now, behave. They're here for manual labor, not entertainment. But that doesn't mean I can't enjoy watching them load up...*

She greeted the boss, older and with a pot belly, the least attractive of the men. Fortunately, he was wearing a shirt. They went inside to look over her furniture and boxes.

XX.   My Stuff!

DD slipped on her sunglasses as she turned back onto I-10, this time headed west. One more trip on this straight stretch of highway, surrounded by piney woods and cattle fields, with populated exits few and far between. Vast stretches of nothing to break the flat monotony, until Pensacola. DD gave a sigh. Just knowing she couldn't move around made her muscles jump. She tried to find the most comfortable position to spend the next few hours in. That was one thing she would *not* miss about Tallahassee: despite its being the state capital, it was at least a three-hour drive from there to anywhere. Well, two, if you counted Jacksonville.

She sucked a few gulps of diet drink through a straw from a giant Styrofoam cup and parked it in the cup holder. She popped her phone cable into the stereo and started her playlist of Blues, Dixieland, and Country. The miles started to slip by. One hour passed, then two.

Just after the first exit for Pensacola, she saw a big yellow truck ahead.

That truck sure looks familiar, but it can't be.

It was! It was her own moving truck! Stopped on the shoulder by the side of the road! She recognized the way the knots of red and blue rope were crocheted around the handle of the sliding rear door. She took her foot off the gas.

She passed it and saw the driver sitting behind the wheel, talking on his cell phone, with the door propped open. She continued ten miles to the next exit and got off, drove across the overpass, then re-entered the freeway headed east.

She passed the moving truck again, going east on the other side of the divided highway. The driver was nowhere to be seen, but he'd set up hazard reflectors behind the vehicle. She reached the first Pensacola exit and re-entered. When she spotted the triangles way ahead, she braked, put on her flashers, and then pulled in ahead of the stopped truck.

She waited for a break in the traffic roaring by before opening the car door, and then got out and walked back. The driver had been standing in the shade, leaning on the side of the truck away from the road. He'd been one of the crew at her old house, and when he saw who she was, he walked to the front of the truck to meet her.

He was a lanky, dark black man with a trimmed beard and light brown eyes. His skin gleamed like bittersweet chocolate and his muscles bulged under the sleeves of his T-shirt. *Damn. Down, girl!*

"What happened?" DD asked.

"I don't know. I'm not much of a mechanic, I guess," he said, with a shrug and a fresh sweet smile. "The engine just started bucking real bad and so I pulled over. Now it won't start."

"Oh, no," said DD. "My stuff!" She pitched her head back in mock dismay.

"I know," he said. "We'll get it sorted out. The company said they have someone on the way. He should be here soon."

"You want a ride? There's a truck stop at the next exit; you could at least get something cold to drink." *At least. He's not* that *young. He's got to be thirty.*

"No, I'm okay. I'd better stay with the truck until they get here."

"OK. Do you think I should stay too?" *One more try.* "You could sit with me in the car, where there's AC."

"No, you go on ahead, ma'am. Matt's Movers is a good company. We'll get your things to you. They're bringing another truck."

Ma'am? Ma'am, indeed! Hmph. Suit yourself. "Suit yourself. Thanks, um…"

"…Jordan."

"DD." She shook his solid hand. "I guess I'll see you in Houston."

"Soon, I hope, Ms. DD."

She got in her car and drove on.

On the road to Texas, she noticed five or six more stopped vehicles, mostly cars, with the hoods up and frustrated drivers on their phones. *It seems like a lot of people are delaying maintenance nowadays due to this endless recession that we're not having.*

XXI.　　See What's on the Slab

Once she reached Houston, she headed straight for the lab. It was obvious there was no point in going to her new apartment, since it was empty and her stuff wouldn't arrive until tomorrow, if she was lucky. She'd have to stay at a hotel tonight. She found a shaded parking spot in Amrencorp's vast lot, cracked the windows slightly so nothing in her suitcases would melt, and walked inside. She pulled on a neat summer-wool blazer as she walked across the lot, and sleeked her hair back into a ponytail at her nape; she had slipped off her flip-flops and put on loafers with her jeans.

She walked through the automatic sliding glass doors into the sleek marble lobby. One entire wall was a fountain, with water running down a glass sheet etched with the Amrencorp logo, a capital "A," italicized almost beyond recognition, with a flower-petal sun bursting up out of it.

There was a uniformed guard, barely old enough to shave, at the big black semicircular desk. His vest had the Amrencorp logo on it too.

"Hi! I'm DD Davis," she introduced herself.

"Doug." They shook hands.

"Do you have my badge, Doug? They said it would be ready today."

Doug looked in a big paper notebook on the counter, found her name, and used a key on his belt to unlock a drawer under the desktop. He asked for DD's driver's license before passing her the badge, then whipped out a glass touchpad and registered her right index fingerprint as well.

"You can scan in with the badge or the fingerprint." He pointed at a panel beside the doorway to the lab. "Give it a minute or so for the system to refresh."

"Very secure. That's great!" said DD. *Up-to-date technology!* It made her feel better about the probable need of working late or working weekends, which might leave her here by herself at times. She inspected the badge, with its hologram logo and her photo side-by-side. She entered the first hallway to the right of the desk, using the badge.

She was used to the perpetual budget starvation of academia, where the football coach lived in a mansion and drank aged single-malt Scotch while reviewing game tapes with the governor on his floor-to-ceiling TV, and everyone else learned to clip coupons and amuse themselves at free concerts in the park. She strode down the hall to the door of her new lab and stuck her finger against the square inch of glass in the scanner by the door. The LED turned green with a beep and the lock clicked open. *Cool.*

She stepped inside and puffed up with pride as her eyes swept over the gleaming lab counters, the sleek steel incubators, and the laminar-flow cabinet hoods with their UV glow. She relished the sight of spectrometers, cabinets full of virgin petri dishes, beakers, loops and swabs, and the goggled lab techs busy at work. She cleared her throat.

All five of the techs glanced up at once and stood a little straighter at their work. One, a pretty girl with dyed red hair in a long braid, (*What was her name again?*) was standing at a counter making notations on a sheaf of printouts clipped with a giant binder clip. She picked up the printouts and walked over to DD.

"Dr. Davis, hi, I'm Abby." She offered one of the printouts. "Would you like to take a look at these growth rates? They're way out of line above what we expected."

"Yes, I remember you from the other day, Abby." DD smiled, took the printouts and leafed through them. "Whoa! This is incredible! This is almost pure exponential growth! What happened?"

"I don't know, Dr. Davis…"

"…Call me DD."

"DD." Abby smiled. "I was just looking over the nutrient specs for the different batches and I can't find anything different. Were these cultures the same organisms the original studies used?"

"Absolutely. I had my assistant, Tim, check the lot numbers for the original cultures, and I supervised the hybridization process myself. The seals on the boxes were unbroken when I opened the shipment at this end."

A few minutes' silence as they stood, flipping through the printouts together. DD stole a glimpse at Abby. About Jessica's age. Jessica was so smart, this could have been her. Jessica had a full-ride academic scholarship coming, too, before she disappeared the first time.

"Abby, I need to get to my computer in my office to look into this more thoroughly. There's got to be an explanation. Are there any more of these printouts?"

"Yes, about 100 pages; they should be done printing now. Would you like me to bring them in to you?"

"Yes, please. And thanks…I needed to see these as soon as possible. Good judgment!"

Abby grinned, a slight crinkle in the corners of her blue eyes belying the babyish dimples that emerged on her cheeks. She was plainly one for whom a little praise went a long way, belying stereotypes of her generation. She almost skipped out of the lab.

DD walked to the end of the lab and into her gleaming office with its brand-new glass and aluminum desk, track lighting, muted pastel draperies, and ample bookshelves. She settled into the black mesh chair and wiggled for a moment in joyful amazement at how well it supported her back. Her smile faded as she regarded the puzzle before her, though. She began to arrange the printouts on her desk with a furrowed brow.

XXII.   Eureka!

Hours later, the shining floor-to-ceiling windows had become mirrors of the interior, backed up to the darkness outside; the track lighting cast a soft glow on the walls, and DD's LED desk lamp was spangling a tight, bright constellation that illuminated the printouts. DD sat up straight. *It's got to be.*

The *p. davisii* normally broke the crude oil into fragments of petroleum compounds, which quickly polymerized into longer chains. These chains had to be promptly and repeatedly dispersed into an emulsion by spraying with Corexit before the bacterium could continue digesting them. However, the Corexit slowed the bacteria's metabolism, so the breakdown was incomplete, and much slower than what they were seeing. DD had a sheet of scratch paper on the desk next to her.

It's the only explanation.

The scratch paper was filled with pencil equations and calculations. The workers had paused the spraying of Corexit when the slick started shrinking, as they always did, but it just kept shrinking, so they never had to start again. The amount of Corexit that was used, in the end, was a fraction of what they expected.

The p. davisii *is eating the polymers suspended in pure seawater. We had no indication of this in the vat trials. What's going on here?*

She tapped her pencil on the desk absently. *I should go out to the site in the morning. I can sit here and speculate*
112

all night with the data I have, but there's bound to be some factor that's not been observed yet.

She shut off her desk lamp and made ready to leave. She was the last one there, and as she walked out through the gleaming lab, she felt a proprietary thrill. She lingered a moment by the door.

Mine. She glowed inside.

She stepped out the front door, keys in her right hand, her left hand on the KelTec in her pocket. Her car was the only one in the lot. She stopped dead as her mind made the transition back to the mundane world. *I have no place to go.*

She looked inside her car. Empty, but for her suitcases in the back. She entered the car, which still held heat from the afternoon sun. She turned the key and rolled the windows down a few inches to let in the Fall air, which had turned a little cooler, and pondered.

Her new apartment was bare walls and empty cabinets and closets. Her belongings were, she presumed, still somewhere on I-10. She had become so absorbed in her work, she'd completely forgotten about the stalled truck! She'd spent the afternoon and evening, which she would otherwise have spent supervising its unloading, poring over the printouts in complete absorption. She'd expected that the moving company would call when they arrived, but they never had. Her things were still in transit.

I'm sure they'll be here tomorrow, probably first thing in the morning. But for now, I need to figure out where to go tonight!

She shuffled through the printouts and found the GPS coordinates of the ocean water where the *p davisii* samples were being drawn from, over the spill. She consulted her smartphone for the location. A wry smile spread across her face. *Eighteen miles offshore of the Bolivar Peninsula. How about that?*

She checked the time on the phone: 8:45. The last ferry ran at 9:00, so she wouldn't make it to Bolivar tonight; it was a two-hour drive to get to the ferry. So she couldn't stay with Joanne tonight. But it was off-season still, so she should be able to find a decent room in Galveston for the night. Then she could call Amrencorp in the morning and arrange a trip out to the platform. She buckled up and started the car.

XXIII. OCD

Amit watched the cab pull away with Juni in it. He stood for a few minutes with his hands in his pockets. The trickle of people leaving the building coalesced into a slow river, which merged with a flood in the street before him. Like some strange species of insects molting *en masse*, they left tatters of pantyhose, soles of shoes, and shredded scarves and ties behind them. One woman clutched her disintegrating dress together, trying to preserve a semblance of modesty. Others had given up and walked along nude or semi-nude. He figured out after a few minutes the degree of nudity depended on which garments were natural fibers and which were synthetic. Some were dazed, others seemed panicked, some women and a couple of men were in tears. A young man with a full beard and a surfeit of tattoos and piercings was grinning fiercely as he strutted along in nothing but his white cotton underwear briefs.

Traffic was at a near-standstill on the street, and as a passing car bucked to a stop, he realized how many components of vehicles were also plastic. But why was plastic suddenly dissolving into gels and liquids? And it was a variety of different types of polymers, too; he couldn't think of one solvent that would liquefy all of them. He set out walking along Polk street towards his apartment. As he left the campus, he saw that the traffic lights were still working, though it didn't make any difference, as the proportion of stalled cars had increased to perhaps one in twenty, enough to block traffic completely. People abandoned cars to walk, weaving among the vehicles trapped in gridlock. Many of the drivers leaned pointlessly on their horns as though they thought that would levitate the traffic out of the way. Others smoked, or bobbed their heads to music, trying to make the best of what they thought was just an unusually bad traffic jam in one of America's biggest cities.

He made it to the entrance of Arriga Park without further incident and crossed the park via its picturesque paths. The fountain wasn't running. He couldn't remember if it had been turned off for the winter already or not. Probably so, since it could freeze pretty hard in Chicago in October. He reached the other end of the small park and saw his apartment building. He reached into his pocket, and felt his polyester pants rip silently around the pocket opening, just from the pressure of his hand. The pocket was cotton, at least, and his keys were still inside. The awning above the building entrance was intact; he fit his key in the lock on the glass front door and it turned, but he had a moment's panic as it refused to open. He put his shoulder into the door and, with a good shove, it released with a ripping sound. The weather strip around the door had become a gooey seal which dropped onto the tile floor in moist chunks.

He approached the elevator and pressed the button, flinching slightly as his thumb met a sticky surface. The button lit up and the light above the door began showing progress: 12…11…10… As he waited, he thought about the cables and pulleys that suspended the elevator, the insulated electrical supply to the belt-driven motor, and the insulated

116

wires carrying current to the interior of the box suspended high in its shaft. He sighed, his elderly knees and arches twinging already from coming down the office steps, and walked down the short hallway to the staircase. Six flights, to his apartment on the seventh floor. He was panting when his key turned in the door.

The door swung open. He hesitated. He stood in the doorway, inspecting his apartment for signs of dissolving plastic. The laminate floor…the telephone on the wall…the acrylic vase on the coffee table…all looked normal. He rubbed his finger and thumb together where the stickiness from the elevator button had deposited itself, and noticed it was gone, leaving only a light, slippery coating. He put his fingers to his nose. He recognized the smell…it was familiar…where from?

His eyebrows shot up in recognition as he placed the aroma. *Pseudomonas putida!* He'd never forget that smell from his early, thrilling days of groundbreaking success at genetic engineering. And that was the same bacterium the Chinese doctor had been asking him about! Could it be? How? But it was the only explanation that made sense. That call, followed by plastic things starting to fall apart, and smelling like *p putida*: were they connected?

He decided to assume the theory he'd come up with was correct until disproven. He stood in the doorway and stripped naked. Nobody came along, thank goodness, to see his stocky dark-skinned frame in the nude, his sagging skin sprigged with graying hair.

He extracted his keys from the pants pocket and then dropped all his clothing on the floor in the hall next to the door. He left the door open, not touching the doorknob. He walked warily down the wool runner in the middle of the hallway and onto the tile floor of the bathroom. He hesitated, frowning at the plastic shower curtain dangling by its plastic rings. He picked up a ceramic water cup next to the sink, tipping the toothbrush within onto the counter without touching it, and used the cup to push the shower curtain back. He stepped inside the tub and let the curtain drop closed, then used the bottom of the cup to tap on the cross-shaped spigot handles to turn on the shower, good and hot. He washed the cup first and set it at the far end of the tub, then scrubbed himself from top to toe, and back up to his head again, with hot, soapy water.

A third top-to-toe soaping was followed by a rinse. He turned off the spigots by hand. He opened the curtain. He opened the medicine cabinet mounted on the wall and took out a bottle of isopropyl alcohol he kept on hand for first aid, and poured it generously onto the strip of tile floor he'd walked across. He stepped out into the puddle of isopropyl and toweled off with a clean towel, which he then wrapped around his waist. He took a hand towel and draped it over his shoulder.

He had a pair of latex gloves on the first-aid shelf as well, and he put them on. Stepping into the hall, he rolled the carpet runner up with care, touching only its edges and back, avoiding any surface his feet might have touched. Feet

118

straddled wide apart to step close to the baseboards, he waddled to the door, where he tossed the carpet on top of his clothing in the hall. He stripped off the latex gloves, which he then deposited on top of the pile. He walked back into the bathroom and washed his hands again, then took the remaining isopropyl and doused the segment of the entryway floor he'd crossed to reach the hall runner when he first came in. He blotted some of the alcohol up with the hand towel and used the alcohol-soaked towel to wipe the outside doorknob.

Then, and only then, did he shut the door. He turned around and surveyed his one-bedroom home. If he was right— and it was the best guess at this point—this was the only place nearby that was sure to be free of the destruction and disintegration going on outside.

XXIV. At Sea

DD had never felt so dainty in her entire life as she did on the boat out to the oil platform. She'd been a tomboy, and then grew up into the sort of woman many men found intimidating. Working in the sciences, she was used to ogling, sniggers, and putdowns both subtle and obvious. But the men on the boat with her, dressed in coveralls, or jeans and T-shirts, carrying backpacks or wearing tool belts, muscular and agile on the bouncing deck in the choppy water, radiated a masculine calm which made her acutely aware of her relatively weak and diminutive frame. Each one swept his eyes once from her ponytail, down past her clipboard, to her rugged hiking shoes, and back to her face. Once, and that was the end of that. No catcalls, no smirks, no posturing. All business. *Guess these oil roustabouts have nothing to prove.*

She was escorted to the galley of the boat, where she sat down at a small, bolted-down table with a technician, who sketched the basic process of underwater drilling for her.

"So, first we drill the well with joints of pipe, then we insert the casing once we've got it as far down as we want it go."

"So, is this like the Deepwater Horizon well?"

"Nah. Those Macondo wells are way offshore, just because the tourists and the greenies up there don't want to see the platforms from the beach. That's what made that spill so hard to cap off. They were in, what, 5,000 feet of water?"

DD gave him what she hoped was an alert look. Considering *I'll be working in this industry I should know more about it.*

"We're in 500 feet. Big difference in pressure. What is it you said you do?"

"I'm a microbiologist. I just developed a new strain of bacteria to eat oil spills."

"Oh, yeah, I heard about that! They said it worked faster and cleaner than any of the bacteria they'd used so far. Almost no Corexit needed, right?"

DD smiled, proud, and sat up straighter. "Yes, that's *p davisii*, my baby! Actually, I'm headed out to the platform because it might be working *too* well!"

Jeff, the tech, tilted his head. Eurasian features, round face, sparse beard. It made him look younger than he must be, for him to be out here. "How so?"

"Well, it looks like *p davisii* might be able to eat other types of petroleum-based polymers."

"Hmm. Interesting." She could tell he wasn't one given to thinking things through and imagining conclusions.

Well, and I'm probably being too *imaginative. At least I hope I am.*

"Yes, well, so…you were explaining how the drilling process works…" She steered him back on topic.

"Oh, yeah. You know, it would be easier if I could draw it. We're almost to the platform and I've got paper there to draw on. Do you drink coffee?" He got up and went to the urn on the counter; she followed him. He picked up a

Styrofoam cup off the top of the stack next to the urn without looking, a motion he'd repeated many times, and the cup underneath stuck to it. He gave a quiet, surprised giggle, looking at it. One side of the cup looked a little melted. The four top cups were fused. He pouted his lips in brief confusion, shrugged, tossed the warped ones in the trash, and drew them each a cup of coffee.

XXV.   The Length of the Handle of the Pump

In the compact, functional office of the platform, Jeff drew a diagram. A box up on top of the water, "That's us," a long, thin, double line down to the ocean floor, "That's the drilling pipe."

Then a big block under the line representing the ocean floor, "Once we find the oil deposit," he scribbled a big black oval just beneath the block, "we put a casing in at the end of the drill pipe. It's really wide in diameter, and we keep putting smaller casings inside bigger casings, like a telescope, until we finally meet the oil deposit." He'd drawn a fair representation of a telescope reaching down to just above the blob of oil.

"Isn't the oil under a great deal of pressure?" Asked DD.

"Oh, yeah! It sure is!"

"Well, so," DD asked, "How do you keep the oil from shooting out?

"That's where these geologists and drilling experts make the big bucks. They tell us exactly how deep the oil is and warn us before we get to it. They stop just short of the oil deposit and run a production line down into the deposit." He drew a line down through the drilling pipe and the casing and into the oil itself. "There's a packer around the production line which seals around it inside the casing."

"Like a ring on your finger?" DD glanced at his hands, and the young guy was wearing no ring. "Or a watch?"

"Exactly."

"But, how do they get this packer thing to seal to the casing?"

"Oh, it expands."

"How does it expand? Is it, like, some sort of spring mechanism?"

Jeff smiled. "Not in this depth. The deeper wells have mechanical packers because they have to hold up to really high pressure. But ours are just elastomeric donuts. They soak up oil and expand, and the endcaps are also designed to squish them vertically a little so that they expand out instead of lengthwise."

DD looked at him. "Tell me you didn't just say the packer is plastic."

"Why, what's wrong?"

"Tell me, Jeff, what is plastic?"

"Well, there are lots of different kind of plastic," he began, but she interrupted.

"What do they have in common?" DD demanded.

"I'm not sure what you're driving at," Jeff said.

"They're polymers."

"Yeah, so?"

"I am 99% sure at this point that *p davisii* eats every type of polymers!"

Jeff frowned. He sat silent for a moment. DD could practically see the gears turning inside his head. "Oh, shit! If that's true...the well could blow!"

"Not just this well; the assay ships have showed growth rates consistent with mutated *p davisii* throughout the
124

entire drilling field. Any well with a plastic packer is going to start gushing oil. It's not a matter of if, but when!"

"Shit."

"Damn straight. You know what happens when the wells start to leak? It's a giant *p davisii* buffet. Each and every oil plume is going to be inoculating the ocean for miles with a blooming colony of mutated *p davisii*."

"I don't like the sound of that."

"I don't either. Remember your stack of ruined coffee cups?"

"On the boat? Yes, what about them?"

"That Styrofoam was probably infected with *p davisii*."

She watched the reality of what they were talking about sink in, and his eyes grew wide as he considered the implications. "There have got to be hundreds of wells with plastic packers in the Gulf alone…thousands in the world."

DD couldn't curse. She couldn't speak. For a moment, she could hardly breathe.

XXVI. Still Beats the VA Clinic

The cab driver was an old-time Chicago native who'd
wanted to exchange notes, if not entire genealogies, once he
found out Juni had family in the Grand Boulevard
neighborhood, but Juni was answering him in monosyllables,
so he gave up. He was having to be extra-creative with his
course-plotting anyway, because several major streets were
blocked by stalled cars and cars with blown-out tires. Juni kept
looking at her phone; it kept saying "no signal." No signal, in
downtown Chicago! What was going on? Was it a war? A
terrorist attack?

Finally, they passed into an area where she had three
bars of service.

Juni called her brother, who worked nights, waking
him. It took a few moments to get his groggy mind to
understand the situation, and she found herself barking at him,
afraid the signal would drop before he got it. He got it–
finally!–and said he would call her husband at work, and
either one or both of them would meet her at the urgent care
center.

The trip from the university to the hospital took
almost an hour, twice as long as it would normally take, and
Juni handed the cab driver her Visa card. He slid the card
through the reader, but it sang a little tune of disappointment.

"Network's down. You got cash?"

Juni pulled a few bills out of her jacket pocket. She
was a dollar short, but the driver accepted it. "Don't worry
about it! I hope someone would do the same for my wife."
126

Juni got gingerly out of the cab, standing on her uninjured foot, the toe of the sprained one touching the ground. She looked around as the cab pulled away around the semicircular driveway, but there was no one there to assist her, so she limped over to the door of the urgent care center, pinwheeling her arms for balance and wincing in pain with each step. She approached the automatic door, but the motion sensor failed to see her for some reason. She waved her arms, but the door still didn't open. She noticed that a little door off to the side was propped open, and she supported herself with a palm on the useless sliding-glass door to totter over to it.

Once inside, apparent turmoil resolved itself into dozens of individual dramas. Children wailed and wheezed, and people held bloody towels to heads or limbs. The molded-plastic chairs arrayed around the waiting room were broken, some of them lying in Daliesque puddles, some merely broken off their metal bases. Her bare right foot and the ball of her injured left foot sunk into the putty-like substance which the linoleum floor's traffic areas had turned into. The reception counter was abandoned by the staff. Juni turned and saw a smaller alcove next to the doorway, where the linoleum floor was still solid and people were sprawled out, curled up, or sitting; one woman coughed relentlessly into a squelchy kleenex. Juni fished a packet of tissues from her jacket pocket and handed them to the woman without a word. The woman nodded gratitude. Another woman, very young, was pale and dull-eyed, with dry lips, panting and resting her head on the lap of a worried-looking youth who stroked her hair with desperate concentration.

Juni hobbled up to the counter and leaned on her elbows, taking the weight off her injured foot. After quite a long wait, a petite and pretty woman in teal-and-purple scrubs came out, her face cycling through expressions signaling that she didn't know whether to laugh or cry. She gave Juni a pile of forms and a lead pencil. Juni's forearms stuck to the formica countertop when she reached out to take them. "Our clipboards and pens are destroyed, sorry. Just fill this out if you *really* think you want to be seen."

"Why wouldn't I want to be seen? I sprained my ankle."

"Well, we can't X-ray it, because the top of the X-ray table is now on the floor, and the X-ray unit won't work anyway. We can't cast it because our casting materials are all polymer and they aren't setting up. All we can do is wrap it in an Ace bandage and send you home with Tylenol."

At that moment a half-sobbing, half-shrieking voice ululated from somewhere behind her. "Yeah." The girl jerked her head towards the sound. "We don't have any hypodermics left, either, for local anesthetic," the girl said, striving for cynical but with a waver in her voice betraying her despair. "Or IVs. Staying or going?"

"Well, I have an Ace bandage and Tylenol at home." Juni found herself speaking slowly. Her mind felt like honey in winter, slow-motion, unreal, trying to fit this scene into something that made sense, and failing.

The girl made an impatient half-shrug. Juni handed her back the pencil and the form and hobbled outside. A rescuing chariot, her brother in his car pulled up in the driveway. Her husband, her dear, sweet Bill, jumped out and wrapped one strong arm around her shoulders, taking her other hand, and tenderly assisted her into the back seat. She sniffled, and collapsed against him in relief.

XXVII. Gotta Get that Gasoline

LeRoy pulled his '77 Malibu into the Quick Stop N Go. Peewee and Jack were sitting in their usual spots by the water hose, running their daily business as usual. LeRoy didn't need anything in that way today, and that was good because he had just enough money in his account to pay for a tank of gas to get him to work the rest of the week, plus the EBT card, and Peewee and Jack didn't have any way to take EBT since Jack's sister's fish market had closed up shop because they caught that Mexican gal working there.

To his surprise, all eight pumps were blocked by cars. But the drivers weren't pumping gas; they weren't inside paying for gas and getting smokes or soda; they were standing around, waving their arms, talking to each other, talking on their cell phones, or talking to Buddy, who was standing there scratching his head and shrugging his shoulders.

The body language of everyone at the pumps was so clearly semaphoring, "What the fuck?" that it made LeRoy laugh. He turned off his engine and lit a cigarette, draping his wrist over the sturdy plastic of the Malibu's steering wheel, and waited to see what happened next.

What happened next was that Buddy, who was supposedly not the owner of the station, but sure acted like the owner, and nobody'd ever seen the owner, walked over to a corrugated metal shed, unlocked it, pulled out a flat wooden block, and then walked over to one of the metal filling holes over the in-ground fuel tanks, which just happened to be a few feet in front of LeRoy's bumper. Buddy squatted and used

130

both hands to take the cap off the hole, then stood up. LeRoy saw that the wooden block was actually a long stick of wood, riveted end-to-end so it unfolded into a yardstick. When the stick was unfolded, it was longer than Buddy was tall, and Buddy lowered the end of it into the hole.

When he pulled the stick out, LeRoy tipped his head to the side. The last foot-and-a-half of the stick was coated with what looked like mayhaw jelly. Buddy stared at the stick for a moment, perplexed, then pulled a rag out of his belt and wiped it clean. The second time, he watched it real close as he dipped it carefully into the center of the tubular channel, not letting it touch the sides. He drew it out, just as carefully, and once again it was covered in a clotted, sticky amber substance. Buddy noticed LeRoy watching, and he pivoted, so that the end of the stick was hidden from LeRoy's view.

Buddy looked furtively at the people standing by their cars. LeRoy watched one woman shut her cheap flip phone, climb back into her SUV, and turn the key hopefully, with no success. She slumped in frustration. A man showed up in a battered blue Kia and the woman at Pump 1, dressed in a McDonald's uniform and scowling in frustration, locked her little Honda with the key-fob remote and jumped in with him. There was one man, tall, beefy, tattooed, bloodshot, and scarred, who was standing next to a pimped-out black Escalade with "2 Fast 4 U Niggas" lettered in script at the top of the windshield, his stare fixed on Buddy. Buddy folded the stick up and walked back towards the shed. He tossed the stick in and closed the shed. LeRoy noticed he didn't lock it. Out of the corner of his eye, LeRoy saw the big, ugly Escalade owner start to move. LeRoy'd always found that the best way to deal with trouble wasn't to be there when it happened. He figured that now would be an excellent time to depart. He glanced down to turn the ignition key, and when he looked up from starting the car, Buddy was gone. That fast!

In a few seconds, so was LeRoy.

XXVIII. In Whom We Trust

DD's hands were cold on the metal railing of the boat now ferrying her ashore from the oil rig. She zipped her windbreaker. It helped with the chilly breeze which had thrashed its way out of nowhere, but she still felt cold inside. She repeated over and over inside her head what she'd told Jeff: It wasn't a question of if the wells would burst, but when. She resisted the urge to look behind her at the gentle waves in the Gulf; there'd be no sign of the eruption, which would occur underwater, until the oil gradually began to bob to the surface, and even that would hardly be noticeable from this angle. The floor of the Gulf of Mexico would be perforated with thousands of open oil wells, weeping black tears of crude. Would the *p davisii* reproduce fast enough to eat the oil? A nauseous feeling rose inside her as she calculated the volumes and realized the volume of bacteria that would result from multiple wells giving way would completely change the biochemistry of the water: metabolic by-products, heat from fermentation of unimaginably huge volumes. It would even cause mechanical changes in the viscosity of the water. A horrible thought struck her: how would that affect larger animals, as marine creatures tried to swim through goo? And what about the food chain, from krill on up to mammals?

She heard masculine voices raised in excitement from below decks. Two crew members in coveralls with the Amrencorp logo hustled to the top of the steps to look down into the boat's innards. She heard a compressor start up: the bilge pump. "I thought the hull was inspected in dry dock last month?" She overheard one of the crewmen say. The two of them, frowning, started down the steep stairway and their dialogue was muffled.

The boat approached the pier, and though the water seemed no rougher, the craft was rocking more vigorously now. The boat wallowed as it came about, and slowly swung into place to line up beside the weathered wood. DD noticed that the ship's rail, which had been at her eye level when she was standing on the pier before they boarded, was now only knee-height above the pier. The crew flipped the ramp out anyway, horizontal instead of sloping down, then disappeared below again. She minced across that bridge to the dock. Several oil-rig roustabouts had been on the boat with her, coming ashore for their much-anticipated months off. But instead of surging across the ramp, they'd dumped their luggage at the rail and joined the group below decks trying to puzzle out what was wrong with the boat. She looked at the belly of the craft at the waterline and was surprised to see it pitted with craters like the surface of the moon, with little shreds of fiber sticking out like mangy fur. Her mouth opened in shock as a thought occurred to her. *What kind of polymer is used in that fiberglass hull? Would p. davisii be able to eat it?*

Her train of thought derailed as a familiar face popped up in front of her: a man wearing a trench coat, khakis, and deck shoes. She smiled in recognition: someone she'd met at the presentation? Then she placed the out-of-context face and her smile collapsed. The sick feeling in her stomach turned into a clutching pain. *Not him again! Not now.*

134

"Mr. Fleck." She said, noncommittal.

"DD…Dr. Davis…I have to talk to you." His eyes were red and watering…the stiff salt breeze? But the emotion in his voice and the quivering of his lips suggested some deranged excitement instead.

"About what?" She drew back. His agitation put her immediately into fight-or-flight mode and she unlocked her knees.

He took a step closer to her, and so she took two quick steps to the side, so he wasn't blocking her way to run up the pier towards land if escape was needed. No one was on the boat's deck or on the pier at that moment, and all the people on shore were at least 100 yards away and not paying any attention. Still in an easy semi-squat, prepared to run, she slipped her right hand in her pocket and curled her fingers around the stock of her gun, her finger parked comfortingly on the outside of the trigger guard.

Fleck was strident, his voice cracking. "This is it. The end. It's happening. Now. We have to get out of here!" He reached out to take her arm and she easily stepped away, shaking off his fingers as they brushed her arm, and he let his hand fall to his side and looked down at the boards of the pier.

He could definitely outrun me with those long legs. She sidled over a little farther, still facing him; she was between him and the shore now.

She eased backed a step. Two steps.

He raised his head, his face more composed. "Dr. Davis, I know how this must sound. But please believe me:

you want to come with me. Things are about to get ugly, not just here but all over the world, and I can keep you safe. Your bacteria is about to cause a global disaster."

DD snickered, incredulous, rolling her eyes, and as she did, her attention was captured by the sight of the boat. The deck was inches from the water; each wave washed over the stern and slopped over the inwale into the stairway, soaking the upholstered benches and streaming down the treads.

She watched the first crew member hurry out, cursing floridly, his coveralls wet to the waist. A stream of uniformed crewmen and jeans-clad roustabouts followed, pouring out, clattering across the ramp at a run, some grabbing their bags piled on the deck, others not even pausing. One vaulted the railing, bypassing the ramp completely to land on the pier with a thump that shook both DD and Fleck. All twelve of them lined up to stare at the craft, cursing under their breaths, but otherwise speechless. The boat rode higher for a moment with the weight of the big men off it, then resumed its accelerating sinking. The ropes holding it ashore stretched taut.

Fleck, momentarily forgotten, gently cupped her left elbow.

"*P. davisii* eats fiberglass," he murmured in her ear. "It eats all plastic. And it's spreading. Here, and in Asia, and we think in East Africa. Nothing can stop it now."

DD turned to look at him. Something inside her shifted; she was scared and she wanted someone to trust. She dropped her hand down behind his to take his right arm and let

136

him lead her off the dock. *I am numb. Shocked.* Details popped out at her with acute clarity: a pelican on a piling; a post stuck in a concrete footing, now leaning against a cement block wall; a bottle cap on the ground. *I've never dealt with something like this before. I need help, to figure out what's going on and how to cope with it.* As they stepped off the wooden pier onto the concrete seawall, she turned to see the boat's gunwales sink underwater, the craft listing crazily away from the pier, and the roof of the cabin being held out of the drink only by the straining ropes. One of the roustabouts who'd come ashore had pulled off one of his shoes and was sitting on his duffel, looking at the sole. The waffled tread was gone; the bottom of the shoe was melted smooth.

Fleck led her into the little canteen by the dock. They sat at a rickety table. A bleached-and-teased fiftyish waitress poured them coffee. Fleck explained. "I don't really work for TERRI."

No shit. "I figured that out. Who *do* you work for?"

"I'd rather not say. But this is bigger than my Agency. The UN, the Chinese, the Russians, and all the US intelligence agencies are all mobilizing together on this one."

"What one? What *exactly* is happening?"

Fleck gestured at the TV mounted on the wall above the window to the kitchen. CNN was streaming images of pile-ups on freeways, collapsing buildings, airplane crashes, a delivery truck with milk streaming into puddles on the ground, a half-naked Asian woman running screaming through streets with Chinese signage, her clothing in tatters…

"You don't think about how many things in our lives are made of petroleum polymers, do you?" Fleck said.

DD nodded, the implications coming fully clear to her now.

"DD," Fleck said, "you made this bacterium. You can help us stop it."

"I don't know…" she mused, the microbiologist part of her mind kicking back into gear to toy with the problem, glad to have something familiar to latch onto.

If I could just regain control of the growth rate, I'd have a chance. But why is it doing this?

Mistaking her doubt for resistance, he said, "You have a moral obligation to help undo the harm it's done."

"Yes, yes, I agree," DD said, too engrossed in the mental puzzle to take the emotional bait. "The other OHCBs always burned themselves out when the spill was gone," she mused aloud. "We never thought this could happen. I still don't know how or why it's started digesting polymers. Especially when you consider how many different types of bonds there are in plastic substrates…"

"The fact remains, you are our best hope." He looked solemn, but as she came out of her distraction, DD's bullshit detector went off on the solemnity, even as molecular models twirled in her head.

There must be genes for enzymes being expressed that I somehow missed in the haplotyping. Those enzymes have to be dissolving the polymers. Is there any evidence of

*alkanivorax or p putida producing polymer-cleaving enzymes?
How fast could they evolve them in real-world settings?*

"I'll try everything I can to figure it out, as soon as I get back to the lab. I was planning to spend the night here and go back in the morning, but I'll grab my stuff and head back right now. Amrencorp's shuttle was supposed to be here to take me to the hotel, but I don't see it."

"You can't go back there."

"The hotel?"

"Your lab."

"What? Why not?" *My lab! My new lab! And I need it to understand, much less have a snowball's chance in Hell of solving this problem!*

"It's been compromised."

"What do you mean, compromised?"

"Does the name Timothy Schneider mean anything to you?"

"Of course! Tim's my right hand! He's been my assistant for eight years!"

Fleck withdrew a sheet of paper from his pocket. It was a photocopied ledger of accounting transactions, headed, "FCU 00505028-99 PITHOS BIOCHEM." Several of the transactions were highlighted.

"Did you order cultures from Standard Labs of Minnesota?" He laid the ledger on the formica tabletop.

"All the time, of course."

"How many at once?"

"Usually forty-eight at a time. They were cheaper that way, and that was how many we'd use up before they died."

"Why does this invoice say '240 pieces' then?" He tapped the page.

She slapped her hand down and drew the paper closer. As her eyes flicked from transaction to transaction, she saw an account number that was familiar: 115, petty cash. But petty cash transactions were only authorized to $100. Why were the numbers in the right-hand column bigger? $355…$622…$1560! And all the negative transactions into petty cash…from Supplies and Equipment…one transaction from an outside company she'd never heard of, Sinopec Corporation, what was THAT about?

"I'm no accountant, but is this…"

"Our forensic accountant estimates that Mr. Schneider has embezzled about $184,000 from FCU in the time he's been working for you, most of it in the last three years"

DD's stomach wasn't hurting any longer. *Bad sign.* Her heart was pounding and her mouth was dry. *I gave him all my passwords, including to the new lab's server.*

"I have to get back to my lab." She had tunnel vision now. "I have to get back to my lab. I have to see if this is true." *I never liked Tim. But I did trust him.*

"DD, if you insist, I'll take you to the lab. But he's been logging into the server with your username. Believe me, you won't want to use that lab until we find out for sure what software he's uploaded and what it's designed to do. It could be spyware, or even malware."

DD torpidly stood. Fleck dropped a $5 bill on the table. Fleck stuck out his right arm and DD took it with her left hand, acting on autopilot. As they left the restaurant, DD stuck her right hand in her pocket and touched her KelTec.

To her distress, the plastic grip felt soft and sticky.

XXIX. Burn After Reading

Fleck patted DD's left hand in the crook of his elbow, seemingly in reassurance. She drew a breath to ask a question, and his hand compressed hers, trapping it. Before she could pull her hand away or react at all, two other men in trench coats, jeans, and deck shoes appeared out of nowhere. One of them seized her right arm and the other stood directly behind her. Her hand was still curled around the KelTec in her pocket, but there was no round in the chamber and her other hand was trapped. *Overabundance of caution. Excessive concern with safety. Should have kept a round in the chamber.* She released her hold on the gun and made a token struggle; then she saw that the three men were dragging her towards a waiting car, a huge grey sedan.

Nope, not getting in there! She screamed, "FIRE! HELP!" She bent one of the men's pinkies back and heard a satisfying "snap!" But these guys were pros, and he barely flinched at the broken finger. As they stuffed her into the vehicle, nobody nearby even looked up. *I guess we're not going back to my lab,* she thought, sandwiched between two goons with Fleck in the front passenger seat next to the driver. The doors slammed and the car pulled away.

DD had just enough time to see that the car was headed west, towards Houston, before someone slipped what felt like a pillowcase over her head. She lifted her hands to pull it off and someone caught her wrists and held them together; she heard the ratcheting trill of a zip tie closing and felt the bite of the plastic. She raised her bound hands towards her covered face to pull the fabric away from her nose and mouth, and hands forced hers back into her lap. *I can't breathe!* She fought the panic back. *Yes, I can.* The air was warm and stale from her exhalations, the fabric was getting damp from the tears rolling down her cheeks unbidden, but she forced herself to realize she was able to fill her lungs if she paid attention and breathed slowly. It wasn't easy to breathe slowly; her heart pounded. She willed herself to relax, with little result. She puffed air through her lips with each exhale to make a small space in front of her nose and mouth.

Time was distorted by her lack of vision, but she thought it was only a few minutes later when the vehicle exited the Interstate, and she could tell by the stops, turns, and bumps it was wending its way back into a local neighborhood. The vehicle made one last, slow turn and stopped on a slight uphill slope. The man to her right got out, while the man to her left held her zip-tie bound wrists. The first man reached into the car and seized her wrists, pulling her out. He put a hand on top of her fabric-covered head as she cleared the door. She staggered to an upright position on a gravel-paved surface.

She gasped as someone (the man from the left side; he was shorter and had something in his pocket that jingled, keys or change) grabbed her waist, beginning a frisk which found the KelTec in her jeans immediately. The searcher's hands took the little gun and then traveled up and down both her legs, goosed her crotch twice, hard *(Bastard! Just like the fucking TSA!),* then went under her jacket, around her back, up under her breasts, then cupped each one briefly before traveling up her bra straps. She swallowed, blinking back tears of outrage, and forced herself to focus on breathing.

The other man (or maybe Fleck, she wasn't sure) fiddled with her bound wrists, and they came free, the zip tie cut. She shook her stiff hands and pumped them open and closed twice before they were abruptly captured again. She broke free from the captor's grip with her right hand and, just as she began to struggle, the other man grabbed the free hand and both hands were pulled together and re-tied, behind her this time. She panted from the brief scuffle; the most chilling thing was the absolute silence in which it all took place. Should she scream? She drew a deep breath to, but a hand clamped over her fabric-covered mouth before she could. Her scream came out of her nose as a moaning whine, and the man pinched her nose shut for a moment while keeping her mouth covered, suffocating her just long enough to make her start to panic. Pulling up on her wrists, torqueing her shoulders, painful enough to capture her full attention, the man behind her let go of her face and propelled her forward. He jerked her to a short stop just before a slight step up into a doorway, then slowly nudged her forward until her toes found the sill, and she stepped up.

This is all happening so fast!

The light filtering through the pillowcase wasn't quite as bright as she was steered forward. After they turned a corner, it was almost fully dark. Her captors let go of her and she swayed on her feet, trying to orient herself. Then the case was pulled off her head and the zip ties snipped at precisely

144

the same moment, and before she could even begin to react, a door slammed and cut off the light in the room, leaving her in full darkness.

Alone?

She shuffled slowly forward, hands out in front of her, until her shins hit something metallic. She bent and felt it…a toilet. A sinking feeling as she identified it and realized its presence implied a cell; she might be in here a long time. She explored the whole room with her feet and fingertips.

As she moved about, her eyes adjusted gradually to the tiny, linear outline of light that came in around the tightly fit door. About eight-by-ten, the room contained the steel toilet mounted on the wall, a steel sink, and a wall-mounted steel shelf bed with a thin mattress of naked foam rubber, a roll of toilet paper sitting in the middle of it. The walls were raw wood, cut close around the bed, sink, and toilet, and attached to the studs with screws. The floor was tile. There was what seemed to be a window, which was boarded over with the same wood, which the edges revealed to her fingertips as thick plywood, screwed into the window frame and overlapping the plywood wall. There was also a cluster of faint red dots in the far-left upper corner by the ceiling: the infrared lights of a night-vision camera. Something barely discernible on the ceiling might have been a light fixture, but she couldn't find a switch anywhere, though she ran her hands over every centimeter of wall she could reach.

The movement and stretching calmed her a little. She sank down on the bed to think, the steel shelf hard against her buttocks through the skimpy foam mattress. She pinched the foam rubber and found it to be just ordinary foam; she could rip it to fluffy pieces or cut it into a shape.

And then do what, exactly? No point in that.

The searcher had missed the tiny Swiss-army knife that was in the same pocket as her handgun, but the miniature screwdriver on it would only endure removing a few of the screws holding the plywood before breaking.

And then what?

She was forced to conclude that her available resources weren't up to the task of getting her out of here.

She zipped her windbreaker. Her feet were cold inside her sneakers and she recognized the room was quite cold. *Maybe 50 degrees Fahrenheit.* She stood and paced to keep warm, her hands in the empty pockets of the jacket. The sink produced only cold water. She cupped her hand beneath it and drank deeply, then thrust that cold hand into her warm jeans pocket. Think of this as a survival situation: water, check.

Next, avoid hypothermia. *Only one thing in this damned room...cell...that's a good insulator.* She picked up the foam mattress and, standing against the wall, rolled her torso up in it. She awkwardly flopped her burritoed body onto the steel mattress, yanked a corner of the mattress up to use as a pillow, and tried to rest. She repeated the serenity prayer over and over and forced her breathing to slow and deepen. As her mind relaxed, a thought emerged.

The extra shipments of cultures! The dual labeling. Maybe some of the organisms weren't p putida? *Or* alkanivorax? *I wish I had some way of finding out.*

She imagined what steps she could take to find and isolate the new enzymes and trace their origins. She could build a plasmid which would inactivate the DNA that coded for it. She then realized the plasmid had to be administered by shooting bullets at it with her KelTec, because the bacterial chromosomes were really zip-ties.

She awakened when three naked 100-watt bulbs, overhead in a wire cage, flicked on. Disoriented, she didn't know how long she'd slept, and she struggled briefly to free her arms from the claustrophobic embrace of the foam enveloping her before remembering where she was. She sat up, blinking and squinting and very much aware of her full bladder. She unwrapped her foam rubber cocoon the rest of the way, just as the two men who'd been in the car burst into the room.

The taller one grabbed her by the front of her jacket; she heard something rip in the lining as he jerked her towards him. She smelled his coffee-fouled breath in her face, as he demanded, "Why'd you do it?"

"What?"

"You know what! Tim's told us everything!"

"Tim?" She struggled to get on top of the dialogue. "But Tim…"

He shook her so hard her teeth clunked together and her eyes sparked in the back of her head. She found herself saying "Hnuhnnuhnuh," and then her knees started to buckle as he released her. She found her footing and felt her teeth with her tongue—*not broken, thank God!*—then stood with her hands on the front of her thighs as if frozen, her eyes once again betraying her by streaming tears.

Lord grant me the serenity to accept the things I cannot change. She drew a shaky breath and let it out, then began another, smoother breath…

Her knees buckled as the shorter man swept a leg into the backs of them. She jammed her wrist and hit her hip hard on the tile floor. He stepped in front of her and pulled back a foot to kick her, but his comrade said, "Wait!"

He put a hand on her attacker's shoulder, and she noticed, stifling a smile, that the last two of his fingers were taped together. The other man subsided.

The courage to change the things I can. A deep breath. She wavered to her feet.

And the wisdom…

"Sit down," Short Jingly commanded, gesturing at the bunk. His shirt was a different color, DD was sure, so it must be the next day already. She sat with another deep breath.

…to know the difference.

"Look, Dr. Davis. We don't believe you came up with this yourself. Tell us who recruited you and things will go better for you."

"Came up with what? *P. davisii*? I most certainly did come up with it myself…"

148

"So, you admit it?" Interrupted Tall Coffee-breath.

"Yes, of course I admit it! It was all techniques I developed myself. It was based on the work of Viswanathan, but he had nothing to do with it directly." The two men exchanged glances and nods when they heard Viswanathan's name, which puzzled DD.

"Who convinced you to make it do this?"

"Do what?" DD stalled.

"Don't play games with us. This is a terrorist weapon worse than any we've encountered. Tim told us about your little 'side' experiments!"

DD made a mental leap. She'd known a few people in the political cesspool in Tallahassee who'd been sold out to prosecutors during political witch-hunts. Her mouth gaped as the truth dawned on her. "I suppose," she began, numb, "that you offered Tim immunity for what he told you?"

She saw red, and found herself half-lying on the bunk's steel surface, before she felt the pain in the side of her head. She touched her temple and her hand came away with a trace of blood.

"That's enough!" bellowed Short Jingly. He walked over to the door and opened it with a key. "Get out of here and calm yourself down!" He was talking to his partner, the one who'd struck her. Revenge for the broken finger.

Tall Coffee-breath complied. DD dimly knew it was a ploy, but she still felt visceral relief to have him out of the room, and she couldn't help feeling absurd gratitude to Short Jingly for sending him out. She remained seated, pivoted towards her right, facing the wall at the end of the bunk, palms flat on the steel, left foot on the floor, not looking at Short Jingly as he locked the door. He sat at the farthest end of the bed, elbows on his knees, head turned towards her.

"DD…my name is Isaac; may I call you DD?" She didn't respond. *Deep breaths.*

"DD, you are in a lot of trouble here. My partner wants to remand you for prosecution and let them decide whether to treat you as a terrorist or an ordinary criminal. But here's the thing: I don't believe you did this on purpose." She pivoted to look at him blankly, both feet on the floor, hands in her lap. *Not buying the good cop bullshit, no sir.*

"I believe you were duped into this and you didn't know what the consequences would be. You see, I know a lot about you academic types—my dad was a professor—and I know you sometimes get so absorbed in your studies that you don't see things beyond the tip of your nose.

"You want anything? You hungry? Thirsty?" He seemed to suddenly realize she might be uncomfortable.

"No," said DD. She was still feeling nauseous and a little dizzy after the shaking and the blow to the head. "But I need to pee."

His eyes flicked to the toilet, then away. He got up and let himself out.

"Be right back," he said as he pulled the door shut behind him.

DD glanced up at the corner. Yes, it was a camera up there. She grabbed the toilet paper, pulled off her jacket, and

150

performed a sort of fan dance to preserve her dignity as much as possible. She sighed in relief as she pulled her jeans up and pressed the button, inset in the wall, to flush.

Short Jingly…*his name is Isaac*…came back in with a foam cup of black coffee, four sugars, a plastic stirrer, and two little plastic cups of creamer, all of which he held out to her. She took the coffee, disdained the additives, and sat on the bed, blowing on the scalding liquid so she could take a sip. The heat felt good on her cold fingers, even through the Styrofoam. Which was not melting, she observed.

"DD, I don't want anything more to happen to you. You may think you're protecting these people, but they don't give a crap about you. Tell me who they are and we can make sure you're not prosecuted."

"Look, Isaac. I only just figured out what was happening myself. I saw the boat sink. I know that *p davisii* is wreaking all sorts of havoc in the Gulf and it's obvious that it's going to get worse. Believe me, I had no idea it would develop the capacity to eat plastic. I don't know how it happened, which as a scientist seriously ticks me off. But it was an accident." She was talking more than she'd intended. *I guess having had no one to talk to makes me want to talk more.* She sipped the coffee and winced at the bitterness.

"Pretty bad, isn't it?" Asked Isaac with a wry smile. "Sorry about our coffeepot. We all put plenty of sugar in to make it drinkable…" he held up the sugar packets, and DD wordlessly took them from him. She shook them by one end, then tore all four open and stirred them into her cup.

"DD, Tim came clean with us."

"About his embezzlement?"

"DD, Tim wasn't embezzling from you."

DD was silent. *I don't know what to believe anymore.* She didn't want to believe Tim was committing larceny. As much of a prick as he was, she'd trusted him for years and she never suspected that dishonesty was one of his faults; quite the opposite, he was honest in his criticisms of others, to the point of verbal abuse at times. *But what about the dual labels on the cultures? Those Sinopec transactions? what about the printouts?* Of course, the ledger transactions could have been faked. She had to consider the source.

"Let me talk to Fleck." *Since when do you trust Fleck? Since that boat sank right before your eyes? Since he showed you the ledgers? And what did that get you, trusting a government agent? Whom can you trust?*

"Fleck's not here right now." Like some Kolkata phone-bank operator being asked for his supervisor.

"I'm not saying anything else until I've talked to Fleck again."

"Since when do you trust Fleck?" *Did he read my mind?*

"Was I talking out loud?" she asked.

"Talking about what, DD?" Isaac asked in a strange and soothing manner.

The coffee cup, nearly empty, hit the floor and DD gaped at it.

"We were talking about the plastic."

The Styrofoam cup didn't dissolve but maybe that was because the coffee killed the alkanivorax. I should tell him.

But instead, she kicked her feet up onto the hard steel bunk, laid her head on the foam rubber mattress, and closed her eyes. Isaac walked to the door and unlocked it to let the taller man back inside.

XXX.   White Rabbit: The Interview

"DD…DD…"

Deedeededee… She sang, "Deedeededee…" She laughed at the sound of her own voice. She realized her eyes were closed and she opened them. She thought she opened them.

"Just let me open my eyes…things are blurry…"

"It's okay, DD. Let me help you up." Isaac took her hand. She grasped his hand and pulled herself up to sitting. She rose cautiously. Her legs felt soft and rubbery; she stumbled into him. He steadied her.

She felt a surge of strength and stood upright, her hand on his shoulder.

Then she remembered he wasn't her friend.

"What do you mean, I'm not your friend?" Isaac asked.

Did I say that out loud? Too funny!

"You know," DD grinned slyly, looking at him from the corner of her eyes. "You know!"

She took a step away from Isaac's side. Coffee Breath was standing by the door. She took another step back, away from both of them, and hit something hard. She realized she was against the wall. She pushed off from the wall and took a run at the door, but next thing she knew she was whirling, with Coffee Breath's arm around her waist.

"Whee! Shall we dance?" She giggled. He took her shoulders and danced her backwards, and then she was sitting on the bed. Her hands startled her. No, his hands startled her.

154

Her heart was beating fast and her mouth was dry. Her coffee cup was overturned on the floor, and her mouth was so dry! She felt a sense of loss over the mouthful of spilled sweet drink and whimpered, feeling tears rise to her eyes, pointing at the tiny puddle of coffee.

"It's okay, DD, I'll get you some more coffee." One of them said. *Said. Said.*

"I want some more. That coffee is good stuff. I'm feeling much more energetic now."

"Good! Maybe you can focus now on who gave you the cultures," suggested Isaac.

"Tim ordered them. He does all the ordering," DD said.

"Don't play dumb."

"I am dumb." *That's not right.* "No, I'm smart. If I'm dumb, you must be an idiot, right?" She chuckled and stood up. "Bye!" *Time to go!* She tried to sidestep Isaac and Tall Coffee Breath pushed her easily back onto the bunk.

"DD, just tell us. Who did you meet with? What did that person look like?" Isaac said. *His name is Isaac.*

"Isaac. Isaac who?" DD asked.

"Who did you meet with?"

"What's your last name, Isaac? Mine is Davis." She held out her right hand. He ignored it.

"Dr. Davis, who did you meet with about the cultures?"

"He didn't give me any choice but to meet with him," DD said sadly.

Isaac's eyebrows twitched upwards. He leaned forward.

"Who didn't?" he said, eager. "Who didn't give you any choice?"

"The man who came to my room early in the morning."

"What did he look like?"

"The same."

He knows what Fleck looks like. Why would he look any different yesterday morning?

"The same as what?"

DD noticed the grain in the plywood near the ceiling above Isaac's head was crawling. *Not crawling exactly...not getting anywhere ...shrinking...no, not really shrinking...pulsing. Did they put something in the coffee? Shit, that hasn't happened to me since I was 15!*

"The same as what, DD?" Urged Isaac gently. *Annoying. He's annoying me.*

"Fleck. It was Fleck." Isaac slumped.

She began to hum. "Bela Fleck, do you recognize the song?"

"Not Fleck, DD, the other one, the one who gave you the cultures," Isaac tried again.

"There was another one! Yes, there was! Two!" DD smiled, happy to be helpful.

"Who were they?"

She blinked. *Who were they? Who were I? Who were we? We... they... you... you two... you all...*
156

"Y'all. My head hurts." She put her hand to her temple and then stared at the blood on her hand. *Dry. I'm bleeding dry blood.*

She held it out to Isaac "Look it's dry blood. Just like the movie."

"What movie?"

"*The Andromeda Strain.* Before your time. Before my time. Old sci-fi."

Isaac glanced at the taller man, who pulled out a memo pad and jotted something on it. This struck DD as funny, him thinking *The Andromeda Strain* was something significant, *big spy stuff,* and she giggled.

"DD," Isaac said, "who did you talk to before you made the last batch of cultures?"

"Talk to?"

"Did you talk to Viswanathan?"

She was getting angry. "Look, I told you I don't know him. He did the classic work."

"It's okay, DD. We know you're not the one responsible. If you help us by letting us know who set you up, we'll make sure the prosecutor goes easy on you. The work you did on *p davisii* wasn't your own, we understand that."

She stood up. She wanted to frame a cogent argument, but all at once she was seeing red, red and black pulsating before her eyes, and she was clawing, kicking, scratching. Something hit her head. The blow came in the same place as before, just as hard, but she couldn't feel any pain, just the rage. Someone was screaming in rage and it was coming from her throat, and something was hitting her hard in the stomach so the scream was wobbling like a Tarzan yell, like a bellows, and she had a handful of hair and it was attached and then it wasn't, and she was biting something soft which tasted like rust. Her elbows were pulled behind her and she thrashed and kicked, making a resonant thrum when her shin hit the bunk *that should hurt but it doesn't. Not like it used to when Daddy did it.*

She was panting, her arms behind her, also in a way that should hurt but didn't, and she screamed, "Fuck you! Fuck you! It's mine! I made it, it's mine by contract, and I can do what I want with it. You can talk to my lawyer if you don't believe me. I worked for this. I worked for years in that fucking state-funded academic gutter. You don't know how many asses I had to kiss. You have NO IDEA how many stupid political games I had to play. Stupid. Stupid…egotistical…"

Suddenly, she was sobbing. She let her body slump forward. She observed remotely that her shoulders felt better as she leaned forward, which was odd that they should feel better, because they hadn't hurt before, but the sobs were wracking her body and distracting her from that.

She was face down on the floor and the door was slamming. She was alone in the room. She was still sobbing. She crawled over and vomited brown coffee into the steel toilet and the sobbing ceased. She gathered up the foam mattress and hugged it with her arms and legs. Her breath slowed. She slept.

158

Outside the door, Isaac and his partner peered at each other under their brows, shaking their heads. "Leave her here a couple of days?"

Isaac nodded. "One more round of questioning. Then dispose of her."

"Sure we can't just do it now? I don't think she…Shit!" He lost his footing on the linoleum floor; his feet slid out from under him.

Isaac stifled his laughter, stepped over to offer the other man a hand up, and wound up on his hands and knees in the puddle of soupy melting plastic.

XXXI. Guillotined

"The declaration of emergency has gone out, but we don't know how many units actually got the message," Steve said, from his seat at POTUS's right hand at the conference table.

"What does Homeland Security have to say?"

"We can't contact them."

"Well, get me the Secretary of Defense then."

"We are trying, Mr. President. We've lost contact with approximately 67 per cent of Secret Service units, 44 per cent of FBI, and 89 per cent of Marines. Whoever's behind this, it's everywhere."

"What about the secure satellite uplinks?" He directed his attention to the NSA director.

"The satellites are unaffected," he said. "From the limited information we have been able to glean in brief moments of contact, it appears that other nations' satellites are also unharmed."

"What's the problem, then?"

The Secret Service Special Agent in Charge pulled the spiral headset cord from the back of his neck. He held it out and pinched the wire with his fingertips, pulling the wire straight as it slipped through his opposed nails. The plastic insulating the wire came away in a gummy wad. He threw the headset down in disgust. "Don't you get it? This is happening to all of us! It's gotten into all our equipment! Even the EMP-hardened stuff!"

"This is like an EMP attack, on steroids! Every level of communication is cut off, in every geographical location. We have no contingency plan for this!"

"I suppose what will happen now," POTUS said, listlessly, "is that everyone will try to get instructions for how to deal with the emergency. But they won't be able to." He looked up. "The government is like an animal with its head cut off. It will be chaos!"

The SAC and Steve exchanged glances of relief that he seemed to be catching on. Steve prompted, "But in this case, each agency has its protocols..."

A light came on in POTUS's eyes. "They'll break apart into cells and each will attempt to further their last stated goals and missions."

"That's right, Mr. President." Said the SSSPA-in-charge. He was the one who had taught him the protocols when he was inaugurated. "And what else?" He nudged, trying not to sound like a preschool teacher.

"Make regular attempts to re-establish contact with the hierarchy."

"Very good." He struggled to keep any condescension from his voice; the last thing they needed was for POTUS to erupt into one of his face-saving tirades, as he tended to do when his authority was challenged. He was just glad that Congress had been on recess when this hit, or they'd have had to deal with a pissing contest as they all tried to take charge.

"So. What are my resources?" POTUS was making an effort to gear his mind up to the speed of the evolving situation, accustomed as he was to having a small crowd of sharp and driven aides and staffers to deliver the summary distillation of gigabytes of data and information, along with their well-considered recommendations. This was just him, and he felt disarmed, naked, exposed, awkward.

"Mr. President, your resources at this time are what you see in front of you, in this room. These people: your security detail and personal retinue. If you fire one, there is no one to replace him. These computers, which don't work without power, which we may lose at any moment. And the tiny amount of information which is printed on paper in this room."

"So." He paused. "We wait. No other choice, is there?" He glanced around, and no one contradicted him.

"The only decision to be made is, where?"

"Yes, Mr. President."

Steve brought POTUS a glass of water and set it beside him on the conference table. This room should be a hubbub of activity. But two-thirds of the monitors ranging the periphery of the room sat dark or displayed the manufacturer's logo or "NO SIGNAL." A few staffers sat at the few functioning workstations, running on back-up batteries, copying data onto thumb drives and SD cards. The high-grade laser printers in the next room were spewing mailing lists, address lists, and database spreadsheets in hard copy form at their maximum draft speed.

"No internet?" POTUS asked.

"Not in DC. One of the major cell carriers has two bars of service. For now. It looks like all the rest of the towers are infected," The SAC said. "The cellular networks around the country are also, apparently, going down at an alarming rate."

"And these computers?" He waved his hand to encompass the workstations lining the walls.

"Are connected in-house only. Glass fiber optic cables still use plastic connectors. No one has touched the internal White House cables since the last security sweep three days ago, so our wiring seems uncontaminated. For now. Who knows if any of these memory cards are infected?" An aide who was sitting at a computer was listening in, and his face fell. He pressed the SD card and it popped out of its socket into his hand. He held it before his face and scrutinized it closely.

"And the electricity?"

"The back-up generators are fueled by gasoline. The tanks are metal, and they haven't been refilled or rotated in over a month, so they should be alright. Again: we think, if no one has touched the tanks with contaminated hands. We have enough of a reserve to run them for two weeks on full power, a month if we drop back to economy consumption. Basically, the White House is off-grid."

As if on cue, a background din which he'd barely been aware of, vanished. The massive back-up generators which kept the White House in power had automatically switched to the next sequential fuel tank, and just like that, there was no more electricity.

In the silence, the big man spoke, his voice uncharacteristically tiny in the big room. "Damn. I assume it's a priority to bring us back up?"

The SAC hesitated, glanced at Steve as if for guidance or support.

"Mr. President, we have no way of knowing that." Steve spoke softly.

"Can't you contact Pepco?" The President named the Washington, DC power company.

"Mr. President, landline and cellular phone service is out for the entire city."

"Can't we send our own techs out to troubleshoot our line?"

He sighed. "First, the line is probably shorted out at multiple points, due to the insulation and connectors dissolving. Second, our infrastructure geek gives us a 92% chance that the power station itself is contaminated to the point of being non-functional.

"And, third, no one is going out of this compound without full military and law enforcement guard details, because the streets are already bedlam. Looting, fires, and people trying to escape the city on foot. The police have no communications and few working vehicles, but there are rumors that over half of them have deserted their posts already."

"Contaminated? What do you mean, contaminated?"

164

"Let Birdwell explain it to you. He's the Army Corps of Engineer's ecology geek."

Lt. Col. Birdwell was, despite his WASP-like name, olive-skinned and black-eyed. He was tall and slender, his jowl just beginning to soften in middle age, his black hair gray at the temples. "Mr. President," he began, "we believe some sort of microorganism, capable of consuming everything composed of petroleum or plastic, is spreading exponentially, turning everything it touches into water and a semi-solid polymer gel. We don't know for sure where it began, though the NSA," he nodded at the NSA chief, leaning unnoticed against the opposite wall, "believes they have a fix on the originator of the culture. Unfortunately, they've lost contact with the unit that was assigned to acquire that asset."

POTUS grimaced at the NSA head, who suddenly found his cufflinks extremely interesting.

"Everyone: Sit!" he barked in the haranguing tone of voice that had put him in the Oval Office. "If you're not cleared to be here, leave. Get out!"

The technicians and staffers at the monitors rose and filed out. His security detail, Birdwell, Steve, and Susan Steiner, Secretary of Education, who'd happened to be present for the bill signing, were the only ones in the room with him. He looked around the table.

"Alright, men, we need a plan. But first, we need to know what we're dealing with. Is this bioterrorism? Is it those ISIS sons of bitches?"

The NSA head spoke up.

"We believe it may be. There are actually four possible viruses and bacteria that could be behind this outbreak. Two of them come from geographically unlikely sources, one in Iceland and one in Nairobi. The Russians could easily have developed something like this, though we had no intel about anything like it beforehand, and we're going over the documents we still have access to, to see if we missed something. But the most likely candidate is a disgruntled academic, a gun nut from the south, DD Davis, and we think she was funded by the Chinese. I am confident we will hear back from the group that is detaining her shortly, and we will have a more definitive answer at that time."

"Well, that's not much to go on. But it's better than nothing." He waved his hand, and added as an afterthought, "Anyone else have anything to add?"

Everyone remained silent. "Alright, then. We need a plan. Thoughts?"

One by one, everyone present weighed in. The final decision was, that they couldn't remain here, but it would be foolish to move right away. The state of mayhem in the city of DC itself would likely peak in 72 hours or so and, they assumed, then die down to a tenuous, gang-enforced peace. They would finish getting as much as they could in hard-copy form, using back-up battery power.

They would assess their resources for moving. If they had vehicles with uncontaminated gas tanks, it might make sense to use the gas in the reserve tanks to get to Camp David instead of trying to get the generators running for a few more weeks. They would also prioritize ascertaining the whereabouts of the First Lady and her children, who'd been at POTUS's New York skyscraper residence earlier in the day. They would continue trying to establish contact with foreign leaders. In the end, there was little they could do, but they set to work doing it with diligence.

XXXII. A Flea and A Fly in a Flue

DD tried hard not to wake up. She succeeded for quite some time. She first became aware that someone had stuffed something in her mouth, *a sock perhaps*? She opened her eyes and the light hurt, so she shut them. The knifelike headache from the base of her skull to her eyes told her she must have majorly tied one on; she hadn't been so hung-over since undergrad days. She shifted position and realized she was lying on a hard surface, in a puddle of something. She'd only been plastered enough to piss herself once, in high school, her one and only encounter with chugging straight gin right out of the bottle. But her pants…she was wearing pants, good…were dry.

All at once, everything came back to her. *The wells…the boat…Fleck…Isaac!* She flailed upright on the metal bench, ignoring the screaming pain from her shoulders. She discovered that she was cuddling a yellow sticky lump which, on further inspection, seemed to be dissolving into the puddle she sat in: the foam mattress. The "sock" in her mouth was actually her tongue, swollen and dry as cotton. She slipped her hand into her pocket—Her shoulder *really* hurt! — and her baby Swiss Army knife was still there. *They must have been so excited about finding the KelTec that they didn't check any further.* However, when she pulled it out, she saw that the red plastic face on each side was dissolved away like nail polish in acetone, leaving only a thin crescent shaped film around the edges. The knife blade, screwdriver, and corkscrew all still worked, so evidently there was no plastic in the pivot

168

points. *Just as well I don't have the KelTec. It's probably a useless wad of gunk now that the p davisii has gotten to it. Now what?*

She rose, her legs still a little quivery under her, and staggered to the sink. She scooped handsful of water into her parched mouth and throat. At once, she turned and vomited water and sour bile into the toilet, gasped for a few minutes with her head down and her palms on her knees, and then forced herself to drink again, more slowly this time. Her headache pulsed in time with her heartbeat. She reached her hand out to steady herself against the wall and felt a rougher surface than expected. That was when she noticed: *the plywood over the window. It's separating. That's why I can see in here; there's light seeping in around the edges where it's warping. Plywood is thin sheets of wood, glued together. Looks like the glue is PLASTIC!!!*

She worked her fingers under the first thin sheet of wood in the plywood, and it ripped away from the next layer. She pulled out her little knife and worked painstakingly on the next one, and the next. She hit a chunk which just fell apart in her hands, full-thickness, then an area where it was still so firm that she had to work her tedious way around it. It was slow going, but the de-lamination, helped by the moisture excreted by the bacteria eating the glue, weakened the wood and made it flimsy.

After sustained effort, she had a pile of wet wood chips on the floor and a DD-sized hole in the plywood. But, the window was closed.

Of course.

Gritting her teeth against the pain in her shoulder socket, she wormed her hand down between the plywood and the pane. She got her fingers around the metal grip on the window sash. The window was, fortunately, unlocked and easy to open, because her shoulder felt like burning-hot knives when she pulled on it. She gritted her teeth and pulled anyway, giving a guttural cry of pain as the window opened.

She glanced back at the door, and then slithered out the window into the humid Gulf Coast twilight. She drew a deep breath and rocked on the balls of her feet. She heard crickets. *Only one place to go now. I haven't seen Akisni and Snowbear in years. But if there's anyplace to weather this crisis, it's with them.*

XXXIII. Body at the Door

Jacob took the lead, pretending to be alone. The group of eight stuck to the middle of the sidewalks, kept the women in the center, and puffed themselves up to look as fierce as they could. They disregarded the smashing of windows and looting of shops they passed, and as long as they didn't bother the looters, the looters took no notice of them. They made it five of the six blocks to the hospital and reached an intersection with a bonfire fed by furniture, pallets, and cardboard in the center. A line of burly young men stood blocking their way.

"How you cousin?" one asked Jacob.

"Not bad. Not bad. Taking girl, hurt bad, to hospital." He nodded at the group behind him, and the Germans parted shoulders briefly to show Maya.

"Two women. Nice."

"We be going on to the hospital now."

"Nah."

"Yah."

"Who the white boys?"

"Germans. Foreigners."

"They be staying here. And we take the white ho."

"No, we all go."

"I've no time to chat with you, homie." The leader jerked his head. A series of cracks rang out, rifle shots, and the Germans, Maya, and Susan fell to the ground.

"You got ten seconds, homie. Run."

Jacob didn't need to be told twice.

XXXIV. Fancy Meeting You Here!

DD's feet hit the ground. She felt concrete and gravel under the sole of her right foot, but her left foot slid out from under her. She almost fell as her left running shoe fell to pieces. The cotton sock was still intact, though. A quick probe revealed that the right sneaker wasn't in much better shape, so she peeled it off her foot in pieces, stripping off her tattered nylon windbreaker as well, and stood in her stocking feet, jeans, and t-shirt, absorbing the sounds of the night. She was on a huge lot of storage silos, stretching off in all four directions in orderly rows, lit by dim yellow lights over the door of each cylindrical structure. She looked up.

The mercury-vapor lights overhead are out. Those must be emergency lights on solar batteries. No power.

She could hear the soothing sough of the ocean from only one direction. *Best guess is, that's East. Unless I'm on an island.* As her eyes adjusted to the starlight and the light of the waxing crescent moon overhead, she saw the dark, mounded mass of a stand of trees outlined against the sky in the other direction. She held out her outstretched fists, stacking them, and observed that her top fist just touched the moon, *two fists, or two hours, since moonrise.* Picking her slow way over the cracked pavement to avoid rocks and broken glass, she walked around the silo she'd been held in. She came across the car she'd been kidnapped in, sitting abandoned, doors open, dark. She slipped into the driver's seat; the keys were in the ignition! But she could tell before she even tried that it was useless; the key was in the "run" position and the car was dark, dead, inert. She tried anyway, turning the key all the way back, and then forward to "start," with the expected lack of response. The glove compartment and console were empty. So was the trunk, except for a jack and spare tire. As she circled the car one last time, she realized the spare was the only tire that was intact; the other four were flat. *Infected.*

She decided to head away from the coast. She slid her way through the silent, fence-framed field, past silo after silo. A stray cat scurried by; a bird, startled from its roost, burst into the sky. A lone tree-frog chirruped from an elevated haven.

As she approached the woods, the song of more tree frogs trilled in her ears. Even with the beginning of the last warehouse, she saw the chain-link fence up close. She walked up to it and found it was at least eight feet tall, topped by a single strand of barbed wire. *Once a city kid, always a city kid…but I'm getting too old for this!* She gripped the wire of the chain link with her fingers and stockinged toes and ascended to the top fairly easily, ignoring the protests of her abused shoulders. Once there, she put her hand around the strand of barbed wire. The barbs were about ten inches apart, plain wire, *not razor wire, thank God. Time to turn into a sloth.* Moving with excruciating slowness, she brought one leg over the barbed wire between two barbs, holding the top of the fence with one hand and grasping the wire in between two other barbs with her other hand. The transfer of weight from one side of the fence to the other was delicate…slow…easy…until she was pigeon-toed, one toe in a link on each side of the fence, bow-legged to avoid the barbs she straddled, and her torso was parallel to the wire and the top of the fence. First, the inside hand came over, her weight shifted to the outside foot.

Ow ow ow I will not think about my toes the pain does not exist. This hurts a lot more than it did when I was 15. Now the trickiest part. Am I still fit enough to do this?

She lifted her inside leg straight out from the hip into an arabesque, and slowly swung it over to the other leg…then she was clinging to the outside of the fence!

She climbed down, springing to the ground, flush with self-congratulation, but her jubilation was cut short by the agony of a thousand needles. *Sand spurs! The curse of the Gulf Coast!* She picked the sharp burrs out of her abused socks. The right sock already had a hole in it, right over the ball of her foot. She got every one of the miniscule barbed pods out of her socks, not once cursing out loud when they punctured her fingertips, and rose to continue.

Aiming for the empty patches of vegetation-free sand, she headed for the salt scrub in the dim light. Once she was hidden by the palmettos and tall grasses of the scrub, she had to pick out thorn- and sand-spur-free paths, but she headed more or less straight, keeping the moon behind her. After half an hour or so, she turned to look at the moon. She once again extended her fists, but now the moon was only one and a half fists above the horizon. *So, I'm headed East, not West. That means I must be on an island.*

She kept going until she reached a two-lane road. The hard asphalt surface felt like luxury carpeting on her poor feet, now bare and probably bleeding, but she'd check for injuries later and deal with them when she could. Right now, the decrease in pain felt almost comfortable by contrast.

Turn right or left? Eenie, meenie, minie, moe.

She turned right and walked down the road until she reached an intersection. Road signs, barely visible in the light of the setting moon, told her she was at corner of Seawolf Parkway (*Some parkway!)* and Coastwide Road. Coastwide Road ran back in the general direction she'd come from. There was a sign, just a plywood panel on two fence posts, farther back off the road. She had to walk right up to the signboard and almost put her face up to it to make it out. *Martin Midstream, Inc. They had an oil barge anchored next to the drilling rig. But that still doesn't tell me where I am now.*

She continued along Seawolf Parkway. It was eerie how there was no traffic. At the next intersection, she came across a truck parked on the sandy shoulder. A dump truck. It looked like…but no. *All dump trucks look pretty much alike.* She opened the pitiful little knife in her pocket and clutched it by her side as she padded up to the truck. She circled it, silent, twenty feet away.

No sign of movement.

She hesitated, unsure what to do next, then made up her mind and approached the cab. She put her foot on the passenger-side running board and hauled herself up on the grab bar (*The shoulder!)* to look in the open window. The cab was empty. She was about to try the door handle when the truck rocked and a face popped up outside the open driver's side window. A familiar face.

"Jeremy?" She asked, incredulous. Of course, he didn't hear her with the truck between them. She dropped off the side of the cab, forgetting about the condition of her feet, and almost crumpled at the burning pain that spiraled up her legs and wound up behind her eyes. She gasped and straightened as Jeremy (*It can't be!*) came around the front of the truck.

"DD? DD?" Jeremy was just as shocked as she. "What are you doing on Pelican Island?"

DD felt a gush of relief at the sound of his familiar and friendly voice.

"You wouldn't believe me if I told you."

"Try me." Jeremy smiled.

"Can we sit in your truck? My feet…"

"You have no shoes! How did you even *get* here? Here, I'll help you up."

He opened the door and boosted her, *totally unnecessarily*, but DD's shoulder was nevertheless glad of the assistance. She sank into the cloth passenger seat gratefully. Jeremy climbed in on the other side. He held out a steel canteen of water. She took it eagerly.

"Okay, so how did you happen to be here?" Jeremy asked.

DD sipped the water and told her story. It was a long telling, since she had to start with telling him what she did for

176

a living. Their initial encounter had been focused on other, more enjoyable things. She wound up giving the Cliff's-Notes version of her OHCB presentation. Jeremy, despite his blue-collar occupation, was intelligent; he picked up on it better than she'd expected. She went on to describe the oil-well visit, the sinking boat, the kidnapping, and the interrogation. He began to look confused.

"So, who is this guy Fleck again?" Jeremy asked.

"I'm not sure. He's not who he said he was, I know that much. I'm not sure who any of those guys were. I just know they were government somehow. I know I'm glad to be away from them.

"Speaking of which, can I hitch a ride with you… as far away from here as possible?"

Jeremy's eyebrows raised a little. He set a hand on her thigh. "I'd love to give you a ride anywhere you want, DD." She smiled at that. "But this truck isn't going anywhere. It's got the machine sickness."

"Machine sickness. Is that what people are calling it?"

"Yep. And you're the only person I've talked to who actually understands what happened to cause it. I was leaving Martin Midstream after dumping a load of gravel, when my motor seized up. Water in the gas, was what it looked like to me. Then, while I was trying to get my phone to work, the cowling and the boots and hoses started dissolving to pieces right in front of me." He shook his head. "My cell phone lost signal. People kept driving by and I tried to flag someone down, but no one would stop. I spent yesterday walking over to Martin Midstream to see if I could use a landline or something, but it's like a ghost town. Deserted. Not even a guard at the security gate. I had some battery left in the truck and I listened to the news on the radio until it died. This is everywhere. One of the talk shows said it spread from an oil rig in China, and the whole world has it now! I had some snacks in the cab here, but they're gone now. This is my second night sleeping in the truck bed. I was planning to start walking to the bridge in the morning. You're welcome to come with me."

"So, there's no cell phone service at all? None?"

"Wouldn't do us any good if there was." He reached across her to the glove box, his sweat acrid and masculine, and took out a full-sized steel mag light. He turned it on, blinding in the darkness, and pointed the beam at the floor, where a melted glob, recognizable as something which had once been a cell phone, lay by her feet.

"Oh, my God! Look at your feet!" Jeremy exclaimed.

DD looked, and they were admittedly frightening. The remnants of her socks hung around her ankles. They were studded with sand spurs and dyed brown with dried blood. Her toes were swollen like sausages. Streaks of dried blood showed between them. She cradled her right foot on top of her thigh to look. The sole was an indistinguishable dark mass of dirt, blood, and shredded skin. "I have a first-aid kit in the back and a full cooler of drinking water that the machine sickness hasn't gotten to yet. Let's see what we can do about

178

that!" He jumped out of the cab and came around to help her down. In the darkness, she felt a tear trickle down her cheek.

Someone's taking care of me.

She was exhausted, and all at once she felt every blow and kick she'd taken, and every sand spur and piece of broken glass she'd stepped on. Her arms felt like lead weights where they hung from her injured shoulders. Not trusting her voice to stay steady, she silently accepted Jeremy's help up into the bed of the truck.

XXXV. Improv

The next day, DD awoke shortly after sunrise. She was lying on her back, on a rough wool blanket, atop the folded-up canvas cover for the dump truck bed. She was embarrassed to discover she'd reached out for Jeremy's hand sometime during the night and was still holding it. She tried to slip it away and he squeezed lightly, trapping her fingers and raising his head to look at her before letting her draw it back. She smiled. It hurt to smile, hurt at the temple where her head had been hit. She remembered the night before. He'd swabbed the blood off her feet (she looked down, and they were wrapped in stretch-gauze first-aid bandages). Then he'd sponged her face and hair before pronouncing the head wound, "Not that bad. They weren't trying to really hurt you."

"Could have fooled me!" she'd said. "But then, I've never played that rough in my life, even in karate class."

The canvas cover for the truck bed was evidently mixed natural and synthetic fiber; it was weakening in places, to where you could pop a finger through it. The blanket, though, appeared to be pure wool, an olive drab, probably old Army-surplus. DD felt bad about destroying it, but with Jeremy's encouragement she used her little knife to cut four big circles and two wide strips out of the blanket. This allowed her to rig up bi-layered, primitive moccasins. They both drank as much water as they could, leaving less than a gallon in Jeremy's big drum thermos cooler, and they set off down Seawolf Boulevard, Jeremy swinging the cooler by the handle and DD carrying the flashlight, staying on the soft sand and
180

trying to walk as normally as possible despite the pain in her gauze-wrapped feet.

It was an unseasonably warm Gulf-Coast winter day. By noon, every step was agony, and bloodstains were beginning to soak through the outer layer of her moccasins. She'd shrugged her T-shirt over her head for partial protection from the sun, giving her the look of a headless dummy, but her arms would be burned. Jeremy was better prepared for the conditions, with a baseball cap and long-sleeved cotton shirt. They passed signs for a copper distributor, a truck distributor, and a road called Halliburton Way. Oil silos and derricks were visible in the distance in both directions, and soon they saw colorful houses way ahead of them, more than a mile away.

As they walked, DD told him more about *p davisii,* her capture, and Tim's double treachery, "I've been thinking: I figure he was embezzling, and swapping out the cultures for cheaper, unstandardized ones. Who knows what the actual bacteria are, that the last hybridization was made from?

"At the same time, he must have been selling some of the newly genetically modified cultures to someone from Sinopec. Then, when he got caught, he must have told the Feds I was a terrorist in order to get immunity for himself. I am so furious!"

She added through clenched teeth, "I never liked Tim. But I *did* trust him."

She told Jeremy the whole story in excruciating detail of her torture and escape, making the drug episode sound funny enough that they both laughed out loud, and mentioned her current plan to get to the off-grid community in Indiana.

As they reached the houses, they saw that they were cheaply built townhomes painted in pastel colors to look like a beach resort. A sign said University Apartments. Cars were in the complex's parking lots, some with the doors, hoods, or trunks open, and a few of the units had doors standing open. Jeremy walked over to the front of one of the homes and turned on the water tap for the garden hose. Nothing happened.

"PVC pipes, probably," remarked DD. Their water situation was about to get serious. They drank the last of the water in the cooler, then walked a little farther.

A small strip mall, with a diner and several small shops was less than a quarter mile away. Again, no sign of life. The restaurant's doors were open, there was no water in the kitchen behind the counter. They checked all three stores and none of them had water either. They walked a little farther, to the gas station on the corner. A car sat by the pump with the dispenser handle still stuck in its fuel door. The parking lot of the gas station was full of abandoned vehicles. The shop itself had been locked up, but the glass doors had been shattered. They ducked inside. The place showed signs of some light looting: the registers had been forced open and merchandise was scattered all over the floor. Every plastic container that anyone had touched was burst open and melted, but there was still plenty of bottled water, soda, juice, and tea inside the closed glass-fronted coolers.

182

"Hey, look! Beer!" said Jeremy.

"Are you kidding? That crap is like sex in a canoe!" said DD.

"Sex in a canoe?" Said Jeremy.

"Fucking close to water."

The refrigerators weren't cold, but DD took an Arizona Iced Tea and Jeremy took a Coca-Cola, and they sat in the shade on the stoop of the store and drank their tepid beverages.

"This is the best tea I ever drank in my entire life," said DD.

"Yep."

They rested for a few minutes. Then they spent some time opening bottled waters, trying carefully to keep from touching the mouth of the bottle, and pouring them into the cooler, filling it to the top. They stocked their pockets with Slim Jims and bags of nuts, things that wouldn't melt or spoil. They each ate a candy bar, softened in the heat. Jeremy stashed a couple of the weak, warm beer cans despite DD's eye roll.

"What University is this?" Asked DD.

"You are new around here, aren't you?" Asked Jeremy. "Texas A & M, the Aggies. Galveston Campus. Marine Biology, Merchant Marine, Navy ROTC…"

"So, we're close to Galveston then?"

"Right across the causeway."

DD grabbed all the band-aids, alcohol wipes, gauze wrap, and antibiotic cream in the meager first aid section. She also slicked herself down with sunblock, especially her arms, which were turning a florid shade of red. She hoped at least she could prevent them blistering. She grabbed a foam sun visor and cheap sunglasses (realizing as she grabbed these plastic items that she was contaminating them and they would be melted soon), and off they went.

The causeway was beautiful, with a thin strip of sandy beach and ocean water on both sides. Derricks and shipping cranes could be seen on the horizon, but they were all still; one was toppled over. The remains of a small pleasure boat, hull half-dissolved, motor nowhere to be seen, lay at the water's edge. The island's eponymous pelicans soared overhead and landed on pilings. The water on the Gulf side was blue-green with soft swells breaking on the shore, and the Bay side was golden and dotted with the froth of rough wavelets.

What was no doubt a short, pleasant drive in a car now seemed interminable on DD's wounded feet, but eventually they reached the end of the causeway and ambled onto Galveston Island proper.

They paused to survey the prospects.

Useless, abandoned cars punctuated the roadway. Jeremy set the water cooler down, careful to put it on the sand and not the contaminated asphalt. and stepped over the guardrail. DD wasn't inclined to follow; stopping had brought the pain in her feet to the front of her mind. Instead, she plopped down on the pavement, sticking her feet straight out in front of her.

"Gonna see what I can see from high ground," said Jeremy. He crossed the road and scrambled up a 20-foot mound of dirt and construction debris. DD looked up at him where he stood atop the hill, silhouetted against the sky, pivoting to look in all directions. The ocean breeze ruffled his hair and his eyes creased in the sun reflected off the water. Freed momentarily from the pain in her feet, she paid attention to her emotions. She felt… *gratitude.*

It seemed like a million years earlier that she'd driven her car onto the nearby ferry dock for the ride to Bolivar, and the B and B where they'd first met. He hadn't said anything about their brief encounter or her abrupt departure. Should she? She'd sworn off drama years ago, had no desire to repeat the Kabuki of falling in love, being disappointed or betrayed, breaking up, licking wounds. It was draining. It was a sign of how shaken she was by recent events that she was even considering it. She closed her eyes, trying to ignore the burning soreness in her feet, her sunburned arms, and her chapped and cracking lips. She quarried deeply within herself for the self-assured scientist, the fiercely independent woman who'd hopped in her SUV to start a new life, such a short time ago.

The world went black.

Jeremy's shadow was blocking the burning sun from her eyelids. She opened her eyes to his silhouette, and then squinted as he moved away from his spot between herself and the sun.

"See anything interesting?" She asked.

"Maybe." He said. "Pedi cab."

"You mean, like those bike rickshaws? I didn't know they had them here!"

"Yep. They use them for festivals and on the tourist strip. There's one up ahead about half a mile, flipped over on its side. Can't tell why it's flipped over from here."

"But it might be working! That would be so wonderful!" Her voice quavered on the last word. *Shit. I'm a basket case.*

Jeremy's face showed a fleeting micro-expression of deep empathetic pain before firming up. "How are your feet?"

"They hurt like Hell." She blinked at his extended hand.

"Come on, not much further. Let's see if we can get to that Pedi cab." She took his hand and tried not to wince or gasp when she stood. *There's no way I can put my feet on the ground that doesn't hurt!* He shouldered the water and they commenced their plodding pace again. When they were within a hundred feet or so he broke pace with her and easily strode up to the bike. "Looks good!" he shouted. She limped the remaining distance.

He set the Pedi cab upright. The metal structure of the cab was fine. The tires, however, were falling to pieces, the rubber softened by the dissolution of the nylon casing underneath. The plastic reflector lenses on the back were crazed and cracked as if they'd sat out in the sun for twenty years. The vinyl upholstery on the seat was melting and cracking. So was the foam rubber underneath it. The vinyl sunshade was in tatters.

"We won't get far on those tires," DD said, crestfallen.

"I have an idea about that. You rest over there in the shade," he nodded at a backhoe a little ways off, casting the only shade available for miles on this treeless shoreline. "I'll be right back." He strode off towards the dock, and DD helped herself to a drink of tepid water and then walked, on her knees, over to the backhoe. She hated being a burden, but she didn't want to be foolish either; she was hurt. Once she reached the shade of the backhoe, the heat was still stifling, but the sun wasn't beating on her anymore. She held her fists out and stacked them up from the western horizon to the sun: one, two three…about 2:30 then.

She leaned back and closed her eyes…When she opened her eyes, the sun was setting, a creamsicle-orange ball surrounded by streaks of lime and citron. The ocean was calm and steely. A fly was mountaineering on her chin and she brushed it off, which made the row of fresh mosquito bites above her left eyebrow start to itch. She smelled salt sea air, *p. davisii*, and most strongly, herself. *Not my freshest.* She sat up, her back and thighs protesting, and wiggled her toes. They felt sore as hell inside their woolen sacks, but judging by their movement, they were slightly less swollen. She had no way to rewrap them, so she decided not to take off the jerry-rigged moccasins to investigate any further.

She turned her head and saw Jeremy bent over the rickshaw bike, which was upside down on the sand. She unconsciously put her fingers into her hair, where they stuck fast in the snarls. *Never thought I'd rock dreadlocks.*

"Hey, you're awake. Can you walk?" Called Jeremy, nodding at her feet.

"Tell you in a minute." She flipped onto her hands and knees, then got her feet under her. *Ow. Shit.* "I think I'll be okay," she said unconvincingly, and hobbled over. He'd liberated a length of ship's mooring rope, the heavy hemp rope almost as thick as her chafed, scabbed, and sunburned wrists. He'd cut a piece long enough to fit around the rim of the bike's wheel, where it fit neatly into the groove, and fastened it on with scraps of stout wire he'd cut from the chain-link fence nearby. The two wheels on the axle under the passenger cab had received the same treatment. He flipped it over right side up. He piled the remaining length of rope on the floor of the thing.

DD was astonished. "That's amazing! You were a Boy Scout, weren't you?"

"Well, I don't know about that. But it should help us get around." But he was smiling. And looking at her. And damned if she didn't feel something rise within her, battered and sunburnt and exhausted as she was! *Whoa, girl!*

But it sure is nice to have found a friend. She smiled back with cracked and bleeding lips.

188

XXXVI. Material Girl

Jeremy and DD rode the Pedi cab into downtown Galveston, Jeremy pedaling and DD sitting with her feet out in front of her on the pile of rope. Here and there, a random house appeared occupied, the door intact and closed. Some of these had hand-lettered warning signs on the gateposts, or hastily built barbed-wire, broken-glass, or thorn-bush barricades. However, most of the city appeared to be deserted, dark and subdued by the twilight. They stopped at an abandoned motel. Jeremy got off the bike and walked around cautiously, checking each and every room, but there was no one there. By the time he was finished, it was dark.

He came back to the bike. "Some of the rooms are pretty disgusting. But there's one right there," he pointed, "that's not too bad inside. Let's stop here for the night."

"Okay," said DD. She braced herself, took a deep breath, and put her feet on the ground. The pain was excruciating. But she thought it wasn't as bad as it had been that afternoon. She hobbled into the indicated doorway, noting that the door itself was intact, but the furniture was randomly piled against the wall next to it...someone had apparently been barricaded inside, and then later pushed the furniture aside to get out.

Using the flashlight, they surveyed the room. The bathroom door was closed; opening it, she was hit with a stench which told her there was no water in the dwelling, but the toilet had been in use anyway. She quickly shut the door. There was a sink outside the bathroom door and the freely turning faucets confirmed the lack of water. There were two beds, both rumpled. Jeremy went outside to get the rope and water from the Pedi cab to bring inside. She sat on one of the beds, yearning to collapse into sleep, but she had her feet to attend to.

"Will you help me dress my feet?" She reached into her bag and extracted the remaining gauze, tape, and antibiotic cream, and pulled her little knife out of her pocket. She took off her crude woolen moccasins, then began peeling off the existing dressings while Jeremy held the flashlight. She took the flashlight and pulled one foot up onto her knee to inspect it. It was still pretty swollen, and there was enough dried blood that she couldn't see what condition it was in. Jeremy brought her the one clean hand towel still perched on the rack above the sink and wet it with water from the cooler.

Once all the blood was sponged away, her feet didn't look that bad. "I might be able to pedal tomorrow! You're a good nurse!" Jeremy had wrapped them up snug, but not too tight, that morning. The ointment had staved off infection. Her soles were for the most part just cracked and nicked. Though she'd felt as if they must be mutilated, there were no serious cuts or gouges, and the swelling seemed to have pushed most of the sandspur barbs from her flesh. Just seeing that the destruction wasn't as bad as she'd feared made them hurt less already. However, the alcohol wipes she used next on the torn-up pads of her feet made them burn like Hellfire! She hissed and rocked until the pain subsided. She extended the first foot out and let Jeremy re-bandage it with plenty of antibiotic cream and gauze while she peeled and cleaned the other foot.

Once both feet were dressed, still throbbing from the isopropyl, she lay back on the bed with a sigh. Jeremy got up and walked around to the other bed and collapsed spread-eagled on his back. DD noticed his stiff gait and reflected that he'd likely not ridden a bike in a while.

"We can take turns pedaling," she said. He grunted, doubtful.

"It's going to be cold at night further North," he replied after a minute or two. "Are you sure you can find this place in Indiana?"

"Oh, I'm sure. I used to visit every time I drove through on the way back and forth between Florida and Bemidji." *That was fifteen years ago, when I was twenty-seven, but it can't have changed that much, can it?*

She considered saying that out loud, but couldn't decide: *is it better to tell him the complete truth, or more important to encourage him*? She ruminated on that question, but before she decided, she heard his breath sink into a light snore. The rhythm of it lulled her.

What felt like moments later, she opened her eyes to the luminosity of daybreak through the window. Jeremy wasn't in the other bed. She had to pee, and she turned down her mouth and wrinkled her nose at the thought of opening that bathroom door again. She stood, testing her injuries. Her feet were sore, but not awful. She looked nearby for her makeshift moccasins. She located them and bundled her feet up, then went outside. She trod slowly and gingerly, watchful about her foot placement, around back of the motel. By the time she was situated in a squat to take care of business in the weeds, her bladder was about to burst.

When she came back into the room, Jeremy was sitting in one of the cheap fabric-upholstered chairs, holding a pair of... "Shoes!" DD squealed.

They were leather shoes, ballet-slipper style. Size nine, and she wore a seven and a half, but with her feet swollen and bandaged they should be about right. The soles were intact... for now. "These soles are probably plastic of some sort...they could be natural rubber, but I doubt it. I'll have to watch where I put my feet."

He held up two more identical pairs. "You've got spares for a while, anyway. There's a shoe store across the street. My boots have—used to have—synthetic soles, so they fell apart this morning." He pointed to two pairs of men's shiny, lace-up dress shoes on the table. "These are leather and my size, and most important, the leather soles are sewed on." She looked down and he was already wearing a pair of them, his feet looking oddly metrosexual in contrast to his grimy, threadbare, faded jeans.

"Yeah, they don't make stitched shoes for women," sighed DD. "They're all glued, even the really expensive ones." She frowned. "Maybe I can find some of those upscale sewn men's dress shoes in a small enough size." She slipped on the ballet skimmers. "In the meantime, these are perfect! Thanks!"

They breakfasted on their spoils from the
convenience store. They both drank a good bit of water,
bringing them down to half the cooler left, but the cooler was
starting to show a few sticky spots. DD spared a small amount
of her isopropyl to wet the colonies down and hoped that
would do it. They loaded the Pedi cab and were on their way,
Jeremy riding this time and DD pedaling, her feet doing
alright, at first, on the rope-wrapped pedals. She had to stop,
though when her feet began to throb after an hour or so. She
pulled off a skimmer and saw a fresh yellowish stain on the
gauze where the scratches had begun to ooze through. Jeremy
pedaled the rest of the day while she sat in the gondola and felt
sorry for herself.

*I hate not being able to pull my weight—literally in
this case. I did pedal for a few miles. At least it's a start.*

They stayed on two-lane back roads and didn't see
many people. Passing houses, it was hard to tell if they were
occupied. The usual tell-tale signal of a car in the driveway
was meaningless now since most cars were infected and
remained parked wherever they'd been when their gasoline
and oil was digested to water by the bacteria. Their first
experience of this was when they passed an unexceptional
ranch-style home set back from the road. The front door was
open, the screen door was shut, and there was no car in the
carport or driveway and no sign of movement. They decided
to see if there was anyone home, or anything inside to forage.
Leaving the Pedi cab at the bottom of the driveway, Jeremy
strode up to the open front door, DD moving slowly and

gingerly behind him on her still-tender feet. He stepped onto the shallow wood porch, lifted a hand to knock, and both he and DD heard the metallic clack of a shotgun being cocked. Jeremy instantly raised his hands in the air and took a step back. "Turn around and walk to your bike," a woman's voice commanded from within. Jeremy complied, DD leading the way, with her hands also in the air. They never saw the woman's face.

A few motor vehicles, still fueled and uninfected, passed them the first day, but none the second day. They would greet the people they saw and tersely exchange basic information: where are you from? Where are you headed? Best way to get through? Run into any trouble? The people they saw were mostly traveling on foot, and some shied away from them, though others sat and had a conversation. Most seemed to be couples, with or without children, some groups of friends in twos or threes, and a few larger bands.

On the third day, they heard lone gunshots, five of them, a few seconds apart. "Probably hunters," Jeremy opined. *How can you know that?* DD thought. *Lawlessness, roving mobs; isn't that what happens when society falls apart?*

In the absence of any electronic communication, rumors swirled. Everyone they met offered an opinion: it was a terrorist attack; it was the Muslims; it was the UN getting ready to invade us for Agenda 21; rich white people's things weren't affected; it was an alien invasion and they'd be swooping in with their flying saucers any day. DD kept silent about her role in causing the catastrophe, and Jeremy observed

194

that silence and kept it without having to discuss it. Partly, she was afraid that people would believe her, and would attack her for destroying their lives.

Destroying everyone's lives.

Partly, she was afraid that they wouldn't believe her and think her insane.

Sometimes it all seems like a vivid hallucination.

On the fourth day, they stopped just before dusk to bathe in a cattle pond. There was a farmhouse nearby, and having learned their lesson, they shouted from a long way back as they approached, then banged on the front door, but no one answered. The cows in the field herded up to the fence, lowing pitifully about their neglected state. The house was locked up tight, but there was a screened back porch with a flimsy latch-lock, easily forced.

They washed themselves head to toe and rinsed and wrung their clothing in the dark water of the pond, standing on pea gravel that the absent farmer had dumped along one patch of shoreline. DD wrapped her feet in the wet wool moccasins and they walked to the porch. After their bath, as Jeremy put band-aids on the few remaining cuts on her feet, he ran his hand up her leg, and she responded by leaning forward, taking his hand, and pulling him on top of her. He came forward eagerly. His mouth tasted good but his bristly beard stubble burned and she turned her head away. The warmth of his body felt delicious after the chilly water. They slid their hands over each other's sides, his hand trapped in between them toying with her breast, until she wrapped her legs around his waist and abruptly pulled him in place to slip inside her. The rhythmic buffeting worked the tension out of her buttocks and belly, and the fullness of him inside her fed her in a way that she didn't know she'd been hungry. She didn't come, and they didn't talk about it, but afterwards he propped himself up on his elbow and smiled into her eyes, and she smiled back. *Easy. Comforting.*

Late in the morning of the sixth day, they approached the entrance ramp to I-10. DD was pedaling. She'd gotten into the rhythm of it and almost didn't stop, but something caught her eye. She was off the seat of the bike and sprinted off like a shot!

"What the hell? Come back here! DD, what's wrong with you?" Jeremy called from his station atop the coiled rope.

She was dashing across the road towards an abandoned moving van, her sore feet forgotten. Abandoned and disabled vehicles were strewn everywhere, so much a part of the landscape they didn't even register anymore. But she leapt with joy onto a burgundy sofa sitting on the shoulder; she sprawled out.

"My stuff! Jeremy, this is my stuff!"

"No shit?" He stood over her, amused.

"They said they were going to send a replacement truck for it. This must be it! Didn't make it to Houston, though, did it?" She got up and peeked over the rear bumper into the truck. It looked like an explosion at a rummage sale. "Looks like they put it in with someone else's stuff." She looked a while longer. "But it looks like most of mine was probably in here. I wonder..."

She scrambled up inside the cargo area and located a leather storage ottoman. The lid was tossed aside and the contents had been emptied, but she grabbed a seemingly random scrap of yarn and pulled up, and the false bottom came out. "Yes!" she exulted, "my revolver!" She pulled out a silver Smith & Wesson K-frame revolver. She tilted the cylinder out.

"Five shots?" Said Jeremy. "Keeps the weight down."

"I know, right? It's a great 'girl' gun. Fires .38 Special or .357 Magnum. I've got it loaded with the .357 now, and these two speedloaders are .357 too." She put the speedloaders in her pocket. "Unfortunately, the rest of my ammo was in that dresser." She nodded at a six-drawer bureau on the other side of the truck. All its drawers were missing and nowhere to be seen. She stood up and began nudging through the debris on the floor with her toe.

Half an hour later, she had a shoulder bag full of miscellaneous items, including family photos, first aid items, and candles. They had a tent (*nylon, but it might last a night or two*). They had a hammock, cotton, brought home from a trip to Cancún. They had two-thirds of a bottle of vodka and even, after a little scrounging, the lid for it. She had two pairs of rugged leather walking shoes and some rigid-soled hiking boots. She looked around and started to cry.

"We can't possibly take any more of this on the Pedi cab," she sniffled. "But these are all my things. That armoire was my mother's."

Jeremy put a hand on her upper back, unsure what to say. DD took a deep breath. "Let's just go," she said decisively. "Now. Standing around here feeling sorry for myself isn't going to make that armoire fit on a bicycle!"

Just at that moment, a new voice came from the square of light at the end of the truck. "I don't think you're going anywhere right this minute!"

Rather than raise her revolver, DD left it holstered and ran to the entrance. "Jessica?" She asked.

"Mom!"

XXXVII. Not Bad for An Old Guy

Amit sat at his breakfast bar, typing furiously and reading intently on his laptop, an empty plate and cup at his elbow, as the light of the rising sun streamed in through the sliding glass doors. There was still electricity in the apartment building, but the internet was cutting in and out. He had no idea how the cables were routed, but the internet had told him, during brief diversions from his primary research aim overnight, that random buildings, blocks, and entire neighborhoods, were haphazardly going down; phone, internet, power, cable TV. Electrical fires were also breaking out, small ones and large, suggesting short circuits of insulated wires large and small, high voltage and low, AC and DC, throughout the system. He was uploading his notes to his cloud server in India, and pulling down published microbiology papers via VPN whenever he noticed the "Connected" icon come on in his encrypted interface. His initial breakthrough had come around midnight when he opened a new browser tab and typed, not for the first time, "OHCB AND *pseudomonas putida* AND mutation," without realizing he was in the browser search bar, instead of in the biomed database search window. The results popped up as he realized his error, and just as his cursor was on the "X" to close the window, he hesitated. At the bottom of the page, the last one of the results was a Power Point presentation from an Amrencorp meeting in Baton Rouge. He clicked on the link and read the first slide: Bioremediation. He uploaded his notes to the cloud while he flicked through the slides, growing more excited each moment. This could get him started looking in the right direction!

India was lagging behind in the spread of the problem, and BBSs there were crackling with news and rumors. China was said to be overwhelmed, but no one knew, since they'd cut off all electronic communication earlier in the day. Japan's entire population was inside their homes, obediently awaiting further news. Jakarta, and all of Indonesia, was completely unreachable. The affliction had reached Australia, Iceland, Ontario, Russia, Poland. Estonia was free of problems for the time being, and the rest of Europe was still connecting spottily. As the night wore on, the time of the last posting on bulletin boards and social media was the only way to estimate when a country or region had gone dark. The mass media ceased broadcasting or posting online around 10:00 p.m., but no one was paying any attention to their scripted speculation at that point anyway.

As silence descended, rumors proliferated among the few remaining connected: it was drones with focused EMPs! It was the global Communist revolution! It was the Kurdish militia and ISIL joining forces! It was the Rothschilds! He refrained from sharing his near-certainty about the bacterial nature of the devastation, sure no one would be convinced anyway.

Amit knew he had little time, perhaps just moments, until he lost connectivity as well. He heard the stairwell door open out in the hallway. He heard heavy footsteps…two big men? Three? He lifted his head. The footsteps stopped outside his door. He closed his computer and slipped it into its case, stuffing the cable in after it. His doorbell rang.

He pulled the strap of the laptop bag over his head and across his chest. "Open up! Police!" from the hall. In three steps he was by the terrace door. The doorbell rang again, followed by three pounding bangs on the door itself; he used the noise to mask the sound of the sliding glass door opening and then gliding shut behind him.

He walked over to the waist-high brick planter which comprised the partition dividing his terrace from the neighbors'. He pushed a plastic lawn chair to the wall, stepped up on it, and gracelessly plunged through the thick shrubs planted on top, pulling his computer bag after him. He hit the terrace floor hard, but got up and dusted himself off. He was pretty sure there was no one home; these neighbors traveled a lot and it had been several weeks since he'd heard any sound from them. He picked up a wrought-iron patio chair and flung it through their sliding door, setting off their alarm system. It began to beep every three seconds. BEEEP! He was dashing through their apartment. BEEEP! He opened their front door. BEEEP! He closed the door behind him. He trotted down the hall to the stairwell entrance. By the time the alarm's deafening siren went off, he was clattering down the stairs onto the fifth-floor landing.

He heard shouts coming from the seventh floor and redoubled his speed, ignoring the knife-like jabs under his kneecaps. He reached the second floor, and instead of heading to the ground floor and out through the lobby, he had the

presence of mind to duck out of the stairwell—he thought his
pursuers were still too high up to see him—and slip around the
corner to the gym entrance. As he'd hoped, the exit to the gym
balcony was unlocked (he knew the building custodian
smoked out there on his breaks). Amit straddled the rail. He
dropped his laptop case into the bushes below, which broke its
fall. He hesitated, realizing a ten-foot drop was too far for a
man his age to attempt. But subtract his 5'7" height, and he
should be okay. He swung his other leg over, then crouched.
He dangled by his hands from the bottom of the balustrade,
and then he let himself drop. He hit hard, jarring his arches
and his back even though he tried to let the bend of his knees
take the force. Then he fell on his butt. But when he caught his
breath, he found himself, astoundingly, entirely unhurt. He
looked around and discovered himself to be apparently
unobserved as well. He smoothed his hair, tidied his jacket
and shirt collar, strung his laptop case across his body, and
strode off down Racine. The general chaos of running,
walking, crying people in various stages of undress had
continued unabated since the previous evening, but they were
intermingled now with a calmer and less colorful stream of
individuals. They had serious faces, carried light luggage or
pushed carts or strollers, and many carried some sort of stick
or club. He saw some families with small children: refugees
who'd seen the chaos the city streets were descending into and
knew they wanted to get out. He did his best to lose himself
among them.

He was seriously tempted to try to reach his car, but he knew better. It was a shame. It was probably not infected because he'd last filled it up two weeks ago. He'd then parked it in his rental garage space and not driven it since. He had a pretty good working hypothesis now about y what had happened. He'd seen his name in DD's presentation; he guessed that the men who were in his apartment, contaminating it with *p alkanivorax*—no, *p davisii*—that very minute, were after him because they'd seen his name there, too.

Amit was no wet-behind-the-ears neophyte. He'd spent his whole life wrangling with corrupt, inept, self-important, bureaucrats of one sort or another: Indian government officials, academic administrators, wages-and-hours inspectors in his role as supervisor, and high-level executive directors in NGOs who only allowed lives to be saved if it enhanced their authority. He'd no desire to become a manipulable implement for them and their blank-eyed lackeys in such a time of emergency. Fingers would be pointing, enmities avenged, and favors called in at premium rates of exchange. Amit had made his career by nimbly and silently evading their grasp; now he just needed to do so literally as well as metaphorically.

XXXVIII. Unconditional

DD almost hurt herself, so eager was she to jump out of the truck and throw her arms around Jessica. She kept repeating her daughter's name over and over again, tears streaming down her face. She'd release her, take her by the shoulders, look at her face, run a hand over her short blond hair, break into tears afresh, gibber, "Jessica! Jessica!" and engulf her plump body in a new embrace. This went on for several minutes.

DD calmed down enough to turn to Jeremy.

"This is my daughter," she began.

"...Jessica." He finished. "I'm Jeremy. Pleased to meet you."

"How...why..." began DD.

Jessica gave her the condensed version. "I was living in Austin, working at a blood bank, when the machine sickness hit, Mom. I'm an LPN now. I thought I'd lose my job when the plastic bags of blood and plasma started bursting, so I just walked out the door and kept walking.

"Later on, I figured out what was happening. Once I saw how bad it was everywhere, I headed east. I was going to Tallahassee. I needed to find out what had happened to you."

"Why now? Why did you care? After so long?"

"I know it's been a long time, Mom, and I'm sorry. I've thought so many times about calling you, but I didn't think you'd want to see me again after everything that happened."

"Oh, honey! You're my little girl! You'll always be my child!" DD shook her head in disbelief. "I admit, I was mad when you disappeared with that low-life. So mad! That is, when I wasn't worried sick. That was one of the worst times of my life. I never knew if you were telling the truth or if he was making you say things. I never knew where you were..."

"He was there every moment I was talking to you on the phone. I'm sorry for those things he made me say. I'm sorry I told you—he told you—I hated you and told you to leave me alone, Mom. I've thought about that a lot." Her face twisted with regret. *Oh, God, I so want to believe that's true. The girl can lie, though. All addicts are expert liars. Is she really a licensed practical nurse? Who knows.*

"That bastard! Is he...are you still..."

"No, I got away from him about four years ago, a few months after you and I last talked. I went to some friends' house in Denver and called the cops; he was wanted for breaking probation. He won't be out for a long time.

"Well, so now you've found us. What now?" Jeremy sounded a bit reluctant.

Jessica looked from her mother to Jeremy and sized up the situation. She tilted her head and gave her mother a look which said they would have a private discussion later.

DD said, "We're going to Sutokata. Do you want to come?"

"Where?" Asked Jessica.

"Sutokata. You remember the community I told you about where we used to go when you were very little?" She squatted and scrambled in her shoulder bag on the ground.

"Oh, yeah, I remember. The picture of me..."

"On the goat!" finished DD, popping to her feet and brandishing a faded Kodachrome print of a blond, pigtailed toddler sitting astride a fat nanny goat and grinning.

"I don't remember it; I was too little. But sure. It sounds like a good place to be right now."

Jeremy interjected. "I hate to be a party pooper, but two won't fit on that bike cab. Especially since we've just loaded up with a few more things."

"Oh, not a problem," said Jessica. "I'll wait up for you two to catch up every now and then." She jerked her thumb at a scooter nearby.

"Is it running? Where'd you find gas for it?"

Jessica giggled. "Mom, did you forget who you're talking to? I modified it to run on ethanol! The carb is a little leaky and I'm not happy with the idle yet, though..."

"Hunh. My daughter the mechanic!" She turned to Jeremy. "She worked as a lawn mower mechanic all summer between her sophomore and junior year of high school."

"That's nice, but the liquor stores are starting to look pretty bare," Jeremy pointed out.

"At least I can always make more ethanol," said Jessica.

"Your great-grandpa the moonshiner would be proud." DD grinned.

206

"I've got enough Everclear in the saddlebags to make it a long way, anyway."

Jeremy, resigning himself to the inevitable hitched his thumbs in his belt loops and touched his baseball cap. Putting on his deepest Foghorn Leghorn, Texas drawl, he said, "Ma'am, it looks like we've got us a convoy!"

XXXIX. Door Closes, Window Opens

Amit was quite exhausted by the time he reached the Walgreen's at the corner of Roosevelt, a block from the river. He'd gotten no sleep that night, except for brief drowsing-off at the keyboard, and he was acutely aware that a man in his late 60s shouldn't treat himself this way.

The automatic sliding doors to the big drugstore stood open, jammed on the half-consumed synthetic rubber seals of their sliding tracks before the power had failed. It was quite plain which sections of the linoleum floors were infected, as a trench of goo ran down the center, flanked by footprints spreading out like uncooked pancakes on a griddle. He did his best to avoid getting any on his shoes; the shoes were leather with leather soles, but stitched together, no doubt, with polyester thread. A few people desultorily rummaged the shelves, but he'd missed the party where looting was concerned. All the food items, water, batteries, and electronic items were gone. The cooler and freezer doors were hanging open. Someone had forced open the metal cage protecting the pharmacy proper, whose shelves were stripped bare. Amit did, however, find a few bottles of isopropyl at the back of one of the bottom retail shelves, and the bottles weren't sticky or deformed, so he tucked two of them into his laptop case.

The sun was straight up in the southern sky. Half the day gone already. He saw no choice but to keep going. Weary, he set out down Canal Street, past warehouses and storage units, overgrown lots, and barbed-wire-topped enclosures with hundreds of trucks inside. There were no hysterical half-dressed folk dashing about here, just a grim procession, strewn along the broad streets, of those who realized a big city was nowhere to be once the trucks and trains stopped running. One foot in front of the other down Lakeshore Drive. He passed the majestic Field Museum and the Museum of Science and Industry, and continued towards the South Shore and its less prestigious sights.

Just at dusk, he heard a car, one of the few still running. A large, dark car with tinted windows, playing loud thumping music, pulled up beside him. He braced himself for the worst. A grey-haired Indian man with a computer, walking alone through a neighborhood like this at night, was a like koi among sharks, and he doubted the police were going to be much of a presence without any running cars. He walked ahead, trying to ignore the vehicle while remaining alert. He calmed himself as much as he could, thinking about how he'd never imagined his life ending like this. He had known it was too good to last: he'd considered it lucky not to have seen any of the human predators from the slums on the far side of the freeway, who would be unable to resist crossing over to prey on the refugees among whom he walked.

But it seemed his luck had run out.

Then, a familiar, woman's voice rang out: "Professor!"

He turned around and saw Juni, standing by the driver's door, waving to him across the hood of the car. Relief flooded through him. He bopped to the passenger side and hopped in. He settled himself into the comfortable leather seat of Juni's Town Car with a deep and appreciative sigh.

"What happened, Professor? Are you all right?" She looked at him with a furrowed brow, deep circles under her eyes, her normally meticulous coiffure in a kerchief.

"Juni, did anyone follow you?" Amit realized he sounded paranoid, but he didn't care.

"What do you mean? Of course not. Who would follow me?" She eyed the rear-view mirror.

"Good. Where have you been since I saw you?" Amit asked. Juni fastened her seat belt. The car was running but she hadn't put it in gear.

"I went to the hospital in the cab you hailed for me, but their X-ray table was in bad shape, so they couldn't X-ray my ankle—it's fine, now, anyway, a little swollen, but not hurting to walk on anymore. So, I went home with my husband when he got there." Her face turned instantly gloomy and greyish. She sat looking straight ahead at the windshield, lost in a private vision.

"…Your husband?" Prompted Amit. He realized the car doors were unlocked and pushed the button to lock them.

"He got out at the Jewel to look inside for food." She spoke slowly. "He left me locked in the car, waiting, with the engine running, and made me promise to start the car, drive away, and keep going if he wasn't back in an hour." She glanced at Amit, then turned her eyes to the horizon again. In her silence, he inferred what she couldn't force herself to utter aloud.

210

"Juni, I'm sorry." Amit said.

She produced four sharp sobs and turned her head away. After a long pause, she drew a breath and said, "I'm sure he's alright."

"Where are you going, Juni?" Asked Amit, knowing when to change the subject.

"He told me to keep driving until I hit Indiana. He said the country is safer than the city. Maybe the machine sickness hasn't reached there yet."

"Machine…sickness?"

"Yes, when the plastic parts in the machines and the fuel starts to decay and then the goo infects other machines. It's like a sickness. It spreads."

"Machine sickness. Yes. Good description. I wonder who thought of it. Listen, Juni, I believe I have a place where we can go. I promise I'll tell you as we go. But first, let me do something."

He pulled one bottle of isopropyl out of his laptop case and, grabbing a tissue from Juni's console, he wiped his shoes and drenched the parts of the carpet where his shoes had touched. Juni had a bottle of hand sanitizer too, and he made her slather her hands while he wiped down her tennis shoes, feet, and ankles (her ankle did look fine, just a bit swollen). She was wearing jeans, a kente cloth shirt with a hoodie over it, and a matching headwrap over her hair. He blotted isopropyl into the carpet under her feet, and wiped the trim around the car door. The steering wheel was smooth, no sign of decay in the plastic, but he wiped it down as well, just to be sure. The gas gauge showed almost full.

"When did you last fill up?" He asked.

"All the gas pumps were broken, so Jim filled the tank with gas from the shed he kept for the riding lawnmower."

"Good, that probably wasn't infected then. We have a shot at making it."

"Making it where?"

"Indiana, as your husband said. Just drive."

Juni put her foot on the gas and off they went. Amit said, "I promised to tell you where we are going. First, I must tell you the story of Sutokata.

"When I was a young man, a million years ago when dinosaurs roamed the earth, I had some hippie friends at college. One of them was Hank. Hank had been a helicopter pilot in Viet Nam and was in school on the GI Bill. He's also one of the most remarkable people I've ever met. Literature, philosophy, physics, calculus, biology, economics, psychology—Hank aced every class he took, without studying. He'd attend lectures, flip through the book while the teacher talked, and bam!" Amit clapped. "He had it. Mind like a steel trap."

"Like a lot of soldiers back from Viet Nam, Hank got disillusioned by the war and disgusted with the state of the country. Like a lot of people in his generation, he turned on, tuned in, and in his third year of college, when they were pressuring him to choose a major, he dropped out.

212

"But in Hank's case, dropping out meant building something totally new. That's just the way he is. He and his wife Suzanne took new names: Snowbear and Akisni. They bought a plot of land in the middle of nowhere and built a self-sufficient compound. They called it Sutokata, which means seed of the future in Lakota."

"Sounds primitive." Juni said.

Amit smiled. "In the best sense. Suzanne—Akisni, which means 'healing' in Lakota—was a trained midwife and has become something of an herbalist. She's the anchor who holds Hank—Snowbear—down to earth when he starts wandering off on one of his space journeys." Amit made spiraling movements next to both temples. "At least, that's how things used to be with them. It's been a while since we've seen each other. But we keep in touch."

XL.   Root Beer and Everclear

DD put on her rigid-soled hiking boots from the moving truck, and with those protecting her feet as they continued to heal, she was able to take a full four-hour shift pedaling the bike rickshaw. They established a routine: Jessica rode onward on the scooter, stopping at least every hour or so, or sooner if there was an auspicious salvage site, to let them catch up. She'd perch on her scooter, helmet under her arm, and patiently wait until they reached her. DD's heart never failed to leap when she first spotted the child whose loss she'd so deeply mourned, but she quashed the emotion, sure she was being played for a fool once again.

"You don't trust your daughter, do you?" Jeremy asked out of nowhere one day, sitting in the back of the Pedi cab.

"I don't trust anyone." DD said, conserving her breath for the slight incline ahead of her.

"Didn't think so."

In a few spots, the way had been blocked by immovable cars and trucks, and they'd crawled their cycles on foot along narrow winding pathways that they picked through the obstruction. They were two of the few vehicles still moving. Cycles definitely had an advantage on the deteriorating roads.

They stuck to highways and interstates, which were mostly still in pretty good shape, though they hit a few stretches where the asphalt was crazed or melted into a sticky goo. These were typically in high-traffic areas where lots of

214

vehicles used to change speed or direction, or else where there were overhead lights for birds to perch on. DD supposed that the birds were carrying the bacteria in their crops and passing it in their feces.

There were lots of people on foot, and a few had devised ways of replacing bicycle tires like Jeremy had: rope was a popular material choice, but so were rolled-up newspapers, and also sewn canvas tubes stuffed with various materials.

Then one day, shortly after a rest break, Jessica came across a woman crouching over a small child who lying supine on the ground. Two older children stood by, silently watching. The woman didn't bother to look up as they approached, even when Jessica walked up and stood over her.

"Something wrong?" She asked.

The woman lifted her tearful face to regard her, and Jessica saw blood on the ground underneath the child's head. It was a little girl, dark-skinned like her mother and siblings, with thick, dark, coarse hair that pegged them as *mestizos* or Indians. She was wearing jeans and a pink T-shirt with a unicorn printed on it. Her feet were wrapped in strips of cloth which had been stitched with care into passable shoes.

"What happened?" Jessica asked, just as DD and Jeremy rolled up, DD pedaling and Jeremy riding. They dismounted.

"This guy—she didn't do nothing..." The woman had a mild Spanish accent. "We was walking and he walked up behind us. He just, just, hit her with a stick he was carrying.

There was something wrong with him. He started yelling crazy stuff and ran off..."

"What did he look like?" Jeremy asked, suddenly watchful.

"Tall, skinny black guy, red shirt, grey hair..." Jeremy's eyes narrowed. He spun on his heel and strode off in search of the assailant.

Jessica was already on her knees next to the girl. "She's breathing with a good pulse. What's her name?"

"Martha." She pronounced it in the Spanish manner, with a hard T: *Marta*.

"Martha," called Jessica. "Can you hear me? *Puedes oirme?* Does she speak English?"

"She speaks English."
The little girl opened her brown eyes. "Mamá?" she asked. Her mama knelt across from Jessica.

"Martha," said Jessica, fearing skull or neck injuries, "do you hurt anywhere?"

"My head," the little girl said. She was about four years old. She sat up before Jessica could stop her, twisting her head to look over her shoulder at DD.

"Well, her neck seems okay," Jessica said.

Jeremy circled around, intent on making sure the attacker wasn't nearby. Jessica looked at the wound on the girl's head, then went to her scooter and took out a bandanna, which she saturated with Everclear from one of the fuel bottles in her saddlebag.

"This will sting," she warned, and Martha whimpered a little as she cleaned out the wound. "It would probably be better to sew it up, but..."

Martha's mother pulled a spool of thread and a needle out of her pocket and held them out to Jessica. "...but I'm not a doctor," finished Jessica.

Martha's mother shrugged. She threaded the needle and bent over her child's head.

"Have you done that before?" asked Jessica.

"Not on a human." The mother's voice didn't shake. She pushed the edges of the wound together.

"Let me!" Jessica took the needle and thread. The little girl was stoic, not whimpering or weeping. Once, she flinched and hissed a breath in between her teeth, but regained her solid composure, and so soon the wound was closed, a little snip of white thread in her mass of black hair the only sign of it. Jessica dabbed it with a little more Everclear, then patted Martha on the hip. "All done." She smiled as the girl ran to her mother's side.

The sun was close to the horizon now. "Should we go on?" DD tossed out to the group. "Or stop for the night?

"Me and the kids were going to camp under this overpass," volunteered the woman.

"My name's DD. This is Jessica... and Jeremy." Jeremy had just sauntered up, satisfied that the assailant was gone for now, and stood considering them. Martha was standing next to her brother and sister, all three of them watching the adults from a row of brunet almond eyes in solemn faces.

"Gabriela." She took DD's proffered hand. Then Gabriela leaned over and kissed Jessica's cheek. "Thanks for stitching up Marthita's head."

"No problem." Jessica shrugged. "I'm an LPN. I worked at an urgent care center where the doc was getting old. He had shaky hands. I wound up doing a lot of his wound closures after the first few months." Jessica turned to her mother. "Let's spend the night here." Gabriela's tiny smile let them know she welcomed their company after her scare. Jeremy nodded.

DD nodded too.

I wonder why she lost that job. A lot of doctors keep narcotics in the office.

The weather was fair and cool and appeared likely to remain so, so they decided the shelter of the dry but reeking, grubby overpass was unnecessary. Instead, they found a flat, dry, leeward spot where a retaining wall ran up against an embankment and set up camp there. They hung tarps and blankets overhead against the morning dew, spread more on the ground, and built a small fire. Pooling their food stores, they produced an enjoyable meal of hot dogs, canned beans, corn tortillas, sliced apples, and chocolate bars.

They drew closer to the fire as the night grew colder.

Sitting around the fire with full stomachs, DD extracted a 6-pack of glass bottles of root beer from the rickshaw. She'd liberated it from the stinking refrigerator of an abandoned home a few miles back.

"Jessica, how much of that Everclear do you have left?"

"Four gallons. Enough for a couple more days."

"Can you spare a pint or so? I bet it would mix well with this root beer."

"Mom!"

"Sounds like a country song, doesn't it? Root beer and Everclear." They swigged a few ounces from each bottle so they could top off with alcohol.

Jessica passed the Everclear bottle instead of pouring. "I'm allergic," she told Gabriela.

"You don't drink anymore?" Asked DD.

"No, I realized the drugs and alcohol were part of what set me off. It wasn't easy. I started drinking when I was 13, you know."

"No, I didn't know that."

Jessica laughed. "Mom, do you really want to know all this? You were so sure you had everything under control all the time, it was easy to convince you of what you wanted to see."

"How could I not have known?" DD replayed Jessica's late childhood and adolescence in her head: She caught her and a girlfriend trying cigarettes behind the garage at age 12 and confiscated her phone for a week. Normal kid stuff, or at least it seemed that way to DD, after her own upbringing.

She'd had no clue the rest was going on. Not until Jessica started driving. Then, she disappeared for a day, right before Christmas break of her sophomore year. Then, she disappeared in her junior year, for the entire week of Spring Break, sending a text message every couple of days saying she was out of signal, her phone was dead, she was on her way home, she'd call in a few days. Then she started showing up, nodding off or jittering on the balls of her feet. She'd appear at odd times at DD's work, or at home, with boyfriends with eyes blue as toilet cleaner or green as snake bile in pustule-ravaged faces, teeth like the windows of abandoned houses, and homemade tattoos on wrists, neck, face. Every attempt to confront her led to a fight and withdrawal. Jessica appeared to straighten out for a while and raised her grades. But then she began cutting, neat slices in her forearms and the fronts of her thighs. Her father withdrew into silence and soothed his unacknowledged pain with online shopping, until the cards were maxed out to the tune of tens of thousands of dollars and he could no longer hide it.

The divorce, though amicable, occupied DD's attention. Jessica appeared to straighten out; she was in therapy, and she qualified for a full-ride scholarship.

Then, Spring of her senior year, not long after her 18th birthday, Jessica moved out abruptly. Soon after, DD got a call; Jessica had stopped showing up at high school, forfeiting her graduation, her scholarship, and her future. Jessica's phone was cut off. Her apartment was vacant, but like a tornado had struck it, childhood stuffed animals alongside sacks of rotting trash, irreplaceable family photos ruined by dripping candle wax since the power had obviously been off for weeks. The landlord hoping DD would make good the unpaid rent, and DD guiltily refusing.

This is bringing up too many painful memories. "I guess I should have listened to you instead of trying to force you to succeed according to my standards. I'm sorry."

"It's okay mom. I only have one regret. I wish I'd been born Swiss."

"What's so great about being Swiss?"

"I'm not sure. But the flag is a big plus."

Everyone was quiet for a while and sipped their drinks. DD was grateful for the silence as it gave her a chance to integrate her feelings and recollections. The children were under a blanket; one of them was snoring ever so softly. The warmth of the liquor spread through their bodies and the gibbous moon drifted higher in the firmament.

Their life stories glided out of their mouths and floated, ephemeral, like the sparks from the fire, before rising on the sinuous updrafts of heat.

Gabriela had traveled about 140 miles with her three children and she was almost home. "Home" being her mother's house in the country, about fifteen miles from this freeway exit. Her husband had been stationed at Fort Chaffee and they'd lived off-base with the children. Two days ago, the President had declared a Nationwide State of Emergency, and the Army had shoved all active-duty personnel into trucks, with no word on their destination or when they might return.

"They had underground tanks full of gasoline at the base, and he said about half of them were still good," Gabriela said. "I don't know how he knew, but he said he knew. I don't know how far those trucks got, or what happened to the soldiers in them, but I figured me and the kids would be better off at my mama's. The prison is right next to the military base, and I heard the convicts broke out yesterday."

"We're headed for a place in Central Indiana I know, a farm. A commune, sort of." DD said.

"Central Indiana? In November?" Gabriela exclaimed. "It's gonna get cold once you cross the Ozarks."

"Yes, I've been thinking about that..." *Don't whine about how you hate the cold. In the face of what you've caused, it's a petty concern.*

"My mom's place has a big cattle barn. I bet she'd let you sleep there, and feed you too, in exchange for chores. She's all alone there with my little brother."

"I've never worked on a farm before. I wouldn't know the first thing to do," began DD.

"I have. Spent time on my uncle's cattle ranch when I was little," said Jeremy.

"I can fix things and I'm a nurse?" offered Jessica tentatively.

"It's settled then. We can be there by noon tomorrow." Gabriela said.

DD started to object but stopped herself. She didn't want to trek through the freezing cold. She told herself she was worried about her recently healed feet, but they were, honestly, looking pretty good.

Even with heavy socks and mittens and respectable boots, I just flat-out hate cold weather!

At that instant, they heard footfalls lumbering up the shoulder towards them. Gabriela sprang across the campsite to crouch over her children, no sign of her phlegmatic reverie as she transformed in seconds into a wild animal protecting her young. Jeremy shot erect to face the intruder. DD stood too, and took a step back, out of the firelight. *What should I do?*

Then she remembered she was armed. She drew her S&W, grasping it low at her side. The stranger moved closer to the fire, arms-length from Jeremy, and his bony build, red shirt, and grey hair left no doubt he was the man Gabriela described, the one who'd attacked Martha.

"The police can't help you now, can they? It's every man for himself! Police can't help you now!" he hooted, shifting foot to foot and jerking his bloodshot gaze around the scene. DD noiselessly pulled back the hammer on the revolver. *Can I do this?* And, *Am I doing this because he's black?*

"What you LOOKIN' AT?" He finished the phrase in a screech and jerked back his hand, holding a rough wood walking stick, heavy and thick like a club. DD raised her firearm. He was sluggish enough, sloshed or insane, or both, that Jeremy had no difficulty seizing the wrist of the hand that held the stick high in the air, so he couldn't bring it down. They grappled a second or two. Then, in a moment of sheer unscripted absurdity, Jessica stepped in and yanked the club out of his grasp, then stepped back; DD blinked in surprise over the sights of her gun, now centered on the man's chest. The poor addled bastard looked at Jessica in dull confusion, then kicked Jeremy—hard—in the thigh, going for the nuts and missing, and yanked his arm free. Jeremy backed up a step, reaching for his gun, but DD was ready with her hammer cocked and her barrel level. *Just like at the range...squeeze, don't pull...* She heard the bang, felt the recoil. *I missed.* Her first emotion was relief. She regained her sight picture, ready to fire again. But then the stranger put his hand to his side, and she realized her first shot had found its mark. She let the gun drop to her side and watched him drop, in turn, to his knees. She put her other hand up as though to say *stop,* just as Jeremy fired the first of two more shots into his body.

Then time speeded up again. The man was on his side. Her heart was thrashing, her ears buzzing from the sound of the gunshot, and her hands were quivering as she holstered the revolver. Jessica bent briefly over the recumbent madman. She looked at her mother, shook her head in sorrow, then stood up and turned away.

Gabriela was telling the one child who'd sat up, the boy, "*Nada pasó. Duermete, amor.*" Nothing happened, go to sleep. The child glanced around, bewildered, but compliantly laid himself back down, sinking into the profound sleep of the innocent.

They stood in a rough circle as the night wheeled around them, connected by some invisible rigidity to the

224

pivotal hub of a moment. No one spoke for a time. "I guess I'll check his pockets," Jeremy said. DD walked back over to her seat by the fire and sat down heavily. She sucked down a long pull on her root beer and Everclear.

"Mom, are you okay?" Asked Jessica, settling next to her.

"Yes. Yes, I think so." *Numb. I go numb when bad things happen.* "I've carried a gun for twenty years. I hoped carrying it would mean I'd never to have to use it."

"I know, mom. You did what you needed to do. You protected us all." She took her mother's shaking hand, and the two of them stared into the fire. It was comforting to realize they were still alive, together, and safe.

Gabriela had soothed the children and was walking towards the fire, facing the two of them. A sharp intake of breath from Gabriela made mother and daughter look up, then follow her gaze to Jeremy.

Jeremy had been bending over their attacker, searching him for anything of use they could scavenge. Now, he was standing upright with his hands in the air. Three men wearing a motley of denim and leather were holding rifles trained on him.

XLI.   90% Of Life Is Showing Up

The next evening, the oblique sun of Autumn was nearing the horizon when Amit requested that Juni turn off US 41 in Indiana, onto an unexceptional two-lane road between two cornfields. They'd bypassed hundreds of inoperative vehicles on their way south.

In some places, they'd discerned the impediments far in advance, and diverted down side roads. Fortunately, due to his age, Amit was proficient in navigating by paper maps, so they didn't get lost.

They'd seen only two police vehicles with their coruscating lights. The few police vehicles still running were way outnumbered by the immobile vehicles. They probably had other things to worry about too, mused Amit, as he'd noticed a gigantic irrigation outlet spouting, turning the farm's utility yard into a lake, its PVC pipes spraying water, above-ground traps and connectors, the thickness of a man's thigh, sagging flaccidly and ready to fall.

Probably a lot of the police had deserted, Amit thought, *to save their own pelts, or their own families'*.

They sped down the desolate country road. Clumps of trees broke the monotony, the only things which kept the scenery from being a featureless pancake from horizon to horizon. The wind swept without ceasing out of the west, and the trees had deformed themselves, bonsai-like, towards the bearing of the gusts. A dog, lolling in the brown grass before a brick ranch house, was the only sign of life. The anesthetizing Midwestern uniformity sped by them in a smudge. The sky

226

was grey and overcast; a draft stirred the odd husk on the dry stubs of corn, chaff from a harvest weeks past, or rustled the dry, drab, leafy stalks of seed corn, reserved to dry in the field for a Spring planting that might, now, never take place.

The sun sank lower and began to turn the few most lofty clouds pearl-pink. At long last, as the leading edge of the ginger disc just melded to the smooth level plane of the horizon, Amit said, "Here."

Juni decelerated and turned south onto an unmarked dirt road between two windbreaks. The road was just two bumpy ruts, which meant they proceeded at a sedate pace, a row of spruce trees like Christmas trees on their left, a row of scraggly arborvitae on their right.

"You could almost believe things were normal," remarked Juni.

"Yes, it's very peaceful out here," agreed Amit. "We might as well enjoy the illusion. I don't think things will ever be normal again."

Juni's face fell, and her lips writhed as she tried to maintain possession of her weeping; her eyes at least remained dry. She concentrated on the track ahead, the potholes in its corrugated surface concealed by the shadow of the windbreak on their right.

"Were you ever married?" She asked abruptly.

Amit sighed, "Yes, I still am. But my wife is in India."

"When do you see each other?"

"The last time was two years ago. I believe that was just before you hired on at the University."

Juni considered that. "But…how does that work? The two of you being married, I mean?"

Amit sighed. "It isn't unusual for Indians to marry someone their parents choose. It was even more common, in fact it was the rule, when I was a young man. Things have changed since then, in India as well as here. And the way the internet, at first, allowed people to communicate across borders and around the world, effortlessly, increased the pace of change. But you asked about my marriage. I suppose… Marriage has different meanings for different people, in different places, and at different times in our lives."

Juni digested this. A few minutes later, "Do you have children?"

"None living."

Juni was silent after that. The windbreaks curved in parallel to the right, then to the left, the trail arching with them, and then ended. The car track continued into the twilight. There was little change in the vista as they crept along; they passed a grain silo, a barn, an irrigation rig, they passed a crossing with another dirt road, empty in both directions as far as they could see. It grew darker, and a rabbit materialized from the grass at the roadside, zig-zagged frantically before them in the headlights for a hundred feet or so, then sprang to the side at the last possible moment, just before Juni would have been compelled to brake.

When there was nothing but dreary farmland from horizon to horizon, the last light in the West was fading, and Juni had a look on her face in the dim greenness of the dash lights like there'd never be anything but fields and dirt roads ever again no matter how far she drove, Amit again said, "Here," pointing to a track which was scarcely discernible in the brown grass, running over a shallow culvert. They crawled from here on, jostling across a field of stubble and going between two spruce trees to cross another windbreak. The track curved around a gentle rise, and then plunged into a stand of bushy forest, like a secret oasis in the midst of the flat farmland. The track jumped onto evenly spaced wood crosspieces, rounded one last curve, then fell to its finish in a clearing.

A small log cabin, its windows gleaming with warm light, perched on the rim of a shallow depression. As she approached the structure, her eyes got larger as she revised her appraisal of its size, from small, to large, to gigantic. The depression, round as a bowl, was large enough that you'd have to shout to be heard from the other side, and though it was shallow in contour, it was perhaps fifty feet deep, and the light from the house and her headlights showed it was lined at the bottom with cattails gone to puffy seed and reeds seething in gusts of wind. The house was three floors tall and had a massive stone flue with a thin tape of smoke winding from it. A man emerged in the door, carrying a shotgun low by his side, and approached the car, unhurried, as it trundled to a halt.

He stopped about twenty feet away, standing outlined in the fading light, and Amit opened his door and swung out.

"Snowbear! Hank! How are you?" Asked Amit, and their host walked into the headlights. The stranger was lanky, a ruddy clean-shaven white man, with long salt-and-pepper hair, sparse on top and dragged back into a ponytail. He was wearing a denim shirt and jeans with heavy leather hiking boots. His belt buckle was in the shape of a silver bear.

He beamed. "Amit! Long time, no see! What brings you here, my friend?" He shook Amit's right hand and they circled each other's shoulders with their left hands in a secure masculine embrace.

"Trouble. Have you not heard?" Amit replied.

"Heard?" Snowbear asked.

"The trouble?"

Snowbear waved a hand vaguely at the house. "Internet went down last night, but no one's been on it for a while anyway. Then we lost power, about four hours ago. What's up?"

"May we…" He shifted his feet and nodded towards the house, aware now of his exhaustion.

"Of course! Sorry! You look whipped! Come on in. We just finished dinner but there are leftovers. Pinto beans and cornbread."

"Sounds wonderful."

Juni trailed the two men into the ample and abundant home.

XLII.   Better than Nothing

Jacob huddled in his garret. He'd broken into the attic window of the condemned house the night he'd watched the Germans and the two women get shot down in the street like dogs. It'd been three days and he'd eaten nothing but some oyster crackers in packets he'd scavenged from the sidewalk outside a crawfish joint. It had rained, and he'd caught some water in plastic bottle he'd found and cut the tops off of, but then the bottles melted, like everything plastic was melting. He was hungry and scared and alone. He slept on a crib mattress he'd pulled from a dumpster, his gun in his hand, startled awake by every scampering cat or distant voice.

Yesterday, he'd heard three women walking down the alley under his window talking about the camps. FEMA had emergency camps just north of town and they still had buses that ran, apparently. He'd heard them say that a bus left every day at sunset from LaFreniere Park. He could just make it there on foot if he left now. He scrambled down the drainpipe and set out through the streets, still plumed with the smoke of hundreds of smoldering fires. He picked his way through broken glass from shattered store windows and around the cars with their deflated tires, the puddles of caustic battery acid freed from its plastic casing, and the shattered blobs of plastic signage. Anytime he saw someone, he ducked out of sight and waited for them to pass, unless they ducked into an alley or a stalled car first, in which case he warily stalked past their concealment.

When he reached the old graveyard adjoining the park, he joined a bedraggled mob by the gates. Yats and blacks, a small gaggle of devastated college kids, moms with filthy starving children, and bunches of solo men and women of varying ages just like himself, leaned against the wall, sat on the curb, or squatted in the shade of scrubby bushes.

"They got food and hot water in the camps. Diapers and clothes for the young ones."

"I getting up under that!"

"They make everyone sleep in bunk beds."

"I hear they make you work."

"Farming is what I heard. Doing laundry. Like prison."

"Better than what we got here."

"Sure enough."

Around 4:30, a semi-truck pulled up, its diesel motor still growling away, its huge tires replaced by wire-lashed bundles of rags. Three men and a woman in green fatigues got out. Jacob had no idea what kind of military they were, he'd never served, and none of his family had, but they had American flag patches above the insignia. The soldiers took it in turns: two would stand with firearms ready, one would search those wishing to board, and one would help them climb up into the wooden-floored trailer of the semi.

Jacob had a sick feeling when he saw that people weren't being allowed to board with firearms. He watched an old, arthritic woman crook her finger at the soldier who'd pulled a Ruger semiauto pistol out of her cleavage, but even when she stamped her foot, the soldier remained impassive. The lady acquiesced and he dropped the magazine, cleared the chamber, and dropped firearm and clip into the slot atop a corrugated steel box. The woman allowed herself to be helped into the truck bed.

When Jacob approached, hands up, it was the woman's turn to search, and he told her straight up, "I have a firearm in the back of my pants."

"Okay, sir, keep your hands up and turn around." The weight of his weapon eased from his hips and he heard a click as the trusty Sig he'd inherited from his dad was unloaded, then a clang as it dropped in the box. He hardly noticed the woman's hands ranging over his body as he thought of his dad teaching him to plink with that gun, hitting cans atop fences at grampa's house. He hadn't thought of his dad in months, and he misted up a little, shook off the helpful hands of the soldiers at the rear of the trailer, and vaulted up himself.

Inside, the truck was empty except for thick hemp ropes laced back and forth across the floor, tied onto steel cargo loops. "Grab hold and hang on!" one of the soldiers shouted at his back. Jacob moved as far forward as he could to leave room for later arrivals, found a spot where he could wedge his legs under a rope, and settled down to fantasize a hot meal, a shower, and a real bed. Today's load was only a half-full truck, and once the doors shut it was dark within. They bumped and lurched for what Jacob thought was an hour and a half or so, during which he thought about his plants dying on the windowsill of his apartment, and when they stopped in the twilight and the engine stopped and doors rolled up, he got his first look at his new, temporary home.

Ten-foot chain-link fences topped with coils of concertina wire surrounded the grounds. It looked to Jacob like what he'd seen of his dad's old photo albums of his service in the Army: flat, treeless grounds with half-cylinder aluminum buildings. He remembered his dad called them "Quonsets" to Jacob's great amusement. He used to jump around chanting, "Quonset, Quonset, Quonset," until his father tossed a blanket over him and threw him shrieking on the couch for a good tickle session. Jacob shook his head. This sentimentality wasn't like him.

The group from the truck had all assembled and were being split into childless men, childless women, and family groups with children. Each was escorted to a different area of the camp. Jacob was shown to his spot: a bunk with a clean mattress, a blanket, and a foam pillow; he was led with the other men to the shower array in the back of the dorm. They all showered, silent and embarrassed, under the bored eye of a uniformed guard. He put his dirty clothing back on, since he had nothing else, but his shoes, which he'd wrapped in strips of cloth to hold them together, had stuck to the cloth and fallen to shreds when he took them off. The dorm was only about a quarter full, so all the new arrivals picked their bunks; Jacob picked a top bunk near one of the small windows. A bell rang and a guard came in a few minutes later to explain to the newbies that this meant supper.

Jacob followed the crowd to a cafeteria building and went through the line to get a tray of food that was more or less what he remembered getting for free lunch in his high school cafeteria. But it was hot, it was edible, and there was enough for a man Jacob's size, so he dug in with gusto. He was clean and sheltered, safe and fed. When the lights-out bell rang at ten, he fell asleep like a child.

XLIII. Love Strange

The expedition to Camp David, which was sixty-odd miles, had been nerve-racking for POTUS in his armored limousine. He snarled every time someone told him they'd heard nothing of his family. It was even more grueling for the Secret Service and Marine detail who trotted alongside on foot as the cars crawled along. Even so, they did everything feasible to make it easier and more comfortable for him, while still maintaining a thick cordon of protection. There was almost an entire military division surrounding him.

Once they established the fundamentals of what was coming to be called the machine sickness, and what was more important, its results, Camp David was the analytically valid choice. The Camp was a bunker, and the petroleum supplies stocked there were undisturbed and (presumably) uncontaminated, enough to last three years. A procedure of couriers travelling by foot and bicycle was contrived, to carry communications between POTUS and Site R in Pennsylvania, where what endured of the military command structure was to be bunkered. Birdwell noted that POTUS withdrew into himself when this was discussed; his eyes constricted. He suspected that the billionaire was silently scheming to use this emergency to get his hands back on the reins of his multinational business empire at the first opportunity. In a way, Birdwell couldn't blame him; everyone was frantic with

236

worry over the whereabouts of their loved ones and the status of their homes. He doubted that the man had grasped the scale of the dissolution confronting them, or the idea that corporations had ceased to exist when electronic communications were lost.

Birdwell shook his head; there wasn't much military left to command; the loss of communications and the inability to feed and supply military bases had left 90% of soldiers, sailors, airmen and marines on their own, either in the US or overseas, wherever they happened to be. The communications they did receive were mostly updates detailing small groups of governmental workers, military and police, who'd achieved momentary contact and were earnestly advised to continue carrying out their previous missions. What those missions were was usually unknown to the officer giving instructions at the time of contact, but often they were able later to dig up paper hard-copy to scrutinize. It gave them a chance to make a better guess who and what was left, and make some sort of conditional analysis.

The protection-camps rescue plan was apparently implemented early on, as laid out during the early PATRIOT years after 9-11, and judging by the spotty reports they received, it functioned more or less as planned in most areas, siphoning the population out of the hellish cities into self-supporting protectee centers.

To say that the first weeks at the refuge were a shock would be an understatement. POTUS was preoccupied and irritable; he seemed stunned. He'd relied on delegating authority and there was no one to delegate to. All he could do is listen to interminable speculation: long days of dispute, uninformed theorizing over what had transpired, bored him almost senseless. He even raised his hand one day as though to strike one brave aide who told him straight-out that his family couldn't be found.

The machine sickness was still held to be part of a larger terrorist or international political plot. This was articulated in top-level communications, transported long distances by foot or bicycle, on coded, sealed, slips of paper, to and from decoy hand-off sites, by couriers who didn't know one another and didn't know what news they were bearing.

One day, the protective detail assigned to the First Lady finally made it through. POTUS stood at the window and watched the eight immense men herd his wife, once an elegant model but now more like a gaunt refugee, and his son and daughter into the building. He actually wept a few tears and rushed to the entry to embrace them. Staff looked on with mixed emotions: relief at the family's being reunited, hope that POTUS would be more emotionally stable now that they'd been found safe, and envy. All but one of the subordinates had been separated from their families on the day the machine sickness struck Washington; only a few of them had been able to re-establish connection, and that was via vague, heavily self-censored paper notes entrusted to the foot couriers.

They waited for their enemies' nuclear bombs to drop, or for troop carriers to sail into their unprotected harbors, disgorging an invasion force on their helpless shores.

Slowly, they came to comprehend beyond any doubt that the affliction must be global. Not only were the US's nuclear warheads sitting useless in their silos, controlled by a tangle of newly uninsulated, shorted-out wires, but so were the warheads of every other nation. Aircraft and aircraft carriers, Humvees and tanks, Blackhawks and F-35s: all depended on plastics and petroleum fuel.

There was a hushed moment of shocked distress when someone brought up the fate of submarine crews. The image of them dying in the dark in submerged coffins, alone, unknowing, wedged itself vividly into everyone's mind, although surely the number dying in riots, plane crashes, structural collapses, and myriad other accidents worldwide was far, far greater.

The world's supreme national military empire was just as helpless as everyone else. Its massive size and rigid structure was, in fact, proving to be a disadvantage. There might be numerous units out there acting semi-autonomously, but those units would trickle away as they starved or ran out of materiél, or else degenerate into gangs of marauding thugs as they failed to receive new orders.

The expensive, hierarchical, and complicated planning and development mechanisms the nation-states of the planet depended on were as incapacitated as a freshman at a frat party.

Unknown to them, everywhere on the planet, individuals: ten thousand, ten million—who could count?—were tinkering and fiddling, gabbing and suggesting, testing and experimenting, with new ways to make things function, to survive and thrive. Just as the airplane was invented by six or eight others at the same time as the Wright Brothers tinkered at Kitty Hawk, just as Antonio Meucci presented a working telephone decades before Alexander Graham Bell, ideas had life of their own and could not be held back, but found a way to trickle through the mesh of connections between the billions of nodes of light known as humans.

XLIV. Don't Shoot or I'll Move

One of the men had the muzzle of his long gun touching the base of Jeremy's cranium; the other two stood farther back. *Think fast, DD.*

She stood, palmed her face with both hands, and let out a high-pitched gasp. She mimicked the sawtooth breathing of hyperventilation, imitating an asthmatic friend she'd once seen almost die from an attack. Jessica, brilliant, picked up on it right away, and launched into a performance of her own. Pretending not to have seen the men, she turned her back on them and began to try to "calm" her mother. She put her hands over hers, on her cheeks, and looked into her eyes.

"Mom, what's wrong? Mom? Mom!" Jessica deserved an Academy Award for her dissimulation. "Oh, no, it's one of her panic attacks! Jeremy, quick, her medication! Before she passes out again!" she called out, her eyes locked with DD's. DD risked a wink.

The middle man was colossal, beefy, and well over six feet tall, his tangled beard looped into a knot mid-chest. The two slighter men's body language telegraphed that he was their leader.

Gabriela stood uncertain, baffled and not twigging, while the two women went through their pantomime. Jessica swung around and covered the distance between her mom and Jeremy in a few galloping paces, then stopped short as she *pretended* to initially take in the situation.

Three things happened at once: Jessica let out an ear-splitting scream. DD lunged towards the five of them, her breathing miraculously restored to normal. And Jeremy slapped the rifle aimed at his ear away, spinning on one knee, seizing the barrel of the weapon, and shoving the stock of it up into his attacker's face, all in one precipitate motion.

DD had her own handgun unholstered by the time she'd closed the space between herself and the menacing tableau. Jessica was inside the radius of the rifle barrel of one of the goons, so he dropped the unusable weapon and went for the semiauto in his pants, just as Jessica sprang on top of him with the paring knife she'd used to cut the apples. The knife penetrated his chest eight or ten times—oh, so fast! —in a series of tiny, wet thumps. He managed to get his gun up and squeezed off a shot, which went wild, before he blanched and dropped limp to the ground. DD was approaching fast; the third thug was vacillating between firing at Jeremy, who was pressing his advantage by forcing his gigantic but off-balance opponent backwards using the stock of his own gun, and shooting DD. He swung the weapon towards her, but over-aimed and missed, and his hesitation allowed her to get a shot off before she sprinted straight at him. She saw him jerk as the shot smashed into him, and she squeezed the trigger four more times as she closed the distance. It barely registered that the last shot made no bang and recoil, just a click. He lifted the rifle again and DD saw, in a shock like a bolt of lightning, the concentric circles of the muzzle, quivering slightly, pointing right at her face, so close she could touch it. She dropped to her knees (she would never be sure, later, if it was quick thinking to get out of the line of fire, or outright terror making her knees buckle) and heard the rifle's report at the same moment, deafening, and saw the rifle recoil high into the air as the brute lost control of his weapon and fell. Heart pounding, she ran up to him, still holding her revolver, leapt atop him, and bashed his heavily tattooed face with the silver handgun, over and over, her cheeks pulling her mouth back into a rictus of fury as she heard the revolting cracks of breaking bones. Her tunnel visual focus shattered all at once, as Jeremy's adversary scuffled backwards towards her; the monster had acquired the presence of mind to let go of his rifle; now he drew a curved machete from between his shoulder blades instead. Jeremy was manipulating the stolen rifle, trying to flip it around and bring it to bear on his attacker, but it was plain that he was going to be too slow to aim and fire the unfamiliar weapon.

DD found herself other than human. Her thighs became the haunches of a beast as she dove horizontally forward out of her crouch, caught Jeremy's opponent behind his knees, and brought him crashing to the ground. All three of them bounded atop the one final man as he turned over, groping for his absent machete, which had gone flying as he fell. Jeremy stomped his face, Jessica kicked his ribs, and DD jumped up to seize his ankle and step on his knee, bending the joint sideways with a wet and appalling *CRUNCH!*

The three of them stood over their vanquished foes, panting, their hearts pounding in their ears. They swung around so they were back to back, observing the four would-be pillagers where they lay on the ground, alert for any sign of motion from them, or for any more confederates who might be lurking in the bushes.

Gradually, their breath slowed, and they began to feel their injuries. Jessica's was the worst: her opponent's handgun shot hadn't gone wild after all, but somehow punctured the thick, heart-shaped muscle of her calf. Jeremy had skinned the thick callus from his left palm, leaving a wound like a bleeding burn. DD's left pinkie finger stuck out sideways at a right angle, broken; when had that happened? She'd no clue. She realized there was blood running down her cheekbone and dripping on her right shoulder from a gash above her hairline, matching the healing one she'd gotten on the left temple from her captors.

And just like little Martha's. She remembered the family and looked around for Gabriela, Martha, and the other two children. She saw no sign of them and stalked past the fire. *Couldn't blame her if she took the kids and ran. I wouldn't have bet on us, against those hoodlums!*

But Gabriela lay under the brush pile they'd collected for kindling, sheltered with a blanket, arms spread like a dove's wings over the children, her hand clamped securely over the baby's mouth. She saw DD padding towards her and scrambled out, holding the baby and permitting him to cry, which he did forthwith. The girls came following, and Martha's big sister boosted her to her hip.

Jeremy, Jessica, and DD allowed Gabriela to fuss over their injuries and bind their wounds. She cleaned and bound Jessica's leg; the bullet had gone in one side and out the
244

other and the bleeding wasn't heavy. Comparatively. Her leg attended to, Jessica tottered over to stitch up her mother's scalp.

"This is becoming a habit for you," said Jeremy to Jessica, as Gabriela wrapped gauze around his skinned hand.

"A habit I'd like to break!" she observed wryly.

The children, seeing all the adults were present and accounted for, crawled back into their bedrolls and fell serenely back to sleep. The adults settled back down by the fire.

They glanced at each other.

"We did it!" exclaimed DD.

"We sure did," agreed Jeremy. "You were a wildcat! I thought I was a goner when that fat bastard pulled that machete!"

"I don't know what came over me!" mused DD. "Wildcat is a good description. I just felt like a feral creature!" She turned to Jessica. "And where did you learn to fight like that?" She asked.

Jessica smiled craftily and took a breath to answer.

"Never mind," DD said. "That is something I don't need to know."

"That's right, mom. You don't," her adult offspring agreed.

"Well, I don't know where any of you learned to do all that," Gabriela interjected, "but you were awesome beyond awesome. You are my heroes!" DD could see every hair of her head, vividly, and every thread of her fraying blouse.

"Is it just me," DD asked, "or does everything seem that much better and brighter right now?"

"It's not just you," Jessica confirmed.

"Is this the first time you've survived a fight for your life?" Jeremy asked.

"Well, yes," admitted DD. On the streets of her childhood and youth, she was the type who either faded and hid, or talked her way out of things.

"Kind of makes you feel really glad to be alive, doesn't it?"

"Hell, yeah!" DD recalled the laser focus, emotional but calm, that had burst into her consciousness when she saw the rifle muzzle pointing right at her.

"Wait till later. I'll show you what really feels good about still being alive!"

DD leered at him.

"Mom! Gro-o-oss!" Jessica mimicked her own tone from back when she was a child and she saw her mother and father kissing.

DD shrugged, giving Jeremy a wicked side glance. He took her hand and they slipped off together.

XLV.   Sutokata

Juni had never imagined anything like it. The home was beyond rustic. Every visible surface was wood: the floors were planking, the ceiling beams were exposed, with the planks of the floor above visible between them. The wall beams were also exposed, but between them stretched bookshelves, yards and yards of them. She'd entered, via a small mud room, into a chamber perhaps 40 by 25 feet, and every single wall was lined with books: paperbacks and hardcovers; biographies, history books, scriptures, coffee-table photograph books, how-to books, classics, erotica, best-sellers...

Noting her wide-eyed gaze, Snowbear smiled. "We have a lot of time to read in the winter."

"Why's that?" Asked Juni.

"We are a self-sustaining farm. In the winter, there's not as much labor to do." Juni considered this, her fatigue making her slow on the uptake.

"Oh. How do you..." just then a willowy, pale woman, with waist-length hair in the process of turning from blonde to white, walked in. She grinned, and crinkles warmed the corners of her unadorned eyes.

"Akisni, you remember Amit," said Snowbear. They hugged. "And this is?"

"Juni." She stepped forward and offered her hand to Akisni, noting the other woman's rustic bandanna kerchief, her magenta flannel shirt, rugged canvas cargo pants, and hiking boots. Her hand was callused but warm.

Juni was suddenly aware of her own designer hoodie, her onyx elephant earrings, her makeup. She felt the city girl's paradoxical emotions, of pride in her sophistication and embarrassment at her frivolity.

"Are you all thirsty? Hungry?" Akisni asked. Juni realized she was both. The sound of running water and clattering dishes and pans from the other side of the great door at the other end of the room resolved itself in her awareness. "Follow me." Juni was a little hesitant. She glanced at Amit, and he gestured with his open hand and followed the women into the kitchen, Snowbear bringing up the rear.

Entering the kitchen, Juni blinked. The juxtaposition of the same exposed beams and planking with modern stainless-steel counters, a commercial refrigerator and freezer, a commercial range with a huge hood, and restaurant-sized mixers, bowls, pans, and utensils was stunning.

Akisni walked to the refrigerator and pulled out two of a dozen or so identical glass casserole dishes. She popped them into the microwave to warm.

"Beans, greens and cornbread," Akisni explained. "We always set aside a few leftovers for snackers, and if it doesn't get eaten it goes to the pigs."

"How many of you are there?" Juni asked.

"Twelve of us live here full-time. We usually have a few people staying here as guests. Spiritual retreats, post-divorce recoveries, hippie dilettantes, and so forth. Used to have birthing moms, but not so much any more." The microwave beeped and Akisni settled them at the trestle table

248

with cloth napkins, silverware, and a ceramic ramekin of butter with little beads of water condensing on top. Juni's stomach growled. She hadn't had collards cooked with bacon since childhood, and she found these delicious. Snowbear sopped up the liquid from the greens with his buttered cornbread, just like her granddaddy used to do, and the familiar custom made Juni feel at home. Perhaps just being alive, after the way the past twenty-four hours had gone, added an edge to her hunger, but Juni ate like this pot-liquor-soaked cornbread was the best food she'd ever had.

Amit apparently felt the same way, because he savored every bite, chewing with an intensity Juni had not seen before in her delicate-mannered boss. He ate silently, and Snowbear sat across from him next to Juni. Akisni sat next to Amit, and when they'd both finished, Gillie, a young white girl with dreadlocks and a nose ring (Juni guessed this was one of Akisni's hippie dilettantes) swept into the room and took their dishes and napkins, swirling her ankle-length skirt as she deposited them into the dishwasher tray and left.

Once his guests had eaten, Snowbear laced his fingers on the table in front of him and asked with forced insouciance, "So, what's all this, then? Something up?"

Viswanathan took an unfathomable breath. "Yes, something is definitely up.

"The short version is that a bacterium has been released into the world which eats everything made of petroleum. Gasoline, diesel, plastic, asphalt, everything."

Akisni remained silent, unreadable. Snowbear grunted his incredulity. "That's a pretty wild claim."

"Snowbear, you know me. When you and your crew were tripping on mushrooms, who made sure you were okay and tucked you into your sleeping bags?"

"True. You have always been the sober, skeptical one. That's why you wound up a world-renowned scientist and Akisni, Les, Brownie, and I wound up living on a hippie commune…"

"Hardly a typical hippie commune. Science groupies, instead of rock stars. But it's important you listen to me and remember who I am, who I've always been. Because this sounds incredible, but it is honestly happening.

"There have always been bacteria which eat petroleum. Oil deposits seep to the surface in the ocean and on land, and where there's a source of nutrients, an organism will evolve to exploit it. The big secret to dealing with oil spills is that, if you just give those bacteria enough time, they will consume every drop of oil. In warmer climates, it can take months; in cooler climates, years or decades.

"The problem is, people are impatient. They don't want to look at oil slicks and tar-soaked wildlife for all the time it takes. It's bad PR for the oil companies. So, in an ocean spill, they spray the oil with dispersants, which makes the oil droplets smaller, but also slows down the function of the bacteria."

Akisni interrupted. "Wait a minute. So, when the oil companies treat the oil, it makes the spill take longer to clean up?" her expressive brow was furrowed.

"Well, it depends on your definition of 'clean up.' The big blobs of oil are gone, but the volume of seawater that's contaminated is actually greater. But that's not important now. I've always hypothesized that this could eventually force the bacteria to evolve more quickly. Several researchers have been working on developing a genetically engineered organism which could withstand the dispersant. But this is different.

"I don't know for sure if this is a naturally evolved variant or a genetically engineered bacterium. I have reason to suspect the latter…" He described the strange call from the Chinese physician.

"That's not much to go on." Snowbear commented.

"True." Amit conceded. "But there's something else. There's a bright—no, brilliant— young researcher who was working with *alkanivorax* and *p. putida* strains. I never had the privilege of meeting her, but she recently left academia to work in the private sector. I saw a Power Point of hers online. I downloaded it; I can show you on my laptop. I was hoping you had internet here, I'd like to finish downloading her most recent papers."

Amit put his hand on his laptop case, by his side on the bench, ready to show them the Power Point, but Snowbear waved his hand dismissively. "Okay." Snowbear stood up.

"Okay. I believe you." He put both palms flat on the table and bent forward, looking his old friend in the eye. "I believe you, Amit. You don't need to show me more proof.

"So. What should we do?"

Amit felt a knot in his chest unclench which he hadn't known was there. "Actually, you are probably in pretty good shape out here; that's why I came here. I did my best to disinfect before we got here, so hopefully we haven't contaminated your dwelling. You'll want to disinfect the tires of Juni's car, and make sure the children…you do have children here still?"

"None younger than ten at the moment."

"Just make sure they don't walk across the tire tracks and distribute the germs that way. However, no matter what we do, it's just a matter of time until it makes it to you. It's in the irrigation rigs of the fields nearby. Animals will track it in; it might even hitch a ride on windborne seeds or pollen. There's so much I don't know yet about this new hybrid.

"So, longer-term, you want to make sure anything you rely on which is plastic is replaced. Electronic devices will melt, or simply stop working. Do you buy propane gas?" He nodded at the stove.

"No, it's methane. It's homemade biogas. We have a micro plant which harvests it from our sewage and farm waste."

Amit's eyebrows shot up. "Really! That's impressive! I'd like a tour later."

"Yes, it's taken us years to work out the inputs; the right mix of anaerobes and how to know when to flare the gas…but it sounds like our urgently pressing concern for right now will be to figure out which components of it are plastic and how to replace them."

"Might I suggest looking at bone and horn as hard-plastic substitutes? They were used for similar purposes a century ago. In India when I was growing up, a lot of things were made out of them that are plastic here nowadays. My biggest worry is pipes and electrical insulation. It didn't take long at all, a matter of hours, for electricity, phones, and internet to go down in Chicago. I think the bacterium must use biofilms to migrate along the insulation."

"We need to call an emergency meeting. We have an electrician and a civil engineer in residence. But the more minds working together on this, the better."

Juni felt more secure, just knowing there were people here who understood the problems they faced and could work together to solve them. Juni's eyes began to drift shut, and as her awareness sank into her belly, full of warm, wholesome soul food, she was ready to cuddle up and fall asleep. She realized she had no one to cuddle, and tears began to trickle silently down her cheeks. Akisni took note and walked around the table to lay a hand on her shoulder. "Honey, are you okay? What's wrong?"

"My husband." Her throat constricted in a sob.

"Is he—it's okay, honey." Juni's shoulders began to shake. "Come with me." Akisni draped a warm, soft arm around her and maneuvered her from the kitchen. As they walked through the swinging double doors at the other end, Juni lost control of her weeping and began to moan.

XLVI. It's Only Natural

Each day that the internet failed to come back on was one rung further up the ladder of resignation. The people of the Sutokata Center gave up checking after about five days. They were all hard at it anyway: swathing electrical wires and PVC water pipes with pine-resin-soaked strips of felt and canvas, excavating plastic parts out of devices and connectors, carving bone substitutes, experimenting with oils and animal fats to see what would serve best as lubricants, and standing watch.

For it didn't take long for the surrounding folk to realize that the people of Sutokata were better-situated to survive the machine sickness than anyone else. Friends from the community stopped by to ask for help: goat's milk for a baby whose mother ran out of formula; a supply of sterile bandages for an elderly neighbor dealing with a slow-healing wound.

There were those they couldn't help: the diabetic neighbor who showed up with his wife, asking if they knew where he could get insulin. They didn't. They'd walked eight miles, since their vehicles were all disabled, and without being asked, Juni drove them back in her car, spreading canvas over the seats and carpet in the back so they wouldn't contaminate the vehicle with the machine sickness. Juni stopped at the end of their half-mile-long driveway to let them out. Knowing that the man would die a slow and miserable death in front of his wife, and there was nothing they could do to prevent it, left the entire household morose for days. However, they aided anyone they possibly could, on the principle of human kindness.

But one day, a few weeks after Juni and Amit arrived, Brownie was carrying feed to the pigs when he spotted a small group of armed men roving up the track towards the compound. They were spread out, but he thought he counted eight or nine of them. He hailed them, and instead of advancing to greet him, the men ran away at a dead run, scattering in all directions. Brownie came straight back to the main house and told Snowbear, who called a consensus meeting that evening.

The residents of Sutokata were, by and large, left-wing. They didn't like guns and they perceived that gun violence was a huge problem. However, in light of the fact that they appeared to be under imminent threat of violence and law enforcement was not accessible, they were forced to consider means of self defense.

Akisni had long insisted that Sutokata be a "place of peace," which meant many things. One thing it meant was that anyone arriving with a firearm was expected to lock it away in a large gun safe in the sheep barn attached to the house. Akisni held one key to the gun safe and Snowbear had the other. Many people had come and gone over the decades, and not all of them had retrieved their guns before leaving, for various reasons. So, to Akisni's chagrin, when the gun safe was opened, it was revealed to be crammed almost full of firearms of various types. If not a literal arsenal, it was at least a solid defensive collection.

256

All of this had been summarized by Snowbear at the beginning of the consensus meeting. All 16 residents of the collective, plus Amit and Juni, sat in the great room in chairs or couches. The young and limber sat on cushions or sprawled on the floor.

Akisni was sitting cross-legged on an oversized leather armchair. She was breathing deeply, sitting upright, but tears were streaming down her face. She was holding a ten-inch dowel wrapped in colorful string, the talking stick. "I believe in non-violence," she stated. "I would rather not live, than live in a world where I have to be violent to live."

Snowbear knelt on the floor in front of her, took the talking stick, and looked her in the eyes.

"I would kill and die rather than see a hair on your head harmed." He rose to address the group. "I don't believe in attacking other people who mean me no harm, but when someone threatens to harm me, or those I care about, I believe in striking back." Akisni fixed her gaze towards her hands in her lap.

Gillie stood up and took the stick from Snowbear. "I agree with Akisni. There is no way to peace. Peace is the way."

Jesse spoke up. "I grew up around guns in southern Georgia." Gillie handed him the stick, which he took absent-mindedly. "I know how to handle guns. I like guns. They're tools for hunting, they're fun to play with, for plinking at bottles back in the woods. But they're also for self-defense. You ladies say you're against fighting. If someone was on top of you," he looked right at Gillie, "choking you and about to rape you, would you fight him?" He held the stick out to her, but she shook her head and looked away, pressing her lips angrily together. "If you'd fight to protect your life, your body, your loved ones, then you owe it to yourself to have the best chance possible of winning."

Murphy took the stick next. "It's not women against men, and I think that's kind of a sexist implication. I'm a man, but I don't believe in warfare or aggression either. I believe in peaceful resolution of problems. But I also don't believe in being a victim."

The discussion went on and on. Everybody present spoke at least once, several spoke many times.

Sheila stood up, her skinny 10-year-old frame poised amongst the adults, and said simply, "I don't like fighting and killing. They're wrong."

Finally, after an hour and a half or so, there was a silence. Everyone was fatigued.

"I call for a consensus," said Josh. "The consensus is that those who are willing, will carry firearms on patrols. We agree that we will not shoot another human being unless it is clear that they have violent intentions towards one of us or the entire group." He turned to his right, where Brittani was seated. "Do you consent?" He asked her.

"I consent." She turned to Brownie on her right.

"I consent," said Brownie.

Every member of the group consented until it came to the next-to-last, Akisni. "I do not consent," she said.

Snowbear shook his head and took her hand "I consent."

"We do not have consensus," stated Josh, formally and rather unnecessarily.

The group took a break; some went outside to smoke in the cold night air, others did yoga poses, some went to their rooms or into a bathroom to wash up or use the facilities. Eventually they all drifted back into the room and re-assembled.

Jesse walked up and grabbed the stick. "I feel pissed off." He stood in the middle of the room, facing Akisni. "I want to live in a world free of violence too. But that's not the world we are living in. In spite of all the idealistic hippie stuff that makes everyone here so happy, we have to play the hand we're dealt. With all due respect, Akisni, you've benefited all your life from the presence of defensive weapons around you, or just from the presence of people who were prepared to defend you. If you deny the morality of self-defense while enjoying its benefits, what does that make you? A hypocrite! We're not talking about invading a foreign country or drone-bombing innocent children at a wedding party here. We're talking about you, me, little Sheila, and about everything we've worked so hard to create and build. Doesn't that mean anything to you?" He dropped the stick on the rug and took his seat on a wooden chair.

The discussion was directed at Akisni from that point on. Not everyone spoke this time around, but those who did, addressed their words to her.

Gillie, prattling her New Age phraseology, was kindest, "Akisni, I love you. I love your gentle spirit. I want the light of that gentle spirit to go on shining from the vessel of your body for years to come. I want you to be safe. You don't have to be a fighter. Just let the fighters be the warriors they are meant to be."

She held the stick out to Akisni. Akisni regarded her for a long time. Gillie was speaking her dialect, and she seemed to be mulling over what the younger woman said. She took the talking stick and unfolded from her perch in the armchair.

"I don't like it. But I consent."

"Do we have consensus?" Asked Josh.

Everyone was silent.

"Do we have consensus?" He asked again. Everyone looked at one another for any trace of disagreement. Other than Akisni's face, now stony and resigned, there was none.

"We have consensus." A collective sigh went up from the group. It was after midnight. Sheila was asleep with her head in her mother's lap.

Ammunition was in short supply for most of the weapons, but for the purpose of defensive patrols, which would shoot only rarely and sparingly, ammunition shouldn't become an issue any time soon.

Snowbear took one of the shotguns with him (best to use the shotgun shells up first, since the shells were plastic and sure to be infected eventually) and waited, silent, at a spot where their unwelcome invaders had been seen. He heard rather than saw them, and fired two blasts in that direction. The aggressors weren't spotted again, but all the willing adults who knew how to handle guns took turns on guard duty from then on. The collective spent some of their precious ammunition teaching Gillie and LaDwon the basics of how to shoot. Jesse, the ex-marine, was delighted to take on that task.

The day Amit and Juni arrived, the electrical meter stopped running and didn't start again. It didn't matter much; the whole-house battery array kept the lights on, though they had to conserve electricity during the day to avoid being without power after midnight. "It's not a problem in the Summer, but we do normally have to buy electricity in the winter," explained Josh, whose adolescent-like, gangling, six-foot-five frame, smooth beardless cheeks, and slow speech belied his degree in engineering and his years of experience as a union Master electrician.

Akisni started a small countertop factory to make tallow candles from the rendered fat from their meat meals. "It's just a matter of time until the lights go out for good," she explained in her serene, firm voice. "I want to be ready when it happens."

A month after Amit and Juni arrived, there came a day when they woke up to find the entire world appeared to be benevolent, enrobed in a thigh-high blanket of snow, the season's first. The gleam of the pristine crystals dazzled like diamonds in the sunshine.

Amit spent most of the morning learning their biomethane system, studying the procedure manual Josh and

Snowbear had created, and tracing the parts of the system as he read about them. The sheds where it was housed were cramped, damp, and disagreeable-smelling, and through the windows the snow gleamed, blinding in the wan sunshine, reminding him of the satisfying, sharp squeak of fresh, dry snow underfoot.

He gave in to the urge and went out for a stroll, to clear the cabin fever that dulled his head. He came upon Josh, hunched over a mass of electronics mounted inside a bulky hinged box affixed to the side of the dwelling.

"You don't look happy," Amit observed. His breath wafted away in ethereal clouds of steam.

"No, I'm not," Josh frowned. "Our solar array should be putting out 8,000 Watts at noon this time of year." He pointed to an LCD which read 7,300. "Something's degrading the output."

"Hm. What could it be?" Asked Amit, stepping backwards and squinting up at the black solar panels. The panels were tent-like assemblies on pivoting aluminum frames, arrayed on the roof 30 feet overhead.

"I don't know, but I'm about to find out. You came by just at the right moment. Help me get the ladders from the shed."

Amit was glad to have something physical to do, and so the two men carried out several aluminum ladders. Josh, who'd done this before, showed Amit how to construct a sturdy 10-foot base from the locking ladders and then extend the 20-foot extension ladder upwards from it. Josh swarmed

262

up the ladders like a monkey, then transferred onto the roof as lithely as if he had no bones. Instantly, he was out of sight amongst the panels. Amit waited, stamping his boots to keep his feet warm and putting his aluminum-chilled hands in his armpits to warm up. He'd left his gloves in the methane shed and now wished he'd grabbed them.

He heard Josh sing out, "Heads up!"

Amit watched as a strip of black plastic, trailing a cable, came gliding over the edge of the roof. He didn't move, as the panel was in no hazard of falling on him, and Josh skimmed down the ladder as easily as he'd ascended. His face was solemn as he picked up the solar panel he'd tossed. "See this?" He pointed out a bumpy, uneven patch on the panel. It had a tiny seed, like a choke-cherry pit, at its center. The pit looked at first glance like it had fallen from a tremendous height, or been shot from a gun: the plastic surface of the panel was spider-webbed with cracks radiating a few inches around it. But when Amit looked closer, he noticed that what appeared to be cracks were in fact channels, etched into the surface of the plastic, around the central depression, in a web-like pattern.

Josh said, "Crows."

Amit followed his thinking quickly. "Crows will eat almost anything. Including small bits of plastic. The bacterium must be living in their crops. And their droppings are infecting the solar panels."

Josh grinned at him. "Bingo."

Amit pointed out the spider-web pattern. "The infections are spreading out in tendrils. It's a common pattern for biofilm formation."

Josh looked thoughtful. "If this infection spreads exponentially, we won't have power in a few weeks. If we can slow it down so it grows, say, arithmetically, the power production won't diminish so fast. The lengthening days after the Solstice will also help us out. We might be able to continue to squeeze some electricity out of the panels into the Spring, or maybe even the Summer…I'd have to do some math to be sure."

"Slow down the growth rate of bacteria, eh? Well," said Amit, "too bad you don't have a microbiologist around."

"Yeah," Josh beamed boyishly. "Too bad."

That night after dinner, Amit and Josh stood in the kitchen while Snowbear and Akisni took their turn washing dishes.

"The problem," said Amit, "is that I don't have any antiseptics, which is what one would normally use to keep the infection under control. I brought less than a gallon of isopropyl with me."

"We have maybe twice that in the first aid room," said Akisni.

"Still nowhere near enough," observed Josh. "And besides, if we use that up, what would happen if someone has a wound which needs to be disinfected? First aid has to be priority."

"I think I have your solution, gentlemen," said Akisni. "Let
264

me show you." She picked up a hurricane lantern and opened the door which led down to the root cellar. Standing at the top of the steps, she picked up a candle lighter that sat on a shelf. She paused, looking at the lighter. It was an ordinary, long-necked lighter with a plastic case and trigger, such as any householder might use to light a candle or a barbecue grill. It was a brief pause, but it was one all the residents of Sutokata were familiar with, seeing it and making it many times each day. It accompanied the thought: *When…not if…the bacterium makes it here, into our sanctuary, this item will not work any more.*

She ignited the lamp and the men followed her downstairs. Shelves and bins of turnips, cabbage, and carrots lined the walls. Their breath steamed in the cool cellar as they ducked strings of onions hanging from the ceiling "It's back here in the herb corner." Hanging from a series of slender chains with alligator clips, amongst aromatic clusters of flowers and dried leafy flora hanging from the joists, were chunks of a yellowish, woody root.

"Turmeric?" Asked Amit, skeptical.

"No: goldenseal," corrected Akisni. "*Hydrastis Canadensis*, one of the most potent natural antibiotics there is." She took the nearest chunk down, holding it by one of its fibrous rootlets, and regarded it reverently. "It's been shown to kill MRSA, *h. pylori*, and tuberculosis. You boil the root to make a decoction." She gestured at the collection hanging next to her. "We have enough here to make perhaps 500 gallons.

When we put in the new pig shed, the spot we picked out was literally overgrown with it, so I harvested it and dried it."

"I don't know about using some root…" began Amit.

"Do you have another option?" Demanded Akisni, her eyes showing a brief flare of uncharacteristic annoyance. "Just because it's a natural herb doesn't mean it's not pharmacologically active."

"Don't get mad, now!" Amit interjected. "Even if it does kill those three you named, we don't know if it will work on this. I'm willing to give it a try. Can you make me a small batch? Maybe one gallon?" He turned to Josh, "We can test it on the infected panel first. It's still out under that fir tree, right?"

"Yes, I figured it was best to keep it away from the other panels, and the house, until we decided what to do about it."

"Good thinking. Is there an undisturbed, sheltered space somewhere I can use as a lab?"

"There's the summer retreat cottage. It's not heated and has no electric, but it's got a roof and four walls and a small fireplace. The windows are boarded up for the winter."

"Perfect! It will take me a while to make it usable, I'm sure, but I'll feel like myself again with something to do with my skills."

"I'll show you where it is," said Josh, shrugging into his parka and grabbing the shotgun next to the door.

"I wonder what to use for culture medium," mused Amit. "Kerosene? Plastic sludge? Do we have any acetone to dissolve acrylics and polystyrene?"

He and Josh commenced jointly free-associating. The two men struck off into the woods, unhurried, indifferent to the way they were lurching about in the deep snow, until they reached the cover of the trees. They set off towards the little hut, still deep in colloquy.

XLVII. Ozarkified

It turned out that Gabriela, who was a descendant of Tejanos and Quapaw Indians who'd intermarried with south Arkansas hillbillies, had moonshiners in her family as well, and not in the distant past. One day, she took them to a barn near her home to meet her cousin Ed, an aged man with a tanned face, networked like a road map with wrinkles gleaned during years of working in the sun. Ed had given up the craft, but still owned the equipment. They explained that Jessica was modifying engines to run on ethanol and that their plan was to distill the stuff for use and sale.

"How do I know you're not ATF?" He asked, peering at her through crowsfeet from under his straw fedora.

"There is no more ATF, Cousin Ed." Gabriela spoke to the elder with respect. "No more phones, no more computers, no more cars."

"There were revenuers before there were computers, phones and cars," observed Ed.

"Yes," interjected DD, "but they had paper systems for keeping track of things. They also had ways of getting from place to place, and ways of communicating with each other. Those are all gone now, and it'll take time to rebuild them from scratch."

"Hm. No authorities, eh?" Ed snorted with disdain. "Never had much use for them anyway.

"So, is that why the sheriff has been asking the young men to meet at the crossroads twice a week?"

Gabriela nodded. "Juan was talking about that. He said the county sheriffs aren't getting any more payments from the State, or equipment from the Feds. He was saying it's every man for himself now and we need to be prepared to fight together if big gangs come through. There's been a lot of shooting over where those crazy prepper militia guys are wedged right in between the prison and the military base."

Ed commented with a long declining whistle. "Sounds like a good area to stay away from."

DD nodded. *At least until those testosterone-addled idiots finish running around the woods shooting each other up and run low on ammunition.* But what she said was, "I heard the first guy to go over the prison wall was a midget."

"Really?" Said Ed.

"Yes. But I thought that was a little condescending."

Ed blinked. "Well, if there are no more ATF guys to interfere with moonshining, I count it all to the good. But why should I let you use my set-up?" Ed, true to his Scots-Irish roots, was a canny bargainer.

Negotiations began in earnest, and they came to an agreement whereby Ed received 20% of the product and the trio were allowed to spend the winter in his drafty but safe barn with four cows, a donkey, and a handful of sheep.

Ed helped them get started with their first batch, instructing them on how to make sure their clear shine didn't burn with a yellow flame, denoting toxic methanol, before beginning to collect it. After that, he'd stop by on occasion, sometimes to offer helpful tips, but mostly to shake his head in amazed delight that the still didn't need to be hidden any longer. As the winter wore on, their feet wore a path leading to the outbuilding where the distilling machinery was constructed.

Finding mash ingredients was hit-and-miss at first. In the absence of trucks to receive their crops, quite a few farmers who had planted in the Spring with full confidence of selling their corn, potatoes, wheat, and sorghum to food conglomerates were stuck with a surplus. Faced with stores of perishable foodstuffs, most were willing to supply them with corn or potatoes in exchange for a portion of the end product. Over the long winter, word spread that the strangers in Ed's barn were buying crops that might otherwise decay, and farmers began showing up on their own to make a deal: for an average 20% of the product, they kept the still supplied.

DD reflected with anxiety: *Next Winter may be different. Seeds will be hard to come by; hybrid seeds, impossible, and the hybrid crops won't breed true, bringing yields down. Pesticides, irrigation equipment, so many things depend on petroleum.*

Jessica spent some time adapting two abandoned 4-wheelers to run on ethanol over the winter. She had experimented with innovative gasket materials, but she ultimately settled on felted wool, soaked in milk that had been boiled down to a thick, gluey condensate. One afternoon, Jessica went to the trading post to trade some moonshine for some milk and food, but then sent Gabriela's son home alone

270

with her purchases. She'd instructed the boy to tell DD she was spending the night at a neighboring farm.

"What else did she say? Why is she staying there?" The boy shrugged.

"That's where my cousin Juan lives," said Gabriela with an arched eyebrow. "He's about Jessica's age. Single." Gabriela looked like she wanted to say more, but was holding back.

Jessica didn't return to sleep in the barn for two weeks; DD was about to go searching for her, and then one night she showed up just before dinner, with scrapes like road rash all along her right arm and shoulder, and puffy eyes from crying. DD put an arm around her and tried to comfort her, and eventually Jessica spilled the story.

"Once I told him I had PCOS and couldn't get pregnant, the way he treated me changed completely!"

DD took a small jar of alcohol and dipped a clean cloth into it to clean Jessica's abrasions. Jessica winced when DD hit a few of the deeper gouges. Tears began to flow anew. After she was done, Jessica raised the jar, tinged ever so faintly red now with her own blood, and tossed it back in one draught.

DD recoiled in disgust, and at the same time she felt an emotional cold deep inside. *God give me the serenity to accept the things I cannot change, the courage to change the things I can, and the wisdom to know the difference.*

"Are you sure you want to do that?" She asked her daughter, nodding at the empty jar of ethanol.

"It's okay mom. Just this one time. For the pain."

DD bit her tongue. She knew from experience, with Jessica and with DD's own father before her, that pursuing the topic now would only spawn conflict.

Juan wasn't a big man, while Jessica had inherited a solid frame from her father, and so DD wasn't surprised at what she saw when she spotted Juan, a few days later. They were both in the valley at the old diner/convenience store which had become a de facto trading post, and the proprietor, whom DD had asked about Jessica when she was missing, pointed him out to her. Juan was exhibiting an icteric black eye and a healing split lip. An array of bluish asymmetric tattoos, inked roughly by hand and difficult to make out, splayed across his collarbones, peeking out above his shirt.

DD had never figured this one thing out about her daughter: Though DD and Jessica's dad had divorced when Jessica was 16, the parting was amicable. They'd never raised a hand to one another, and only rarely raised their voices. *I made sure he wasn't that kind of man before settling down with him and starting a family. I didn't want any children we had to go through hearing Daddy asking Mommy why she'd "made" him hit her.*

DD wondered about the role of epigenetics in human behavior; more and more, her contemporaries in the field of mammalian genetics were finding that different parts of the DNA code were methylated or demethylated, depending on the parents' experiences, and those active or inactivated loci were passed down to children, and even grandchildren, and perhaps further. DD was not that familiar with it, because it didn't appear to occur in bacteria, but she knew that experiments had shown that behaviors of fearfulness, and reactions to stress hormones, were different in the grandchildren of mice which had been subject to stressful experiences. *Or maybe it's just plain genetics, but recessive traits. Of course it's not that simple, not single-allele inheritance. There's no "I Like Getting Punched by Boyfriends" gene. Behavioral inheritance is complex. Still, I just don't understand.*

DD still didn't understand the following week, when Juan came to visit Jessica at the barn and spent the night. She didn't understand when Jessica brought him his dinner, setting the plate down in front of him where he sat before getting her own. She understood, all too well, when Jessica tried to stand up from that evening meal and staggered, and Juan put an arm around her waist and helped her climb the ladder to the hayloft.

The next morning, Jessica lay on her stomach with her face jammed into her pillow, sprawled naked, and snoring the gagging, moaning snores of the hung-over. Juan got up and went outside to water a tree. DD rose and followed him.

He turned, tightening the drawstring on his canvas pants, but was brought up short by the muzzle of DD's Smith and Wesson in his face.

He put his palms up. "*Calmaté, mamá.* Calm down. I ain't trying to hurt no one."

"You won't get another chance to." DD said. "You go inside and get your shirt and leave. Don't say anything. If I ever see you near my daughter again, I won't ask questions." She pulled the hammer back on the revolver for emphasis. "Do you understand me?"

Juan nodded. DD took her finger out of the trigger guard but lowered the gun to point at his crotch. "Go."

Juan went. He did just as DD said. She holstered the gun and sat on a bale of hay next to her daughter, waiting for her to wake up. She was planning to have a talk, one she'd had with her before. *I've fucked up everything in the entire world. Maybe I'm getting another chance to do this one thing right.*

XLVIII. Now You Tell Me

Amit and Josh were on patrol together as usual. They'd become almost inseparable, spending their free time together in the workshop or in Amit's lab. The electrician had picked up the elements of microbiology quickly and become a great lab assistant; the microbiologist had learned the elements of electrical wiring and aided Josh in his projects. They were a mismatched pair: Josh tall, pale, and gangly, and Amit dark and compact.

"If you'd ever told me I'd be walking in snowy woods, with a gun in my hand, in the middle of Winter, I'd have told you you were crazy," Amit said.

"Isn't there a Robert Frost poem about that?" Josh asked.

"*Stopping by Woods on a Snowy Evening...*" Amit recited the first seven lines of the famous poem. "I can't remember the rest."

"This isn't the darkest evening of the year, though. The solstice was almost a month and a half ago." Josh the realist.

"True. And we don't have miles to go before we sleep."

"How far do we walk on this patrol?"

"Let's see...hard to say for sure...some of the paths are irregular curves...but the compound has 38 acres. The back 20 is that empty slope there," he gestured towards the white expanse of an empty, fenced field, "so we only patrol 18 of them. An acre is about 200 by 200 feet..."

They puzzled out the arithmetic, figuring they walked about two miles per circuit, four circuits per two-hour patrol. "But it feels like more," concluded Josh, "because of the snow."

"You think it feels like more to you! I've got twenty years on you and you've got ten inches on me! If I break through the snow, it's up to my waist!" Amit pointed out.

"Yeah, Shorty," Josh joshed.

"Who are you calling Shorty?" Amit punched his arm, hard, and the two men sparred playfully for a few minutes, then called it quits, panting and laughing.

"Don't let Akisni see us!" Amit said.

"Yeah, she'd get her panties in a wad about it, that's for sure."

"Akisni is one of the only true pacifists I've ever known," said Amit. "Lots of people of her generation claimed to be pacifists and protested the war in Vietnam. But when that went out of fashion, and the crime wave of the late 70's turned everyone into realists, she stayed with it. She objected to Reagan's war build-up, and to Clinton bombing Kosovo. Most recently, when the progressives were suddenly in favor of drone-bombing the middle east because a black President was doing it, she continued to be pacifist. She truly believes the world will change if enough people like her decide to be the change they wish to see."

"Snowbear is more of a realist," Josh commented.

"That's the way it usually is. Ultimately, all pacifists benefit from the protection of those who aren't pacifists."

276

"I think sometimes Akisni thinks less of him because of what he...we all have to do nowadays."

"Yes, I heard her crying one night, saying how quickly we all degenerated into savages. I don't like the violence either. Maybe someday everyone will learn to love one another and give up violence, and..."

Josh recited the next part in unison with him, "maybe fairies will fly around on rainbows riding unicorns." Their favorite refrain.

After their chuckles subsided, Amit became serious again. "Yeah, and I wonder sometimes if there isn't, all told, less violence now than there was before."

"What? Are you nuts? We've killed, what, seven intruders?"

"Eight. Joe and Heidi killed one last month, remember?"

"How many people did you kill before this happened?"

"Personally, none. But as a child, my government was always, it seemed, at war with Pakistan. Since I became a US citizen, how many people were being killed on my behalf around the world in wars fought for oil? Add in the refugees drowning at sea, the poverty enforced by petrodollar governments in the third world," he shrugged, "sickness is a way for the body to rid itself of invaders. Sometimes I wonder if this machine sickness isn't just the planet having its way."

"Ooh, pretty deep, man," Josh mocked. "I don't buy that airy-fairy lacey-spacey spooky-kooky Gaia nonsense."

"Oh, I'm not saying the Earth is aware and consciously trying to fight us! I'm a scientist, Josh! I'm just saying that complex systems, like individual animals, often develop ways of restoring homeostasis. Systems that start out chaotic develop islands of self-organizing stability."

"Hnh," grunted Josh, sounding unconvinced. "Hang on, my sock is twisted." He sat down on a stump to undo his bootlace, and Amit sat on the other side of the stump, back to back.

Amit extemporized:

My little boot must think it odd
To stop my circumscribing plod
On this forsaken frozen stump
I freeze my ancient, rugose rump...

A rattle brought them instantly to their feet, rifles leveled. It had been some weeks since they'd had any raiders. The days were getting longer, and the snow was crusted over at the end of a sunny day in a way which told Midwesterners that Spring was coming. The people who stepped out from behind the snowdrift were neither raiders, nor the thugs the law had morphed into. There were three of them: an aged black woman and two middle-aged white women. They were warmly dressed, but their faces were gaunt from weight loss and the bags under their eyes spoke of too little sleep. They carried canvas backpacks which hung almost empty on their shoulders.

The women put their hands up. "Please," said the closest one, a short woman with salt-and-pepper hair. "Please don't hurt us."

The men lowered the muzzles of their weapons. "What do you want?" Asked Josh.

"We saw the smoke from your chimney. The men in town. They took our things. Our food. Socks. Everything."

Amit and Josh looked at each other. "Socks," repeated Josh.

"A new low," said Amit. In the Midwestern winter, you didn't take a person's socks. You might as well just cut off their toes.

"Put your backpacks on the ground and hold your hands up," commanded Amit. The women complied. Josh stood before them, gun diverted, while Amit gave the women a cursory frisk. The black woman's body felt like a bundle of twigs, she was so stiff and thin and frail, her hair a wisp of cotton, her skin so thin it was translucent despite its pigment. The men glanced into their backpacks: a few useless, innocuous items: photographs, a passport, a wooden hair barrette.

"I'll walk them back. You continue the patrol and I'll meet you at the fourth fencepost," said Josh. "Follow me," he turned and headed for the main lodge.

Josh walked slowly so the three women could keep up, despite his long legs. They all wore homemade boots of some type. It had come as a nasty surprise to many people that even canvas or leather footwear was held together by synthetic glues which melted away with exposure to the machine sickness. They entered the main house by a side door, which opened upon a small mud room. The women sat down gratefully on the benches that lined the two walls.

"Wait here," Josh directed. He went in search of Akisni and found her at the large loom, teaching the hippie nose-ring dilettante (Gillie, turning out to be quite capable now that her affectation had worn off) how to make a pattern with the wool threads. He told Akisni about the women and they went to the mud room together. The three were sitting on the boot benches, waiting uncomplaining.

"Sorry to keep you ladies waiting," said Akisni, looking deferentially at the old woman. The others were about Akisni's own age, mid-to-late 50s to early 60s.

"It's alright," said the salt-and-pepper woman, who'd defaulted to the role of leader. "We're just enjoying being warm again. My name's Suzanne. This is Deborah and Augusta."

"Akisni." They shook hands. "Josh said someone robbed you?"

The second white woman, a little taller and with hair that looked more blonde than grey, made an exasperated "Tsss" sound and looked away.

"The police. Or that's what they called themselves."

"Did they dump you on the road? Or did you walk all the way from town?" Akisni sounded concerned.

280

The black woman spoke up "We walked," she said, in her rusty-hinge voice. She had few teeth remaining. "We walked the whole way."

"Oh, my goodness! That's twenty miles! Are you alright? Are your feet dry? Any frostbite? Come on in to the common room by the woodstove and let's get you sorted out..." Akisni assumed her nurturer guise and the ladies followed her.

Josh went out and met Amit, who was waiting at the post, right where they'd agreed, and they finished the patrol together.

"What will we do if more people like that show up?" Amit asked.

"Take them in." Josh answered, almost distractedly.

"What if there are hundreds of them?"

"We'll have to build more shelter." Josh said. Amit's brow creased.

"Amit," Josh explained, "anyone who comes in peace has always been welcomed at Sutokata. It's part of what we're about. We have more resources than we need, even now. And now, more than ever, people need the peace and safety we offer."

They walked in silence a little further. "You know," confessed Amit, "I always thought Sutokata was an impossible dream, a fantasy, a remnant of the 60s that would blow away one day. But you all have created something solid here. You're not unwilling to defend yourselves..."

"The Dalai Lama himself said that if someone is trying to shoot you, you naturally should shoot back," interjected Josh.

"Quite so. You're realists, and even though you're living communally, you have clear rules and obligations about shared and personal property."

"Yes, and we make all major decisions by consensus. That's been found to work in groups up to about 30."

"I hated those long consensus meetings at first. But then I noticed something: when every group decision has to be made by a consensus, you realize how few decisions really, truly, need to be made as a group."

Josh smiled. "Well, yeah. A lot of communes get hung up on voting on things, making rules and more rules, and the losers get all butthurt and leave. Snowbear and Akisni can tell you about the early days. They had a few stubborn, disagreeable, contrary people who decided to leave in that way, but there's only been one since I've been here. So far Sutokata hasn't had any decision which truly *had* to be made, which we couldn't find consensus on. Of course, we have to be forgiving when someone makes a judgment call in an emergency."

"Hmn. That's where the trust comes in."

"Right." Josh stopped in his tracks for a moment. "I think I see what you're worried about. What happens when we exceed 30 people? When some newcomer refuses to join the consensus and refuses to leave?"

"Exactly. The stakes of leaving are higher now. Also, what about real crime?"

"We go by the Non-Aggression Principle: Don't Hurt People or Take Their Stuff."

"Right, right." He waved his hand in dismissal. "I know you handle thefts and fistfights by consensus hearings. And I know you aren't afraid to kill," he waved his hand in the general direction of the pile of frozen corpses of raiders, "in self-defense. But what if someone truly hurts, rapes, or kills someone else? What if they do something that puts us all in danger?"

"Amit, you just answered your own question. The stakes are higher now because staying or leaving here can mean the difference between dying and surviving. There's no law to hand someone over to because the 'law' is now just bullies who come to take our stuff."

"Isn't that all it ever was? It's just more obvious now."

"You might have a point. Anyway, according to our principles, someone who does something which can't be forgiven or made amends for, would be dead to us. Expelled. And they might just end up actually dead as a result. It's no longer our concern."

They were back at the entrance after their fourth circuit. They'd finished their patrol, so they went inside. Gillie and another man, George, were waiting to relieve them.

XLIX. Intervening

Jessica rolled over on her back. Her eyes were swollen and stuck almost shut from dehydration. She was panting, just from the effort of turning over. She groaned.

"Sit up," DD said.

Jessica groaned again. DD stood up and stepped up to the straw-stuffed mattress on the floor and kicked it, hard enough to give Jessica a good shake, hard enough to send straw flying. The golden shreds fell like snow around her in the morning sunlight.

Jessica flailed upright. "Where's Juan?" She croaked through parched lips.

"Juan's left and he won't be back," DD explained.

"You can't do that!" Jessica was instantly awake and furious. She struggled to her feet and swayed, confused but belligerent.

"Yes, in fact, I can and I did," DD said. Jessica turned on her, and she flinched. Her girl had shown she was a capable combatant, but DD wouldn't hurt her, no matter what. She prepared to suffer a beating.

Instead, Jessica grabbed an empty feed sack. She began moving around her little corner of the barn, gathering her few belongings and stuffing them in the sack.

"You got drunk last night," observed DD.

"So what if I did?"

"You know what happens when you drink. You're an alcoholic."

"You know what, mom? No. I'm not an alcoholic. I never was. I was just self-medicating for all the stress and bullshit I've been through. Now I've found someone who really gets me. I can drink moderately without going overboard. And I'm loved. Loved, do you understand that? *Can* you understand that?"

Ouch. No, maybe I can't. But focus on her, not me… "Can *you* understand what you're doing to yourself? Or to me? To those around you? Now, more than ever, we need to stick together and help one another. Look how your hands are shaking!" Jessica was holding a treasured photo of her father in her right hand, ready to put in the bag, and it was fluttering like a leaf on the breeze. "If you won't stop drinking for yourself, do it for me. Do it for your father." She nodded at the picture and Jessica scowled as she tucked it deep inside the feed bag.

"My advice?" Jeremy said, from the bottom of the loft, where neither of the women had noticed him come in. "Listen to your mom. When someone who loves you tells you that you have a drinking problem, you have a drinking problem."

Jessica didn't say another word. She shakily clambered down the steps and stumbled out into the morning sunlight. DD sat down hard on the primitive bed. She leaned her elbows on her knees and watched her daughter walk out of her life. Again.

Probably for the last time.

She knew she'd done the right thing, but that didn't make it less painful. She quivered, restraining herself from running after Jessica and throwing her arms around her neck and clinging to her, begging her not to leave. Perhaps the stakes were higher now with communications knocked out; perhaps not. Jessica had walked completely out of her world before.

L.   You Didn't Want to Use That, Did You?

As the Midwestern winter began to turn direly cold, the raids on Sutokata by locals who heard they had food became more frequent. It was too cold to dig graves. Akisni lost her appetite, dropped weight, and became gaunt and pale as the stack of frozen bodies grew taller. By mid-December, the raids ended. When none of the raiders came back, word must have got around; even the famished and desperate determined it wasn't worth their lives. The Sutokatans used up the shotgun shells first, before the plastic encasing them became infected, handling them with clean hands and scrutinizing them before use. They were left with a mismatched assortment of rifles and handguns with varying amounts of metal-cased ammunition.

When they went through the raiders' pockets, they kept turning up baggies full of capsules and tablets. Reference to the PDR in the study let them know that most of the pills were amoxicillin, but there were other antibiotics, too. "Broad-spectrum beta-lactam antibiotics," observed Amit. The words triggered a sense memory of the last time he'd hung up a telephone (perhaps the last time he'd ever speak on the phone?) in his office, when the Chinese doctor had called, and he was suddenly overcome by a sense of aching nostalgia for something as simple as a telephone. He considered that the call must have been from someone making a doomed bid to stem the spread of machine sickness in China. He mused at the way that the technological lines of communication had made the world smaller, and that thoughts and memes and ideas would have to make their way around the world hand-to-hand and eye-to-eye, the way they had in centuries past. Except perhaps, the knowledge that others were out there, and human, and the collapse of governments which enforced borders, would make it faster this time.

The way everyone was carrying the drugs in their pockets, he speculated that they'd become a sort of de facto currency, an easily portable, premium trade good which had intrinsic value.

On the bright side, the solar panels were cured of the machine sickness by Akisni and Amit's goldenseal infusion. Spraying them lightly with a saline-goldenseal solution whenever it thawed seemed to be all that was needed for now; Amit had ascertained that *p davisii* died after being at -5°C for just a few minutes. Once the weather warmed up, they'd have to spray more often, but all they needed to do through the cold months was the normal chore of keeping them free of snow and ice. Up on the roof, clearing the panels, Amit reflected that it was strange to look up at the vibrant blue winter sky and see no contrails; commercial and recreational aviation had come to a screeching halt. No pilot wanted to be the one in the cockpit when the fuel turned to water, or some critical plastic clip, hose, or bearing in the aircraft turned to mush.

Snowbear's antiquated hybrid CB-police radio array, a dusty Frankenstein's monster with analog dials, was resurrected from under stacks of books and papers. It appeared to be intact. It lived in a little cubby of an office off the main common room and no one was allowed to touch it but

Snowbear, who dreaded the inevitable day when *p davisii* made its way into the electronics and wiring inside it. The wooden knobs with which he'd replaced the plastic ones on the metal face were kept always on, tuned to one channel or another, so there was always a faint static in the background, like a stream of running water. Their profound isolation sunk in a little deeper with every day that passed hearing no voices on that radio. Some of the younger ones had trouble comprehending it; Amit and some of the older Sutokatans could remember life when news came over a few broadcast channels or on printed paper. They could imagine the world recreating that without plastics, but they wondered how long it might take.

One day, Amit came into the common room beaming with delight. "Where's Josh?" He demanded excitedly.

"I don't know. Why, what's up?" Asked Akisni, looking up from weaving braid. "You look like the cat that ate the canary!"

"I have to tell him about something! I isolated *shewanella oneidensis*!" Without pausing to explain, he ran out of the house and found Josh outside, using a maul and sledge to split firewood on a stump.

"Josh, I got it! I got the *shewanella* strains to culture!"

Josh stood up, mirroring Amit's delight. "The electrically conductive bacterium? The one they use in biological fuel cells?"

Amit was bouncing on his toes, he was so excited, and Josh nodded with him. Giddy as children, the firewood forgotten, the two men walked off to the laboratory shed together, gabbing a mile a minute and waving their arms.

The long winter gave them time to work on the building's wiring, wrapping the wires with home-made cotton braid to prevent short-circuits once the *p davisii* infection spread. For, Amit told them, it was an issue of when, not if. "There is no way to sterilize a space this big and varied. Every surface you touch every day is populated with bacteria. Making and maintaining a small, sterile area to work in comprises most of the daily routine of a micro lab. The world around you is an invisible ecology of microbes incessantly competing with one another."

One day, the radio sputtered and voices were heard. Everyone inside dropped what they were doing and looked at one another for a few ticks, stunned, unsure if they'd imagined it. Then the voices returned, clearer, and Snowbear lunged for the dial and turned the volume up.

"Passing the windbreak now." A man's voice came on the frequency, tinny and distorted.

Another voice responded, "Any sign of activity?"

"Negative."

"Oh, shit!" Snowbear exclaimed. "They're coming here! Now! This isn't good."

"Who's on patrol?"

"I was," said LaDwon, a handsome young black man, coming in and stomping the snow off his boots. "Murphy was supposed to relieve me." Murphy's dreadlocked dirty-blond hair and pierced eyebrows popped around the corner of the doorway to the kitchen. He finished chewing and hastily swallowed.

"Don't go out, Murphy," said Snowbear. "The two of you, go up to the gun safe. Take half the rifles and all the handguns and put them in the crawlspace in the root cellar. Hide most of the ammo too but leave a few rounds so they won't get suspicious. Leave the shotguns, they're useless now."

The two younger men stood, confused, not comprehending, shocked at the change in their mild-mannered elder's demeanor. "Come on!" snapped Snowbear. "They're coming for us. NOW! MOVE!" To punctuate his order, the radio began to spout communications again. The younger men vanished to do as instructed. The invaders, more organized than the random bands they'd seen so far, had found the stack of dead bodies in the snow, meaning they surrounded Sutokata on at least two sides. Meaning also, that they knew the collective was armed and unafraid to shoot; no taking them by surprise! Snowbear spotted a man's form running by the window, silhouetted against the winter whiteness. He turned off the radio and covered it with a pile of papers, trying his best to make it look like a random mess, instead of like he was trying to hide something. He was halfway to the front door when it splintered, as a raider kicked it in.

"Aw, man!" He said the first thing that came to his head, "That door wasn't even locked! Now I'm gonna need to fix the hasp!" Five militaristic men, in puffy black winter jumpsuits and black balaclavas, leveled weapons at him and then swung them around the room, pinning him, Amit, and Akisni in place with their hands up.

"How many of you are there?" The closest aggressor demanded.

"Seventeen." Snowbear answered.

"Where are they at?" Snowbear hesitated, unsure how to answer, "I said, WHERE ARE THEY AT, FREAK!?" The thuggish cop… guardsman…whatever they were (they wore no insignia and didn't bother to identify themselves), gestured threateningly with his weapon, though his finger was, at least, still off the trigger.

"Calm down. I am cooperating." He could hear Akisni's ragged breath, fought back the atavistic masculine urge to protect his mate at all costs. "I don't know where they all are. Some are outside…"

At that moment, LaDwon and Murphy entered the room. They paused to take in the tableau, then put their hands up high.

A big four-wheel-drive SUV pulled up in front of the door and seven more armed men piled out. They came in through the broken front door and wordlessly began searching the house. They opened the kitchen cabinets and stuffed a few items in their pockets, mostly commercial sweets Akisni had been saving for special occasions. Then they trooped up the stairs. "Gun safe!" came a shout from upstairs. Their captor turned to face Snowbear, brandishing his weapon.
292

"Here's the key, in my pocket," volunteered Snowbear, slowly and deliberately extracting it and handing it to the thug nearest the stairs. The attacker took the key and headed up, and moments later, came down cradling four shotguns and two hunting rifles in his arms with a few boxes of rifle ammo in his hands; he carried them out to the SUV and put them in the back.

The searchers finished searching the bedrooms upstairs—it sounded like the whole floor was getting a good tossing, and Akisni's terror was turning into anger with every crockery-breaking and fabric-ripping sound. They came down to the main level, and then five of them trooped into the root cellar. All the residents tried not to show any increased concern.

"Jackpot!" One of the raiders called from downstairs. The Sutokatans assumed their gun cache was discovered, and they were silently dismayed (except for Akisni) at the thought of being both defenseless and unable to hunt. But then a trooper came out of the basement door, weapon slung behind him, holding up a long, coiled length of hemp rope in one hand and a bundle of the reeds they used to weave baskets in the other. Two men came up behind him, carrying Akisni's huge canvas bags of raw wool and cotton. The last two came out, one carrying two large glass jars of precious fat which they used to make candles, which they needed more and more for light over the winter, as the sun went down early and the deteriorating batteries' charges ran out before bedtime. The last of the thugs came out, holding nothing but his own rifle.

The one still holding Snowbear at gunpoint told the other two who'd been with him, "Search this room." To Snowbear's relief, they didn't make a thorough job of it and didn't toss it as they had the upstairs. They pulled a few shelves of books onto the floor, but he could see them decide that the chore of unshelving the whole library would have been tedious and unproductive. They barely shuffled the top layer of papers covering the inset cubby which held the radio.

"Hah!" exclaimed one of the intruders. He held aloft a big basket full of tubular braid which Akisni and Sheila, the ten-year-old, had been weaving to insulate the wiring. The leader smiled and nodded, and when all his men had exited, he grabbed the kerosene lantern, full of untainted fuel, that hung on its hook by the front door and carried it with him to the car.

The five Sutokatans walked to the door and watched them drive off. There were four more vehicles, five total. One was marked as County Sheriff and one marked Fish and Wildlife, while the remaining three were unmarked. One of the cars knocked over the low fence around the kitchen herb garden, half buried in snow. The rest of the community came downstairs or gravitated towards the main building from the barns and sheds, and soon all seventeen of them were in the main common room. Akisni was quietly sobbing; Amit held her hand.

Snowbear directed Murphy to complete his planned patrol, and Murphy clattered down to the cellar. The young man, frustrated that he'd not had an opportunity to bash the marauders, was glad to have some type of real action to take,
294

and strutted out the door loading a 30.06. The rest of the diverse group sank down into chairs or sat on the floor. They tried to assess the damage calmly.

"We lost half our guns, but we still have five rifles and a good supply of matching ammo. We are short on handgun ammo, but the guys," he nodded at LaDwon, who nodded back, "saved all our sidearms."

"They also didn't find the radio. I'm surprised by what they did take, though..."

"...Natural materials." Observed Akisni in a tear-choked voice. "All our hard work."

"She's right!" exclaimed Amit. "It makes sense. Plastic has got to be becoming increasingly useless. They may have sterile fuel depots (for now) at military bases, but one thing they don't have is a supply line for *p. davisii*-resistant materials. They have to take it where they can get it locally."

"They took the cowhide," volunteered Brittani, a young woman all dimples and lips, café-au-lait skin and sparkling eyes. "I was out in the barn when they came, and the hide that was hanging on the siding, they just yanked it down and rolled it up."

"My cotton." Akisni shook her head. "In a couple of months, we'll shear the sheep and have more wool, but cotton country starts at least a hundred miles south of here. Might as well be in Timbuktu." Sheila gravely processed this information, still crestfallen that all her handiwork had been stolen.

"I'm guessing cotton is going to be hard to come by anywhere. Cotton is a thirsty crop and they're going to have to figure out new ways to grow it, with all the PVC piping to the irrigation rigs falling down," observed Jesse, drawing on experiences of his youth in central Georgia. "I imagine they've figured that out too. That's probably why they were so excited to get yours."

The group sat up, planning ways to hide their natural materials against future confiscations, and speculating about ways to produce more. In truth, they went on talking even when there wasn't much more to say, stunned by the violation of their private retreat, reluctant to abandon the sound of each other's voices to sleep. When the battery power running the lights ultimately ran out for the night, they stumbled to bed in the dark.

LI.   Road Trip!

Even after the ethanol yield was divided among Ed, the farmers, and the distillers, they had more pure, blue-burning grain alcohol than two small vehicles could carry.

"This should be plenty to get us to Sutokata," DD said to Jeremy. The achievement would have been more satisfying if only Jessica had been there to savor it with them. DD often caught herself staring at Jessica's scooter where it sat in its spot by the barn door. It'd been six weeks and DD'd expected her to come back to get the bike, even if she wouldn't go with them to Sutokata after all. DD deluded herself (ineffectively) that she just wanted some sort of closure. She tried to pump Ed and Gabriela for information about Jessica's whereabouts.

Ed said, "I don't know where she is, but that reminds me of a riddle: What's the difference between a piano, a tuna, and a pot of glue?"

"Ummm … I give up."

"You can tune a piano but you can't piano tuna."

"Wait…but what about the pot of glue?"

"I knew you'd get stuck there"

\#

DD tried to keep her ears open and her mouth shut, and she noticed a couple of times when conversations stopped dead when she entered the trading post, but again, it seemed that no one wanted to get involved. DD was exasperated. This wasn't like the first time around, where it was a matter of a girl sneaking off for fun and romance away from her mother's prying eyes. It was more like the end game, before she'd disappeared for good. This was a serious matter, tainted by addiction and violence. People avoided her. She felt unclean.

The days were starting to get longer; soon it would be spring, time for them to leave Arkansas and head for Sutokata. Jeremy and DD began to load two of the ATVs Jessica had converted to ethanol.

They scanned the skies thoughtfully. Their neighbors still farmed the hills, some of them following in the footsteps of ancestors who'd farmed here for centuries, some even before the French and Spanish came. They contributed reflections about the weather conditions and how they usually changed hereabouts as the seasons changed. They hazarded guesses as to what this waning winter's weather portended for Spring. They began to concur, in their indirect ways, pinching a bud on a tree, gouging the leaf litter with a cane, rubbing fallen tree bark between shrunken fingers, that a drying and warming trend would probably settle over the region in about two or three weeks.

The scooter in the corner of the barn seemed to DD to grow. It appeared to be covered in flashing neon lights which only she could see. DD couldn't keep her eyes off it as the time to leave grew near. One night she sat up out of a sound sleep and looked at the scooter. It had called her, out loud, she'd swear it! She got up and walked to the scooter, then realized she had heard something that awakened her. The noise she was hearing was a whimper, coming from just outside the barn door. Perhaps a puppy someone had abandoned, an infant beast orphaned when its feral mother was shot.

DD strained to lift the bar on the barn door, level with the top of her head. She pulled the door open a few feet. There was no snow on the ground, but the wind was bitterly cold in this post-midnight, moonless period.

Lying on the ground by the door, wedged against the barn's foundation, was Jessica. The whining sound was coming from her. She was curled up around her hands, which were pressed into her stomach. Her hair was filthy, matted, and sodden with blood from a cut near her temple. She smelled like a locker room, a brewery, and a strong red tide in the Gulf all mixed up together. DD helped her to her feet and into the barn. She turned and slid the door shut. Jessica collapsed on a bale and curled up again.

"Stay right here. I'm going to wake Jeremy to bar the door again, okay?" DD could just bar the door in an emergency, straining precariously on tiptoe and grunting with the effort, but Jeremy with his greater height and strength could do it in an instant without even waking up all the way. DD slipped to his pallet on the other end of the living space and shook him awake.

After Jeremy barred the door, he came and looked down at Jessica, still twisted around her pain and unable to articulate a coherent word through her quivering throat and jaw.

He shook his head. "Damn!" was all he said. He walked back over to his pallet and lay down.

DD nursed Jessica through her DTs. She caught her puke and cleaned her head wound. She stripped her pants, drenched with blood-crimsoned urine, off her body and took the earliest opportunity to soak them in ethanol and burn them. It took two full days before Jessica could speak more than a few simple words: yes and no, and hungry and thirsty, and it hurts. She said that last phrase a lot. The shakes began to fade on the third day.

Gaby and her mom came by a few times to check on her, bringing herbal teas and soups. On the fourth day, when it was plain that Jessica was getting better, they spelled DD while she took a walk to clear her head, get her blood flowing, try to walk off the fury she felt towards Juan for what he'd done, towards Jessica for choosing to go back to him. *There is no excuse for what he's done, none!* She remembered pulling the hammer back while pointing the gun at Juan's craven face; although her other kills had been self-defense, she had no doubt she could murder this man in cold blood.

Yet, this was Jessica's choosing, the path she'd elected for herself. In a way, Juan wasn't even human to her; he was just an object, like a razor blade, which Jessica used to harm herself. DD resolved to toss him out mentally like the garbage he was, rather than embroil herself in a campaign of revenge, which could only escalate fruitlessly.

She came back from her walk, calmer than she'd been since finding her girl in the frigid mud. Jessica was sitting up, draped in a tarp, propped against a bale. Gaby was sitting at her side with a bowl of water and a comb, patiently

300

working the mats out of Jessica's head while trying not to pull apart the freshly stitched head wound.

"I wound up stitching up a human head after all," Gaby smiled at DD. "Remember how she stitched up Marthita's head when she found out I'd only done it on dogs and sheep? I got to return the favor."

Jessica smiled, her face wan. "Mom, you were right. I should have known better. I'm a drunk and an addict. Will you take me back if I promise to stay clean and sober?" *She knows she doesn't have to ask. But it's respectful that she did.*

"And Juan?" DD asked sternly.

"He can rot in Hell forever for all I care!" Her eyes filled with tears. "If you knew what he did to me," she faded to a squeak. *I'd rather not imagine.*

"I don't understand why you chose to go back to him after the first time he beat you and raped you. I didn't teach you to put up with that. You don't deserve that!"

"Because I loved him! He *gets* me. We are both damaged inside and he gets that about me!"

"I don't understand. How are you damaged? You had a happy, happy childhood. I gave you everything I never had and always wanted. I don't understand why you put yourself in the same category as that, that, *monster*."

"I always knew I didn't belong in the world you raised me in. I always knew things would never be normal for me."

"Jessica, what could I have done differently? How did I fail you so horribly?"

"Mom, it's nothing you did. You couldn't have changed it. It's not your fault."

DD sighed, allowing that absolution to sink in. *I needed to hear that.*

"You know you're my child and I love you unconditionally. But I can't let you continue to rip my heart out this way." DD felt inside for tears to go with this, but they were plugged up in a well deep inside her. They'd been held in place by a packer of artifice for years, as life moved over it in waves like the ocean.

Jessica was silent.

She is the thing I want most of all in the world.

"Well, we can't change the past. We can only create the future. Do you promise?" DD entreated. "No alcohol? No drugs? And no Juan?"

"I promise," Jessica said. She was solemn and vulnerable. *I know, I know. Fool me once, shame on you; fool me twice, shame on me. And this is more than twice. But I want it to be true, so badly.*

"Well, good." She said, turning away, gruff and businesslike, as though she hadn't just exposed herself to more needless pain. "We need a mechanic for this trip to Sutokata. You're hired."

Jessica leaned back against her hay bale. She closed her eyes with a feeble smile. Gabriela had cleaned her face well, and the dim light of the barn hid the bruises. For an instant, DD flashed back to a different Jessica, six years old, fresh out of the bathtub, fighting heavy sleep-eyes in her lace canopy bed amidst the pink-flowered sheets.

And so it came to pass, one fine, frosty Ozark mountain morning, just as the sun was rising, Jessica, Jeremy and DD pulled through the gate in the fence around Gabriela's cousin's farm, rolling on tires of heavy cotton canvas stuffed with oats. The use of oats had been DD's suggestion, based on an old family legend, of her great-great-grandfather, whose family had kicked him off their Ontario farm for the wickedness of stuffing the tires of his home-built motorcycle with oats meant for animal feed. He'd ridden that motorcycle proudly into Flint, Michigan, and down the main street, where it made a mention in the local paper. He'd gone on to be the first machinist foreman on the original Buick assembly line, and his mechanical aptitude had popped up again, generations later, in Jessica. She wondered how he'd have felt to see the urban war zone Flint had eventually turned into. She wondered how the remaining people of Flint, demoralized by unemployment, foreclosures, and exodus, and dulled and confused by lead poisoning from contamination, had fared when the workers arrived to put them in the protectee camps. Were they grateful? Did they fight? Did they even understand?

Gabriela walked over with the children to say goodbye. Marthita ran up to Jessica and leaped on the scooter, burying her face in the young woman's belly and squeezing her waist as hard as her delicate arms could manage. The girl had been a fixture around the barn through the long winter. She was now telling everyone she wanted to be a mechanic when she grew up, "like Jessica." DD wiped a tear from her eye as Jessica embraced the little girl, rocking gently with her eyes closed. Jeremy was closing the gate, and as he mounted his ATV, Jessica set Martha down. Their engines revved, and one by one they pulled off.

Jessica took the lead on the Vespa and the other two fell in behind.

DD reveled in the beauty of the mountains. The sun ascended and struck the frost on the tan ground, sparkling like diamonds. The trees were still brown, but a hint of green, hanging over them like a mist, spoke of the imminence of Spring. The sky was blue, stained with high cirrus clouds like the film of buttermilk left inside a glass. For a moment, the strangeness which had haunted every day since last October lifted, and she was just a mom on a road trip with her daughter and...

The feeling collapsed. She and Jeremy were friends. They had each others' backs, literally and figuratively, and ever since their first engagement, with the poor violent lunatic, the trust of comrades-in-arms was implicit. But there was no "Honey," "Baby," "Dear" stuff going on. Their physical attraction was undeniable, and they'd had some memorable encounters in the woods on warm days, and in the distillery shed, and plenty of clichéd rolls in the hay of the barn, sheep baaing under the loft. But the more they were involved in other ways, the less satisfactory the sex was. Occasionally, they'd fall asleep in an embrace after sex, but DD usually had to bring herself to climax afterwards. This was normal for her, and she decided the first time had just been a fluke. They slept separately most nights.

Jessica had asked DD bluntly one day, "Mom, you and Jeremy: what's the deal there?"

DD just shrugged. Jeremy wasn't a thinker, but a doer, and DD was still at bottom a scientist, given to exploring ideas and concocting ways to test them. They'd be discussing the day's plans, the need for more water in the mash, and how the sheep had been restless the night before. Jeremy would speculate there was an animal prowling outside the barn at night, and DD would start brainstorming: an animal, the wind might have changed, maybe one of the ewes was getting ready to lamb out of season (herd mammals circle to protect birthing females, she'd read), and she'd look up and Jeremy would smirk at her and go on stirring the vat of mash he was working on. She would feel momentarily silly, like someone caught talking out loud to the cat, and fall silent.

But today, they were all doers. In the crisp mountain air, they were a trio of intrepid warriors on an adventure! They crested a ridge and the ascending contours of the range of mountains, hills really, called the Ozarks, spread out before them to the Northwest. A group of whitetails, three does and a two-point buck, were motionless in the road, silhouetted against the sky, the only visible movement the gentle rising of vapor from the creatures' nostrils. The trio braked to a stop. Life has few of these transcendent moments. Man, women, deer, sky, all hung suspended in perfect harmony. A rabbit broke abruptly from a bush on the other side of the road.

Startled, the four deer ran off, their impossible, graceful, bounding steps taking them through the underbrush as they vaulted, otherworldly, down the acute slope.

DD sighed in elation and turned to Jessica, ahead to her right, but her daughter's eyes were still glued to the eponymous flags of the retreating ruminants. She smiled a mother's smile. *The experience is new to her. I guess, always, anything we see together, I will think of how it must look through her eyes.*

DD pivoted to look at Jeremy and saw him remove his hand from the rifle mounted upright on the ATV behind him. *He knows we can't carry that much meat, and we don't want to stop our journey, just as we're getting started, in order to dress it. But here's the difference, right here: his country-boy instinct and my city-girl whimsy.*

The weather got colder as they moved north, traveling faster than the warming glow of spring, but they were equipped for colder-weather camping. There were a number of old-time, deserted downtowns that had undergone a scraggly rebirth of sorts, as people moved closer together to avoid melting roads and long-distance walks. Some, of course, had been renovated before the machine sickness, but they no longer hosted expensively-but-casually clad crowds sampling goat-cheese wild-foraged-mushroom bruschetta and pomegranate-pear martinis. Here and there, they encountered others who'd come up with the same idea as Jessica and rebuilt small vehicles for ethanol. The smoke streams of the fires of many stills rose up across the land, no longer hidden for fear of the law. In this area, many people still had livestock when the machine sickness hit, so horses, donkeys, mules, and sometimes even cattle were making a comeback as forms of transportation. Dirt or gravel roads, or roads with wide dirt shoulders, were becoming more popular and reliable, as the machine sickness broke down more and more asphalt paving into chunks and puddles.

When the Ozarks gave way to the flat plains of Missouri and Kansas, the trip became monotonous. They passed a windmill farm, giant graceful structures like a regiment of giants in feathered headgear. Some of the turbines were turning their slow, brutal arcs. Some were turning part-circles, jamming, and swinging backwards. Many were cocked crooked at their fiberglass nacelles, where something plastic inside had given way. One turbine's titanic blade had flown free of its steel column and sat alone in a fallow field. They stopped to investigate and found two of the three blades embedded in the earth. The one that had struck the ground first had gouged a long furrow twice as deep as Jeremy was tall and plowed up a divot as big as DD's old house. They marveled at the destruction, felt themselves miniscule before it. Then they cast an eye at the other windmills nearby, one of them listing crazily, and hastily moved on.

One day, a drab gloomy sky blew in. They watched slow, inexorable clouds advance across the flatlands, an impressionist smear of silver rain below, and then found an abandoned metal warehouse and made camp.

"Isn't this tornado country?" Jessica asked. "Would this warehouse hold up to a tornado?"

"There's not much that can hold up to a tornado, if that's your destiny," Jeremy said.

They wound up staying there for five days, sleeping a lot, huddled around a lumber-scrap fire, as the Midwestern springtime demonstrated its fickleness. They kept one eye on the sky, fearing the yellow tinge that presaged tornadoes, but the rain was constant and the wind was steady, barely rattling the corrugated sheet metal with its worst gusts.

When the front finally passed over, they resumed their travel and headed north, a rising sun on their left and a spectacular rainbow on their right.

That night, they reached Lake of the Ozarks. They needed a bath, so they headed down a dirt road with a sign that said, "Riverview." When they got to the end of the gravel road, they discovered they were at an RV park. The guard on watch hailed them, holding a rifle at rest across his body and obviously perceiving them as no threat. The park was occupied by residents who'd been stranded there, camping out, when the machine sickness hit; as their largely fiberglass portable homes dissolved and collapsed, they'd worked diligently to create solutions. A few collectors had antique aluminum Airstream trailers which were pretty much intact, although of course the PVC plumbing was worthless now. The metal frames of even the fiberglass trailers and motorhomes remained, atop tire-free chassis, propped on concrete blocks or chunks of limestone to level them as their hydraulic jacks failed. Some campers had already been living in "park models," and had units encased in aluminum siding and roofing; others had been built with vinyl siding and asphalt shingles, and were in the same boat as the temporary visitors. It seemed to have been a difficult winter, and two burned-out hulks of motorhomes showed the danger of trying to heat a flammable structure with natural fuels. People had used what came to hand, which yielded a surrealistic neighborhood landscape of concrete, sheet metal, canvas, grass thatching, wood, and rope. The swimming-pool enclosure's chain-link fence had been stripped off; they saw a corner of it peeking out as the underlayment for an RV wall someone had rebuilt by weaving strips of fabric into it. The pool itself had been repurposed as a reservoir, and DD the microbiologist was impressed at the strategies they'd come up with to keep it sanitary after their sodium hypochlorite ran out. The park had become a tribal unit, congregating at a community fire each day and sharing food. They'd survived the winter with few deaths, obtaining food by foraging local grocery stores, wildcrafting fruits and herbs in the Fall, fishing and hunting over the Winter, and trading their few items of value with the local farmers who, just like those in Gabriela's community, had nowhere to ship their crops to once the trucks stopped running. They were turning over ground to make a huge vegetable garden with seeds they'd foraged from a nearby home repair warehouse store. They were all too aware that cereals would be the issue: the equipment to till huge tracts of land was lacking, and most farmers had been using hybridized or GMO seed, which wouldn't breed true. Foreheads furrowed among those whose temperament tended towards planning ahead when the visitors brought the topic up, but no one had any answers other than to hoard small amounts of starches for their families when they could get away with it and hope the mice didn't find them. DD looked at a 3-year-old toddling around her older siblings' feet. *Next Winter is going to be brutal.*

The three camped by the tiny public beach on the wide Osage river, tarried a day, and took the most invigorating cold-water swim of their lives in the warm sunshine of the next afternoon.

They crossed the lake itself via a steel-girder bridge on US 54 and took it east of Kansas City to US 36, which became I-72. They had to detour way out of their path on local roads around Springfield, where the heavily trafficked freeway, rotted by *p davisii*, had transformed over the winter into an impassible Burren-like landscape. DD knelt to examine what was happening. The cracks in the asphalt had exposed layers of gravel, silt, and sand, in which a variety of tiny green things flourished in the warmth, producing astonishing miniature landscapes of elfin beauty.

Once they reached Indiana, DD's memory proved faithful despite her frequent doubts. There were many times she was just about ready to turn the party around and retrace their steps, and then she'd spot some trivial landmark: a school-bus shelter with the name of a local dentist painted on it (*Dr. Payne, terrible name for a dentist!*); a trench which

310

curved away from the road around a huge boulder; an intersection with what had once been a plastic molded Shell Oil box sign on the abandoned gas station, but was now just a tall metal pole with red and yellow splashes trailing down its sides. It was an overcast and chilly day when the evergreen windbreak gave the signal they awaited that this was the right place. With no little trepidation, they turned down the anonymous track that led to Sutokata.

Before proceeding, they formed up abreast, as had become their habit. Jessica was in the center on her scooter, looking down at her mother and Jeremy, on their lower ATV seats, on each side.

"Now, it's been a while since I was here," cautioned DD. "I don't even know for sure the collective is still there, or that the people there are the ones I remember."

"We should go slow then," said Jeremy.

"And make lots of noise so it doesn't seem like we're sneaking up on them!" said Jessica.

They picked their way down the road as it tapered into a trail, beeping the horns on their little vehicles every so often. Two armed men—*no,* DD corrected herself, *an armed man and an armed woman*—stopped them before the compound proper came into sight. Their rifles were leveled at the three strangers, but they were relaxed and their fingers were off the triggers.

The travelers cut their motors. DD noticed the smell of rotting meat, carried from behind the defenders on the light breeze. It made her uncomfortable, the acid taste of nausea welling up in her throat. DD, Jessica, and Jeremy raised their open hands.

"Who are you and what do you want?" challenged the man. His white face was flushed with the chill under his knit cap and above his wool coat.

"I'm DD Davis. I'm a friend..." *what if they don't know who I'm talking about,* "of Akisni and Snowbear." *What if we came all this way for nothing?*

The weapons came down and the guards visibly relaxed. "Let's just take you to the main house and see about that," the woman said in a friendly tone. "Mind if we ride on the back of your vehicles?"

Jessica led the way, and the two ATVs, with the Sutokata residents perched on the cargo boxes behind the drivers, guns aimed at the sky, followed behind. They passed a side trail and DD got a glimpse of two people laboring hard, digging a deep trench in the muddy, freshly thawed spring dirt. The rotting-meat smell was especially strong here.

Maybe a horse or cow died and they're burying it?

They entered the main house and were settled into chairs while one of their captors/greeters, who introduced himself as Joe, went to find Snowbear and Akisni. Heidi, a medium-height brunette in a Baja shirt with a wool knit poncho over it, leaned on the butt of her rifle and smiled pleasantly. Akisni was right in the adjacent kitchen, and she bustled in.

"DD!" Her voice was full of elation as she wrapped her arms around her old friend. "How did you make it here?
312

You must tell me everything!" She released DD from her warm enveloping hug, holding her arms as she took a good look at her face. Then she turned to her companions. "Who are your friends?"

"This is Jeremy, my friend from Galveston, and this," she paused for effect, "is Jessica." Akisni's eyebrows shot up.

"*Jessica?* Little Jessica? Buttercup?"

"The goat tamer herself!" grinned DD. "Oh, my God! I can't believe it. Moments like this make me feel old!"

"Tell me about it!"

"Jeremy, was it? Nice to meet you." Akisni shook his hand. "We are always happy to get news of what's going on outside. Let me fix you some tea." She stepped out of the room, only to return a few moments later. She offered a choice of blends, "Mint? Chamomile? Red Clover? Cinnamon?" and disappeared into the kitchen again. Snowbear was found outside, where he was patching fences around the summer pasturage, and by the time he came inside, they were all quite cozy in chairs with tea and rolls.

"So, that's the quick version of how I wound up in Houston just before the machine sickness hit," finished DD, "and a summary of how Jessica disappeared as a teenager and broke my heart."

"I'm so sorry, mom." Jessica pressed her lips together and looked at her mom earnestly.

"It's okay, Buttercup. You weren't in your right mind. What's past is past."

"Here's Snowbear," said Akisni, rising and handing him a cup of his favorite tea, which he turned to take from her after giving DD a brief hug. "Honey, I was getting caught up with DD, but I didn't let her tell me about what's happened to her since the machine sickness. She came all the way from Galveston and I knew you'd want to hear everything she had to say about what things are like out there."

"Well," Snowbear sat down. "Let me get comfortable then."

The trio told the tale of their winter near Fort Smith, their journey, and all the people they'd connected with. The Sutokatans were pleased to hear that small communities had sprung up spontaneously to deal with the new isolation, and fascinated to hear about some of the innovative solutions other groups had come up with to the loss of plastic and oil.

Snowbear and Akisni became excited about the possibility of converting gasoline engines to ethanol. "It honestly never occurred to me to do something so simple! Is it difficult?"

"Not really," Jessica said.

"What about heavy machinery? Like a tractor or backhoe?"

"If it's gasoline powered, the conversion should be pretty straightforward. Diesel, not so much. I'll look at your equipment tomorrow and see what it will take to do it."

"I'm sure Amit and Josh will want to pump you all for ideas and information," said Snowbear.

"Who?" Asked DD.

"Our biologist and our electrician."

"Amit? You don't mean Amit Viswanathan by any chance?"

"Yes, that's Amit. Do you know him?"

"Are you kidding? I know *of* him. He's a legend! He did the pioneering work in my field. He was the first man ever to patent a genetically engineered organism! Is he actually *here,* at Sutokata?" Her voice rose in excitement.

"Hmh. I've known Amit since he was a grad student and I was a freshman. I never realized you two were in the same area of biochemistry—"

"Microbiology."

"—microbiology, until just now. How likely is it you'd both wind up at the same place?"

"You have no idea." DD gave a deep sigh. *Might as well get it over with, since the subject's come up.* "There's something I have to tell you."

"What?"

"I'm the one responsible for the machine sickness. I created it."

Akisni gave a little laugh. "Don't be silly. It came from the big oil corporations."

"Which I work for—worked for. I actually built on Amit Viswanathan's work to create an oil-eating microbe which would grow faster, under a wider range of conditions, than any we'd had before. It was intended for the purpose of cleaning up oil spills in an environmentally friendly way. It worked better than we could have imagined. Then, it suddenly got out of control; I'm still not sure how. I think my assistant bought some mislabeled cultures. He might have done it deliberately. I just don't know.

"But anyway, this is all. My. Fault."

It's strange how saying something out loud makes it more real, DD thought as she began sobbing into her cupped palms. *Even if it's something you've thought inside for a while.*

She took long, gasping breaths between sobs. Jessica came to her side and put a hand on her back. Something nudged her hand and it was Jeremy, offering a handkerchief.

"DD, nobody is blaming you," Akisni said softly. "I'm sure it was an accident." DD exploded in a new spasm of crying, and there was no other sound in the room for quite a few minutes. Eventually, the spasm of emotion began to burn itself out, and she began to catch her breath.

"DD," began Akisni again, "every human action has the potential for unforeseen consequences. If we determine never to cause any harm, we can never cause any good either. And that's the biggest harm of all. You did what you did because you wanted to help..."

"...And because I'm good at it," interjected DD, giving a slight smirk through her tears.

"You are suffering the results of it just like everyone else in this country, probably on this planet. You can't carry that. Put it down."

Put it down. "Put it down. I should put it down!" All at once, it seemed like DD's entire body melted. She realized

316

she'd been carrying every blow and kick and lie and insult inflicted on her by Isaac and Coffee-Breath, cherishing it as her just retribution for the destruction she'd wrought. She was overcome by a wave of exhaustion. She leaned back in the armchair and closed her eyes.

Jessica said, "I remember just bits and pieces about this place. When I saw the rafters, I recognized them... and they brought other things back."

"Like what?" Asked Akisni. Jessica described snippets of memory and the older woman expanded on them, or told her what had actually happened, where Jessica's memories were half-obscured behind the veil of childhood.

Jessica looked over at her mother. "Is she...asleep?" She asked, incredulous.

Everyone sat for an awkward moment. DD solved the conundrum by beginning to snore. "It looks that way," said Akisni. She shook her head. "Odd reaction. I guess she's been through a lot."

Jessica piped up brightly, "Hey, are the goats still here?"

Akisni smiled. "Sure, they are. Wanna go see them?" The two of them and Snowbear began to put on their coats. Jeremy looked at DD, hesitated, shrugged, and joined them. Out they went, as DD spiraled deeper and deeper into intense, serene sleep.

They visited the barn, where goats, sheep, and cows shared living quarters (the pigs were in a separate building). Jessica giggled and petted them like she was a pigtailed girl again, and everyone's mood lightened a little. They took a different path back, accompanying Snowbear who said he just wanted to check on something, and when they came out in a clearing, Jessica froze.

"Oh my God!" She exclaimed. The clearing was the one by the driveway which DD had glimpsed earlier on their way in. The long, deep trench had been finished and was now already half-filled in. LaDwon and Les were wearing light jackets, open in the cool Spring temperatures. They were perspiring with the effort of their labor, but they had scarves wrapped over their noses and mouths. At the bottom of the unfilled portion, Jessica saw the remains of the winter's raiders, at the same time she smelled the results of the recent warmer weather.

"What happened to them?" She was shocked. Akisni turned her head away and looked at the ground.

"They meant us harm." Snowbear. "We respect life, but we have to protect what is ours. We couldn't bury them until the ground thawed. Sorry, I forgot you didn't know. Of course, it's shocking."

"So, it was self-defense?" Jessica's voice was a little shrill, as though willing them to say yes.

"Unfortunately, yes." Snowbear clenched the corners of his mouth and looked down, unflinching, at the reeking carrion which had once been human beings.

Jeremy took the lead to re-enter the path, "Good enough for me!" he called out heartily. "Let's go!" The others followed.

318

Jessica was ten feet away at the edge of the clearing. She clasped her hair behind her head, turned, and vomited, long and hard, into the weeds with all the practiced precision of a recovering alcoholic. Wiping her mouth, she followed Jeremy down the trail into the brush. Akisni, head still down, silently took the rear.

LII.   It's Always the Quiet Ones

Brownie grabbed his jacket, loaded his favorite handgun, a Ruger, and chambered a round. He retrieved his waterproofed leather moccasins from by the door and went out for his shift on patrol. Murphy came in and gave him a quick fist bump as Brownie went out.

Brownie started down a trail which made up one of their usual patrol patterns. This trail swung to the right around the copse of trees. It intersected a deer trail which led up from the water and fanned out into a fallow cornfield. Instead of continuing along the footpath, Brownie veered onto the deer trail, stopping where it was hidden by the trees. There, he met his connection, a short man with an irritating habit of jingling his keys in his pocket. The other man, the tall one with coffee-stained teeth, was nowhere to be seen. Sometimes, the two men came together, but usually it was one or the other.

"What do you have for me?" Isaac asked with no preamble.

"A new microorganism. Something about generating energy, something better than the biogas. Supposedly no risk of explosion."

"Still haven't turned up any EarthFirst! literature? VHMNT?" He pronounced it *vehement*. "A group called The Justice Department?"

"No, nothing like that. Um, a book by Robert Hunter about the founding of Greenpeace."

"Hmm. Well, bring it next time if you can slip out with it without being noticed. We don't have access to
320

information networks anymore and we're trying to get a handle on the motives of these bioterrorists." Brownie nodded.

Brownie handed Isaac a slip of paper with the word, *shewanella*, written on it. Only Brownie had misspelled it as "SHEWENDELA."

"What's this?" Said Isaac. "Some black chick?"

"No, it's the name of the bacteria."

"Are you sure no one saw you write this down?"

"Well, there was LaDwon. But he was reading, I don't think he was paying attention."

"How many years have you been undercover?"

"I—I'm sorry." Brownie's face fell. "It wasn't political information so I thought..."

"Don't you get it? The name of the game is bioterrorism, and these are major players. This could be as big as the machine sickness! First, they bring this nation to its knees, then they create a new source of power which only they control, and then they take over!" Isaac may have been a little hard on Brownie here, he realized; he was still angry at himself for leaving DD in the cell when they evacuated, planning to be back within a day or so, expecting to find her hungry, thirsty, and more cooperative. No one could have known it was more than a simple evacuation drill. No one could have known it was a global catastrophe, sweeping through every millimeter of the planet with the wildfire intensity of life itself.

Realization dawned behind Brownie's eyes. "I didn't realize. I thought the machine sickness was an accident."

"That may be what Davis wants you to believe. Trust me, there are no accidents. Now, finish your patrol. We will meet again at this location. At oh seven hundred in nineteen days."

"Nineteen days." Brownie did some quick addition. "The twenty-third. Seven a.m. Got it." He walked back to the main path. As he resumed his patrol, he turned to glance back, and Isaac was gone.

LIII.   Best Served Cold

Tim Schneider reached the end of the row of cotton. His fingers were bleeding and swollen. His back ached and throbbed. He reached into his shirt and extracted a cloth-wrapped bundle and dropped it into the sack at the end of the row along with his load of bolls. He was halfway down the next row before the bag was retrieved. The protectee who picked it up glanced inside and grinned before throwing it over his shoulder and hauling it off. Tim knew that, once behind the truck, he would extract the special package for further distribution of the substance inside. Just like any prison, and this was a prison, no matter what they called it, this camp had ways of getting contraband inside, and a microeconomy to distribute it according to supply and demand. Sugar, which was what was in the package, was in high demand. It would buy Tim another week of protection from the Tango Blasts. Tim's natural shrewdness, and his lack of the behavioral constraints observed by lesser mortals, worked to his favor here in the camp. Plus, he had lots of opportunity for the kind of sexual power games he preferred. Sam had always been too soft for him anyway. He was getting leaner and meaner every day. Literally. Tim tugged the drawstring on his pants, tight as it would go already. Resources were short, they said, but everyone noticed, as the months rolled by, that the administrators weren't getting leaner like the protectees were.

The afternoon rains were about to roll in. The Gulf Coast had always had a summer weather pattern of thunderstorms which popped up every day, deluging the area and cultivating grass, mildew, and mosquitos. This summer was the worst in memory; the storms were more intense every day. The ocean itself, to the east, was covered with a constant cloud of rolling fog, which reeked of an organic stench. Every afternoon the fog grew denser, building into a mountain which fused with flat-bottomed thunderheads and surged inland. Tim had heard others say the land he was harvesting had been too dry to grow cotton before, and farmers who'd resorted to the camps said the cotton farms inland, which depended on irrigation, were all fallow since the irrigation equipment had failed.

The first peals of thunder rolled across the countryside. Tim joined the daily exodus from the fields back to the shelter of the barracks. Before he could merge with the milling crowd, a supervisor clapped him on the shoulder, gesturing towards the peacekeeper at the corner of the field. The man stood holding a rifle, wearing the same cotton pajamas as the inmates, but his were newer and in better repair, as the peacekeepers' always were. The protectees noticed that no matter how much cotton they harvested, their own personal cotton garments weren't replaced until they were falling to pieces.

Next to the peacekeeper was one of the Feds, someone familiar. Tim's eyes narrowed.

"Another debriefing, Lee?" Tim asked as he came closer.

"Yes. This one is about your former boss."

"They've all been about DD, in one way or another." Tim had managed to gather by inference during these interviews that they'd had DD in custody and lost her. He wondered how she'd managed to get away. He didn't think she had the guile to talk her way free.

"Yes, but now we want to get to know more about her personally. My unit leader thinks she may be designing another bioweapon, and we want to know more about how her mind works."

Lightning flashed, and the second resounding din of thunder rolled over the horizon, louder this time. Tim walked ahead of the two men into the administration building and sat at the wooden table in the wooden chair facing the Fed. Tim smelled cologne on Lee, a drugstore brand. Tim hadn't had cologne to wear since the morning he was arrested; he missed it. Funny how it was the little things you missed. The peacekeeper stood outside the door.

Lee started the conversation.

"How long has Dr. Davis known the Simpsons?"

"Snowbear and Akisni? I don't know. She said she used to go to the commune when she was working on some site in Minnesota."

"Was she a communist?"

Tim snorted. "No, she wasn't really political. If anything, I'd say she was a right-wing gun nut."

"Did she use her office e-mail to communicate with them?"

"Not that I ever saw."

"You handled all her travel plans, correct?"

"Yes. She wouldn't have known where to go or what to do without me."

"Did you ever cover for her when she was visiting Sutokata? Make it look like she was going somewhere else?"

"No. Honestly, I didn't even remember about the place until *you* reminded me."

"Don't use the word 'honestly' with me, Tim; I know better."

Tim just rolled his eyes. "How many times are you going to ask me the same questions?"

"How did you ship the cultures to the Chinese?" Repetition.

"Are we doing this Chinese thing again? Look, I don't know what you're talking about." Tim said, for probably the hundredth time. Lee's bovine gaze slid away from the lie.

The daily downpour began to pound on the roof. Raindrops streamed down the outside of the windows. The wind hit the building like a wet towel. Rain blanketed the view out the window in uniform grey.

"Tim, you could go to prison for a long time."

"I'm *in* prison, remember? Oh, sorry. I'm in a protective camp."

"These camps are for the citizens' own protection. There is no law enforcement structure left since the government collapsed. Would you rather be out there?"

"Would you let me go if I said yes?" Tim retorted.

"You agreed to remain under our protection when you were protecteed. Obviously, there'd be chaos if we let people come and go from the camps as they pleased."

"Unlike everyone else out there, who was stampeded into being protecteed when they were terrified that the world was falling apart before their eyes, I wasn't protecteed voluntarily, remember?"

"Which is exactly the point: you know that you could go to prison for a very long time, both for embezzlement, and for selling biotech cultures to the Chinese. Not to mention cocaine possession. Do you want to know what actual prisons are like now?"

From what Tim had heard, there were few, if any, actual prisons left. Most of the prisons had been secured with systems which relied to some extent on electric devices and electronic recordkeeping. They'd had redundant generators in case of power failure, but no one ever planned for the contingency of the wiring insulation rotting through everywhere, all at once, and shorting out the entire system. The weeks after the machine sickness hit had been catastrophes of brutality and deprivation for the prisoners and their keepers, and the death toll had been horrific. The ones who'd escaped had blended into the general population; the few who survived being trapped inside had been rolled into the camps. Tim had met many in the camps who were former prisoners, and they all told similar nightmare stories. No, he knew prison now was an empty threat. But Tim would allow his captors to think he was still afraid of prison, until it was to his advantage not to.

"You wouldn't send me to prison." He put a false note of anxiety in his voice.

"Maybe not. But how'd you like it if your sugar supply dried up?"

This was a new gambit! Tim wanted to know more; he was intrigued. "What do you mean?" He feigned worry. He doubted the authorities had the ability to cut off sugar smuggling, but he wanted to know why they thought *he* thought they could.

"Tim, this small-time stuff is too petty for you. How would you like to get a piece of something big?"

"I'm listening."

"DD Davis has teamed up with Amit Viswanathan, the first microbiologist to patent a living creature. We are pretty sure the two of them created the machine sickness in order to cripple our infrastructure. They are cooking up a new organism, which we believe to be Phase 2 of their plan. They, along with their eco-terrorist confederates, are planning to introduce another bacterium. We don't know what it will do yet, but we think it will make the machine sickness look like a case of sniffles by comparison."

"And what does this have to do with me?"

"You know better than anyone how her mind works. Tim, we want to put you in charge of a squad to compile all the material we've been able to find about DD and Viswanathan's research at Sutokata. We have managed to

328

make contact with an undercover informer the FBI had there for years to monitor their terrorist activity. You should be able to interpret the information we get from that asset; from what you've told me, you were basically doing her research for her, just without a degree."

Tim at this point sincerely believed that this was true, so he wasn't lying this time when he nodded his head.

"I'll need complete control over the staffing and budgeting process," Tim said.

"Subject to my review, of course. You understand." Lee waved his hands, somehow clearly denoting Tim's history of embezzlement and fencing stolen goods with that gesture.

"Oh, of course," Tim said, nonchalant. Inside, he was rejoicing. This was just too good to be true! After facing off with this man Lee several times over the past months, Tim knew that, not only was he stupid, he didn't know he was stupid. Hiding transactions from him—on paper ledgers, even! —would be a cakewalk.

Besides, Tim's resentment of DD had developed, since he'd been sent here, into a smoldering hatred. It must have been she who betrayed him to the police, resulting in his being in custody when the world fell apart. If not for her, he reasoned, he'd have been in Houston in a luxury apartment, snorting coke with pretty little Sam, as they'd dreamed. He lay awake at night imagining how he might get back at her. This would be a delightful revenge!

LIV.   Pastoral

That Spring was an orgy of invention and discovery at Sutokata. The commune's normal Spring workload was imbued with new urgency by their awareness that self-sufficiency was no longer a high-minded abstract goal, but rather a necessity. That necessity was compounded by the need to develop innovative ways to cache and conceal their weapons, wool, skins, clothing and bedding, ethanol, and preserved food against, not just the odd raider, but the potential of visits by the larcenous police. The lengthening spring days were full of back-breaking work, but that work was slightly less back-breaking because Jessica had converted a gasoline tractor to run on ethanol.

They turned over the muddy earth and seeded it with corn, wheat, soy, and vegetables. The herd animals were turned out to graze on the sprouting grass of the pasture. Fences were mended, ditches dredged, outbuildings patched and rebuilt. As the days continued to lengthen after the equinox, and their bodies hardened to the labor, Amit and Josh began to pal around with Jessica in the evenings, as they inspired each other to devise new ways to circumvent the loss of plastics and oils. A 50-50 mixture of goldenseal and amoxicillin, suspended in ethanol and water, had to be carefully applied to the solar panels twice weekly to keep them from becoming infected. Jessica was working on building an ethanol-powered generator for the inevitable day when the solar panels would fail. Amit and Josh had a project going involving chlorophyll extracts and different growth and

330

conduction media to see if they could develop a supplemental, organic solar power generator. But the real excitement came when Amit told DD about his *Shewanella* cultures. It turned out that DD had supervised a graduate student who was using DD's own groundbreaking genetic engineering techniques to increase the electrical production of *shewanella*-based bioelectric cells. The grad student had increased the output by two orders of magnitude, and DD remembered the techniques well enough that they could, through trial and error, replicate them. Handicapped as they were by the lack of internet access to find out what research had come before them, it took hundreds of long hours of work to remake lost progress.

The work felt so much like play, Josh said one day, "I think if we had a quantum physicist here, we could make a faster-than-light biological engine."

"As long as he wasn't good-looking," said DD.

"Why not?" straight-lined Amit.

"It would be too frustrating," DD replied. "Because when he found the position, he can't get the momentum; when he found the time, he wouldn't have the energy!"

"Mo-om!" groaned Jessica.

"The last physicist I knew checked into a hotel with a photon. The desk clerk asked if she had any luggage, but the photon said no, she was traveling light," said Amit.

"That's bad," groaned Josh. "I'd tell a chemistry joke but I'm sure I'd get no reaction."

As the weather got warmer in central Indiana, birds returned (Josh and Amit stepped up the goldenseal washes on the solar panels accordingly). Streams thawed; the air took on an earthy aroma. The frantic plowing and seeding of Spring passed; the livestock were situated in their Summer homes, and the farm settled into its summer rhythm.

The days grew longer, and more evenings were passed outdoors. The badminton set was resurrected from its storage in a shed and found to be destroyed by *p davisii*; a few hours of work were required to replace the nylon net with wool, restring the racquets with gut, and make new birdies out of salvaged corks and feathers from the chickens. The Sutokatans turned into children again, batting the shuttlecock back and forth.

One day, the shuttlecock arced high into the air, paused at its apex, but never came down. The players on the ground, four on each side, stood with their racquets hanging at their sides, staring dumfounded at the sky. Something had swooped in, captured the birdie, and buzzed off into the treetops.

"What was that?" Said LaDwon.

"A hawk?" Suggested Brownie.

"No, it wasn't alive," said Doug. "I'm sure of it."

The thing emerged from the trees and circled overhead. It was brownish like a hawk's feathers, but its hum told them it was mechanical. It released the birdie from its claws, then landed on the ground near the players. Sheila picked it up.

"It's a drone," she said. Sure enough, the thing was built of carved wood and metal, six tiny turbofans around a central container of liquid divided into two compartments, and spring-loaded dowels for pincer arms and landing legs. Wires wrapped in fiber connected all the parts. It resembled a crane fly, but it was the size of a woodchuck. The group stood around marveling at the thing, and Josh stepped out from his hiding place in the bushes grinning and holding a curious remote control made of two pieces of fused and melted glass, one piece a socket imbedded with wires, and one a smooth round ball. On closer inspection, a cavity within the socket piece contained liquid compartments just like the drone.

"What?"

"How?"

The group began to form questions, but Josh cut them off. "Biobatteries.

"This *shewanella* bacterium produces an electrical current by creating two different oxidation states on the aerobic and anaerobic sides of the membrane. That makes an electrical current, which flows from one side to the other. It works!" His glee was obvious.

"Epic!" exclaimed Jesse.

"It's interesting looking," commented Gillie. "Kind of beyond steampunk tech. Kind of rustic pioneer tech."

Everyone had to have a turn controlling the drone. That lasted forty-five minutes or so, until it stopped responding.

"Need to put it in a warm place and add nutrients so it can recharge itself." Josh whisked the drone indoors.

During these languorous Summer days, they started having dinner outdoors on wooden tables when the weather was clear. Afterwards, a guitar, a banjo, a fiddle, a *bodhrán*, a bongo, a concertina, maracas, a saxophone, a flute, a trumpet, and a variety of harmonicas might find their way outdoors to combine with voices high and low in a tapestry of kaleidoscopic musical variety which covered almost every conceivable genre, style, and era, veering from sublime harmony to catastrophic cacophony.

The local police didn't raid them again over the summer. Visitors and new arrivals brought rumors as to why. Rumor had it that the mysterious Federal cops had shot one of the local police over some demand the local guy made. The demand itself grew in the womb of rumor, from a simple case of ammunition in the Spring, to a helicopter and SWAT gear by Independence Day. Regardless, the local police had apparently degenerated into a squabbling pack of hyenas after that incident. Some speculated that they also were running low on uncontaminated fuel, and so the radius of their predations was shrinking. DD expected the Feds to reappear at any moment, which marred her enjoyment as Spring flourished into Summer, but they never showed up. *Yet.*

One July evening after dinner, DD was in the herb garden with Jessica, pulling weeds. Mother and daughter were on their hands and knees between rows of leafy, fragrant flora. The moist dirt still gave off a faint trace of heat left over from the sun, now a hand's breadth from the horizon.

"The mint has just gone crazy with all this rain!" DD observed.

"I know, so has the pennyroyal," agreed Jessica. "I've gotta go pee." She grabbed the pile of discarded weeds next to her with her right hand to carry it off, and pressed her left hand against her lower back as she rose to a wide squat and then staggered upright. The loose, long-sleeved men's' denim shirt she was wearing had come unbuttoned. DD glanced up, did a double take, and then stared. *How could I not have known?*

"Jessica!" Sharply.

"What, mom?" She saw her mother's gaze and pulled the placket of the shirt together, smearing dirt onto it from the uprooted herbs in her hand. An awkward, motionless moment ensued.

"Yeah, so..." Jessica began.

"You're pregnant." DD observed.

"I'm sorry mom!" Jessica was nine years old again, causing DD to flash back to the night she was caught climbing out her bedroom window to meet the girl next door with a pack of cigarettes and a can of beer. Her lip trembled.

Don't let this be like that. Don't let me lose her again. DD stood up, more quickly than her child had, and stepped over a row of fragrant basil to wrap her arms around Jessica. "It's okay, baby. It's okay." She held her for a moment with her eyes closed, rocking gently, then took her by the shoulders and looked into her eyes. "In fact, it's great! It's wonderful!"

Then the dam burst. Jessica nestled into her mother's neck and sobbed. It took a few minutes to purge the tear ducts. *Like mother, like daughter. Nothing like a good cry to get you over something.*

"Mom, I was going to tell you but there was never a good time."

"It's okay, sweetheart. I understand."

"But what will we do? I can't get to the hospital! If there even are hospitals any more."

"You really don't know? Oh, honey! Akisni is a midwife. She apprenticed at the Farm in Tennessee. In the 80s, women used to travel for miles to Sutokata just to have a natural birth with her."

Jessica looked hopeful. "Really?"

"Cross my heart. Let's go find her now. I'm sure there's a lot she'll need to get ready."

Strawberries, blueberries and cream. Fresh peaches and apples from the orchard. Meadows full of brilliant wildflowers which lasted just a single day in a jar on the windowsill. Rest breaks under the trees, the vivid green of the leaves overhead sharply distinct from the inebriating blue of the cloud-spotted sky. The Summer passed as a series of haikus.

August came, and harvest began in earnest. The honey light of the sun began to slant and the sunsets were earlier and earlier. The wind blew stronger across the fields. One surprising morning, a thin coating of frost dusted the grass and their breath was visible on the crisp air of dawn. DD

336

heard the obscene and tragic sobbing of a pig that was being slaughtered, and the smell of burning hung on the air for days as bacon and ham was preserved in the smokehouse. Flocks were culled and sausage was made. Fruit and vegetables were canned; the women (and two of the men) had a constant factory going in the kitchen, generating rows and rows of colorful glass jars with wax seals standing proudly on the shelves in the basement.

After the Fall's raid, the collective decision had been made to create concealed root cellars to store a third of their preserved food (just enough to survive the winter on short rations, not so much that the raiders, if they came back, would know anything was missing). To make these cellars, deep holes needed to be dug, using their mini backhoe (fuel-converted, thanks to Jessica) and consuming an alarming amount of precious ethanol.

Jessica's ankles had begun to swell to the size of softballs when she stood very long, and Akisni had frowned and ordered her to take a supervisory role–only! –over Josh and some of the others in her mechanical projects. Jessica obediently lazed around the distillery shed and directed them as they upgraded the size of the tanks and the diameter of the piping. They pretended to need her guidance, consulting her every few minutes so she wouldn't feel the urge to get up and start working. They were determined to triple their output of ethanol by the time harvest was done.

LV.   If You Want It Done Right...

"That's absurd. We can't have protectees coming and going at random! There is enough chaos and disorder as it is!" Lee's successor told Tim.

"I'm not a typical protectee," Tim pointed out, "and it wouldn't be at random. This program is critical, Jeff. Top secret! I don't even know if Lee'd want me to share as many details with you as I already have!"

Jeff stood, chewing his lip, head down, and mulled it over. Jeff had contacted Lee not long after the machine sickness hit, when Jeff realized that he'd no way of contacting his own superiors. Jeff and Lee had gone to the law enforcement academy together and they still watched a game together every now and then. Jeff had figured out over the years that Lee was probably working for either NSA or DHS, but Lee was always one to play by the rules, so he never told Jeff which one, and Jeff never asked. Jeff had stayed with the FBI and never risen far in the hierarchy, but he was ablaze with a strong sense of patriotic loyalty; he wanted to remain faithful and serve his country in its hour of greatest need. He tracked Lee down, first visiting his house, then using old-fashioned plodding police work to track him to the camp. Lee was glad to have the help of someone he knew he could trust, a familiar face in a world where everything was topsy-turvy.

But Lee had stayed true to his protocols and never trusted Jeff with the need-to-know material about this program the arrogant, but brilliant, Tim Schneider was involved in. So, when Lee passed on suddenly after drinking his coffee one

338

morning, Jeff was thrown into a position he knew nothing about. The camp physician said it was likely rat poison in his coffee that'd killed Lee. Plenty of people at the camp had reasons, both good and bad, to hate Lee; how the poison got into his coffee turned out to be a muddled question worthy of an entire detective story, and unfortunately Jeff was no Sherlock Holmes. Regarding Tim Schneider, Jeff knew only that Lee had trusted him. Tim was no ordinary protectee, not least of all because his paper protection-camp file was missing.

The Bureau's protocols and procedures were there for a reason, and normal procedure would have been to contact base and wait to be contacted back for briefing. However, lines of communication had broken down. There was no base, no superiors, no level of secrecy above his, no one who could fill him in. So, he had to take Tim's word for what was going on.

Fortunately, Tim had filled him in thoroughly on the whole situation, and the skills Jeff had learned during his training in interrogation told him that Tim was basically honest and trustworthy, if somewhat curt and snippy at times. So, DD and these hippies were eco-terrorists. Their plan was nefarious: introduce the machine sickness, and then, when the country had reached complete disarray, introduce a second bacterium which would allow them to control the production of energy and rule the revival of technology, which would allow domination of the world under the new order of life. Apparently, Tim and Lee had a mole in the commune and they'd had an agent, Isaac, traveling back and forth to communicate with him. But now, according to Tim, either the mole or the agent Isaac had been compromised. The only way to tell which one it was, was to allow Tim to go to Sutokata himself to sort things out. As Jeff saw it, this was plausible.

Besides, Tim was irritating, and it would get Tim out of Jeff's face for a while.

"Okay," Jeff decided. "You can go."

LVI.   What a Coincidence!

The radio, which Snowbear powdered liberally with beta-lactam antibiotics on a regular basis, sat hissing in its carrel on auto-scan. No chatter had been heard on it for months, until one gorgeous June day, a voice came through. DD was sitting with Akisni in the common room carding wool; she looked up and furrowed her brow. The voice was garbled and the words couldn't be heard, but she thought she recognized the voice. *I must be losing my mind. That sounded like Tim.*

A minute or two later, she was sure of it. She felt her blood rush to her head as she identified the voice of Tim Schneider. "Is anyone there? Attention, is anyone there?" *It couldn't be him!*

Akisni didn't notice that there was anything wrong with DD (*funny how you can be overwhelmed with blinding emotion and the person right next to you not notice*). Akisni got up and rubbed her hands with alcohol from a small bottle before picking up the microphone. "This is Sutokata. Who's calling please?"

"Oh, thank God! I am completely lost and there is a gang chasing me!" He was panting with exertion and fear.

"State your position, please." Said Akisni.

"I am at mile marker 6 of State Road 2332."

"You are only a little ways from us! Look to your left and you'll see a row of spruce trees, like Christmas trees."

"I see them."

"That's the entrance to Sutokata. How far behind are your pursuers?"

"A good four or five miles. I can definitely make it."

"Sending our people out now to meet you."

Akisni ran out to mobilize the patrols to head down the path. DD ran after her to try to stop her, but Akisni, determined, was an irresistible force. She kept brushing DD off and shushing her until the two ATVs with four armed residents had been dispatched down the trail to meet their refugee.

Finally, DD got her attention: "Akisni, I know who that is! I recognized his voice!"

"Who is it, then?" Akisni asked.

"It's Tim!" Akisni's blank stare showed she had no recollection of Tim's name. "My assistant! The one who was embezzling from the University."

In Akisni's eyes, her memory clicked. "But you don't know he was embezzling. They just told you that when they were trying to get you to give them your secrets. Anyway, are you sure it's him?"

"It's him! Akisni, I've thought a lot about this. It all adds up. His spending above his means, the weird reaction of the cultures, which he ordered, that caused the machine sickness, the Sinopec transactions and Amit hearing from the Chinese. It must have been him."

"DD, you can't know that!

"I do know!"

"Well, anyway, he still doesn't deserve to be beaten up by a gang. Hopefully it's not the police chasing him and those four can handle it."

Down the trail came a canvas-tired bicycle. Riding the bicycle was, yes, Tim Schneider. But DD would have been hard-pressed to recognize him if she hadn't recognized his voice on the radio. His once-delicate, aristocratic nose was a twisted lump in the center of his face. His formerly clean-shaven face was covered by an unkempt beard. He wore a grimy wool pea coat and stocking cap and canvas cargo pants with wood-soled canvas shoes. Two pairs of Sukotakans on ATVs, LaDwon riding with Jesse, and George and Heidi, followed behind him at an idle; Jesse was riding as rear passenger and he held the radio Tim had been using, a small walkie-talkie model, which explained its limited range. It was covered with amoxicillin powder.

Tim stopped when he saw Akisni and DD, straddling the bike, and the defenders pulled up to flank him. DD stepped forward. She saw him act startled as he recognized her. *Fake reaction. But I'll bet the others don't realize it's fake.* At that moment, DD knew beyond the shadow of a doubt he wasn't here by coincidence, but she also knew that she couldn't prove it. Given her past with Tim, she couldn't even assert that truth without compromising her own credibility. She realized her hand was on the butt of her holstered sidearm and forced herself to release it.

"Tim Schneider." She named him like she'd name a species of poisonous snake, striving to conceal all the fury she felt inside the words.

"Dr. Davis?" Tim responded, apparently ingenuous. "What are you doing here? How? Why?"

"Wow, what a coincidence." DD did her best to keep the irony out of her voice. One of the patrols, George, glanced at her sharply but she kept her features impassive.

"Who was chasing you?" Asked Akisni sympathetically.

"Just some of those kids who set up camp under the overpass," Darwin said. "They stopped at the turnoff by the windbreak and then drove off when they saw us coming. No real threat." The others nodded.

"They're riding gas-powered bikes. Don't know where they scavenged the sterile gas from, but they won't be going anywhere, soon enough," said LaDwon from the other ATV.

"Can I camp here for the night?" Asked Tim, looking around. *Yes, camp here and be gone tomorrow.*

"No, of course we wouldn't dream of letting you sleep outside! Come inside and have a hot shower and a proper meal and tell us everything that you've seen," insisted Akisni, turning to lead the way.

"A hot shower!" exclaimed Tim. "I'd love to! It's been months!"

This is not good. Not good at all.

Tim swung his leg up over the seat to dismount and followed, walking his bike to the porch.

LVII.   Would I Lie to You?

Tim was in the shower, the time of day, mid-afternoon, meaning he could take his time because of lack of demand on the hot water supply.

"Look, Akisni. This guy is poison. I'm telling you, you do NOT want him here. Feed him and send him on his way!"

"DD, just because you have a personal issue with him..."

"This isn't *just* a personal issue. He's a criminal. He's a thief. But I worked side by side with him for years. You know what made him such a great assistant? He manipulated everyone into giving him whatever it was he wanted. He was a door dragon against interruptions when I was working on deadline. He took no shit from bureaucrats or committees, didn't even bother me with most of their bullshit, just made it go away, like that!" She snapped her fingers. "Nobody liked him. *I* didn't like him. But I *did* trust him. Wrongly."

"DD, I know how you feel. You don't want to be the one solely responsible for the machine sickness, but that doesn't mean he did what you're so convinced he did."

Akisni had hit her sorest point. DD lost her cool, and as she heard the crack in her own voice she knew she'd all but lost the argument. "This isn't about my guilt! This is about taking a serpent to your breast! He's a psychopath! This is a huge mistake!" Her eyes began to well with tears. She heard the shower shut off and the curtain pulled back. She turned on her heel and walked outside into the spring sunshine to compose herself.

When she returned, Tim and Akisni were talking. Tim was seated in the same chair where DD'd sat on the day when they'd first arrived. DD took a seat a few chairs distant, resolved to be a silent listener, a fly on the wall, as Tim told his tale.

"I was at my mom's in Miami when everything started shutting down. FEMA came to her retirement community and insisted on evacuating everyone to safety. They took the sickest ones from the assisted living side first. They even had nurses and medical equipment to take care of them. Later on, they evacuated the ones like my mom, who were just old but basically okay by themselves. I wanted to go with her but they wouldn't let me. They said she needed a different level of care." Akisni nodded. They'd heard, from other visitors, about the mass round-ups in the cities, sorting people by age and gender, abilities, disabilities, and special skills, sending them to different protection camps, but Tim was the only person they'd met who claimed to have come back from one.

"They took me to a different place, a protection camp. It was like a giant military installation, but there was nothing for anyone to do, and all kinds of people there. Homeless people. Ghetto trash." His lip curled in contempt. "I was the only white person in my barracks! Anyway, someone had dug a tunnel under the fence and I found it. I snuck out at night. The guards were pretty lax. Most of the people there didn't try to get out. They felt safer inside than outside." This wasn't what others had said. They'd said the camps were basically prisons and that people who tried to escape were punished, or just disappeared. *But is it possible that the regimes in different camps, in different areas, vary?* DD considered that possibility while Tim and Akisni continued their conversation.

"Where was this camp they took you to?" Akisni asked.

"Just west of Rainesville. I remembered DD talking about this place here, Sutokata, and so once I got out, I decided to make my way here."

"How did you get here?" Akisni probed.

"I rode my bike."

"No, I mean how did you find it? It's not on any map."

"I knew it was in central Indiana. I asked everyone I met if they'd heard of it." *Bullshit. I should call him on that, question him more.*

"Can I go to the bathroom?" Tim nodded at the big glass of clear, pure water, now empty, at his elbow, before she could formulate a question. *Missed my chance.* She took a breath to say something more to Akisni, but before she could form words, Akisni stood up and walked out of the room, returning with a notepad and pencil.

After Tim came back, Akisni resumed the interview.

"What roads did you take?"

"I-75 all the way to Cincinnati and I-74 into Illinois." Akisni nodded. Plausible.

"Let me take some notes." She flipped open the notepad on her lap. "Tell me about the condition of the interstates to the East of us."

"The few people who were on the road, were all headed North. The oceans are boiling. Everyone wants to get away from the Gulf before next year's hurricane season." Tim went on at some length about the degree to which the highways were compromised at different points along the way. He described towns in which the uniformed police had erected barricades which they used as toll gates to extort goods from travelers passing through. "Sometimes they claimed they were redistributing them to those who needed them more. Sometimes they just blatantly took your stuff and kept it for themselves. I lost my metal thermos, all but one pair of shoes," he nodded at the wood-soled canvas shoes bound to his feet, "all but one of my cotton shirts, a nice wool coat and socks. I got beat up a few times trying to resist."

DD couldn't contain herself any longer. She blurted out, "What's your game, Tim?"

Tim tossed his hair back. "I don't have any idea what you're talking about." He tried a lighthearted tone, "I was delighted to see you. I thought you'd be happy to see me too!"

"Cut the crap. I saw your purchase orders. I know you were stealing!"

"What? Stealing? You're crazy! I was never anything but a loyal and dedicated assistant to you! What's wrong with you?"

"Really? Then why did you order three or four times more cultures than we could possibly use? And why didn't the ID numbers on the cultures match the ID numbers on the purchase orders?"

He furrowed his brow. "Can you show me what you mean? Everything always added up."

So brazen! "No, of course not! I don't have the printouts here! What do you think, I carried them all the way from Texas?"

"Well, then, perhaps you'd better stop making unfounded accusations, because I know a lot of things about you that you might not want repeated in front of your friends here."

What? What is he talking about? DD thought, taken aback, before realizing in a split second that it didn't matter; since he was unhampered by the truth, he'd just make things up.

Then, she realized that her silence could be taken by Akisni for guilt. She was off-balance, instantly on her back foot. She was casting about desperately for something to say that wouldn't make her look defensive.

So, this is how it felt to be on the other side of his attacks when he was running interference, for me, all those years.

DD looked at Akisni with a silent pleading. She shook her head "No," abjectly.

Please don't.

But she saw nothing yielding in Akisni's obdurate gaze.

"I'm sure you must be hungry," Akisni beamed at Tim. "Let's go in the kitchen and get you fed, then Suzie will get you settled in to a guest room." She led him that way without a backward glance at DD.

He said the ocean was boiling. Boiling? Surely not. He's lying. Boiling!

LVIII.   Can't Quit Now

"Jesus Christ! What the hell do you want from me?" yelled Josh, his usual equanimity completely disrupted.

"I just want you to do it right!" screamed Jessica back. "If you don't get this joint welded perfectly, it's the weak link in the whole project. This has to be perfect! Perfect!" She pounded the arm of her Adirondack chair in frustration, restrained from surging out of the chair by an act of will. And by gravidity mingled with gravity.

"I'm doing the best I can! You've made me start over four times since breakfast, and the last three were just fine. This isn't rocket surgery, it's just a still!"

"Listen!" began Jessica. Then she gasped, and Josh's attitude instantly changed.
"Jessica? Is it time?"

"Don't change the subject!" Jessica snapped. "I've been having Braxton-Hicks contractions for days, and even if this is labor, Akisni says the first baby is slow. I've got hours yet. Bring me that pipe and let me inspect the weld again."

Josh complied, realizing she needed him to humor her now, more than he needed to be right. He continued working on building the distillery for several more hours. During that time, Jessica reacted to a few more random jolts from her distended belly. "They're more like squeezes," she said around lunchtime.

The mealtime bell rang and Josh took her hand and leaned back to pull her out of the chair. He held himself back from his normal loping gait and walked protectively behind her. She waddled, spraddle-legged, ahead of him to the picnic tables. She tried to swing her leg over the attached bench and couldn't get her foot high enough, and Josh bent over to help. This caught the attention of Suzanne, standing by the staging table, and Suzanne pointed it out to Deborah with a jerk of her chin.

Deborah said, "Josh? I know, but a bit young for you, don't you think?"

Suzanne said, "Oh, I don't know…twenty goes into sixty a lot more than sixty goes into twenty… *No, silly!* I mean Jessica. Look at how her hip is sprung!"

The two matrons made their way over to Jessica, the elderly Augusta shuffling behind them.

"Let me help you, dear," said Deborah. "Thanks," said Jessica, leaning on the table and breathing a little harder.

"You in labor." Augusta caught up, and she sounded quite certain. "You shouldn't eat nothing," she croaked.

"No, it's just another Braxton-Hicks." Jessica tried to wave them off.
"I'll get Akisni," Suzanne trotted towards the kitchen and the two other women fussed over Jessica, who went from annoyed to alarmed as the reality of what was about to happen sunk in. She gave up trying to swing her leg over the bench and sat down on the wood facing away from the table instead. Deborah stood with her hand reassuringly on Jessica's upper back, and Augusta sat down on the bench next to her.

Soon Akisni was by her side. "Come on inside, let's check this out." Jessica allowed Akisni to help her up and began following her into the house, flanked by Deborah and Augusta, with Suzanne at her back. Halfway there, Jessica put her hand on Deborah's shoulder and paused for a moment, bent forward with her hand on her belly. "12:21," Akisni noted, flipping her grandfather's pocket watch shut. "We'll see how far apart they are."

DD met them in the infirmary, where Akisni had curtained off an area to make a birthing room. She'd done her best to make it cozy-looking with quilts and pillows. A tray of exam instruments and sutures was on a table in a corner, next to a green metal oxygen tank. Akisni had everyone wash their hands. She examined Jessica's belly with her on her back, on her side, and on her hands and knees, and she listened to the baby's heart with a conical stethoscope which she called a fetoscope. "The baby's head-down," she assured her. "And the head isn't engaged yet. That's pretty common with the first baby. You've got a while to go. You can rock in the rocking chair, lie down and try to get some rest, or take a short walk if you like."

Jessica plopped into the rocker. "I'd love some tea," she said, putting her puffy feet on the cushioned footrest.

"Should she be eating or drinking?" Deborah frowned.

"It's okay. She can have a little fruit or a light snack if she gets hungry, too. She's got a long ways to go and she doesn't need to get dehydrated or hypoglycemic." The trio of crones headed for the kitchen to make tea. DD sat on the floor and began rubbing Jessica's feet gently.

"Oh, mom! You have no idea how good that feels!" She groaned ecstatically.

"Oh, yes I do!" DD smiled. "I was working long days as a graduate assistant in the lab when I was pregnant with you! Support stockings and maternity girdles were my best friends!"

"And you worked right up until you went into labor. I know, mom. You've told me the story a hundred times."

"I was always a workaholic. But when you came along it was like I was torn in two between wanting to be with you and wanting to be in the lab. You're lucky, in a way, that you won't have to go through that."

"Yeah, mom, but what if something goes wrong? There's no way of doing a transfusion, much less a C-section!"

"I know, honey. I know." DD's brow furrowed.

"We'll do the best we can here," Akisni put in. "Even though a third of births were C-sections before the machine sickness hit, most of those weren't strictly necessary. Maybe one in 20 births really, truly *needs* to be a C-section to save the mother's or the baby's life or health. And for a young, healthy mom like you, with a baby in the head-down position like this, the chances are much lower."

A contraction hit. This one was a little bit stronger, going by her facial expression. Jessica leaned forward, and DD stood up and hugged her head.

"Twelve minutes apart." Akisni smiled once it was over. "And a thirty-second contraction. You need to rest and save your strength. This baby might not be born until tomorrow. We'll let it take its time."

So, the day went, DD and Akisni sitting with Jessica as the contractions got stronger and more frequent. Different residents popped by to visit after their day's work ended. Jessica ate a peach and a few bites of dirty rice around dinnertime and sipped sweetened herb tea and water.

As twilight fell, the contractions seemed to change in quality as well as intensity. Jessica began to pant and gasp and dig her heels into the floor, breaking a little sweat, with each one. Juni came to the door for a visit, and Akisni turned her away. "And tell everyone else not to come anymore. It's getting close now and she doesn't need any distractions."

DD watched her child, her little girl, sink deeper into the endorphin trance of labor. She thought back to the day—it seemed like just yesterday—that it was her in this state.

"Mooooom!" Jessica groaned, "I don't want to do this. This is starting to really hurt. I'm so tired. I can't do it! I just can't!"

"You're doing it, sweetheart!" encouraged DD. "You're doing beautifully. Just let it go. It will be over before you know it," she lied, as generations of mothers before her had lied to their daughters.

Akisni checked Jessica's belly again and pronounced her fetus fully engaged and face down.

"OK, I need to check you from the inside. We'll keep this to a minimum to prevent infection, but I need to know what station you are and make sure you're dilating properly." She was at the sink, lathering her hands to the elbows with soap three times, and then drenching them with alcohol from a bottle beside her on the counter.

Jessica lay back and Akisni checked her.

"Four centimeters and plus-one station. Coming right along."

Jessica swung her legs off the bed to walk into the bathroom, and halfway there her water broke with a gush, producing a spreading puddle on the wooden floor. Akisni grabbed a towel, from a stack of white towels neatly folded and smelling of bleach, and laid it down on the puddle while Jessica went to the loo. Jessica came back and sat on the bed, and as she swung her legs up she began to gag and heave. Miraculously agile for a split second, Deborah managed to get a basin under her face just in time to catch to vomit.

Jessica lay on her side for a few minutes and the contractions slowed. At Akisni's direction, DD and Deborah helped her up, and held her arms as she slowly walked the length of the room a few times, "It helps wiggle the baby down through the pelvis," Akisni explained. A contraction hit and Jessica sank into a squat; the women automatically sank down with her and she wound up sitting on their thighs as the pushing urges hit her and her moans turned to grunts and groans. This happened twice more as they walked her back to the bed.

Jessica put her hands on the bed, but before she could climb on, her knees buckled. Akisni hustled around behind and dropped to the floor. "Quick! Get me that stack of towels! This baby is *right here!*"

Jessica was flat-out screaming now, a sound which brought tears to DD's eyes as she handed Akisni the towels. *My little girl is crying in pain and I can't make it stop!* Akisni got the towels spread out on the floor just as the infant's slick black head made its appearance. DD sat and took her daughter's hand, getting her own hand almost crushed for her troubles. Jessica whimpered as the next contraction pushed the baby's head all the way out, and made panicky noises as the baby's head turned in Akisni's hands. Finally, the shoulders and the rest of the body slithered out, and Jessica gave a low moan of relief, burying her face in her mother's hands.

Akisni dried the baby off, inspecting him carefully as she did so. "A boy," she said, bundling him loosely. "Go ahead and get up on the bed now, Jessica, and you can hold him." Jessica complied, leaning back on the pillows. The baby began to cry until she took him, meeting her son face to face for the first time. Once again, DD's eyes filled with tears, this time of pride, as she saw the face of her grandson. She looked back and forth from his pink, wrinkled, perplexed face to the face of the grown woman she'd met, just the same way, in a time out of place and a place out of time, years ago.

The two women barely noticed Akisni gently guiding the placenta out. "Who wants to cut the cord?" Akisni asked, stepping over to the instrument tray in the corner.

"Oh no!" Akisni exclaimed.

"What is it?" Said DD fearfully.

"Oh, no, it's okay. It's just that the clamps are plastic and I guess the machine sickness got to them. Never mind, there's some boiled hemp over there. I'll just tie the cord off." She crossed the curtain and retrieved the spool of homemade string from the infirmary. DD took the scissors and snipped the cord—it was tougher than she expected—and then helped Jessica put the baby to her breast.

"He looks like a nursing champion!" Akisni observed. She left the room and so did Deborah. The three generations of family were left alone to rest, bond, and get acquainted.

A little while later, Akisni returned and woke Jessica, taking the baby and handing him to his grandmother, who was sitting in the rocking chair in a sentimental reverie. Akisni checked Jessica and pronounced her in great shape, with no tearing and not much blood loss. "You did great!" She beamed. She, Deborah, and Suzanne levered Jessica onto her wobbly legs and stripped the stained bedspread and the waxed-cotton sheet beneath it from the bed, revealing a whole, clean set of bedding underneath. They pushed a three-sided crib up against the bedside and secured it with a strap, and DD kissed her grandson on the head—*the top of a baby's head is the best smell on earth*—and laid the child inside.

The next morning, DD, still in the chair, woke with a start. Augusta stomped into the room as hard as her frail octogenarian feet could stomp. Still bleary from waking up to help Jessica nurse the baby and tuck him back in during the night, it took her a moment to realize she'd fallen asleep sitting up in the rocker, but the sharp spasm in her left shoulder blade confirmed it.

"What you name this baby?" Augusta demanded.

"I haven't picked a name yet." Jessica blinked, startled.

"You gots to name him now." Insisted Augusta "Mama knows baby name when God give it the breath of life." She drew closer to look at the infant's face, then drew back in surprise. "Daddy black?"

Jessica smiled. "Mestizo. Spanish-speaking Mexican Indian."

Augusta jerked herself upright to her full, intimidating, four feet, ten inches. She gazed at Jessica and the baby critically for a moment, then concluded, "You gots to name that baby," and shuffled out of the room.

DD smiled wearily at her daughter. "You take your time. Have you thought of any names?"

"I have a few in mind: Amit. Sutokata. Ozark. Hunter. Stark."

"Those are all good names. I like Ozark especially."

The baby began to fuss and suck his hands, and Jessica sat up and brought him to her breast. DD watched her feed her son, DD's grandson. *I never thought this day would come. Not a day when the world was back to the dark ages; and not the day when my errant girl would be nurturing a baby of her own.*

360

LIX.   Honor Among Thieves

Brownie rose extra-early on the morning of the 23rd. It was the kind of cool late-Summer morning which lets you know the rollercoaster year has well and truly begun its downhill glide into Fall and Winter, so he shivered as his bare feet hit the floor. He didn't bathe or brush his teeth. He'd stashed his shoes under his bed, instead of leaving them in the mud room like everyone always did. He pulled on a heavy wool sweater and a knit stocking cap and crept down the stairs. Gillie was on patrol this morning; she'd started her circuit about twenty minutes earlier. Brownie had been watching her; he knew she usually ducked into the goat shed to warm up. They'd all been taking patrol less and less seriously after the raids had petered out; the last one had been five —or was it six? — weeks ago.

He slipped out the door and walked quietly out to the lab shed in the bluish glow of the pre-dawn sky. He stood in the shed doorway as his eyes adjusted to the darker interior from the dimness outside. He'd been spying on DD, Amit, and Josh whenever they went inside, so he followed the protocol: clean smock, clean face mask. A panicky moment when he realized they would see that the mask and smock had been used, but then he realized that the scientists didn't keep track of one another's comings and goings, so they wouldn't notice an extra in the hamper, would they? He drenched his hands in ethanol and poured ethanol into a shallow dish in front of the

door jamb. He slipped off his shoes and waded through the —
very cold! —tray of alcohol. He gasped involuntarily, and then
froze, afraid his sharp intake of breath would draw attention.
A minute went by and nothing happened; he told himself he
should relax, he was being silly. Everything sounded so loud
in the early-morning tranquility.

He took a small, stubby test tube from a rack under a
leather curtain. He opened a box, an unplugged dorm
refrigerator, with bricks inside that had been heated the prior
day in the stove. He took a flask full of cloudy liquid out of
the box and removed the thin layer of lambskin stretched over
its mouth. He poured a tiny portion, not even an ounce, of the
liquid into the test tube, filling it almost completely. He
located a jar of beeswax and fumbled with it one-handed,
stuffed some into the opening of his little tube. He returned the
flask to the incubator, hoping the temperature drop didn't raise
anyone's suspicion in the morning; he didn't know how
carefully they monitored it. He exited the shed, stuffing the
mask and gown he was wearing into the hamper as he left. He
put his shoes back on and poured out the tray of alcohol. He
squinted in the direction of the rising sun as the door was
slammed shut behind him by a spring hitched to the
doorframe, sounding loud as a gunshot in the silence, and he
stifled a curse.

He slipped down the trail back to the house. Gillie
exited the goat barn just as he was reaching the front door; he
caught a glimpse of her in silhouette before she blew out the
candle she no longer needed in the burgeoning daylight. With
362

care to be soundless, he eased through the door. Then, he froze. The baby wailed! Jessica's footsteps in the far bedroom, then a pause, then more wailing. Brownie stood still as a statue. What if she decided to just get up and begin her day in the crepuscular light? Could he slip back outdoors unnoticed? What would he say to explain his presence? But Ozark's infant cries became muffled and stopped, as Jessica put him to her breast and lay down in bed beside him. Brownie stood, frozen, for a long time before he decided it was safe to move.

Brownie was back in his bed, apparently asleep, by the time the rest of the house's occupants awoke with the sunrise.

The next few hours were excruciating. He went about his normal morning routine, hygiene, breakfast, chores, sure that his guilt was transparently obvious. At long last his afternoon patrol shift rolled around, and he went outside with relief.

Brownie had reconciled himself, years earlier, to sharing information with the Feds. After all, he was just talking. And nothing they were doing at the community was dangerous, or illegal, so as he saw it, the Feds were just being their normal paranoid and incompetent selves and paying him for nothing. And the money he'd squirreled away over the years had been nothing to sneeze at. That money, electronic markers in a bank that had vanished with the death of data, was inaccessible now, of course. Isaac was now paying him instead in antibiotics, sugar, and silver coins.

But this was different. This wasn't just talk. Brownie had actually, affirmatively, taken action, stolen something from those he considered his friends, people who trusted him. He waited by the deer trail. Sutokata was, in a way, his only remaining family. He wanted to be rid of the ampule as soon as possible, and he was determined to tell Isaac that he wasn't going to spy any more. There was no more Federal Government as such, from what everyone said; Brownie didn't even know where this information was going, or who it actually was who wanted a sample of the new "battery bacterium," as DD had described it.

Brownie handed the tiny test tube to Isaac with a quiet sigh of relief.

"You have to keep it warm. Keep it in a pocket close to your body. If it freezes, it's dead," Brownie said. "That's all I know. It was hard enough to sneak into the lab shed and take this without making them suspicious. Usually only the three scientists go anywhere near there. And they can be there at any hour of the day and night."

"Good work, Mr. Brown," said Isaac.

"Yes," a third voice said, "Good work." Tim Schneider stepped up to Brownie. With a graceful dance step, Tim whirled, ending up behind him, and with one clean motion, slit Brownie's throat. Brownie dropped to the ground, unable to gasp or speak, blood trickling and fountaining from the gruesome second grin beneath his chin.

"I'll take that now, Isaac," Tim said, holding out his left hand. In his right, he held a simple kitchen knife, honed to razor sharpness.

Isaac backed away. "No, sir. I don't think so."

"Isaac, are you disobeying a direct order?"

"You're not in my chain of command. Lee Flatt was my C.O. and word is, you had a hand in his death."

Tim made a sudden lunge for Isaac, who turned and ran into the woods. Tim started to follow him, but the smaller man had vanished from sight. The thorns and twigs snagged Tim's clothing and his feet began to sink in the mud. Tim, ever fastidious, recoiled in distaste. He hesitated a moment, fury twisting his features at losing control of his prize, and then shrugged. Isaac, on foot, couldn't beat Tim, on his bike, back to the camp. On the other hand, Tim couldn't explain Brownie's half-decapitated corpse to the Sutokatans. Tim cogitated rapidly; he could beat Isaac back to the protectee camp, ambush him there, and take the ampule away from him. He wondered what Lee's superiors, who didn't even know about Jeff, would give him in return for this prize.

So! Tim figured he'd better get moving. He ran back to the house and grabbed his bike.

LX.   For a Season

Snowbear, Akisni, Josh, Amit and DD raised tiny snifters of French cognac from Snowbear's private reserve. "To *shewanella*!" they all repeated and drank a small sip, then leaned back to savor the drink, the moment of victory, and the company.

The heady liquid was consumed as much with the nose as the mouth, by inhaling the biting fragrance and taking minuscule sips. DD closed her eyes and savored the wood-smoke, caramel, gardenia essence.

"You know what I'm thinking?" DD said.

"Probably something obscene," observed Josh. DD stuck out her tongue.

"I'm thinking about *shewanella*-powered radios. Hovercraft. Airships!"

Amit jumped in, agreeing.

"No reason we can't scale up the drone. No reason we can't scale it down, for that matter, if we can find a plastic-free way to insulate the circuitry."

"No DOT or FAA to keep it forever in development with regulations!" Interjected DD. "No more 'Where's my jet pack?'"

"But why," mused Akisni, "keep it to ourselves? It's like sourdough."

Snowbear snorted a little and nodded. "Sourdough. Spread it around and it will keep growing. The instructions are pretty simple to make the cell cultures. It could go viral."

"Bacterial, actually," DD corrected him.

366

"Whatever. The point is, if we want people to have the opportunity to learn to use it, we need to start spreading it around asap, before the weather starts getting really cold again," said Snowbear.

"Yes, it's easier to keep alive when the conditions are warmer," agreed Amit.

"Not only that," DD offered, "but this Winter is going to be brutal. Most farmers were using hybridized or GMO seeds. They didn't have any way to replant last Spring. Then they lost all the technology they used to plant, cultivate, and harvest. Yields of grain had to've been pathetic this summer, across the whole country, just like they were around here. People are living on canned goods and crops in silos and warehouses. The bioelectricity has the potential to allow them to grow a reasonable amount of food again. But they have to get started. If people don't have a way to return to modern agriculture, we can expect mass starvation."

"Mass starvation means mass migration," commented Akisni. "Like during the Dust Bowl, or Ireland after An Gorta Mór, the Great Hunger."

"So," Amit said, "there's no internet to spread this around with. Who's going to disseminate the new technology? It's going to have to be done the old-fashioned way, by travelers bringing the word with them."

"I've been wondering how my family is doing in Galveston," admitted Jeremy in a seeming non-sequitur. DD caught his eye.

"I'm ready to hit the road again!" exclaimed DD.

"Are you sure?" Smiled Snowbear. "You haven't been away from that grandchild more than a couple of hours since he was born!" DD frowned. She hadn't thought of that. She dipped her lip in the cognac and licked it.

"No," she said after a moment's thought, "I'm ready for a trip. Jessica has been complaining that I'm too domineering. She needs some breathing room to come into her own as a mother."

"Who are you? And what have you done with DD?" Akisni mock-scowled at her.

"I think," DD said, suddenly introspective and serious, "that holding myself back from trying to track Tim down and kill him personally, with my own two hands, was my great turning point. I was torn between the need to be close to Ozark and Jessica, and the burning urge to strangle that son of a bitch. I realized after a while that, well, you just simply can't be in control of everything that happens to you, or everywhere around you."

"Wonder what Brownie did to piss Tim off so badly?" Josh idly wondered. They were all silent for a moment, remembering their fallen friend.

"To Brownie."

"To Brownie," they all raised their glasses, then sipped their cognacs. It trickled down their throats like liquid fire, kindling a glow in the stoves of their existence.

A few weeks later, they were ready. The two ethanol trikes were tuned up and loaded. Pages and pages of instructions on maintaining *shewanella* cultures were printed by hand lithography methods using homemade vegetable dyes and charcoal ink. The glass-blowing kit was running 24-7 making small sample lights, powered by bioelectric cells.

Amit, DD, and Josh still found time to brainstorm and tinker. "We're almost ready to start testing out the miniaturized semiconductor colonies. Are you sure you want to go now?" Amit asked.

"No, it's time for me to see the Gulf of Mexico again. I want to know if it's really boiling."

LXI.   Fly Away Home

Isaac crouched in the woods. The glass vial of
shewanella culture felt like a lead weight in his shirt pocket.
So fragile! This technology was too powerful for him to hold
the responsibility alone. He had to get the ampule to Site R.
Site R had been something of an open secret during his
training, and he didn't know its exact location, but he knew
which county it was supposed to be in, and that it was on the
highest ground for miles around. That should be enough
knowledge to allow him to locate their security cordon so he
could turn the vial of *shewanella* over to them.

The girl they called Jessica, no longer pregnant, had
just pulled her little Vespa over to the side of the path and was
picking something, the little purple Fall wildflowers maybe,
by the roadside. This was his chance to get transportation to
Site R! If he could get this ampule to the President before the
terrorists took advantage of it, he could save his country! His
chest swelled with patriotic pride as he imagined fulfilling his
duty, as he'd always dreamed of doing.

Isaac ran out to Jessica's scooter and swung his leg
through. He started it and revved the little motor in one
movement. A slight hang-up as he figured out the shifter, and
then the scooter jerked forward. As it did, the basket on the
back fell to the ground.

Just as Isaac bumped onto the gravel track, he
realized what the basket must hold: Jessica's baby. He ducked

370

his head and glimpsed the child's drowsy face, still smiling trustingly, in the sick instant before the basket hit the ground with a thump.

He listened for the baby's cry as he pulled away but heard nothing. He hoped the reason he couldn't hear it was because of the sound of the Vespa's little motor.

LXII.   Loose but Lucid

The two trikes rolled into town on market day, in a cloud composed of dust and the steam from their ethanol-powered engines. Shoppers and traders, men and women in a variegation of pre-Sickness T-shirts and jeans and homespun hemp, cotton, and hand-tanned leather, clustered around stalls of merchandise and a few savory-smelling food booths. The inhabitants drifted out in twos and threes to eye the new arrivals. Jeremy operated the drone; it lifted from the back of his trike, swept a few lazy circles overhead, and landed lightly on the raised wooden platform that served as a community stage.

DD mounted the weathered wood steps easily. It didn't take long for a crowd to assemble in the crossroads in front of the trading post. She swept her eyes over the faces, looking for Gabriela or Ed, Marthita or the other kids. She saw a few familiar faces, but her Ozark family wasn't there. She was pleased that she didn't see Juan either.

"It's good to see familiar faces," she began, timid.

Then she grinned; Jeremy had gotten off his trike and quickly dropped his pants. He pulled up his shirttails and flashed his underwear.

"This winter, my friends, is going to be *hard*!" She started over, more emphatically. Murmurs and nods of agreement.

"Back when we switched to PVC irrigation pipes, and started using herbicide on GMO seeds it seemed like mere details. Farming was the thing and we were still farming. It was just details. It was!

"The devil is in the details!" The people were starting to glance back and forth at each other, wondering where she was going with this, and who this crazy woman was; if it weren't for the drone at her feet, she might have lost their attention.

"The devil is not in you or me," she finished.

"Filthy heretic!" shouted a woman whose long hair and skirts marked her as Pentecostal.

"We're all filthy!" countered DD. She raised her arm, as though to gesture, then sniffed her armpit and made a face as though at the smell; the crowd tittered at the crude humor and the religious woman frowned and huffed.

"People, we are all: you, me, even her—" she pointed at the holy roller— "covered with filthy germs all the time! The filthy germs everywhere make friends with our guts and make us healthy. The filthy germs that clean up oil spills have now eaten our oil and our plastic. But just as our hearts beat stronger when we have healthy germs in our guts, the heart of the earth continues to beat. Every blood cell circulates everything we need to every cell, tissue, and organ. We don't know why it happens, but we don't have to think about it. It's the exact same way with the world around us!"

"You!" she pointed at a tall man, an alpha, the sheriff who'd been drilling the men in self-defense last Winter, a leader.

"You are a blood cell! I," she thumped just below her collarbones with her fists in a way that vaguely suggested an ape, "am a blood cell! This," she pointed at the drone and Jeremy (pants discreetly back up) took his cue, using the remote to lift the drone off the platform, and turning on its flashing lights, "is oxygen. It's life, and breath. And you can have one yourself."

Even though maybe one in ten got the gist of her raving, the crowd were interested now. Their body language signaled it as they leaned forward, chatter dying as they eyed the drone and DD.

"There are those who have said that people are a cancer on the earth. Scientists have said that cancer is caused by infections. The infection is cancer and cancer is the infection. But here's the thing:

"The light comes from the darkness and the darkness has not overcome it. John, chapter 1, verse 5." She paused, making eye contact with the Pentecostalist woman, who'd been joined by her bearded husband and their seven children, stairstepping in age a year or two apart from toddler to teenager. The patriarch nodded unconsciously, mama relaxed almost imperceptibly, and DD went on.

"The key to fighting off the infection and to outliving the cancer is change, change, change. We, as humans can remake, remodel, and regenerate. This world can only improve by changing. This technology represents change.

"You will tell your grandchildren about this day. You will remember this moment as the moment you learned that restoration is in your hands."

She saw chests heaving in deep sighs, chins lift, eyes soften. She had them! She went on.

"The single moment when change takes place is an illusion. The process is going on continuously no matter how hard we try to cling to the way things are. *It has changed even as we are perceiving it.*" Confusion; better bring it back to something concrete.

"I am going to give away five of these drones, along with instructions on how to make more." The crowd began to jostle each other to get to the stage. "These drones are powered by a bacterium called *shewanella* that is easy to culture. It works just like sourdough starter." A number of the women's eyes lit up in familiarity. "I am going to leave instructions on how to keep it alive and how to build the power cells that use it. I only ask that those who take it promise to share the information freely.

"Whoa, there, big fella!" She drew her revolver and trained it on the man who had his foot on the first step. She did her best Mae West impression, "I'm happy to see you, too, but we haven't been properly introduced!" The crowd tittered. Jeremy, guarding the remote between his feet, had a machete in one hand and his carbine in the other and was sweeping a little clearing in the crowd around him, the drone hovering right overhead.

"Everyone can—and will—have a bioelectric cell and the means to make more within two weeks, *IF* you listen carefully and do as I say. The five drones are hidden by the roadside between here and Little Rock. If anything happens to the two of us, you will never know where they are." The front row of people, big men all, who'd shoved their way up front, backed away half a step and calmed down to listen.

"One of you will ride five miles south with us, and then we will tell that person where the drones and instructions are. You have the count of five hundred to pick that person. Pick someone you trust.

"I'm walking to my trike now."

Shoulders square, she strutted down the steps and the crowd parted to let her through. She smiled a little smile to herself.

I've gotten to the point where I positively enjoy this part.

She stepped within Jeremy's perimeter and the two of them straddled their trikes. "One hundred!" Jeremy shouted.

They'd repeated this scene from Indiana to Arkansas in over a dozen small localities and they had the routine down pat. They read this crowd as being no threat (there had been a couple of places they'd needed to fight their way out and leave the hidden drones to die undiscovered). The people focused on the stage where the old sheriff was calling for nominees. This crowd knew whom to trust, and Ed was pushed up front almost organically, like a cell performing exocytosis, and the sheriff just confirmed, "Ed? Is it Ed?" The crowd buzzed
376

affirmation, and Ed walked over to the trikes. The count never reached two hundred. DD gave her old distilling mentor Ed a genuine hug, and the crowd applauded. She gestured him on behind her, and the two trikes rolled south.

"No one is to follow us for ten minutes. Understand?" Jeremy shouted again, and again the crowd murmured yes. As they passed the turn-off to the barn, DD caught sight of Gabriela walking along the road with the kids. She felt a pang, wishing she could visit her friend and see her cozy barn home of last winter, but instead she contented herself with a wave to the woman and children, who swiveled in puzzlement to watch them go by.

After they dropped Ed off with the list of hiding places, they continued towards the Texas border. They went far enough to outrun word of mouth and camped for the night near Texarkana. They went silently about the business of setting up camp, digging a latrine, and building a fire. The sun went down and the Fall cool settled over them; they made a simple dinner of smoked meat and fire-roasted potatoes, then sat quietly by the fire.

I'll be the first to bring it up. It's probably not even on his mind.

"That was the last of the cultures."

"Yes. Yes, it was." Jeremy, laconic as always.

"So, what now?"

"Well," Jeremy said, as if surprised it was a question, "aren't we going back to Galveston?"

DD paused. "No, I have nothing and no one in Galveston."

Jeremy considered this a moment. "I guess not."

I guessed right. No commitment. Never was. She searched herself for a sense of loss, of betrayal. *None on my end either.*

"I thought I'd go look up some old friends in Tallahassee, see how they're doing and if I can winter with one of them," she said.

"Sounds like a plan," said Jeremy.

"We need to spread out the stuff and divide it then," DD said, beginning to unload the saddlebags on her trike. She spread out a blanket on the ground to put their belongings on. "If we hurry, we can finish before it gets dark."

"If we hurry." Jeremy walked up behind her. He grabbed her by the hips and pulled her buttocks against his pelvis; his raging erection took her by surprise, but she ground against him. All at once, they were on the ground, struggling with breathtaking urgency to get their clothes off. To her surprise, she was lubricated and ready almost instantly and he found just the right place; a starburst fired inside her once, twice, and on the fifth stroke she was convulsed by a blinding climax which sent her out of her body for a moment, shooting towards the first evening star overhead, emerging from the dusky blue evening sky above her. She settled back into her body, opened her eyes, and watched Jeremy come, for the last time. She smiled.

Most things work better when you just let go.

378

LXIII. Constellation

Isaac felt his pocket. The ampule was still there, unbroken. He swiped his forearm across his brow, removing the sweat and blood trickling into his eyes, despite the night's chill. He had only another half mile to go before reaching the Site R perimeter.

"Halt and identify!"

Isaac stopped, called out his name and ID number. The sentry lowered his weapon and escorted him to his CO. Standing by the CO's shoulder was a man in a dark coat and stocking cap.

"I brought this culture from an enemy encampment." Isaac held the ampule out in the palm of his suddenly quivering hand. "It's the secret to renewable power. No one must be allowed to get this except our scientists."

The man in black stepped forward. "We've been waiting for this," he said, though Isaac, had told no one he was coming. The spook took the ampule and wrapped it in a cloth or tissue and put it in his coat pocket. He then stepped back and nodded meaningfully at the sentry. When the Commanding Officer saw the nod, he also stepped back.

Isaac swallowed hard. The sentry raised his weapon. Isaac was paralyzed by confusion. He'd fought and killed for this nation, killed good people! Innocent people! The infant's eyes flashed in his mind, trusting in its woven basket until the moment it hit the ground. Had it survived? It didn't matter.

With a tiny shake of his head, he began to take a breath to speak, to explain.

Which he did not. Ever again.

The man in black pivoted, with a small smile, to return to the secure site. As he turned, a light appeared in his peripheral vision. A sentry, out of position, no doubt! He turned to hail him and command him to identify himself, and another light appeared. The first was about twenty feet away, the second one, forty, and his vision resolved a row of pinpoint lights stretching away from him, down the rise he was standing on and ascending the next one. Then he realized the entire far ridge was a constellation of tiny lights.

He furrowed his brow. He slowly approached the first light. He reached it and saw it was on the ground. He squatted and saw two small glass jars connected by a tube with something white and fibrous inside. The lids of the jars were also connected, by wires, and one of the lids was an LED panel, which was where the glow was coming from. He reached for it, hesitated, then decided to pick it up. He'd carry this inside and check it out more thoroughly later. Right now, the priority was getting the agent Isaac's delivery to Birdwell. A shame about Isaac, but someone who acted with that kind of impetuosity couldn't be relied upon for future actions. And there were no spare resources to support unreliable, possibly useless assets.

He took the device with him and entered the compound. He walked past the torches mounted on the walls and the lanterns held by the patrols.

380

Everyone recognized him and let him pass. He glided down the hallways, all the way to the main laboratory, which was one of the few places recently wired with their precious natural-fiber-insulated wires. Those wires only transmitted electricity, generated by their dwindling supply of fiercely guarded gasoline, for a few hours in the evening. He set the strange lighting device, if that's what it was, down. He turned to Lt. Colonel Birdwell, PhD, and handed him the ampule reverently, mindful of the lives that had been sacrificed to bring this invention to be the salvation of America and the Free World.

"Here it is. It's what you wanted. With this, the US can rise again to make a whole new world."

But Birdwell was staring instead at the glass gewgaw on the bench beside him, aghast.

"What's this?" Birdwell asked.

"I don't know. I found it in the woods," he replied dismissively.

"It looks like..." He bent down closer to look at the object. "It looks like a biological-fuel-cell lantern?"

"Yes? So?"

"This is a message from someone. A threat? The terrorists must be close to inventing what we are working on! We have to beat them to the punch, or the enemy will have the technology first and it will all be useless!"

"Should I send someone to bring in the rest of them, then?"

"The...rest...of them?" Birdwell said.

"Yes. The whole hillside was covered with them. I thought they were just toys or something."

"Where?" Demanded Birdwell.

Minutes later, he was in the darkened woods. The jars each held a liquid with a square of something black in it; one was clear and half-full, the other cloudy and full to the top. The lights, strung out in the darkness, looked like strings of Christmas lights, something Birdwell never thought he'd see again, in these apocalyptic times. The LEDs were suspended in clear glass, instead of plastic. Several soldiers followed behind him with hand carts, carefully loading the lights onto the wagons to be taken back to the lab. He walked from one to the next, to the next, until he reached to top of the hill. And stopped. Because a line of lights went on, for at least a mile that he could see. He turned to his aide and instructed him to send for more soldiers and more wagons.

He stared at the lights for a few moments more. Then he turned to go back to the lab. He needed to think.

A soldier walked up to him and proffered a box. "I think you might want to see this, Sir."

The box was made of plain unfinished wood, about the size of a breadbox, with a circular hole covered with a stretched piece of paper-thin leather. The speaker, for that's what it was, was playing music. Then, a person's voice came from it. It had been so many months since Birdwell had heard a voice over the airwaves he'd almost forgotten what it was like, but the voice, though distorted, spoke words that were as plain as day.

382

HELLO, AND WELCOME TO THE FUTURE. THIS MESSAGE IS INTENDED FOR ANYONE WHO FINDS IT. THIS BROADCAST IS POWERED BY BACTERIAL FUEL CELLS. THE BACTERIA WHICH MAKE UP THESE FUEL CELLS HAVE BEEN CULTURED AND DISTRIBUTED FREE OF CHARGE. THEY LIVE ON SEWAGE AND ROTTING VEGETATION. THE FUEL CELL TECHNOLOGY CAN BE REPRODUCED BY ANYONE WITH ONLY SIMPLE MATERIALS. I GOT THE FIRST CULTURE FROM A FIELD OF LIGHTS JUST LIKE THIS. THE FUTURE OF THE WORLD IS DISPERSED ENERGY PRODUCTION AND DECENTRALIZED CONTROL. ENJOY...AND PLEASE PASS THIS TECHNOLOGY ON TO OTHERS, AS I DID.

The music started to play again, the same soft rhythm and upbeat melody. It was a recorded message, repeated again and yet again. With only a moment's thought, Birdwell knew what he'd find within the box: one of the biofuel cells, and a simple assembly of coiled wire wrapped in natural insulators, a simple hobbyist's radio like those of the early 20th century, preset to one frequency, the frequency on which the message was being broadcast over, and over, and over. He would set his soldiers to finding the source of the broadcast, but he was willing to bet it would be unmanned.

Early the next morning, groggy from sleep, POTUS was being briefed on the development. Birdwell saw the shadows beneath his eyes and the furrows etched in his forehead; the dry skin and the vacant gaze testified to the stress of the past year and a half. He'd gotten where he was by being bombastic and overbearing, achieving what he wanted through a vast organization. The only thing he was ill-prepared for was a situation like this one, where his control was so limited and his underlings were so few and ill-equipped.

"But, this is just twentieth-century technology! Surely once we control the biobatteries, we can defeat *wooden radios*!"

"Mr. President, it may be simple twentieth-century technology now. But people who've had smartphones and insulin pumps and social media and, and, drones and dance clubs and light shows, and everything else we all took for granted until very recently, aren't going to take long to figure out how to scale this tech both up and down, and make it ubiquitous." Birdwell paused, taking a deep breath to quell the unfamiliar sensation of panic twitching to life in his diaphragm. "We have no control of who uses this, or where they use it. There's no way to *take* control! The materials are cheap and easy to find anywhere. Even if there is some component which turns out to be more expensive or hard to find, let me remind you that we no longer have unlimited financial resources. We have no way to collect taxes: the people in the camps can't pay them, and the people outside the camps won't. This tech is not something fueled by substances dug out of the ground in far-away places, where we can

384

control the flow of importation. Anywhere there are human beings, there is abundant fuel for this technology. The technology actually *removes* or minimizes the problem of waste disposal, instead of creating new wastes." Birdwell paused, thinking about how an infantry battalion wouldn't need generators...or latrines!

"This changes everything, Mr. President. Everything."

Birdwell and everyone else in the room digested this in silence.

"We can't control it." Said POTUS.

"No, sir."

"We can't confiscate it? Monopolize it?" He said.

"It's too late for that," said Birdwell. "The cat is out of the bag. There's no patent enforcement any more anyway."

"Damn, I wish I still had control of my corporations! We have the protectees still. Can we set the camps to manufacturing it? "

Birdwell winced. "We could. Communication is spotty and slow, but the manufacture is absurdly simple. The main problem is that we won't have the protectees much longer. The camps we are in touch with, those east of the Rocky Mountains, are mostly projected to run out of food in approximately mid-February this year. We can stretch the supplies, perhaps until April, but famine conditions will prevail after that."

"They can still work if they're hungry." The big man waved a hand and made a dismissive moue. "At least we'll be protecting them and giving them a place to live!"

"Yes, Mr. President." Birdwell knew at that moment that the one-time leader of the Free World was too fixed in his thinking to grasp the reality of change, accelerating as it was, out of control, in fractal patterns. He was clinging to the mental model of power which he'd clawed and kicked his way to the top of. Birdwell had studied military history. He knew he needed to make an immediate decision between supervising a gulag spiraling into death, sickness, and violence, or striking out on his own. He eyed the radio, still parroting its message, and the light, still glowing softly on the countertop.

He closed his eyes. In the darkness behind his eyelids, he once again saw the string of lights on the hillside, stretching off like signal fires along the frontier of empire, into the wilds of the future.

THE END

Preview scene from the second book of the trilogy, *Watch It Burn…*

Jessica screamed and ran to the basket on the ground.

She'd been unaware of the man who'd appeared out of nowhere and stolen the alcohol-powered scooter as she gathered purple asters by the path. The asters lay now, forgotten, on the ground. She raced towards the basket that held her infant child.

"Ozark," she breathed, every millisecond that went by without hearing his cry lasting a millennium. The melon-thump sound the basket made when it hit the ground echoed in her ears. She seized the basket, a woven cradle, and turned it over.

There was a bundle of blankets within. Still no sound. But no blood.

She crouched on the ground and began to flip the blankets aside, dreading what she'd see. Her baby's face appeared, motionless. Oh, God! He was dead!

Buy it now, on your favorite retail site, or direct from the Eupocalypse website (cryptocurrency accepted).

Science Fiction— Caution: contains real science

The boundaries between science fiction and fantasy have blurred and merged over recent decades, but the recent success of stories like Andy Weir's *The Martian* and Dennis Taylor's Bobiverse books show that there is a persistent appetite for science fiction which is, well, *science-y*. Everything that happens during the Eupocalypse is based on real events and real technologies, which are being used right now, this very moment, all over the world. Below, in completely random order, are links to articles about some of them:

Operation Jupiter:

https://www.ul.com/wp-content/uploads/2014/03/2008_Review.pdf

General survey of OHCBs in oil pollution cleanup:

http://hzi.openrepository.com/hzi/bitstream/10033/19793/1/Yakimov%2520et%2520al_final.pdf

Non-scientific article about OHCBs in Deepwater Horizon spill:

https://www.usnews.com/news/articles/2013/04/08/study-oil-eating-bacteria-mitigated-deepwater-horizon-oil-spill

Metabolism of OHCBs in Deepwater Horizon:

https://marine.rutgers.edu/dmcs/ms606/2010_fall/Valentine%20et%20al%20Science%20Express%202010.pdf

Shewanella-based microbial fuel cells:

https://vdocuments.site/a-mediator-less-microbial-fuel-cell-using-a-metal-reducing-bacterium-shewanella.html , and http://onlinelibrary.wiley.com/doi/10.1002/bit.25624/abstract;jsessionid=52415C268FC9BB3185227E679964E944.f01t03

Microbial fuel cells currently in use by the US Navy:

https://www.nrl.navy.mil/techtransfer/available-technologies/energy/benthic-fuel-cell

Background on patenting OHCBs:

https://en.wikipedia.org/wiki/Ananda_Mohan_Chakrabarty

OHCBs at oil-spill site in Bemidji, Minnesota:

https://www.mprnews.org/story/2014/06/03/bemidji-oil-spill-site-research

Background on deep-water oil drilling in the Macondo oil range:

https://www.nap.edu/read/13273/chapter/4

***P. putida* infections in humans:**

https://www.ncbi.nlm.nih.gov/pubmed/20809240 , and http://www.journalofinfection.com/article/S0163-4453(08)00021-2/pdf

Genetically-engineered *P. putida* used in industrial manufacturing:

https://www.researchgate.net/publication/221847539_Industrial_biotechnology_of_Pseudomonas_putida_and_related_species

Bacterial populations on human hands:

http://jwbrown.mbio.ncsu.edu/MJC/JWB_paper.pdf

Antonio Meucci inventing the telephone:

https://www.theguardian.com/world/2002/jun/17/humanities.internationaleducationnews

A ton of research about goldenseal:

https://www.ncbi.nlm.nih.gov/pubmed/?term=hydrastis+canadensis

9 781962 454018